SONORA

ALSO BY E. HOWARD HUNT

Undercover: Memoirs of an American Secret Agent
The Berlin Ending
The Hargrave Deception
The Kremlin Conspiracy
The Gaza Intercept
The Dublin Affair
Murder in State
The Sankov Confession
Evil Time
Body Count
Chinese Red
The Paris Edge
Dragon Teeth

JACK NOVAK SERIES

Cozumel
Guadalajara
Mazatlán
Ixtapa
Islamorada
Izmir

STEVE BENTLEY SERIES

The House on Q Street
Mistress to Murder
End of a Stripper
Murder on the Rocks
Calypso Caper
Murder on Her Mind
Guilty Knowledge

SONORA

E. HOWARD HUNT

A TOM DOHERTY ASSOCIATES BOOK
NEW YORK

SONORA

Copyright © 2000 by E. Howard Hunt

A Forge Book
Published by Tom Doherty Associates, LLC
175 Fifth Avenue
New York, NY 10010

www.tor.com

Forge® is a registered trademark of Tom Doherty Associates, LLC.

Design by Lisa Pifher

ISBN 0-312-87205-4

First edition: January 2000

Printed in the United States of America

0 9 8 7 6 5 4 3 2 1

This book is dedicated to the memory of
Dr. Bert Buxton, classmate and lifelong friend.

THIS BOOK IS A PREQUEL PREDATING BY FIVE YEARS
THE FIRST JACK NOVAK BOOK, *COZUMEL*.

These violent delights
have violent ends
And in their triumph die
like fire and powder . . .

—William Shakespeare
Romeo and Juliet
Act II, Scene 6

SONORA

PROLOGUE

It was dusk when Isidro Moreno saw the plane come into the valley. The sun was already behind the western ridge of mountains leaving them outlined in a deep violet haze, and Isidro watched as the wing lights swept blindingly above him, casting swaths as bright as midday across the Sonora desert floor.

He would have been seen, he thought, had he not been sitting with his back against the rough hide of a saguaro trunk. To one side was the *tambache*—bundle—of mesquite twigs and branches gathered that day and cut with the old machete that lay across his thighs. He was honing the blade with careful, almost loving strokes, holding the hard black stone at a precise angle despite the pain in his arthritic hand.

Isidro paused to watch the plane turn and head back. Its wheels were down, he saw, so perhaps it was in trouble and looking for a place to land. Then he remembered a long stretch less than a kilometer away that had been cleared of mesquite bushes and saguaro clumps, and must be the place the plane was searching for. Isidro had assumed that the mesquite and saguaro had been harvested for firewood, but as he thought about it now he realized that the landowner, Don Felipe Paredes, had no need for such humble stuff to burn in the fireplaces of his rancho mansion. Don Felipe could easily pay for good *leña,* logs of pine and *cedro* that would burn all day and all night, giving off the sweet odor of their crackling sap to scent the entire two-story household.

As the plane roared overhead a second time Isidro pressed back against the cactus trunk and kept his face down. He was revising his thoughts about the low-flying plane. Both propellers were turning and there were no coughing sounds from its engines, so it must be coming down according to plan.

Doubtless the plane was bringing a cargo of contraband from Texas; television sets and refrigerators were what Isidro Moreno had heard were in greatest demand. So laden with *falluca,* the plane would probably land hard, he thought, and it occurred to him that help might be needed to unload the heavy cargo.

The plane was down now, out of sight, and the sound of its engines was muffled by the cactus forest. The sounds died away; and Isidro turned over his machete and gently stroked the other side of the blade to rid the edge of metal burrs. Standing, he slid the machete into its worn leather scabbard and glanced down at the firewood he had gathered. His wife, Olivia, would be waiting for it in their adobe hut if the beans were to be kept boiling long enough to be edible. But Isidro decided to go to the landed plane and try to earn a few pesos.

He was fifty-eight, but his lined, leathery face looked much older. Though his knuckles and wrists were swollen, he was confident of the strength of his back and thighs where heavy labor was involved.

So he stooped over and picked up the *tambache*'s binding strap and set it across his forehead, then rose, lifting the load onto his back where it rode against the thick, grey serape.

There was very little light now as he made his way across the desert floor, and a coolness was settling into the valley. The dark mountains gave him what little directional help he needed, and in the half-light his footsteps startled a hare that bounded out of sight.

With an *escopeta* he could have dropped the hare, he knew, but the only firearm he possessed was an old *pistola* of his father who had ridden against the Callistas many years ago. The *pistola* was oiled, wrapped in rags, and buried in the earth floor beneath the wood-frame bed he shared with Olivia. But the hare moved too rapidly for a pistol shot, and in any case Isidro had no cartridges to waste on uncertain ventures. Besides, the hare had looked scrawny, without much meat for Olivia's cooking pot, so it was best to put it out of his mind. More than likely a horned viper would strike the hare and kill it before dawn. That was what happened in the desert.

He plodded on toward the remembered clearing, hearing no engine sounds but only the occasional fluttering call of a cactus-nesting owl. Isidro was comfortable in the desert. He knew its heat and cold, knew where to find firewood and water, herbs for cooking and dry grasses for bedding. Moreover, the white worms that burrowed in cactus trunks were sweet as piñon nuts, nutritious, and easy to find and remove.

Isidro heard voices before he saw the plane. The voices sounded angry, and so he slowed and walked without sound to a gentle rise where he undid his *tambache* and crawled until he could see what lay beyond.

The plane was there, lights flooding ahead, and he saw that one wing drooped lower than the other.

Two men were standing by the nose of the plane. One cursed and kicked a wheel tire that had lost its roundness.

The other man said, "Even if we had a spare we need a jack to put it on. So we have to wait for the truck."

In a northern accent his companion said, "This is turning out badly, Rogelio. The truck may carry a jack but Felipe will have to send to Nogales for another tire. How long will this take?"

The man called Rogelio shrugged. "A day. Perhaps two."

"Meanwhile we sit here." The first man kicked the deflated tire angrily.

"We can stay in the farmhouse," Rogelio said. "Don't worry about a place to sleep and eat. We have to worry about flying back the load."

"Hell of a place to land. There may be worse strips but I don't know where."

"Listen, *piloto,*" Rogelio said, "you're paid well to fly wherever you're told so don't complain."

"I don't know this Felipe Paredes—can he be trusted?"

"If not we would not be here," said Rogelio. "Don't worry, the truck will come any time now."

As they moved away from the wheels Isidro could see their firearms. The pilot, who was gringo from his accent, carried a hand-gun in a holster whereas Rogelio wore a small, squarish machine gun on a sling over one shoulder. He went to the plane's open door, leaned in, and took out a bottle. After drinking he gave the bottle to the pilot, who also drank. Watching them made Isidro feel thirst. The two men were enjoying tequila or wine, he thought. It had been a long time since he tasted even raw mescal, and his mouth and lips were dry.

On knees and elbows he crawled to where he could see part of the interior of the plane through the open door. There was a dim light that would have shown large cartons had there been any. So the plane had arrived empty in order to fly off with cargo to be turned over by Don Felipe Paredes who owned the land.

The men were lounging beside the doorway, talking in low voices, and Isidro could not hear their words. In any case he was listening for the sound of an approaching *camión,* the one that would have to travel to distant Nogales to bring back a new tire before the plane could leave.

He was lying on his side, one ear pressed to the packed sand in order to receive the *camión*'s distant vibrations. Instead, he heard a dry slithering sound nearby, and without moving his body turned his gaze beyond his shoulder.

Because his night vision was excellent Isidro was able to see the snake's tongue flicking outward between the down-curved fangs. He knew that the forked, delicate tongue was sensing his body warmth without hostility. And he also knew that the *cascabel* would wriggle closer until it was stretched out alongside his body to absorb its warmth. For the moment the tail rattles lay on the sand, and that was a good sign. Isidro saw that the snake was almost as long as his own body, the middle part fat and bulging as though it had eaten recently and well.

But for the armed men beside their plane Isidro would have rolled quickly away from the snake before it could coil and strike. Unfortunately, he lay next to the spined points of a maguey plant, so there was little he could do without making noise and attracting the men's attention. They were undoubtedly nervous over what had happened to their plane, and concerned about their future in the desert darkness. Hearing noise they might fire many bullets in his direction, and Isidro had no desire to die either from bullets or the agonizing venom of the large snake that was, in its natural way, inspecting him.

Holy Mother, he said, silently praying to the Virgin of Guadalupe, protect me now in the time of my mortal peril.

He did not dare to cross himself lest the snake misinterpret the movement and strike his unprotected leg. Instead, very slowly, Isidro began working his upper hand under the fold of his serape until his fingers touched the machete hilt. While he was doing that, the snake's head lifted until light from the plane's wings reflected in its eyes like dots of gold. Isidro felt deathly cold, and his gnarled hand with its enlarged knuckles seemed to be no part of him at all. Even so, he gradually worked his fingers down and around until they grasped the smooth wood handle of the machete.

The snake had noticed motion under the serape and drew back a little. Its rattles lifted and shook like the sound of dry leaves stirred by breeze.

Isidro prayed again and took a deep breath. Slowly, watching the snake's lifted head, he began to slide the machete from the sheath along his thigh while the *cascabel* gazed at him more intently than ever.

Then, from beside the plane, came a burst of music as a radio turned on. Ranchero music, he thought, from the Hermosillo station. It diverted the snake's attention, its head turning toward the source of the sound, and in that moment Isidro freed the machete, turned over on his belly, and with a powerful swinging stroke cut off the snake's head. As the dying body thrashed he rolled onto it to smother the sound of its convulsions. *Caray!* What a big one, he thought, pressing down on it as muscles rippled along its thick powerful body.

When there was no further movement, Isidro crossed himself and thanked the Virgin for her intervention. Then he rolled off the snake's headless body and looked at it admiringly.

During his years of desert roaming he had killed hundreds of poisonous snakes, but never one so closely threatening. Although there seemed no need for his labor at the empty plane, he had at least the fat snake for his effort. The meat was white as chicken, and the steaks, simmered with frijoles, chiles, and chayotes, or roasted over fire, would be succulent and sufficient for three days' meals. Again he thanked the Virgin of Guadalupe, then turned his attention to the two men.

One of them—Rogelio—pulled a blue cloth sack from the plane and carried it to the edge of the clearing. There, he placed it in the high fork of a tall saguaro and walked back to the plane.

The pilot turned off his radio and said, "This was supposed to be a touch-and-go, Rogelio. Instead, we're stuck here, and in daylight the plane can easily be seen from the air. I'd like to burn the damn thing and get out."

"How? The nearest town is Santa Victoria, twenty miles away. You'd never make it across the desert. Besides, there is the cargo we came for."

"The cargo should be here by now. Where the hell is the truck? Even after delivery what can we do with it?"

"Guard it," said Rogelio. "Guard it with our lives."

The pilot grunted. "I fly planes," he said. "I'm not a gunfighter. I had enough of that in another country." He drank deeply from the bottle.

Isidro was getting ready to crawl back down the little slope, pulling the snake's body after him, when he felt the earth vibrating lightly and heard the distant sound of a moving vehicle.

He decided to wait and see it arrive.

Making himself comfortable, Isidro listened as the *camión* approached. He saw the moving glow of its headlights, and thought that Rogelio and the pilot would be safe now. The truck would take them to Don Felipe's house where they could sleep and eat and wait for the necessary tire.

In a little while the *camión* turned into the far end of the clearing and sped toward the plane. Rogelio and the pilot stepped away from it and waved at the oncoming vehicle. It was smaller than a *camión*, with an open bed behind the driver's cab. A *camioneta*. Clearly, they were glad to see the *camioneta* arrive.

It was painted the dull color of old fire ashes—even the headlight rims and the wheel covers—and it stopped so hard that gravel and sand spattered around it.

From the cab two men got out and walked to meet the airmen. All four shook hands and gave each other *abrazos*.

Rogelio stepped back and pointed at the ruined tire. *"Compadres,"* he said, "we have a problem."

"So you do," the truck driver said. He walked over and kicked the tire. To his companion he said, "Bring the jack."

The pilot said, "There's no tire to put on. You have to bring us one."

"From Nogales," Rogelio said. "Meanwhile, take us to the house, where we can wait for the tire."

The man who was supposed to fetch the jack said, "How did this happen?"

The pilot said, "A sharp stone, a cactus thorn—what difference does it make? We need another tire to fly out of here. I'm cold. Let's get started for the house."

The truck driver said, "Don Felipe is not expecting company."

"Too damn bad," the pilot said. "If he'd kept the strip clean this wouldn't have happened. I don't want to hear about inconvenience to Don Felipe. It's inconvenient all around." He glanced at his wristwatch. "They're waiting for me on the other side of the river. I don't show up I'm in trouble. Bad trouble."

The truck driver shrugged. "My orders are to deliver ten kilos to you and receive payment. I have the *cocaína*. You have the payment?"

"Of course," Rogelio said, "but there is no point in exchanging until we can fly out. Until then I don't even want to see the *cocaína*. All I want to see is a sound tire."

The driver said, "My orders have nothing to do with tires. That is up to Don Felipe."

Rogelio said, "It's in his interest that we fly out of here before the plane attracts attention. He'll understand."

The pilot said, "Take us to him. I'll tell him that future sales depend on his cooperation."

The truck driver said, "There are many buyers, señor. Who buys does not trouble Don Felipe."

It was fully dark now, and Isidro Moreno saw that the moon was beginning to show above the western ridge near where the sun had disappeared below the horizon.

Rogelio said, "That may be so, but it does not affect this transaction."

"Then let us conclude it," the truck driver said. "Pablo, bring the cargo."

The man called Pablo went over to the *camioneta* and lifted a tarpaulin from the rear bed. He pulled out a canvas sack not unlike the one Rogelio had stored in the cactus tree, walked back, and handed it to the truck driver. "Here it is," the driver said. "Inspect it, taste, weigh it. Then hand over the money."

Without looking at the delivery sack Rogelio said, "If I take this and pay you, will you then take us to the house?"

"I will have to consult with Don Felipe," the driver said, "explain the situation, and come back with his decision. Don Felipe is a reasonable man. With payment in hand he will be inclined to do as you desire."

Isidro Moreno sensed that bad blood was beginning to ferment among the men. Perhaps now, he thought, was the time to leave, but he was interested in how it would all come out, and heard the pilot say, "I have an idea, *caballeros*. Let us all go to Nogales, return with the tire, and conclude the transaction."

The driver shook his head. "That will take too long and Don Felipe is expecting me. If I do not return with the payment it will go hard with me."

Rogelio nodded. "Our boss is equally demanding and I must have something to show for this trip. So I will pay you and trust Don Felipe to do what is right." He turned and began walking toward the plane's open door.

Isidro knew that the money was no longer in the plane and wondered what Rogelio was planning to do.

Rogelio unslung his odd-looking machine gun and placed it on the floor ledge, then climbed into the cabin. While he was doing that the pilot moved over toward the flat tire. The truck driver put down his canvas sack and set his hands on his hips, one hand beside a big revolver stuck in his belt.

Rogelio reappeared in the cabin doorway, a small bag in one hand. He tossed it toward the two employees of Don Felipe, and as Pablo went toward it Rogelio picked up the machine gun as though to sling it over his shoulder, but instead he grasped it with both hands and fired at the two men. Pablo took most of the bullets and fell down, but the truck driver was only wounded and from his knees shot Rogelio and the pilot. Rogelio's body pitched out of the plane as the pilot staggered backward against the wing. His pistol was out, and holding it in both hands he fired three times at the truck driver, whose body bucked and collapsed sideways. The pilot pressed one hand to his body and sat down against the wheel. Isidro could see blood running between his fingers.

Why are they killing each other? Isidro asked himself. He could see no reason for the shootings. The truck stood there silent, its lights directly on the wounded pilot. "Son of a bitch," the pilot said in a strained voice. "Oh, son of a bitch!" He dropped his pistol, and with both hands pressing his belly, bent forward moaning in pain.

Isidro rose on his knees and looked around at the scene of the shootings. As far as he could tell, Rogelio, Pablo and the truck driver were dead. Only the pilot was still alive and it did not seem that he was alive for long.

The shooting, while it lasted, had been loud, Isidro mused, but he did not think the sounds would carry as far as the *hacendado*'s house. The cactus forest would muffle the sounds as through a heavy blanket. So unless Don Felipe sent out men to determine the reason for the delay no one was going to come. At least until first light.

Rising, Isidro shook sand from his serape, moved stiff joints, and began walking toward the pilot. When he reached a position in front of him Isidro squatted and said, "What can I do for you?"

The pilot's head lifted, his eyes opened, and he said, "Help me. Help."

"I am not a *curandero,*" Isidro said, "or even a *médico.*"

"Then take me to one." He licked his lips and moved his head in the direction of the *camioneta.*

"I am sorry," Isidro said, "but I cannot drive. I know nothing of it. But if you can drive I will show you the way."

In the headlights' glare the pilot's face stubble glinted like fine copper wires. He was, Isidro judged, no more than thirty-five, but Isidro had not seen many gringos close up so he could not be sure. They seemed to live much longer than his countrymen—unless killed by cars or guns.

"I can't drive," the pilot said, the effort of speaking twisting his face into a teeth-baring grimace. "It will kill me. Can you get someone to drive?"

Isidro shook his head slowly. "The only ones are at the house of Don Felipe Paredes. And by shooting his men you have made him your enemy. *Sí,* someone would come, but only to kill you." He sighed. "In any case the house is at least ten kilometers distant. To walk there through this desert would take me at least three hours."

"I'll pay you," the pilot gritted through set teeth. "There is money in my pocket."

And in the fork of the saguaro tree, Isidro thought, but said, "A man should not be paid for helping another. It is that I do not know how to help you, señor," he added respectfully.

"Oh, God," the young man moaned. "Oh, God, God, God, Holy Jesus." His head lowered until his chin rested on his upper chest. After a while Isidro said, "Why did Rogelio begin shooting? I do not understand his reasoning."

Thickly the pilot said, "You saw? They were not going to help with the tire. They were going to steal our money and leave us. But by taking their truck we could have gotten away from here." Breath rattled dryly in his throat. "It went wrong." His face lifted and his gaze met Isidro's. "I don't want to die in the desert. In the name of God help me." Blood flowed between his fingers.

Isidro thought for a while before saying, "The government has a small clinic at Huizapulli." He looked up at the positions of the moon and stars. "Leaving now, I could reach the clinic by dawn."

"Then go," the pilot gasped. "I beg you to get help."

Isidro considered. "The *médico* may not be there, señor. It depends on the day of the week." He rose. "Nevertheless I will go to Huizapulli and explain the situation."

The pilot seemed not to hear him. "I'm cold," he whispered. "There are blankets in the plane."

Isidro stooped under the wing and walked back to the open door. Toward the narrow end there was a pile of old blankets that must have been there for delicate cargo. He stepped around Rogelio's body and pulled out two blankets and carried them back to the pilot. He laid them gently over the young man's body and saw that the pilot's face was wet with tears.

What a tragedy, Isidro thought. They were bad men, all four of them, not evil men, just bad. The pilot was probably the least bad of them all, and now he has accepted that he is going to die beside the plane he brought here.

For what? he thought. For money.

Stepping back, Isidro said, "I will go now, and may God keep you."

The pilot said nothing. His eyes were closed and blood was seeping through the heavy blankets.

"*Adios,*" Isidro said, and began walking away. He remembered the bottle both men had drunk from, found it lying beside Rogelio's body, and took it back to the pilot, thinking the liquor might ease the pain and comfort him. He uncapped the bottle and poured some of the liquor into the young man's mouth but most of it dribbled away. Isidro swallowed a little of it, finding the taste burning and unpleasant. He left the open bottle within easy reach against the pilot's thigh and walked back over the rise. There he lay down beside the dead snake and his *tambache* and looked up into the clear night. The stars were brilliant and there was so much moonlight that he could have made his way in any direction without bumping into shrubs and cactus or stumbling into an arroyo.

But he had decided not to walk away. His promise to go for help had been made to console the young man who would be dead in a little while. He would die in peace thinking help would eventually come. Better to die when there was still hope in your mind, Isidro thought, than in the knowledge that nothing could be done.

Because that was how he himself would want it; he had conferred the gift of peaceful dying on the young gringo with the copper beard.

Beneath his body the earth was still. So far no *camión* had been sent out by Don Felipe. In the countryside it had always been said that Don Felipe Paredes was a *rico* and more or less a *bandido*. Isidro had taken no position with regard to the landowner but from what had taken place this night he knew that Don Felipe was both a rich man and a criminal.

Attempting to denounce the *hacendado* to the authorities was both dangerous and pointless, Isidro knew, but it occurred to him that he had been given an opportunity to keep Don Felipe from becoming even more wealthy. Perhaps God had arranged this for that very reason. It was a question he would like to put to Padre Gardenia, the priest everyone visited on feast days. The priest's name was not really Gardenia, but the gentle priest cultivated the white flowers in his small garden and had come to be known as El Padre de las Gardenias, and finally simply Padre Gardenia.

The priest was a man truly of the people, who understood that not everyone could always attend mass on days of obligation or contribute more than a few coins to the collection box. Padre Gardenia lived simply, in a small room beside the adobe church, and Isidro Moreno had often thought that he lived as poorly and hungrily as the poorest of his flock. In contrast to Don Felipe, Padre Gardenia was a thoroughly good man, and without his white collar when he was chopping firewood beside the church he looked like any other Tilma *indio*. Which was how and why the priest enjoyed the trust and loyalty of everyone in that small village.

Staring up at the endless heavens, Isidro reminded himself that he could have gone for the priest except that the church was two hours distant, and bringing Padre Gardenia would have accomplished nothing except perhaps to involve the priest in difficulties with Don Felipe and the authorities. So he told himself that he had done all he could for the wounded pilot, little though it was, and would be guided in other things by asking himself what God required him to do.

By now he hoped that Olivia would be sleeping soundly and comfortably in their bed. Except for his encounter with the big snake he would have to think carefully about what else he might tell her. She was not given to gossip, but an unguarded word might bring disaster to them both, so for a while at least he would tell her nothing. And it was not her way to question where he might have been or why.

Slowly Isidro turned over and got onto his knees.

The scene was as brightly lighted as before. He looked at the pilot and saw that even more blood had come through the thick blankets. The pilot's head was resting on one shoulder and though his eyes were open they were unseeing. Isidro crossed himself in respect for the dead, and left his hiding place.

The truck driver's body lay close to the canvas sack he had come to deliver to the plane. Isidro avoided the body while pulling the sack a few feet away. He opened it and saw a number of bags of powder that looked like white flour. The bags themselves were transparent and smooth to his touch. This was the truly evil stuff, he told himself. He got out his machete and, holding each bag above the desert floor, slit them with his machete and watched the white dust blow away.

The bag that Rogelio had tossed toward Pablo held a razor, a bar of soap, two books, and a pair of rubber-soled shoes. He might have taken the shoes but they were too small for his broad feet.

As he walked past the *camioneta* Isidro wondered if there was anything he should do about it. If he cut its tires with his machete Don Felipe would know some *peón* had done it, and the men of the hacienda would start looking for who it might have been. Suspecting someone, they would torture him to confess, and Isidro did not want that to happen to some innocent *peón*. What he was doing was dangerous enough, but he did not intend to leave a trail that would lead to anyone alive.

Leaving the lighted area, Isidro went over to the cactus stand where Rogelio had placed his blue sack. It was located above his reach so he used the blunt edge of his machete to pull it down. Squatting at the border of the airstrip, he opened the bag. There was enough light to show him packets of green bills that he recognized as gringo money. Once at a roadside he had changed a tire for a gringa and she had given him such a bill with the number "5" on it. At the time he had been disappointed, thinking it was only five pesos, but at the store where he bought cooking oil the storekeeper had given him many more than five pesos in change. So he knew that these green bills were worth a large fortune in pesos, a fortune he had already determined that Don Felipe was not going to receive.

He began counting the number of currency packets but stopped when he reached twenty, never having learned to count beyond that number. But he was satisfied that a man such as himself could pass the rest of his life spending them and never completely succeed.

He looked across at the fallen bodies and their now useless weapons. He counted four weapons and there could be more in the plane or the truck. Had one been an *escopeta* he might have taken it for hunting, but all were small-bore weapons not suited to his need. If he took them away to sell he would run the risk of arrest, and no matter how great the profit from selling them he would be of no use or comfort to Olivia in jail.

Besides, the weapons had killed men and were now evil in themselves.

As he looked at the side of the plane, breeze swept across the clearing picking up little whorls of dust and sand. By now the white powder could no longer be seen. Isidro thought about the vast fortune that had come to him without his wishing it or seeking it in any way, and he acknowledged the truth of Padre Gardenia's words when the priest had said that God moves in mysterious ways.

But Isidro Moreno thought that he understood a part of God's intention when he had been guided this night to a normally deserted place, and been shown all that he had seen. He looked up and saw that the stars and moon had moved, and he understood that in less than six hours the sun would again appear above the eastern mountains. The desert would warm and above it in the rising heat buzzards would climb and glide and soar. Soon their keen vision would pick out the plane and the *camioneta* and the motionless bodies, and they would spiral down cautiously at first, settle on the desert floor, and lurch awkwardly to where the bodies lay.

By then, Isidro thought, he wanted to be far away from where the men had killed each other. He knew that the circling *zopilotes* would be noticed by Don Felipe's workmen, who would then drive out into the desert to learn what the attraction was.

Isidro closed his eyes, crossed himself, and plunged one hand into the sack. He drew out all that his hand could hold and slid the banded packets into the long thigh-pocket of his cotton trousers, telling himself that God or the Virgin had intended that much for his portion and no more. He closed the sack and carried it over the rise to where he had left his snake and his *tambache*. Because he was not going to walk directly home, he slit the belly of the snake and spilled its entrails on the sand so that the meat would keep until he was able to reach home.

After tying the snake's body across his *tambache* he lifted it onto his back and carried the money sack in one hand. As he turned away from the lighted zone he decided to hide his portion of the money beneath the bed, where his father's old *pistola* was buried. Perhaps once a month he or Olivia would take out one of the bills and ride a bus to one of the distant villages where it would be exchanged for pesos. They would spend only enough for their needs lest rumor spread that the Morenos were enjoying sudden wealth. For a time at least they would conduct themselves with great caution, and perhaps eventually leave their little home and find another place in this great land to spend the rest of their lives.

There was a narrow path ahead that cattle sometimes used, but Isidro did not want to risk encountering a herder on the way. By staying in the desert he would have to walk further to the village, but if he could reach the adobe church before sunrise his purpose would be accomplished.

It was Isidro's intention to enter the chapel and place the sack he carried at the altar, where Padre Gardenia would find it when he entered to say his private morning prayers.

The church needed paving over its dirt floor, and a bell for its empty tower and many other things. Of all men, the priest would know how best to use God's gift for the betterment of the church, the sick, and the poor of the village.

So thinking, Isidro rolled his shoulder muscles under the weight of the *tambache,* breathed deeply of the cool night air, tasting a purity that was more delicious than the finest tequila, and lengthened his stride so that he would reach the village and the church while the good Padre Gardenia was still asleep.

Book ONE

ONE

The year the Guadalajara cartel tortured and murdered Kiki Camarena I was working out of the Nogales DEA office. For six months I'd been on temporary assignments in Phoenix, San Diego, and El Paso, so I was becoming accustomed to living out of a suitcase in third-rate motels. The acid stomach came from diner food.

Nogales was an improvement over the other cities because Manny Montijo was there. We'd been partners working cases in Baltimore and Philadelphia, and I liked him. He was dependable and resourceful, and a couple of cuts above the average DEA agent. He endured his share of slurs about being a *cucaracha,* a Mexican-American, even though his heritage was Spanish and he had a degree from USC. That bothered me more than it seemed to affect Manny, who was a lot more diplomatic than I wanted to be. In fact, my recent gypsy-style assignments reflected my lack of popularity among empty-suit regional supervisors, who prized docility over production.

After flying Navy fighters in 'Nam I'd come home to find my young wife, Pam, addicted to heroin. At the time, she was a top-earning model, and though I tried for weeks to get her into detox her addiction was too strong, and she ended up with a needle in her arm, chalk-white and dead. Whether the fix was too heavy by chance or intention I never knew. But I resigned from the Navy and signed up with the Drug Enforcement Administration, which seemed glad to have someone with a valid four-year degree from a recognizable college—in my case the Naval Academy.

It was about ten o'clock on a Monday morning when Manny came over to my desk with two Styrofoam cups of coffee. He set mine down, sipped from his, and said, "Whatcha doin'?"

"The usual. Finishing reports due a week ago." I signed at the bottom of one, on the line provided, and slid it into my outbox. "What's on your mind, *compadre?*"

He grimaced before saying, "Not sure, Jack, but here it is." He drank more coffee and I sipped mine as he said, "I go to a local church, San Ramón, where one of the priests asked me a couple months ago if I was a Spanish Montijo. Turns out he came from northern Spain, where the wealthy branch of my family has vineyards and makes wine. Someone had told him I was with DEA and he gave me his blessing."

I smiled. "Always good to have."

"Right. Nothing after that until yesterday. Following mass, Father Jerónimo asked me into his study and told me he has a priest cousin serving in a little village south of here, Santa Victoria."

"Never heard of it."

"Who would? Anyway, a while back his cousin came here for medical attention—high blood pressure—and stayed with Father Jerónimo for a few days. The cousin, whom the villagers call Father Gardenia, told him a strange story about receiving a big bundle of U.S. dollars anonymously. No note, no apparent source, *nada.*" He cleared his throat.

I drank from my cup and asked, "How much money?"

"At least three hundred thou."

"Not a bad day's offering. I hope Padre Gardenia didn't inquire too closely for the donor's identity."

Manny shrugged. "The good father's using some of it to floor the church, buy a bell for the tower, and establish a soup kitchen—in that part of Sonora a few bucks go a long way."

I nodded. "Piss-poor country, barren as the moon."

"Yeah. Inhabited mostly by surviving Tilma indians." He cleared his throat again; the air around Nogales was laden with dust and diesel fumes that affected us all. "That it?" I asked.

"Not quite. A federal policeman told Father Gardenia they'd found four bodies outside a plane in the desert ten or twenty miles south of Santa Victoria. Apparently the men had shot each other. I figure it as a soured drug deal, but there were no drugs and . . . no money."

"Definitely a deal gone stinko." I sat forward. "The padre went to the site?"

Manny shook his head. "It's on property belonging to a bigtime Mexican named Paredes—Felipe Paredes—who doesn't like strangers on his land."

"Not even a priest?"

Manny grunted. "I gather Paredes isn't the church-going type."

"Plane still there?"

"My priest didn't say." He looked at a scrawled sheet in his hand, and said, "We have a pretty heavy file on Paredes—enough to arrest him if he showed up this side of the border. But down there, of course, he's immune."

"And protected by the police."

"And army, probably." He sighed. "You know how it goes."

"Sure. So Paredes is either a trafficker or lets his land be used for aircraft flying to or from the States. Big profits either way." I frowned. "But if only three hundred thou showed up that wasn't exactly a big deal—not big enough to interest us, right?"

"Except, who knows how much Padre Gardenia *didn't* get, Jack. And, there's this: presuming the green came from where the bodies were found, who took it to the church? Did the guy shoot all four, and get conscience stricken afterward? Did he donate dirty money to Padre Gardenia to square himself in his own mind? Or did he just stumble across the scene, and scoop up the money afterward?"

"Hell, Manny, either way he did the right thing."

"Yeah." He squinted at his note-sheet. "I'd like to get a satellite scan of Paredes's rancho. If the plane's still there the wing numbers could tell us something."

"Why would the plane still be there?"

"You tell me, you're a pilot."

"Could have run out of gas, or landed with engine trouble. How long would it take to get a sat scan?"

"Least a week, considering all the paperwork and approvals." He eyed me. "Quicker to drive there for a look."

"Quick and dicey," I muttered, "but you're right. How far is the place?"

"From here I figure about a hundred and fifty miles, mostly desert roads. Interested?"

"Maybe. But let's see what sat photography produces."

A week of bureaucratic paper shoving between Nogales, Phoenix, and Washington, and I'd almost forgotten about Padre Gardenia, the plane, and the corpses in the desert. Manny phoned a pal in Washington headquarters and learned the sat scan request was rated low priority, no way to tell when the satellite would be diverted to cover Paredes's land.

We were dining on good Texas beef at the Embers steakhouse and quaffing Coronas and Tecates when Manny said, "I don't hold out much hope for the satellite, Jack, but you could take an office pickup—"

"With sleeping bag, food, water, extra gas and spare tires. Why doesn't the idea thrill me?"

He smiled. "Or you could fly there and back in a couple of hours."

"True. And who's going to ask permission to fly in Mexican air space and eyeball land of one of their affluent nationals?"

"Not necessary. Put a couple fishing rods in the plane and say you're headed for Guaymas, it being marlin season."

"Who says it's marlin season?"

"Who says it ain't?"

I downed more Tecate. "It's a reasonable plot, amigo. What've we got on inventory?"

"Couple of jets and some single-engine prop aircraft."

"I'll check them out."

When I went to the federal joint operations hangar, a mec strolled out to intercept me so I showed him my DEA buzzer and FAA qualifications card. He read every line before returning them to me. "Okay, Mr. Novak, what can I do you for?"

"I hear you've got jets and prop aircraft on the books. What's recently rated airworthy and flyable?"

He tugged at a broad mustache and gave me a half smile. "Not necessarily the same, right?" I followed him deeper into the hangar and stopped when he swept an arm across the far end. "Them five's forfeited aircraft. Cessna Citation's got bullet holes in the fuselage, so forget pressurization. The Lear's got two flat tires—from just sittin' around there—and most of the avionics are shot."

"Why?"

"Sat too long in the sun, wiring insulation melted."

I walked to the nearest prop aircraft, a high-wing Piper, and opened the cockpit door. Hornets swarmed out and I got busy slapping them away from my face. After I slammed the door shut I said to the mec, "Wouldn't hurt to fumigate the fuselage." I moved toward a yellow Comanche.

"True, but who's gonna pay for it? Not on my budget here."

I glanced down under the Comanche's nacelle where a pool of oil spread out over the concrete. I looked around at the mec, who shrugged. No point in asking about the leak—he'd tell me he couldn't afford a Phillips screwdriver to open up the cowling—so I walked over to the last of DEA's local aircraft holdings: a Gruman Skyhawk.

Its tires looked okay, and there was no oil pool under the engine. I moved the elevator up and down and shoved the rudder from side to side. No cables whined or snapped, so I said, "Charley, by dawn tomorrow I want this museum relic checked out, dipsticked, fully fueled, washed, and tires inflated. Ready for takeoff."

"My name ain't Charley," he growled.

"Sorry about that. Tell you what: I've got fifty says you can't do all that and have this crate on the flight line, engine idling by, say, zero six hundred."

He scratched his chin. "Possible. Hope you're a better pilot than a gambler. Bring your money."

At flight operations I took a chart covering Baja, the Sea of Cortez, and most of northern Sonora, then drove back to the office. I scanned the bullpen for Manny until a secretary told me he was in the conference room with a visitor. So I spread out the chart on my desk and used simple navigation instruments—ruler and protractor—to draw a flight line to the Santa Victoria area, noticing that it pretty much paralleled a fourth-class road.

I sensed Manny beside me, and looked up.

"Been talking with a young lady from Phoenix who's looking for a missing brother."

"What's the matter with Missing Persons?"

"Said she tried there last week, got nothing."

"Surprise, surprise. Why did she come here?"

"FBI suggested it. C'mon, Jack, talk with her, she needs an understanding face and a kindly manner."

"That's me? Okay, I'll dust her off so we can get down to business." I rapped the chart and followed him to the conference room.

Before he opened the door I felt a premonition that this was the wrong thing to do, but I went in anyway and saw a young woman seated at the table.

Her cinnamon hair was layered, her creamy complexion was lightly freckled, and a snub nose accented full lips. She was wearing a light beige turtleneck sweater, a gold chain necklace with a ying-yang pendant, and a pale sapphire ring. She looked up at me and I saw startlingly green eyes. Manny said, "Miss LaTour, my partner, Jack Novak. Jack, Miss Favor LaTour." She nodded, and kept her hands on the table. I sat down and said, "Your brother's missing—how long?"

"About three weeks."

"His name?"

"Eddie Flanigan." She half-smiled, "LaTour is my showbiz name; I was born Molly Flanigan. Do you think Favor LaTour is an improvement?"

"Maybe. Does your brother have any involvement with narcotics?"

She shrugged. "He was in Vietnam—Air Force—so I guess he's smoked pot. And inhaled."

"Addict?"

"I don't think so. Ah—I work in Las Vegas, casino dancer, and Eddie and I have an apartment in Phoenix, but between his job and mine we're not often there at the same time." She paused. "In Vegas I share a room with another dancer, but I guess I think of Phoenix as my home. We grew up there."

"What work does your brother do?"

"Eddie flys charters."

"Profitably?"

"Pays his share of the rent."

"And you haven't seen him for three weeks?"

"About that. Said he had a flight to Guadalajara."

"In his own plane?"

"No. He leases planes when he needs them."

"Do you know who he was flying to Guadalajara?"

She shook her head. "He didn't say—but he hardly ever does."

"He leased a plane in Phoenix?"

"I assume so."

"Then he would have filed a flight plan at the airport. Did you check for one?"

She bit her lip before saying, "No, but I guess I should have. I'll do that this afternoon before going back to Vegas."

"Good idea, Miss LaTour—or should I say Flanigan?"

"Either way, it's me." She smiled lightly.

"And we can check on any . . . ah . . . accidents between here and Guadalajara, though I hope there's none reported." I paused. "It would be helpful if we knew what kind of aircraft he leased."

"I'll ask."

"By the way, if he was flying from Phoenix to Guadalajara, why are you asking about him here in Nogales?"

"Because, when he flys to Mexico, he usually stops here to refuel—he's done that twice when I was with him."

Manny said, "Jack, would there be a refueling record?"

"Not if he paid cash."

She said, "That's most likely, his credit cards are pretty much maxed out. Besides, he prefers having the client pay for gas, then he doesn't get stuck with it at the end."

"Sensible," I said. "Sound business practice."

She stared at her hands before asking, "Anything else, gentlemen?"

Manny said, "Give us contact numbers in Vegas and Phoenix, Miss LaTour—ah, you perform in a casino?"

"The Splendide, one of the new ones." She wrote on a pad and handed the sheet to Manny. "If I'm not at either place you can leave messages on the machines. I check them daily."

He nodded. "And you'll call from Phoenix airport?"

"I will." She got up, and I saw she was wearing fashionably faded designer jeans that fitted her legs like latex. When she moved from the table I noticed sensible flats on her feet, not the spike heels I detested. Manny handed her his office card and said, "This number will reach both of us, so feel free to call any time."

"Thank you." She hesitated, and I thought her lip trembled as she said, "Do you think there's . . . hope after so long?"

"There's always hope," I responded. "If your brother went down somewhere in Mexico he could be walking as we speak. After all, as a Vietnam pilot he had survival training."

"That's so, isn't it?" She brightened, gave us her hand briefly, and left the room. Manny turned to me and said, "Are you thinking what I'm thinking?"

"Probably. Eddie flew a low-grade drug mission and either crashed or got himself killed."

"Yeah. And it's possibly connected to Father Gardenia's find—right?"

"Right. I'm planning a flyover tomorrow, see if there's anything to see on Paredes land."

We went back to our adjacent desks where I showed Manny the course I'd plotted. "The Skyhawk is old and slow and I'm hoping the mec will get it airworthy before takeoff."

"Which is when?"

"As soon as there's light. It'll be Visual Flight Rules all the way."

"Returning when?"

"No later than midday. I'm taking along an extra five-gallon can for if I'm low on fuel and have to land."

"Good idea. Take along a camera, too. And a piece."

"I'll draw them from Supply. MAC-10 with spare clips—just in case."

"Jack, for Christ's sake don't go shooting *Federales* and provoke an international incident."

"Only if I'm fired at first. Besides, my policy is no surviving witnesses."

He shook his head and sighed, "I'm less sure this was a good idea."

I looked at my wristwatch. "This time tomorrow we ought to know."

After lunch a call came in from Molly Flanigan aka Favor LaTour. She said her brother had rented a plane for a round-trip daylong flight to Guadalajara, and taken off with one passenger. The plane was a Cessna 414, and the company wanted it back. "I'm leaving for Vegas now, so I can be reached there if there's any news."

"Thank you," I said, "and we'll be sure to let you know."

As we replaced phone receivers Manny and I exchanged glances. "A serious young woman," Manny remarked. "Dependable."

"And attractive as all get-out. It would be nice if we could locate Eddie—alive—but the odds are against it."

"What I've been thinking," Manny agreed. "I like it she has a Vegas roommate of the female persuasion, not a floor gorilla, pit boss, or a high roller. You?"

"I sort of like it, too. Encourages me to do what I can for the lass. Did you see those emerald eyes? They melted me down like wax."

"So you want to see her again."

"Away from the office—in a nonrestrictive atmosphere."

"Where your natural inclinations can have full play . . ."

"Why not? She's single, over twenty-one, and hip to the way of the world."

"In which case she's probably smart enough to avoid the likes of you."

"Possibly, Manny, just possibly. And in my world it's always ladies' choice."

"Making you a gentleman of old-fashioned values, the kind mothers dote on."

"So I've been told by many a mother. Let's check the files for Eddie Flanigan and fax a query to the Pentagon. I'd like to know if he was messed up in dope shit in 'Nam. And a file run on Sis wouldn't be amiss."

"Jack, I ran her name before talking with her."

"As LaTour or Flanigan?"

"Only LaTour—I'll check Flanigan, too."

I looked down at the air chart on my desk. "Can you pinpoint Paredes's place?"

"Be in his file, I'll look for it."

Before leaving the office I checked out a Nikon with telephoto lens and rolls of high-resolution film. I signed for a MAC-10 and three loaded mags, and on the way to my half-star motel, stopped at a hardware store. I bought a gas can, a canteen, a fishing rod, and a shovel—the latter in case I landed and had to dig out a wheel. Manny had dinner with wife Lucinda and their two small daughters, so as I usually did I repaired to the Embers for grilled fajita with rice and black beans, chef's salad, and peach pie. I took along a roast beef sandwich to munch on the flight and watched room TV, sustained by several ounces of Añejo over ice.

The alarm woke me at five. I collected my gear and drove to the airport, stopping for donuts and coffee before reaching the hangar at six.

Lo and behold, the Skyhawk was chocked in front of the hangar, prop idling. I drove the office car into the hangar and got out my gear. The mec strolled over and said, "Lost your bet."

"So I did." I handed him a fifty-dollar bill that disappeared in his greasy palm. Yawning, he said, "That was an all-nighter, so I'm calling in sick today."

"Don't blame you." I pointed at my gas can and asked him to fill it and take it to the plane.

After stowing my gear in the Skyhawk I filed a flight plan in the office under the control tower, giving Guaymas as my destination, and checked weather to the south. "Oughta be CAVU all the way," the clerk told me, "but watch your ass over them fuckin' Sierras. Wind blows every whichway and shears like a knife."

"I'll bear it in mind," I told him, left the office, and pulled chocks from the Skyhawk wheels.

The cockpit and controls weren't unlike those of my Seabee, an old pusher amphibian I kept tethered off the dock at my safehouse on Cozumel. After waggling ailerons, rudder and elevator, I clicked on the radio and found the Nogales tower frequency. Headset on, I requested takeoff permission, and was told to use the east-west runway for lift advantage from the light morning wind.

Taxiing to the runway, I revved the engine and was pleased by its smooth response. For fifty bucks the mec had done well by me. After braking, I scanned sky and airfield, ran up the mercury until the plane shuddered, and freed the brakes. Tail up, nose slightly down, we raced down the runway like a cheetah until at two hundred yards we were airborne. I climbed to five thousand feet, and set my southward course as I crossed the border into Mexico.

Ahead lay—what? Maybe a crashed plane and a couple of corpses. Maybe nothing but clueless desert, but I was going to find out.

What I hoped *not* to find was an armed reception committee. I'd left DEA identification in my motel room but Mex *traficantes* seldom paused to ID trespassers before killing them.

Pushing negative thoughts from my mind, I filled it with pleasing visions of Molly Flanigan. I liked her Irish eyes, open manner, and not least her lithe dancer's bod. Even if I had to bring her somber news I knew I wanted to see Molly again.

Far below I spotted a dirt road and dropped to two thousand feet to verify it was the one to Santa Victoria. The chart showed it was, and Paredes's ranch lay only a few miles beyond.

I corrected my heading for windage, flexed my fingers on the yoke, and sat back until Paredes's hacienda came distantly into view.

Sun-heated air rising from the desert floor yawed the plane and briefly dropped the nose. Before I could level off I glimpsed something far off I hadn't expected to see in the desert.

A column of black smoke reaching into the pale blue cloudless sky.

Two

For a few moments I stared at the oily smoke before remembering my camera. Naturally, it was under the adjoining seat, long lens unattached, and not easily reached. I'd loaded film, however, so that was one less thing to do as I got the Nikon on my lap and fitted on the telephoto. Through the viewfinder the oily column was larger and better defined, and I clicked off three frames. Then I had to turn back onto course before another look through the lens.

The smoke was rising from what seemed to be a large pile of junkyard junk. I dipped the nose and exposed another few frames before noticing a truck beyond the conflagration. I didn't need the magnifying lens to see four men get into the truck and begin moving away, and I wondered why it took so many helpers to start a refuse fire.

Turning west, I gained a thousand feet before leveling off, then banked right so I could get a better view of the scene. As I watched, flames erupted from the junk pile and spread out across the clearing, adding to the rising smoke.

Evidently the monotony of flying a straight course had dulled my mind, for it was only then that I connected the fire with the plane Eddie Flanigan had leased in Phoenix. The smoke was too dense to make out details of what was burning, but when a plane crashes and burns not all the metal is consumed: engines and propellers are inflammable even after wings and fuselage burn to ash—particularly after a fuel tank explosion.

I had enough photos of the fire—for whatever use they might have—and as I turned back on course I saw the truck making a dust trail in the direction of a wide, two-story house.

I didn't have to check the chart to identify it as Felipe Paredes's hacienda; no other dwelling was anywhere in view. Stables and out-buildings were set to the south of the house and there were corrals of horses and cattle. I photographed the spread, and turned back to avoid attracting attention. For all I knew, one of the shacks could hide an armed aircraft able to shoot me out of the sky.

Still, I wanted to scan the surroundings, so I used the telephoto lens as a telescope and located the fire at the end of a narrow clearing I estimated to be some two hundred yards long. Typical desert land-ing strip, I reflected; no gas pumps, no cantina or lunch shack, no amenities at all. It wasn't your hospitable neighborhood fly-in strip, but a piece of real estate whose proximity to the U.S. border gave it immense value to the owner.

That much decided, I realized I still couldn't testify with cer-tainty that I'd seen a burning plane. I'd have to get closer after the flames and smoke died down, and that was going to take at least an hour.

Already the fuel gauge showed I'd burned a third of the tank, and if I stayed airborne another hour barely enough would remain to fly back to Nogales. The chart showed an airstrip near Santa Vic-toria that could take light aircraft. Padre Gardenia was in the vil-lage, and the time was propitious to compare notes, exchange information—if he were willing.

From the air the village strip looked little better than the one I'd photographed, but at least it had a windsock. I lowered flaps and ap-proached from the south, touching down on loose gravel that drummed the underside of the fuselage, kicked up by the rolling wheels. I let the Skyhawk coast to a stop not far from a thatched shack where a couple of layabouts were drinking on shaded stools.

There was no wind so I didn't need tie-down, took out the ignition key, and sauntered over to the cantina.

One customer was bald, with a Pancho Villa mustache, the other sported a salt-and-pepper beard. Behind the sagging service counter a fat female with greasy hair listened to the radio; it was broadcasting lottery results. She frowned, and turned to me. "*¿Qué?*"

"Tecate—preferably cold."

"No Tecate. Cuauhtémoc or mescal."

There were two kinds of mescal, with or without flies. I said, "Cuauhtémoc." She uncapped a bottle and slid it toward me. The bottle was slightly under air temperature. I drank to moisten mouth and throat, and peered at the stained tin wall behind her. A curling yellowed sticker read: *La Guerra Contra La Mosca.* I looked around at bluebottles buzzing the bar and recalled Tin Tan's famous phrase: The war is over, the flies won.

"How far to *el centro?*"

"Six blocks, maybe more," Baldy told me. "Where you wanna go, gringo?"

"The church, *calvo.*" I took another swallow, paid the fat charmer, and set out for downtown.

Where there was sidewalk, it was either broken, or angled up from tree roots; busted curb bordered a cobblestone lane. Shops I passed were either curtained, or open to passersby. I didn't see much commerce being transacted.

A lad on a bicycle pointed me in the direction of the church. Another two blocks of careful walking, and I saw the village church. In front of it a cement mixer was churning away, and workmen were carrying hods into the church. Carpenters were pounding on the roof, and it cheered me to see some of Paredes's money being used for good works. Drug profits traditionally went for broads, cars, Italian castles, bribes, and offshore bank accounts. This trickle might never be missed.

Still, I reflected, there was the missing plane . . .

A hod-carrier jostled me as I peered into the church's dust-filled dimness. Near the narthex a short figure in priestly habit was covering religious artifacts, crossing himself each time he passed the altar. Benches were stacked against the walls, and between us, masons were tiling the prepared floor. No way I could reach the priest through the church.

So I went out and came around to a side entrance through which I could see the priest busily dust-proofing the altar, icons, and font. Cupping my hands, I called, "Padre Gardenia—could I have a word with you?"

Turning, he peered at me. "As soon as I finish here," he said, and continued working.

Presently he brushed off his brown robe and walked on sandled feet toward me. He was short and thin, his hair was long, and he needed a shave. He tightened the cord around his waist and said, "Yes?"

I have him my name and said I was a friend of a friend of his cousin, Padre Jerónimo. He looked around apprehensively, and beckoned me toward a small cottage set a few yards from the rear of the church. Chicken wire enclosed twenty-odd gardenia bushes, some of which were budding, others in full bloom. Their perfume followed me into the kitchen, where the priest produced a wine bottle and two fairly clean glasses. After filling them, he said, "Welcome. How is my cousin?"

We sat at a rough wooden table and lifted our glasses. "In good health and spirits," I replied, and we drank.

"What brings you to Santa Victoria?" he asked politely.

"It has to do with a gift of dollars, a vanished aircraft, and several corpses. I'm in the anti-narcotics business, Padre, and what the policeman told you has a familiar ring." Outside, the sounds of pouring, hammering and sawing continued. The priest paled. "You want the money back?"

"No, it's yours, a gift from heaven." I sipped more wine. "Apparently a plane went down on land belonging to Felipe Paredes a month or so ago. Isn't that about when the money appeared on your altar?"

He nodded. "But I do not know who left it there."

"Any ideas?"

His eyes focused on mine. "Perhaps."

I sat forward. "I don't want a name, Padre, but if you can speculate on the donor, so can Paredes."

"Regrettably so."

"How do you explain to the village this burst of church construction?"

He looked down at his glass. "I say a gift came from Rome. I do not regard that as a lie, for it is possible."

I nodded. "Whoever brought you the money did a good deed, and neither of us wishes the donor to suffer any harm." I paused. "Should you notice a parishioner wearing new clothes or shoes, or displaying unusual affluence, I suggest you take him or her aside for a word of caution."

"Yes, I will do so." He glanced away. "I have seen some of Paredes's work, and he is a cruel, deadly man." He crossed himself and closed his eyes. Opening them, he asked, "Is there anything I can do for you?"

"There may be. I flew from Nogales and saw a large fire on Paredes's landing strip. I suspect the missing plane was being burned, because a truck with several men drove away from the scene. When I leave I plan to fly there and see what the fire leaves. It may be the plane, or—" I shrugged. What else could it be?

The priest nodded. "I advise caution, whatever you do."

"I'm cautious by nature," I told him, and finished my wine. "Should you ever need me, tell Padre Jerónimo."

"I will." He left the table and took down a jar from the shelf above the sink. From it he produced a paper packet and set it before me. "The soldier brought this," he said, "from the plane. It may be of some use to you."

I opened the paper and saw a bead chain with a dog tag. It bore the name Edward J. Flanigan, bloodtype "A," and a serial number beginning with the "O" officer designation. "This will help," I told Padre Gardenia, and rewrapped Eddie's ID. "Tells me more than I want to know."

A workman came to the doorway, doffed his cap, and said, "Pardon, Padre, but as we near the altar, I need your guidance."

"Of course, Serafino." He smiled and we shook hands. I followed him out of his dwelling and began walking back to the airfield, dog tag in my pocket. It was pretty clear evidence that Eddie Flanigan was dead, but for his sister's sake I wanted to make sure. Whoever killed him and the others probably did so on orders from Paredes, who would never be charged with the murders. In any case I was satisfied that Paredes was a vital link in a narcotics transmission chain that began down in Colombia, Venezuela, or Peru, and deserved DEA attention.

Only the bearded loafer was still at the cantina bar. He and the barmaid ignored me, listening to lottery numbers. The broadcast was probably a significant event in the daily life of Santa Victoria, a lifeless village if I ever saw one.

After pushing the tail around to head the Skyhawk's nose into the light breeze, I got behind the controls and started the V-8 Lycoming engine. Brakes on, I ran up the merc and lifted off after a short run. Five minutes later I was approaching Peredes's strip, where the fire had burned down to a few patches of gray smoke that drifted across the clearing.

I shot two frames from five hundred feet, seeing nothing identifiable as a plane, and decided to get closer. Setting flaps, I touched down at the far end of the narrow strip and taxied along until I was only twenty or thirty yards from the twisted, blackened rubble.

Through the viewfinder I was able to make out a warped aileron and two triple-blade propellers still attached to their engine blocks. The props looked undamaged as they would have been had the plane crashed. What had appeared as a black metal tube turned out to be a human forearm, and I swallowed as I photographed it, too.

I hadn't cut the engine, so I hadn't heard the truck approaching from behind. It braked in front of me and a man got out. He was carrying an Uzi assault rifle and the muzzle pointed at me.

THREE

ello," I called. "What happened here? Any survivors?"

"*Bájase,*" he snapped. Get down.

I shrugged. "Sorry. Don't speak Spanish. *No hablo.*"

Through the open door he poked the barrel against my thigh and pointed down.

I had a couple of options. I could get out of the plane and be at his mercy, or I could resist. He might buy my curious-tourist pose, but that would only hold until he saw my camera and my MAC-10; then he'd make me sorry I came. Took me about a second to decide.

I put my leg out, grabbed the Uzi barrel, and kicked his face. As he fell he released the rifle, and I jerked it into the cabin. His partner was getting off the truck when I hit the rudder pedal and gunned the engine, spinning the plane around. I was now headed for the strip's far end, and I shoved the throttle ahead for max takeoff power, lifted the tail, and shot down the clearing between cactus rows. Looking around, I could see billowing dust that concealed the unexpected arrivals and their truck. But after I lifted off I glanced down and saw one man helping the other to his feet. He shook himself and shook his fist at me as I banked around and gained altitude. I hoped I'd broken his jaw.

Heading north for the border, I dropped the Uzi and watched it spin downward out of sight. If I'd been able to stay longer I would

have tried to spot serial numbers on the engine blocks for full identification, but I had enough to satisfy me.

What the arsonists had done was detach the wing and set it atop
the plane's fuselage before setting the fire. They'd probably used
gasoline to get it going, then the wing tanks had exploded. It was the
burning oil I'd first seen making that inky column against the sky. I
got out my roast beef sandwich and ate it, drank from my canteen,
and checked the compass heading.

Fifty miles south of Nogales I called the tower for landing instructions, and twenty minutes later made a soft landing on the
hardtop. I taxied into the hangar and cut the engine, got out, and
carried my gear over to my car. Headed for the office.

The supervisor sat at the head of the conference table. Walter Mc-
Manus was a red-faced ex-border patrolman with bad breath. "Novak," he snapped, "you know damn well you should have cleared
your jaunt with me."

I turned to Manny beside me. "Didn't you do that?"

He shook his head. "Sorry, Jack, I thought you had."

I looked at McManus and shrugged. "Miscommunication,
Wally."

He glared at us. "You push your luck, Novak."

"Sir," I said, "I try to do things by the book, everyone knows
that."

He grunted. "Everyone knows the damn opposite." He looked
down at Eddie's dog tag and sighed. "Poor son of a bitch."

"What I've got," I said, "is photo confirmation that Paredes's
strip is used for narcotics."

"Maybe. Why burn the plane?"

"Landing gear buckled on landing is one possibility. If the plane
was flyable they could have gotten a pilot to fly it away. But the plane
was sitting there in desert heat for about a month, plenty of time to
cook the wiring. Sand fouling the air intakes is another possibility."
I turned to Manny. "Paredes been to Colombia lately?"

"Flew commercial to Cali about a month ago. Our office tried tailing him but he disappeared. A week later he flew to Mexico City and presumably back to his ranch."

McManus snorted. "Guilt by association."

"Which we often depend on," I remarked. "On the face of it Paredes runs a small-scale operation, but it could be traceable back to a Mexican official, or even the Cali cartel. So I think we ought to pay attention to his spread and activities."

"You do, do you?" He lifted the chain and dropped it on the desk. "Why did this Flanigan fly there?"

"One scenario is he flew there with money to make a buy. Something happened, like a rip-off. He and three others got killed, the money was found and taken away, ending up at the church."

"That's one lucky priest," McManus said enviously. "But what happened to the drugs?"

"If there were drugs they've vanished. Or maybe the whole episode was a scam to get money from Flanigan without turning over narcotics. They'd have to kill him and anyone with him. Paredes and his thugs would know, but let's lift our sights and consider Paredes's principals—the ones who manufacture and send him cocaine."

"You sure it's cocaine?"

"Why not? Ten, twenty keys make a worthwhile transaction, where for the same money you'd need a whole planeload of grass, and as we well know marijuana usually comes from Mexico by boat and truck."

McManus nodded thoughtfully. "Think there's enough info to justify an operation?"

"Give me a couple of days, Chief, and I'll have the answer. Flanigan's sister has to be notified, and since she and her brother lived together she may know his contacts—like who paid him to fly."

McManus said, "Whadda ya thinka that, Manwell?"

Ignoring the mispronunciation, Manny said, "It's a starting place," and looked at me. "You'll see her?"

"I can try."

"Then do it," McManus said, "and keep me informed."

"Naturally." I picked up the dog tag and chain.

Leaving the conference room, Manny asked if I was going to call Molly before going to Vegas.

"I'll try her Phoenix number, then her Vegas place. She doesn't come off as a thin-skinned hysterical type, but you never know." I looked at my watch. One-thirty, and all I'd had since predawn bran flakes was the take-along sandwich. "How about Mama Jennie's for clams linguine, partner?"

"Sounds good."

From my desk I called Molly's Phoenix number and got her answering machine. I left my name and asked her to call when convenient. Then I dialed the Vegas number and heard a chirpy voice reply.

"Is Molly there?"

"Who's callin'?"

"Name of Novak. We were talking in Nogales yesterday."

"Oh. Actually, she's at the Jazzercise right now, should be home soon."

"What time does she have to be at the casino?"

"Six o'clock. Uh, this about Eddie?"

"It is."

"You can tell me, I'll make sure she gets the message."

"Appreciate that, but—what's your name, Miss?"

"Beverly Dawn. So?"

"So it's better I talk to her alone. Thanks, Beverly, I may see you later."

"Okay, Novak, I'll tell her."

I replaced the receiver, looked at Manny, and shrugged.

"C'mon, let's eat," he urged.

I called Sid Weisskopf in the Phoenix office and asked him to get me a seat on a flight to Vegas. Then I phoned the local commuter airline and booked a seat to Phoenix on the four o'clock flight.

As we left the office I said, "No way I can get to Vegas before Molly's at the Splendide."

"Too bad," he mocked, "putting you backstage with all them near-naked chorines."

"Line of duty, *compadre,* and someone has to do it."

During the bumpy flight to Phoenix, Mama Jennie's garlic toast repeated but the clams stayed down. So while waiting for the connecting flight to Vegas I drank a beaker of Presidente brandy to settle my stomach and wondered how best to break the bad news to Eddie's sister.

From Vegas's McCarran airport I taxied to the Splendide and took a table while the evening's first show was underway. The chorus line looked like lab replicates, but Molly wasn't among them. She came out later with another dancer, both wearing green sequined crotch pieces and matching headpieces with enough feathers for Parrot Jungle.

Their breasts, however, were enticingly bare.

Music from the pit band was close to deafening. I watched the colorful spectacle as dancers kicked and gyrated, and after a while two males wearing what looked like green jockstraps joined the ladies and scampered happily around, twirling this one, then that, and at the finale lifting Molly and her partner over their heads like waiters' trays. Music swelled and crashed and the curtain closed. I downed the rest of my short Courvoisier, got up and made my way to the stage entrance as audience applause died away.

The keeper of the gate was a dark-skinned bodybuilder whose weight I estimated at two-ten. "Whatcha want?" he challenged.

"Passage," I said, and flashed my gold-and-blue buzzer. He peered at it, frowned, and said, "Okay, but if there's gonna be a bust I wanna know. Now."

"No bust," I assured him, "just a little chat with one of the amigas."

"Yeah? Which one?"

"Classified," I said, and pushed past him.

The door opened into a large communal dressing room with many mirrors and makeup lights. An image factory.

As I stood looking for Molly a broad-shouldered female in painter's coverall bore down on me and halted, hands on hips. She had short dark hair and a silky mustache. Navy tattoos on her forearms and two gold teeth. A fox among the chickens. "What's your business?" she growled.

"Private. With Molly—ah, Favor LaTour."

"You wait right here, I'll tell her. Name?"

"Novak. She's expecting me."

"Yeah, we'll see. Meanwhile, hands off the help."

"I will if you will."

She glared at me, did a military about-face, and made her way among the nearly-naked lovelies. A few glanced at me, decided I was harmless, and continued touching up eye shadow and lips, massaging tender feet. Presently Molly appeared followed closely by the dressing-room warden. She hurried to me and said, "Eddie—is he okay? Where is he?" Her hands clenched, her lips trembled. I shook my head. "Sorry, Molly, he's dead."

She shrieked and one hand covered her mouth. Tears rolled down her cheeks discolored by mascara and rouge. Her eyes closed and she leaned against me. The warden barked, "So?"

"Bugger off," I snapped. "Death in the family."

Abruptly the dyke became solicitous. "Oh, Molly, honey, I'm so *sorry*." She rested a consoling hand on Molly's shoulder until Molly moved away, covered her breasts with her forearms, and said to me, "I need to know more, but not here." To the dyke she said, "Tommy, I'm through for the night, square it with Rex, will you?"

"Sure, honey, just let me know when you'll be back."

Tommy and I eyed each other until she turned away and walked down the rows of chorines getting themselves ready for the next show.

As I waited I could hear bursts of laughter from the dinner show audience. There was no music, just an occasional drum roll to emphasize the stand-up comedian's remarks, and I realized I was better off standing in a hot dressing room than out there listening to crude jokes and lewd comments that comprised today's showbiz humor.

A few minutes more and Molly appeared. White sweater and blue jeans, hair brushed back from her forehead and makeup removed. Behind her came a petite blonde whom Molly introduced as her roommate, Beverly Dawn. "Not my real name," she said, giving me a limp handshake, "but I kind of like Beverly."

"So do I," I said as Molly linked her arm with mine and we moved toward the exit. Behind us Beverly called, "See you later, babe," and Molly said, "Okay."

Wordlessly she guided me to a reserved parking area and got out keys to a silver Mercedes coupe. I slid in beside her as she began to sob. Hands clenching the wheel, shoulders shaking, she managed to ask, "For real, he's dead?"

"I'm very sorry."

"Plane crash?"

"So it seems."

"No . . . chance he survived?"

I got Eddie's dog tag and passed it to her. For a while she stared at it, then took a deep breath and started the engine. "You'll tell me more?"

"I'll tell you all there is."

With that, she backed around and sped out of the lot into moving traffic. Dodging back and forth, she steered the coupe like a NASCAR expert, and I put on my safety belt.

After a while she turned onto a dimly lighted street and pulled up in front of a two-story apartment house. We went inside, up to the second floor, and into a small apartment with sleeper beds, a coffee table, and a miniature kitchen. Walking to it she said, "I need a drink, Mr. Novak, how about you?"

"Seldom drink alone."

"Scotch, rye, bourbon, and vodka," she said, scanning an open cabinet.

"Whatever you're having."

She took down White Horse scotch, cracked ice from trays, and made two drinks. I sat on the opposite sofa and told her most of what I knew. She absorbed it without interruption, wiping her eyes from time to time until I'd finished. Then she drained her drink and said, "So it was a drug run."

"We have to assume so. The plane went down on land owned by a known trafficker."

"What's his name?"

"Paredes. Felipe Paredes. Did Eddie ever mention the name?"

She shook her head.

"Do you know who hired him to fly there?"

She took my glass and carried it, with hers, to the kitchen, where she made fresh drinks. No water in her tumbler, just iced scotch. Our glasses touched and she said, "I want to bury my brother."

I got out a print of a photo I'd taken just before the truck inter-rupted me. "That's what there is."

"Oh, God!" She began sobbing again. I put my arm over her shoulders and she buried her face in my chest. After a while she breathed deeply and sat back. "What was it you asked me?"

"If you had any idea who hired your brother to fly there."

"If I did I'd shoot the sonofabitch. No—wait—" She brushed hair from her forehead and squinted at the far wall. "There *was* a call on our answering machine in Phoenix. I think it's still on the cassette." She bit her thumb. "Frank . . . Frank something." Her eyes closed. "Ros . . . no, Rodriguez. That's it, Frank Rodriguez." Abruptly she stood up. "I've got a remote, I can call the machine for playback—if I can find it."

Distractedly she roamed the apartment, finally coming up with the remote caller. The tape confirmed Frank Rodriguez as one caller, another man left his name as Rogelio Gonzalez.

"Very good," I told her. "In Nogales I'll run both names for background."

"And tell me?"

"Unless there's reason not to."

Her forehead wrinkled. "Like for instance?"

"Like an ongoing case."

"Confidential."

I nodded. "Do you do drugs?"

She shook her head violently. "Neither did Eddie—but Beverly usually does a line before showtime. Other girls, too."

"Don't worry," I said, "I'm not going to shake down the place for her stash. If we jailed every recreational user we'd need a million new jails."

She smiled weakly, touched my hand. "I wasn't even thinking you would, Mr. Novak—"

"Jack," I interjected.

"Jack, then. Only a total chickenshit would do that. But I can't blame Bev. Dancing's a big strain on her and she gets nervous just thinking about each night's show." She glanced at a wall clock— nine-fifteen—and said, "It's going on now. Did you see me earlier?"

I nodded. "I was impressed."

"By my . . . bosom?"

"That, too, but you're a cut above the average casino dancer, it's obvious."

"Thanks. I've only been doing the specialty number for a couple of months and it was hard to get, believe me. The other dancer, Pauline, had to sleep with Rex, the choreographer, but I told him to get lost."

I nodded approvingly. "Talent wins out over lust."

Her smile was fuller. "Jack, I haven't thanked you for coming here, all the trouble you went to. Has to be above the call of duty."

"Possibly. But you've given me two leads. That justifies the trip."

"Even so, I'm deeply grateful. I know the story now—as much as I'll ever know, and no more uncertainties. I loved my brother, I'll miss him terribly, but all the years he's been flying I had to expect that a day like this would come. I—I wish there could be a grave for him, not just that awful place in the desert." She began to cry again and I thought of crashed, burned aircraft that littered the Vietnamese landscape where some of my buddies still lay. "I understand," I said soothingly. "Are there other relatives?"

"Dad's in a nursing home, I'm not going to tell him." She blotted tears on a handkerchief and drained her glass. "We've never been close to aunts and uncles—I suppose that's why we were so close to each other." She got up a little unsteadily. "Freshen your drink?"

"Please." Drinking herself to sleep was okay with me. As she poured more scotch I asked, "When will Beverly get home?"

"Two at the earliest—unless she has a late date. Then it'll be noon tomorrow." Turning, she handed me my glass. "I don't like her doing that but she's over twenty-one and she wants the money—says she's banking it for college tuition. Maybe she is, other girls say the same."

"If you don't mind, Molly, I'd like to go through your other apartment tomorrow. There may be something of Eddie's that would help."

"Help? What way?" she slurred.

"A lead to the distributors and manufacturers. Eddie only flew back and forth across the border, he didn't make the cocaine."

She sat down and thought it over. I said, "I think you'd like to place responsibility somewhere."

Nodding, she reached for her purse, fumbled with a key ring and indicated a key. "Yes, I want to know who got him into that dirty work, paid him—caused his death, the bastards." Her face was flushed, a light film of perspiration on her forehead. "Per—Persimmon Street," she began and licked her lips. "Two thirty-seven, name on door." She blinked and smiled crookedly. "Jack, I believe I'm getting drunk. Mind?"

I shook my head. "Let's get you into bed."

"Sure, good idea." She gazed at me. "Wha' 'bout you, Jack? Too late to fly Phoenix. I'd tell you get a motel, but I don't want to be alone tonight. Not with Eddie out there—alone, so far away . . ." She began sniffling so I said, "I'll stay, Molly, don't worry."

She sighed in relief and closed her eyes. I eased off her flat-heel shoes and pulled out the other sofa bed. When I looked around she was slumped and breathing noisily. I managed to pull off her sweater and jeans—no bra, and only tiny pink briefs. She couldn't stand, so I half-walked her to bedside and laid her gently down. Alcohol and stress had overcome her, and I felt it was better that way. In the morning, despite a hangover, she would be better able to deal with her loss.

Covering her with a sheet, I realized I could use some rest as well. So I turned off lights, pulled off my shoes, and lay down beside her. After a while her breathing eased, and an hour or so later I felt her move against me. Sleepily I realized there was no erotic implication, just human need for contact with another human. I patted her hand and went back to sleep.

Before dawn I got up and phoned the airline, learned I could get on a seven o'clock flight to Phoenix. Beverly hadn't shown up so I made coffee, shaved with one of the girls' razors, and had a hot shower. I finished my coffee and got ready to leave while Molly slept on. I looked at her sleep-smoothed features and reflected that despite the carnal milieu in which she worked she had remained her own person. I liked everything about her, kissed her forehead gently and left.

At the airport I had time for a quick breakfast, then nodded off on the flight back to Sky Harbor International.

The door card read: E. & M. Flanigan. Her key worked the lock smoothly and I went into Eddie's last known abode. The air was still, and musty from disuse. I opened windows, and curtains blew inward. After taking off my jacket I rolled up my cuffs and got to work.

There were two bureaus, her clothing in one, Eddie's in the

other. I went through his drawers one by one, looking on each underside, and peering into the recesses for—what? For anything he might not have wanted his sister to see. Standing on a chair, I scanned the top of the bureau, looked behind a wall clock, and stepped down. Then I looked under all the chairs and paused for a glass of water.

Their common closet was next. Shoes on the floor and garments on a pole. I went through all of Eddie's pockets—including his old Air Force uniform—and found nothing.

At the answering machine I listened to messages left by Frank Rodriguez and Rogelio Gonzalez. The former told Eddie to pick up his package after one o'clock, and Rogelio said they'd meet at the hangar at two. The "package" could be either dope or money, but no one was flying dope into Mexico these days—they had a superabundance of it already—so money was more plausible. If Rogelio had flown to Paredes's strip with Eddie I assumed his body had been burned in the junk pile. Obviously, thought had been given to disposing of the bodies: burying them would have left traces of disturbed soil, but having them burn in the aircraft would support the scenario of a fatal crash. Paredes could disclaim knowledge and responsibility—if anyone had the *cojones* to ask.

I wondered why Molly hadn't mentioned the package and meeting time referred to on the tape, decided she was too distracted by grief and whiskey to bother with details. I'd asked for names, and she supplied them.

It was now mid-morning and warm air came in through the windows. I wiped my face on a bathroom towel and checked the toilet tank for anything foreign. *Nada.* As I stared into the mirror, I realized something was nagging at me. Slowly, I saw in my mind the closet whose clothing I'd searched, swore, and returned to it.

There, to one side, was a dark brown Naugahyde suitcase. I lifted it out and found it locked. A small kitchen knife broke the hasp and I opened it. Inside were two laundered shirts, chino slacks, and a metal briefcase with a digital lock. I didn't have to rupture it because the combination showed four zeroes; when I raised the lid I saw bundles of green currency. Atop them was a sheet of paper with penciled figures—intake and outgo. The last figure was $178,000, which might or might not have included Eddie's final fee.

I assumed that Molly was unaware of the hoard but I wanted her to have it.

On the reverse of the tally sheet were two telephone numbers: Frank and Rogelio. I copied them on the bottom of the sheet, tore it off and put it in my billfold, then looked around. Aside from stashing the money in Molly's bureau I couldn't see a safe place to hide it until she could claim it, so I closed the briefcase again and replaced it in the brown suitcase, intending to take it to Nogales and send the money from there. I set the suitcase beside the door and went to the bathroom to rinse perspiration from my face. Before turning on the faucet I heard scratching at the door and a muffled voice. Not Eddie, not Molly—she wouldn't have had time to get here from Vegas. So, who could it be?

I half-closed the bathroom door and got out my H&K issue .38. Waited.

I heard the bolt retract, and someone said, "Told you I could do it, Frank."

"Good job, Pat. Let's move."

The door opened inward and two men came in. One was middle-aged and swarthy, pencil mustache and slicked black hair. The younger man was blond and balding. He tucked away his lock-picking tools and closed the door. They came into the room and looked around. Frank said, "No hurry, Pat, we got time to really go over the place. You check around here and I'll take the bedroom. If I know Eddie he'll have it here. Didn't trust banks." He chuckled.

"Not with that kind of money," Pat said, turned, and saw me.

"Jesus!" he yelped, "who're you?"

Frank froze, stared hard at me, and swallowed. "What you doin' here?"

"Writing my memoirs. Now, both of you kneel, get out your iron and put it on the sofa. Slowly. Knives, too."

When they were kneeling I went toward them and watched

both men extract handguns from under their coats. A pistol and a large-caliber revolver. That done, they looked up at me. I said, "That better be all there is, because when I pat you down—"

"Okay, okay," Frank snarled, and drew a small handgun from an ankle holster. He dropped it beside the others.

"You, too, Pat, you're included."

Reluctantly, he produced a knife from a leg sheath and set it beside the ankle pistol. I gathered the weapons and transferred them to the dinette table, well out of reach. "Now," I said, "before I call for backup let's hear your explanation. You don't live here and you picked the door lock, that's felony B&E."

They looked at each other, said nothing.

"And I heard talk about money. Whose money?"

"Mine," Frank snapped, "and I want it back."

"Understandable, if true. How much money?"

"Couple hundred thou—look, let's make a deal, okay?"

"Go on."

"Anything here you get ten percent, okay?"

When I said nothing, he said, "Twenty percent," and Pat muttered beside him.

"Actually," I said, "it's not okay, but maybe you can tell me where Eddie is."

"You a friend of his?"

I took out my DEA shield and flashed it briefly. "More than a friend," I said, putting it away. "He and his sister let me stay here when they're away. Now, where's Eddie?"

Frank spat, "Fuck you."

I smacked his left temple with the .38 barrel and he yelped.

"Get face down, both of you, and put your hands on your backs so I can see them." Blood spread across Frank's forehead as he lay down. I got behind them and took a chair. "If you don't know where Eddie is, you knew he wasn't likely to be here when you came for an unauthorized withdrawal, so that answers part of my question. According to his sister, Eddie flew away a couple of weeks ago and hasn't been heard from since. She's frantic with worry, and you're not helping solve the mystery. Where was he heading, Frank?"

"Dunno," he muttered, so I set the message machine on replay and let him hear his and Rogelio's voices. I turned off the machine and said, "That help your memory?"

His chin lifted and he growled, "Copper, you don't know what you're dealing with. Push me more and I'll come after you."

"If you live that long. Get real, Frank. You two are armed housebreakers. I'm here lawfully and I could legally shoot you both, so I advise you to consider your situation. Carefully."

Neither man said anything, so I told them to take off their shoes and pants without turning over. Keeping the pistol on them, I took clothing and shoes to the bathtub, dropped them in and turned on the shower. When everything was soaked I turned off the water and went back to my chair. "Frank," I said, "what would a *pendejo* like you be doing with a couple hundred thou? You don't look like an affluent citizen. Or wasn't the money yours after all?"

"Okay, okay, a friend gave Eddie money to buy a plane. No plane, no Eddie. The friend wants the money back. I said I'd look for it."

"Good try. Still not explaining the 'package' you had Eddie pick up the day he left."

"I got nothin' to say."

"Who's the friend?"

"Fellow I know from business. Evaristo."

"Evaristo what?"

"Never told me."

"What kind of business?"

"Import-export."

"I believe it—first truthful thing you've said." I picked up the phone, dialed the operator and asked for Sunbelt taxi, gave the dispatcher my address, and said I wanted to go to the Starburst Motel, a place I'd noticed coming in from the airport. The dispatcher said ten minutes—time enough for me to spill cartridges from the two revolvers and eject the pistol magazine, all of which I pocketed. The knife I tossed out of the open window. "So," I said, "I've given you villains something to think about. And if I see you nearby night or day I'm likely to shoot first. Or if you bother Miss Flanigan I'll track you down and drop you."

Silence from the floor.

I stayed by them until I heard the cab pull up and honk. Then I picked up the suitcase and went out. As I got into the cab I looked back and saw them at the window, staring at me. By now they must have realized I had the money and pursuit was not feasible. Not in wet pants and squishy shoes. The driver pulled from the curb and I told him to take me to the airport.

In the men's room I put my pistol in the suitcase and checked it through to Nogales.

The secretary said Manny was meeting an informant in Heroica Nogales, our sister city, and might go home from there. "Any dictation, Mr. Novak?"

"Thanks, but I think I'll stay late and type my report."

She shrugged. "Your dictation is better than your typing."

"Well, some of us aren't equally gifted."

"And others aren't gifted at all." With that she flounced past and back to her desk, picked up a nail file and began working it while I wondered in which category she saw herself.

Having put in a pro forma office appearance, I credited myself with a couple of stressful days and repaired to my motel room. It was much less homey than Molly's shared apartments but sufficient unto my needs. I double-locked the door and opened the suitcase. The metal case was still there, as was my .38. I removed both, and decided to phone Molly before she went to work—if she went. Beverly, her roommate, answered languidly and said Molly was in the shower, could she call me? Please, I said, and hung up. While waiting, I wrapped Eddie's clothing around the money case and locked it in the suitcase. Then I poured Añejo over ice, and waited long enough to watch the fourth race at Santa Anita on the sporting channel.

The phone rang and I heard Molly saying, "Jack, how can I ever thank you for all you've done—last night especially, when I was really down."

"No thanks necessary," I replied, "but it's nice to hear. How are you? Advil helping?"

"A lot," she confessed. "I'm just not used to hard liquor—wine, yes, but—Jack, I've been suffering."

"Well, you needed a knockout punch after the grief I brought you, but I'll remember. Wine next time."

"There'll be a next time?"

"I've been sort of hoping. After all, I had your naked, unconscious bod at my mercy and absolutely did not take advantage of you."

There were a few moments' silence before she murmured, "Maybe you should have."

"Maybe next time I will. Now, here's why I called. I spent a couple hours in Phoenix going through your apartment. I came across something of potentially great interest to you—can you guess what it is?"

"No—haven't a clue."

"In Eddie's brown suitcase?"

"Never looked in it—why should I?"

"Well, I guess you shouldn't have, at that. So, what I'm going to do is send it to you. Just be alone when you open it, okay?"

"Okay, but why so mysterious?"

"You'll see. And I might as well tell you that before I left, a couple of burglars picked the lock and came in."

"No! What were they looking for?"

"The item I found."

"They didn't get it? No, how silly of me. Of course they didn't get it—whatever it is—and you have it."

"If I FedExpress the suitcase you'll have it tomorrow. So hang around until at least noon, okay?"

She sighed. "Anything you say, Jack. You seem to be in control of my life." She paused. "Suppose I come to you, save you the trouble of shipping it."

"I'd be embarrassed to have you see my cell. No, stay there and the suitcase will be delivered. Besides, between me and thee, travel isn't easy."

"True enough. You're living in a motel—why?"

"Temporary assignment."

"Well, where do you call home?"

"Cozumel."

"I've been there! Cancún, too. Ah, Jack, you have a wife there? A resident girlfriend? Tell me," she demanded.

"Uh-uh. Take a few days off and see for yourself. Hospitality rules."

"I think I'd like that—even a weekend."

"What about your job?"

She sighed again. "You *would* remind me. Rex gave me tonight off but I'm supposed to return tomorrow."

"That's big of him."

"Isn't it. But now I'm worried—when will I see you again?"

"Sounds like Jeanette McDonald and Nelson Eddy—the song, I mean."

"Jack, I've actually heard of them, I'm not stupid, but I *am* serious about seeing you."

"Work out a date with Rex and we'll do Cozumel."

"All right. Anything I need to do about . . . Eddie?"

"Like what?"

"Forms . . . I don't really know. I suppose he had insurance or a will."

"Probably," I said, knowing that required proof of death wouldn't be easy to obtain. Paredes's crowd would definitely be unhelpful.

Today her mood was a thousand percent better than last night, and I thought her a person who could face tragedy, accept it, and get on with her life. Life was, after all, for the living, and she had years ahead to enjoy it to the full. Eddie's hoard would help considerably. I was glad he'd been thrifty and frugal with it.

"So," she murmured, "Cozumel is a possibility."

"A distinct possibility."

"I'll hold the thought, Jack, and I'm eager to see what you're sending."

At the Federal Express office I had the suitcase strapped, and paid for overnight delivery in Vegas. As I drove back to my motel I reflected that the small fortune she was soon to receive would have come to her as Eddie's surviving relative, will or no will; I was simply expediting the process.

Too, the money would enable her to make a career change if she preferred to leave showbiz, and I thought she would. But I had no concept of her hopes and dreams. And as I entered my room I realized that I couldn't define my own.

Until Pam's death I had never considered a career other than the Navy; then DEA had given me a chance to battle the narcotics that had killed her. But as months and years wore on I'd lost my original enthusiasm for a fight I now considered as unwinnable as the Vietnam War. How many drug czars had been appointed only to resign in defeat? How many billions had we spent trying to stem the invasion of lethal drugs? And how many drug kings had been released by a court system that handicapped DEA and every other law enforcement agency?

Worse, the governments of Mexico, Colombia, Venezuela, and Bolivia were complicit in the manufacture and export of narcotics, and the Department of State too tolerant to sanction them for it.

Despite the negatives, Manuel Montijo remained a dedicated agent, so I'd never confided my downbeat views to him. I'd sworn to observe and enforce prevailing law and I'd continue to do so as long as I carried a badge.

After downing a tumbler of Añejo I lay down on the bed and watched *Purple Death from Outer Space* until vision clouded and I slept until wakened by a phone call in the morning.

I hoped it was Molly, but Manny was saying, "Jack, get your butt over here. McManus wants us to bag Paredes."

FOUR

In route the office, I stopped for crullers and coffee, and entered the conference room where McManus, Manny, and a man I recognized as an assistant U.S. attorney were seated around the table.

"Appreciate you joining us," McManus said dryly. "Novak, meet Furman Edison from the USA office." We shook hands perfunctorily, and I took a seat while wiping crumbs from my mouth. McManus said, "The USA likes the idea of grabbing Paredes and getting him to identify his bigtime suppliers, the overlords."

"Yes," said Edison, "it's an attractive idea. The photos Mr. Novak took are pretty convincing. Assuming Paredes is responsible for—or implicated in—the death of an American citizen, gives us probable cause to pursue him."

"And how do we do that?" I asked.

Edison shrugged. "The details are yours, and once he's on U.S. territory we'll offer him a deal."

When I said nothing, McManus glared at me. "Well?"

"Sort of like belling the cat. Who's going to do it? I mean short of an outright snatch, he'd have to be lured here on some compelling pretext."

"Exactly," Edison remarked. "You produce the body and we'll work him over."

"Splendid," I said, "and I wonder if you have a judge in mind who won't let Paredes bond out before you have a chance to squeeze him." I looked at McManus. "You know how these things usually go."

"Well, we're gonna change all that, proceed carefully, and get an ironclad indictment no shyster can get waived."

"Sounds great," I said with feigned enthusiasm. "Can't wait to get started. Manny?"

"Yeah—me, too."

Leaning forward, I set elbows on the table and eyed McManus. "And naturally we can count on you, Chief, being as we're all in it together. A steady, experienced hand is gonna be a *sine qua non* to achieve the *desiderata.*"

He stared at me through slit eyes. "That's enough of your bullshit, Novak, you're close to insubordination."

Edison cleared his throat nervously as I said, "Gee, Chief, no such intent. It's that we gotta have a well-rounded, capable team to pull this off—I'm sure that's your intention."

"Yeah. And you'll find me conducting close liaison with Mr. Edison here while the two of you are carrying out your assignment."

I frowned. "Couldn't spare a couple of field hands to supply close-in tactical support?"

He considered. "Probably not, being's we're spread so thin—but I'll keep it in mind."

"Can't do better'n that, Chief." I hadn't wanted office cotton pickers, but I wanted Edison to hear the supervisor's response. An experienced bureaucrat, the attorney would remember it in the event McManus tried to stick our heads on pikestaffs.

At this point I regretted ever having listened to Molly Flanigan's tale of woe or flying to Santa Victoria. Well, not entirely. Molly was worth considerable risk-taking by any man.

McManus said, "Mr. Edison, any further thoughts?"

"Thanks, but none at this time." He managed a thin smile, filed papers in his litigation bag, and nodded all around before leaving. I started following him out, but McManus bellowed, "Not so quick, Novak. Playin' the smartass don't score points with me. Mr. Edison is an important government figure around here, and we're well advised to have him in our corner."

"I understand, sir," I said, "and I'll try to do better next time."

"Where you going?"

"Paperwork to do. Budget, physical assets—everything applepie." With that I went out, Manny behind me. He suppressed laughter until we were at our desks, and then he pounded my back in glee. "Jesus, Jack, you really put it to him. I love it when you Anglos start pissin' on each other's boots."

"Manny—simmer down. Wally's Irish, and I'm Czech-Polack with Hunky genes thrown in. We're no more Anglo than you are." Then I smiled. "First, we draw up an unacceptably expensive budget with plenty of slush-fund green to spread around; a four-wheel-drive van, a pile of automatic weapons, grenades, C-4 plastic, and not least, a twin-prop Beechcraft for me."

"He'll go nuts."

"We could appeal to Furman Edison."

"Naw, let Wally trim the budget and we'll go with what's left. Paredes is only one man, after all."

"Protected by armed guards and a hundred and fifty miles of Mex territory."

"So he won't be expecting trouble. That gives us the edge."

I scratched chin stubble, not having had time to shave. "Good point. We could firebomb his house and buildings, but he'd just move elsewhere in Mexico."

Manny nodded. "So we have to get him this side of the Rio Grande—*then* bomb his real estate."

"Right. Now, as we both well know, players like Paredes aren't so crazy about their homeland that they confine their activities to Mexico. They own resorts and businesses around the world, skyscrapers and banks in the U.S., especially Florida. If mama and the kids stay around the ol' rancho, papa keeps condos and apartments well stocked with complaisant bimbos in Texas, Arizona, and California. Maybe he's set up his biological mother in a nice Miami Beach condo—or Palm Beach or Nassau. He'd want to visit her surreptitiously—particularly if she gave a valid reason for wanting him to come."

Manny said, "I see where you're heading. Okay, I'll get a print-out on Paredes's family and extended family plus any *segunda* familia. INS is a good place to start since they have the visa information."

There was perspiration on my face; the A/C wasn't working, as usual. *"Compadre,"* I said, "you was away yesterday PM so I didn't get a chance to brief you on my Phoenix findings, so listen up."

I described my Vegas encounter with Molly and yesterday morning's search of her empty apartment. I told him about Eddie's personal savings, and the two hardasses who'd broken in for it. "One name figured on Eddie's answering machine—Frank Rodriguez, who hired Eddie to fly here and there, including Eddie's last flight to the desert airstrip. We can net him any time and learn what he knows about Paredes's movements, cartel connections, and location of loved ones, including family." I paused. "His lock-picker was a geek named Pat I sized up as a gofer, not a player. Now, since Frank has seen me, I figure—if the time comes—that you ought to take him."

"Okay. Phoenix?"

I nodded. "I'll check with Sid Weisskopf beforehand, see what he has on Rodriguez. The Phoenix office won't want to dirty its own nest, so they won't likely object to our little scheme. We're the out-of-towners so they're not responsible for anything we do."

"So far, so good. But, what about Eddie's cash?"

I looked at my watch. "Molly ought to be signing for it about now." When he frowned I said, "Relax, Manny, whether Eddie had a will or died intestate his sister is his sole beneficiary. I saved her lawyers' and probate expenses plus the likelihood of being stalked by Frank Rodriguez and company. You object to that?"

"No, I wasn't thinking." He drew in a deep breath. "I'll get busy with our files and INS while you draw up a monster budget proposal and get it signed."

As he turned away my desk phone rang. "Novak," I answered.

"Jack, I'm thrilled!" Molly said excitedly, "and I can't thank you enough for what you sent me. God, I had no idea that Eddie—"

"Enough," I interjected, "walls can have ears. So, what you do is get a safe-deposit box and avoid conspicuous consumption."

"Wha—?"

"Extravagant spending. What was Eddie's is yours, but how you came by it is not to be discussed. The two strongarms who broke in had a good idea what they were looking for, and if they figure you have it, well, things could get very unpleasant."

There was a tremor in her voice. "Jack—I'll do just as you say—but can I quit the casino? I'm sick of it."

"Wait a week or so and work up a credible story. Maybe you have an offer in New York or Hollywood—or some high roller is setting you up for life. Be creative, because the story is one you'll have to live with." Or die with, I thought gloomily.

"Then I can spend more than a weekend on Cozumel."

"Hope so. I think I can promise an unforgettable vacation."

"Oh, Jack, it makes me happy to think of it. Now I'll get to the bank like you said, and—" her voice dropped—"here's Bev, so we'll talk later."

I replaced the phone and told Manny it was Molly calling.

"Right. I didn't have to be a code breaker to grasp it. You really like her."

"A worthy candidate for the Mile High Club, but we'll see how well she can cook. In the long run food is more important than sex."

"Yeah, my daddy done tole me."

Over the next several days Manny compiled a comprehensive all-source file on Felipe Paredes, his family, financial holdings, associates, and lady friends. For McManus I prepared a sky-high budget that he attacked savagely with a blue pencil, leaving me with what I'd wanted all along. He signed with a flourish and a smirk that told me he was satisfied he'd stabbed me where it hurt. I let him enjoy his moment of self-deception and got busy acquiring materiel to meet our needs.

Funding was the least of our problems; the office confiscated so much drug money that a year's average take could have paid all our salaries and expenses and bought a Jaguar for every employee. Still, the finance clerk was a meticulous accountant who agonized over releasing each greenback for operational expenses. "It's not taxpayer money from Treasury," I once admonished him. "Think of it as a gift from heaven. The Almighty took it from the bad guys and gave it to us so we could reduce sin and godless self-indulgence among our compatriots. Isn't that a worthy cause?"

"Yeah, but it don't say so in the regs. I gotta have receipts and vouchers like for anything else."

So after a surf-and-turf dinner at the Embers, Manny and I returned to the office and listed our moves in order of priority.

Paredes had a middle-aged sister Juanita, living in Tucson, and we agreed that she was a likely lever to lure Felipe into the U.S. How Manny arranged it was up to him; if I didn't know I couldn't testify in any later litigation Paredes might bring against DEA through some unprincipled lawyer. Dead men, of course, can't sue—a thought that clung to the fringes of my mind.

A possible avenue to Juanita was Frank Rodriguez. It was my task to squeeze him after Manny bagged him. Even if Frank lacked access to Juanita he could supply names of his superiors in the net, which was the goal of the operation.

I laid aside my pencil and sat back. "Maybe we don't need Juanita," I mused. "Frank might be able to bring Paredes here on his own."

"How?"

"Have Frank tell Paredes he located a bigtime buyer who wants a sit-down with Felipe before fronting heavy cash. Frank says he's checked out the buyer—you—and he's solid. Set the meet in a safe house rigged with cameras and recorders and we get evidence to indict."

Manny grunted. "Didn't convict DeLorean."

"That was a Bureau op, we'll do better. Public arrest would scare off his South American principals, so Paredes has to be convinced he either cooperates fully or spends the rest of his life where the sun don't shine."

Manny nodded thoughtfully. "Assuming Paredes cooperates, how do you figure exploiting him?"

"Turn him into an active participant in destroying his suppliers."

Manny made a check mark on our list and said, "We'll need fake ID from Houston, credit cards, pocket litter, drivers' licenses."

"Backstopped," I added. "And I'll need an FAA card so I can fly around in our plane."

"We have a plane?"

"Wally approved three hundred thou but maybe I can find a forfeited twin-engine job for free. I'll put it on the computer and see what comes in." I paused. "Also, a panel van suitable for all-terrain travel, with good rubber."

"Why-for the van?"

"Transporting villains."

"Gotcha. Nogales okay for the safe house?"

"Sure—cut down needless travel."

Manny's phone rang, he answered, and as he listened his face paled. "Be right over," he said, and hung up, Turning to me, he said, "Padre Jerónimo. Padre Gardenia's with him and wants to see you. Urgently."

"Let's go."

Manny led me into the parish house, where the priests were waiting. I hadn't met the resident priest so Manny introduced us, and I turned to Padre Gardenia, his cousin, who looked tired and distraught. "Yes, Padre, what can I do for you?"

After a deep breath he let out a long sigh. "I don't know—probably nothing—but something tragic has happened you should know about."

"The money?"

"More than the money." He looked at his cousin, who patted his arm comfortingly. "Last night a woman, Olivia Moreno, came to me. Her face was battered, one arm broken. I got her to the government clinic in Santa Victoria for treatment of her injuries. But before that she told me men had come to her *chacra* seeking money from a crashed aircraft. They seized and tortured her husband, Isidro, to make him return money they believed he had taken, and when he refused they searched the place and found a small cache of American dollars. They wanted the rest of the aircraft money, and after Isidro said there was only what they found, they beat Olivia and took away her husband. She heard a shot, and found him dead."

Throat dry, I said, "I'm deeply sorry, Padre. Who were the killers?"

"She said they work for Felipe Paredes." He looked at Padre Jerónimo, and shook his head miserably. "What can I do? Send back the gift money to Don Felipe? Would that guarantee Olivia's life?"

"No," I said, "but it would endanger yours. Besides, if they were going to kill her they would have done so last night."

Manny nodded agreement and looked at me. I said, "We will take care of Paredes, bring justice to him. Not tomorrow but soon, believe me. Do you know how Paredes's men identified Isidro?"

"She said they had bought a few chickens, a mule and a plow, a mattress bed, and shoes." Padre Gardenia shook his head again. "Where they live such purchases would draw attention—especially if made with green dollars. Señora Olivia believes that is what happened."

"But so far your church is not suspected of involvement?"

He spread his hands. "Who can say? Of the money gift I have spent only a small portion repairing the church. Now I see it as evil money causing only misery."

Manny nodded. "Dirty money, Padre, but cleansed by using it for the church. Unless Olivia confesses, Paredes would not suspect Isidro gave most of it to you."

"She will say nothing, I am sure of that. But with her husband dead, what is she to do? She is not young, Señores, she cannot work the *chacra* and live from it so I fear for her future."

"Then use some of the gift money to ensure it," I suggested. "She may have relatives distant from Santa Victoria with whom she can live. Arrange to have her disappear with a reasonable sum of the money that caused her husband's death. Where is she now?"

"In my house."

"Then talk to her, and when she is able to travel, help her on her way. But secretly."

"I understand." He looked at Padre Jerónimo, who nodded. "I can think of no better solution, cousin, can you?"

"None."

"Then I must get back to my church and do all I can for Isidro's widow. Thank you for your guidance, Señores. May God bless your righteous work." The priests crossed themselves, as did Manny, and we prepared to leave.

"One thing," Padre Gardenia said musingly, "you say you would bring justice to Felipe Paredes. Commonly it is said that a man is brought to justice."

"True," I replied, "but I doubt Paredes would willingly come to be judged. So, justice will seek him out."

"Wherever he is," Manny added, and we left the parish house.

"Sick damn bastards!" I exploded. "Torturing and killing an old man, beating his wife! I hope they don't get to Padre Gardenia."

"Me, too." He got behind the wheel and we drove back to the office. On the way I said, "The best way to protect the padre is to nail Paredes, agree?"

"Absolutely."

"So we better move fast. Fake ID, safe house—we can start with that. Frank's phone number is in the file."

"And the plane? Do we really need it?"

"Sure we do. You're the bigtime buyer, the plane is yours, I'm your pilot." I paused. "Besides, if we actually bring Paredes here a pickup don't do it."

"What do you mean, 'actually'?"

I shrugged. "Need a diagram?"

"Guess not."

I was booting up the computer when my desk phone rang. The voice was Molly's on the edge of hysteria. "Jack, oh, Jack," she wailed, "Beverly's dead and—and I don't know what to do."

FIVE

ead? How? When?" I motioned Manny to pick up the extension phone.

"Killed . . . murdered. I—oh, God. Eddie, now Bev." Sobs overcame words, and I waited until the spasm lessened. "Were you there?"

"No, I—oh, thank God I was away, came back and found her with . . . with . . . throat cut open." More sobbing. Loudly I said, "Police there?"

"Yes, I called right away."

"Good. Now, listen to me." Muffled whimper. "Molly? Get it together, okay?"

"O—okay."

"The cops'll want a statement, give it to them. Bev's boyfriends, enemies, answer their questions. Okay so far?"

"Yes. I'm listening."

"Good. Now, they'll tell you not to leave town, but it's obvious you have to. Say you can't stay in the apartment, you're going to a motel—okay? Got it?"

"I—I understand." More sniffling. "Then?"

"Pack a bag, drive away but not to a motel, the airport. Park your car in long-term and fly here."

"Where you—?"

"You got it. Call me from the local airport and I'll pick you up. Say nothing to nobody, Molly, it's important to get away clean."

"I will, Jack, just like you say. Oh, the detective wants to talk again, so it's goodbye."

"So long," I said, as the line went dead. Then, "Jesus, Manny, she has to leave *now*. By morning the papers will tell the killers they killed the wrong girl."

"You mean they came for Molly?"

"Isn't it obvious? They wanted Eddie's money, didn't find it in Phoenix, so they went to Molly's Vegas apartment. Poor Bev. God, how tragic for her. How lucky for Molly." I sucked in a deep breath, looked at the wall clock. "It'll be at least four hours before she gets to Nogales, maybe more. You go on home, I'll man the computer, tell our colleagues what we need."

"Okay, Jack. Ah—where you going to stash her?"

"With me—for safety. Until I figure out where she ought to go to stay alive."

"The Vegas cops won't like her disappearing."

"Screw 'em. What can she tell them, anyway? Let them do some detective work."

"Yeah. You hang it on Frank Rodriguez?"

"I do. But in jail he's no use to us. We'll let the cops have him after he's served our purposes." I gazed at him. "That okay with you?"

"I'm not enthusiastic, but the cops won't be looking for him for a while, so we're not obstructing justice. I guess it's okay." He got up and pulled on his coat. "See you in the morning?"

"Sometime."

He left the office, and I turned back to the computer and accessed Houston. Alternate ID for two agents, phone and credit backup; FAA card in Novak's new name. Needed ASAP.

That done, I put out a circular request for an airworthy twin-engine Cessna Comanche, Beech Travel Air, or equivalent. Reply to Novak/Nogales.

Leaving the computer in receiving mode for overnight replies, I paced the office, thoughts focused on Molly. I hoped she would follow directions even though I hadn't told her why, not wanting to frighten her further. That could wait.

She'd be okay with me for a couple of days, then——? Then what? Where could she go? Her dad was in a nursing home somewhere, and she hadn't mentioned her mother, so I assumed she'd passed away. Her only sibling was charred bones in a smoking junk pile he'd flown to his death. Jesus, Eddie, what a load of grief you laid on the innocent . . .

Where to stash her?

How about Cozumel? The house was empty—I hoped—but the freezer was stocked with enough food for a couple of weeks, and she could buy vegetables from street vendors who came by every day.

Yeah, Cozumel. I'd tell her where the door key was, and join her when I could.

After dealing with Frank Rodriguez and Felipe Paredes.

From the office I walked to the nearest liquor store for a pint of Añejo, and sipped at my desk. Nothing had come in via computer, way too early for replies. I wondered if her inheritance from Eddie was secure in a SD box; otherwise, she'd have to get it out of the apartment under the cops' noses. No, the money hadn't been there when the killers arrived. Had they found it they wouldn't have killed Beverly.

I thought of greasy Frank Rodriguez and Pat the shankman, and my hands clenched into fists.

More Añejo. Two swallows and I stashed it in a desk drawer for future reference; had to stay sober to drive, get Molly tucked away. I put my arms on the desk, cushioned my head, and dozed off.

The phone ringing woke me. I stared at it before picking it up, remembered Molly just as I heard her voice. "Jack?"

"Right. I'll come for you. Stay out of sight and wait. Ten minutes, okay?"

"Okay."

I rinsed face and hands, gargled and drank water, and drove to the airport. A few passengers were leaving with luggage, otherwise the place looked dead. I cruised slowly past the entrance, caught sight of Molly perched on a suitcase, and honked lightly. She got up and carried her bag to the car. Getting in beside me, she said, "Jack, I know I've said this before, but what would I do without you?"

"Probably very well. Now, we're heading for my motel, you can stay with me or in a separate room, your call."

"I don't want to be alone." Oncoming headlights showed her face unnaturally pale. I put my arm across her shoulders and she moved against me, then began to cry. "It was . . . awful . . . the blood. Cigarette burns on her face and breasts . . ." Her shoulders began shaking.

"Okay, okay, try not thinking about it."

She looked at me directly. "They came for the money, didn't they? It should be me dead, not Beverly." Her lips trembled.

"That's speculation, and this isn't the time for it. Let the detectives detect, and they'll grab the killer, or killers."

"You—you think so?"

"I'm sure of it. For now, let's thank God you're alive."

Before reaching the motel I reminded her of my place on Cozumel and said it was hers, a hideaway. She thought it over before saying, "If that's what you think I should do."

"Got a better idea?"

She shook her head. "No, not really."

Then I turned into the motel drive and parked in front of my room door. No need to bother the desk clerk, he was used to people coming and going at strange hours. It was that kind of place.

Inside I set her suitcase on a baggage rack and undid my tie. I filled two glasses with ice and added Old Grouse. After sipping, she said, "Thanks, I really needed that."

Gesturing at twin beds, I said, "You can have the wall bed or the other. The bathroom's yours, I'll go later."

She finished her drink and held out her glass. I added scotch to it, gulped mine, and rebuilt it. Molly sat on the edge of the wall bed and kicked off flat-heel shoes, then massaged both feet. "Oh, that feels good!" she exclaimed, and poked the mattress. "Feels even better." She opened her suitcase, took out a small overnight bag and a flimsy nightie, disappeared into the bathroom.

I lay back on my bed and nursed my drink, reflecting that when the day began I'd had no idea it would end like this. And the days preceding made it a week from hell. Too many bodies, too much loose money, and a girl fleeing from remorseless killers. I heard the shower go on, sipped more iced Añejo. I was tired and relaxed, more tired than relaxed because my mind was a kaleidoscope of shifting scenarios involving Frank Rodriguez, Felipe Paredes, Manny and me. I needed Frank to bag Paredes, and Paredes was an essential lead to South American growers and exporters.

At that time, Cali was still the drug barons' golden city, their New Jerusalem where they were sheltered from interference and prosecution, so I assumed that Paredes's principals were there. Only years later did their power base shift to Medellín.

The bathroom door opened, releasing a lightly scented billow of steam. Through it emerged Molly, cinnamon hair fluffed, face clear and bright, wearing the hip-length nighty hemmed with soft pink ribbons. "All yours," she said, and drew back the bed covers enough to slip between them.

Wearily I pried myself off the bed, sucked the last few drops of Añejo, and tottered into the bathroom. The mirror was dripping condensation, but I cleared enough space to shave before getting under the shower, and seldom had hot water felt so good.

After drying off I slapped aftershave on my cheeks, wrapped a towel around my hips, and entered the bedroom. No lighting, but I could make out Molly's form face down under the bedclothes, left knee drawn up, right arm under pillow. When she said nothing I assumed she was asleep. For her, too, it had been a week from hell, and as I got into my bed I knew I wanted to help her, make things better for her along life's unpredictable road. Not being a reflexive do-gooder, I found the impulse almost foreign to my nature. But times change, as do people, and I thought it best to let each day bring what it would without trying to influence events unduly.

With those thoughts I must have fallen asleep because my next sensation was of warmth beside me. Though less than half-awake, I realized Molly had moved in with me; we were on our sides, and her back and smooth buns fitted against me, spoon fashion. "Hello," I whispered, "nightmare frighten you? Thunder?"

"Shhh, don't say anything." She wriggled closer, her body's heat inflaming mine. I kissed the nape of her neck and felt her shiver. "Ummmm," she murmured. "Nice."

I nibbled her ear lobe, and her body jerked, then relaxed. If this was foreplay it was slow and easy and excitingly erotic. And, thank God, she wasn't a talker. I licked her ears some more, lightly bit her neck, and brought my arms around her. "Oh, Jack," she breathed, "I care for you so much," then gasped as our bodies joined. "I care for you, too," I told her, feeling the warmth and primal moisture that so blessedly enveloped me. Then, moving together, we found a sweet slow rhythm that accelerated only toward the end when we were shuddering and gasping as one. Hardly had we spent than her face turned and kissed my lips, her tongue laving them before lolling indolently inside my mouth. Slowly she turned on her back so I could tongue and suck her nipples, not to excite her more, but to pay homage to the delicious, fulfilling gift she had given me.

My eyes were nearly closed when she said softly, "How long will I be on Cozumel before you join me?"

"Can't say but I'll try for two weeks."

A long silence before she asked, "What you're doing—it has to do with Eddie's people?"

"It does."

"You're going after them."

"Tooth and nail. Full court press. Now go to sleep, big day ahead."

She kissed my cheek and squeezed my hand. "If you can take a compliment from a Vegas chorine—remember I said I care for you?"

"I remember."

"Understatement, dear, we hadn't made love. So, the truth is I'm probably falling in love with you."

"But you're not sure."

"Not completely."

"Good—because you don't know me."

"I know what's important about you, and for now that's enough. Details can come later."

"What details?"

"Your family, what you were like as a boy, where you lived, what you liked doing. Your first girlfriend."

"Easy. Little dark-eyed, frizzy-haired Becky Schwartz, whose father had a shoe store down the street. In the stock room she taught me to play doctor."

She giggled. "Is it hard?"

"Can be."

"Were you a fast learner?"

"When you're nine some things come easy." Her hand found my groin as she asked, "Can you remember?"

"Pretty much."

"Wanna show me?"

I did, we did, enough times to qualify us both.

And then there was daylight in the room, the phone was ringing, and Manny's voice was saying, "Ten o'clock, partner, get over here. Things are happening."

Six

anny hadn't exaggerated. My inbox held replies from around
the country, enough that I was able to limit options to the
American Southwest. There were vans in Tucson and Carson
City, and aircraft in Dallas, Houston, and Phoenix.

Over a cup of starter coffee I said to Manny, "How about checking vans, while I find us a set of wings?"

"Fair distribution of labor. Here's a form to fill out for new ID.
Fax it back to Houston with a photo, and another fax with your
FAA rating card."

I nodded. "Do we get to choose our names?"

"No, they select them by computer." He laughed. "They better
not cast me as Chauncey Pierpont the Third."

"Or me as Orlando Garcia." I scanned the blank form and began filling in height, weight, eye color, hair, and so on. Manny had
already forwarded his, and watched until I finished. Then he asked,
"How's our midnight arrival doing?"

"Molly? Left her sleeping, but not before bringing in coffee and
a croissant from the motel lobby. If she's still hungry I think she's
smart enough to locate the McDonald's across the street." I drained
my cup and moved to the fax machine. "She'll go to Cozumel. She'll
be safe there, and have quiet time to figure out what to do next."

"The Vegas paper covered Beverly's murder 'by person or persons unknown.' The story mentioned Miss Favor LaTour, who van-

ished after questioning by police. A source who declined to be named suggested the killing was drug related inasmuch as a small quantity of cocaine was found in Beverly's pocketbook." He gazed at me. I said, "So?"

He shrugged. "The killers now know they cut the wrong girl."

"As we predicted."

"Indeed. We are very wise and forward-looking men. Okay, I'll fly over to Carson City and work my way back. Preferably with a van."

"And I'll fly commercial to Dallas and Houston, check what's available and, with luck, fly back this evening in our very own plane."

"And Molly?"

"Probably sleep most of the day, but I'll see her before I go." I paused. "With an air ticket to Cozumel."

"Right."

"She qualifies as an informant, so the office can supply her ticket. Besides, she'll be staying at a safe house under our private Witness Protection Program."

"Good thinking. So I'll see you tomorrow."

"Yeah, but no early morning calls, okay?"

He smiled. "Wouldn't dream of it."

So we went our separate ways. Molly was dressed and bright-eyed when I stopped by with her ticket, but when she saw it she stopped smiling. "Can't wait to get rid of me? When do I leave?"

"Tomorrow noon."

"So—you're a one-night stand kind of guy," she said, smiling again. "I shoulda known."

"I'll be back tonight if only to disprove your malicious characterization. The housekeeper is Ramona, a vigorous sixty-plus who tidies up, does laundry and occasionally cooks a meal."

She shook her head. "Afraid I don't speak Spanish, just a few words."

"Get a pocket language helper at the airport and things'll go swimmingly. Ah—I'm all for nude swimming, at night, so if you go

sunning wear something not too revealing. Never know who's peek-
ing."

"I'll remember." She came to me, put her arms around my neck,
hugged me and kissed me. "Safe trip, Jack."

"I plan to—and take care of yourself until tonight."

"And then?"

"I'll take care of you."

The Dallas office wanted me to take a sag-winged old Beech twin
off their inventory, but I recognized it as a WWII transition trainer
with too many hours in the air and too many hard landings, so I
passed and flew down to Houston for a look-see. The office kept
their seized aircraft at Hobby Field: a pair of biplane cropdusters, a
fairly new Citation Jet, Piper Navajo, Beech Baron, and a blue-and-
white Comanche I fell in love with at first glance.

The office honcho, a young man unsurprisingly named Elvis,
had the papers, and I learned that the twin Lycoming I0-320-BIAs
had under two hundred hours on them since major overhaul.
Hartzell full-feathering props showed trivial pebble damage, and
the interior was a decorator's delight. White leather, wet bar and
miniature galley, and a pull-out table. Avionics included dual Mode
S transponders, Bendix vertical profile radar, and an Argus moving
map.

"Like it?" Elvis asked.

"Love it—but will she fly?"

"The office pilot took it for a check flight before you got here.
Ah, let's see—he made some notes: max fuel one-twenty gallons,
max takeoff weight thirty-seven hundred pounds, max cruise en-
durance over six hours, stalling speed sixty knots." Elvis handed me
the notes. "Two new tires." He paused. "You'll take it?"

"I'll take it. This baby ought to cruise around one-sixty."

"Pilot said one seventy-five." He ruffled papers on a clipboard,
braced it on the elevator, and said, "Sign here."

I did so, and asked, "Check pilot top off fuel?"

"Dunno." He pointed at an aviation gas pump. "There's likely a dipstick over there."

So I used it and found the tanks could take another twenty to top off, added fuel myself, and signed for it with the office credit card. Then I went to Civil Aviation and checked winds aloft on my route to Nogales. Twenty-knot headwind at five thousand feet, fourteen knots at eight thousand. Base ops gave me a heading for Nogales, nine hundred miles west by northwest, for a projected flight of slightly over five hours if I maintained average ground speed of one-seventy knots. That would put me in Nogales after dark, and a refueling stop would make it even later. El Paso would be about right, and while the Comanche was being fueled I'd call Molly with my ETA.

Before getting into the cockpit I did a walk-around, kicking tires, checking flaps, ailerons, elevator and rudder, looking under engine nacelles for oil stains, and was satisfied I could at least get this beautiful baby off the ground.

The preflight checkoff list was fixed to the instrument console, so I followed it meticulously, started the engines and ran them up separately and together. Then I put on the headset, found the radio tuned to Hobby control, and called for takeoff clearance.

Circling clockwise above the field, I gained altitude, and at eight thousand leveled off, noted the chronometer and set the elapsed-time clock, then turned on course for El Paso.

Because I was flying alone I didn't set the autopilot; I needed the stimulus of hands-on flying to keep me from dozing off during the uneventful three-hour flight. On the ground I got another weather advisory, and used to pay phone to call my motel room. Five rings and I was getting worried, then Molly answered with a guarded "Hello."

"You okay, honey?"

"Oh, Jack, I'm so glad it's you. I was sort of afraid to answer, but—anyway you're here."

"Not quite, El Paso for fuel. But I'll be with you in another three hours."

He voice dropped to a lower register. "You won't believe how eager I am to see you."

"I'm just as eager to get home."

"Home, is it?" She laughed nervously. "I guess it *is* home to you, but being cooped up here is like serving time."

"You didn't go out?"

"Had food sent in. Jack, I—I'm scared—will be until you're here."

"Hang tight," I told her, "and we'll go out for dinner."

"Great, look forward to it. 'Bye."

It was dusk when I took off and I reflected that twenty-four hours before, Molly had been airborne, flying to Nogales. Now it was my turn, and I set the new course with care.

The final leg was routine: over cities, villages and towns, rivers and farm as the Comanche chased the setting sun ever west.

Landing at Nogales, I taxied into the government hangar where I was met by the mec who'd fixed me up before. I told him I wanted a thorough check on engines and controls, and said if he had spray paint handy he could alter the N reg numbers creatively.

"Y'mean, any whichway?"

"Any whichway within reason. I'd just as soon not get shot down by friendly fire." I paused. "Or unfriendly, for that matter."

He grinned at me. "How much time I got?"

"Noon tomorrow?"

"Can do."

Molly stood on tiptoes to kiss me, bit my ear, and tongue my lips. A really great greeting, but I grumbled, "You're dressed."

"You noticed—so why shouldn't I be? You said we'd go out for dinner."

"I didn't say when."

"You mean you thought I'd be waiting with a ribbon in my hair and nothing else?"

"I've fantasized it for nine hundred airborne miles—but no, honey, only kidding. Let me wash up and I'm ready to go."

She brought iced scotch to the bathroom and I knocked it back in a long swallow. In an awed voice, she asked, "You drink like that all the time?"

"Only when a special event awaits me and I'm pressed for time. Like now. Ah—did Manny call?"

"No calls at all. I watched three soaps, two old movies, and two talk shows. She grimaced. "Really educational."

I dried face and hands, straightened my tie, and said, "No doubt about it, you look absolutely gorgeous. Shall we go?"

"You lead, I follow."

So we had the Embers' surf & turf special, washed down with a fragrant Bordeaux, chocolate mousse, cognac, and espresso. After charging the bill I stopped at the pay phone to call Manny's house and tell him I was safely back. With a plane.

"No kidding? I've been driving the van all day, just back myself. Ah—got a moment?"

"Barely."

"Disquieting news. Paredes's brother-in-law is a bigtime Mexican politico. And guess what his job is."

I had a sinking feeling. "Don't tell me."

"Have to. Attorney General's office, in charge of the antinarcotics task force that's supposed to root out corruption and drug trafficking. How do you like that?"

"I hate it, Manny, but all the more reason to nail *cuñado* Felipe See you in the morning. Ah, remember what I told you?"

"Yeah, no early calls. Have a great night, *compadre*."

Near the motel I stopped at a liquor store for two bottles of Veuve Clicquot and a bag of ice. Thus prepared, we entered our room, and while champagne chilled, made loud and lascivious love on beds, armchair, and sofa.

In the aftermath, Molly toweled her perspiring body and murmured, "We neglected the floor."

"Later—after the first bottle of bubbly."

She came over and sat on my lap. Companionably. Seductively. "Promise?"

"Promise."

SEVEN

At the airport I hated to see her go. Beside the gate we embraced lovingly, her loins pressing artfully until I said, "Enough, already, let's save it for Cozumel." A passenger grinned at us and Molly blushed. "Okay, Killer Joe." She squeezed my hand. "Waiting for you yesterday was bad enough, but two weeks alone in your house—gonna be torture."

"There's TV and hi-fi, and you can stay trim for dancing."

"Not sure I want the stage life again. Any suggestions?"

"I'd recommend continuing education so you can acquire a marketable skill."

"Oh? Like what?"

"Running a business, maybe take over a fitness franchise, or start one of your own. Eddie didn't leave you an overwhelming supply of money so I advise investing in your future."

We heard the boarding call in English and Spanish, kissed, and as she walked way she turned and waved goodbye. I saw sorrow and uncertainty on her face.

After her plane was airborne I walked to the government hangar and inspected the Comanche. The mec came over, wiping oily hands on a rag, and said, "That's a real acquisition, Mr. Novak. Notice I changed the reg number like you said. Engines purr like a kitten, and she's ready to go."

"I'm happy," I acknowledged and palmed him fifty. Smiling, he said, "Now I'm happy, too. Anything else you want, let me know, okay?"

"Okay."

By prearrangement, Manny picked me up in his new Ford panel van—new to him, that is; it was an older model with gray paint so dull and patchy it looked as though it had been sandblasted. "Not pretty," Manny acknowledged, "but like a grave it's wide enough and deep enough for the job. Rubber's good, and while you slept away the morning with our female informant I had heavy-duty shocks put on. New plugs, lubrication, and oil change."

"Rides pretty smooth for an old duster. Where are we heading?"

"Safe house."

It was on the north side of Nogales, an old run-down dwelling in a barrio where chickens roamed sandy yards and goats *baaaaaed* among corpses of rusted-out cars. The street had the typical lining of trashed refrigerators, burned sofas, smashed shopping carts, and broken furniture. As we got down from the van I muttered, "Did it have to be this bad?"

"Wait'll you see the inside."

The screen door hung from bent hinges, two wood panels had been assaulted by boots or bats, and the interior was musty, dusty, and reeking of old beer—or worse. "Just," said Manny, "be thankful we don't have to sleep here."

"I'm ready to leave now."

"A phone's being installed tomorrow to add realism to the set."

"And Frank can phone Paredes and take his calls. How about the audio-video setup?"

"Installation's for after phone connection so the phone guy won't disturb our gear."

"Running water?"

"Let's see."

What came out of the kitchen faucets was a colorful combination of rust and mud so we let it run until we were ready to leave. The dinette table was scarred enough to suggest a knife-throwing target, and what upholstery remained on four chairs was worn, torn, and savagely slashed. I said, "Anything resembling a futon for our guest?"

"Box spring in the bedroom."

"Good. Don't want him complaining of cruel and inhuman treatment."

We completed our tour of the premises, turned off the faucets from which reasonably clear water was running, and left the front door unlocked for the phone installer.

Back in the office we found an envelope couriered from Houston containing our new ID. I signed my driver's license, FAA ticket, and SS card in my assigned name: Matthew James Barden. Manny did the same with his Pedro Vicente Mora alias, and we divided credit cards and other pocket litter. "Okay, Pete, let's not forget I'm Matt when dealing with killers and traffickers."

"Gotcha," he replied. "I'll draw a flash roll from finance and you hold operational funds. Phoenix tomorrow?"

"I'm ready when you are."

Because my face was known to Frank Rodriguez and shankman Pat I stayed at the office finishing up case reports and delving more deeply into Felipe Paredes's file. His strategically placed brother-in-law was Pablo Antonio Aguilera, against whom the Mexico City office had registered no black marks. On the surface Pablo Antonio was a respected lawyer whose loyalty to the ruling political party had brought him lucrative clients such as the oil-and-gas monopoly and a government-owned shipping line, and directorships in two state-owned banks. Nothing to cause raised eyebrows. Indeed, his appointment to the anti-narcotics task force had been commended and hailed by government-owned television and cooperative newspapers. So far as the world was concerned, Aguilera was that rare commodity, a clean Mexican politico. In his Acapulco spread he entertained movie stars and ambassadors, including the current

American dork, whose government background consisted of Peace Corps work in Ceylon and Uganda.

A couple of months ago I'd read a back-channel message from Mexico City to DEA/Washington complaining of the ambassador's lassitude in failing to press the Mex Foreign Office and the AG to identify and arrest Kiki Camarena's killers. Witnesses had seen Kiki taken by police outside our Guadalajara consulate; they even had the police jeep's license plate. From federal and city police came words and assurances—but no arrests. The situation was a nauseating example of DEA frustration in drug-producing countries, toward which State and even the president turned blind eyes.

Well, fuck 'em, I thought; I'd do what I could as long as I was vertical and the office let me operate. Starting with Frank Rodriguiez we had a reasonable chance of shutting down one source of narcotics. One out of hundreds, I thought glumly as the sterile phone began to ring. Answering, I said, "Matt Barden, who's this?"

"Pedro Vicente," came Manny's smooth reply. "I'm at the Rex Motel in a suite fit for a king."

"Expecting visitors?"

"Later today—like after siesta. Heard from Molly?"

"Not yet. She'll call when she gets lonely."

"You holding up?"

"Barely. Stay in touch."

McManus came by and asked for a status report. I gave him one, and he was pleased and gratified that we'd acquired plane and rolling stock at no cost to the USG—less interested in the fact that we'd activated the operation.

At day's end I was preparing to leave the office when Manny called on the sterile line. I sensed controlled satisfaction in his voice as he told me Frank Rodriguez was interested in acting as go-between for "a friend in Mexico." "He was pretty cautious," Manny continued, "and wanted to know how long I'd be at the Rex. I told him I was moving around, contacting various suppliers, and would get back to him tomorrow—that's when he said he could probably have an answer."

"Terrific. What else?"

Manny chuckled. "He patted me down for a wire, so naturally I had to pat him down, and Pat."

"You didn't mention him."

"He's just a knifer, gofer, bodyguard. Aside from handguns and Pat's knife they were clean. I told Frank I didn't want Pat at our next meet—we don't want to bag him, anyway."

"That's right. You gonna stay there or come back?"

"Think I'll hang around until noon. Nothing from Frank by then I'll come back, okay?"

"Suits me. Frank took your bait—next, set the hook."

"Meanwhile, you might check the safehouse, see if phone and our gear is installed."

"Will do."

"See you tomorrow, maybe late in the day."

"Carry on."

I was getting ready for bed when Molly called my room. No problem getting from airport to my place, she said, and Ramona was there to greet her. "It's so really nice, Jack, just like you said. And that little plane is yours?"

"Mine to use as I choose." Like the house it was DEA property, but why be garrulous? "We'll fly over to Cancún."

"I'd like that, and what I'd like even more is your arrival. Ah—how are things going?"

"Propitiously. Now, anything you need, tell Ramona, okay?"

"I need you, lover, but she's no help for that. And I miss you."

"Miss you, Molly, 'night."

Until noon I studied computer holdings on Pablo Antonio Aguilera, Paredes's brother-in-law. He was a heavy player, no doubt about it, and perfectly positioned to tip off *traficantes* before raids and stall investigations into such matters as Kiki's kidnapping, torture, and death. By fax I shared my concerns with the Mexico City office and received a pro forma acknowledgement I interpreted as an invitation to mind my own fuckin' business. Okay, lads, I thought, turn over and go back to sleep while I attack our common problem.

The ambassador, I knew, would have a spaz attack were he to learn his underlings were targeting a Mexican sub-cabinet official, so it was just as well they were passing on the play. Nor did I care if Aguilera was a prized CIA informant; I saw him as dirty, and planned to stimulate Manny with the prospect of bringing him down.

Of course, that wasn't going to happen right away; Frank Rodriguez hadn't yet been fully developed, nor Felipe Paredes, so immediate results were not anticipated. Nor was I gong to inform McManus of the Aguilera factor. Wally could read my fax but not my mind.

Holding that thought I went out to lunch and enjoyed a brisket on rye and a can of Tecate at Sol's Southern Deli. Sol had passed to his reward and the business was now owned by Ferdy Cabezas and spouse, who had worked there for Sol and bought the deli from his widow on lenient terms. The business had changed hands but food and service remained as before, so I dropped by from time to time.

Finishing my Tecate, I wondered what Molly was doing about now. If she liked fishing, there were rods inside the rear entry, and Ramona could supply bait for the grunts, snapper, and grouper that circulated around the pier. I hoped Molly liked fishing; it would be restorative in the wake of her brother's death. And it would add to our list of mutual enjoyments.

In mid-afternoon Manny phoned to say things were moving according to plan and he would be flying back from Phoenix.

"Phone and equipment installed," I told him, "ready for Frank's entrance."

"Could be as early as tomorrow," he said. "See you soon."

•   •   •

Before meeting Manny with our Ford van I stopped at a hardware store for duct tape and a bottle of bleach. I bought a pack of disposable hypodermic syringes at a drugstore, and continued on to the airport, where Manny was waiting with his carry-on bag.

As we drove away, he said, "Frank's frantic to close the deal. Hasn't named his Mexican friend, but said he wasn't located far from the border, and had his own landing strip. I said I'd fly there to pick up the coke, but I insisted on paying in Nogales. That way his friend is risk-free."

"He thinks."

"Yeah. Said the plan made sense."

"Numbers?"

"I said I'd take a trial ten kilos for fourteen thou each, and if the product tested out I'd want a good deal more. He was practically drooling." Manny smiled. "So it was a good day. Ah—looks like we're heading for the safe house."

I nodded. "Check out our gear."

The techs had done a good job of concealment: two camcorders focused on the dinette table, one tape recorder was under the sink, another beneath the table, all equipment battery-powered and voice-activated.

We sat at the table talking in normal tones and the replay was crisply audible. Camcorders captured us in living color, so we rewound all tapes, tuned off lights, and left.

During dinner at Taco Bell I summarized my exchange with the Mexico City office involving Aguilera, and Manny said, "Don't know I can blame them. Bucking an ambassador can be dangerous to your career."

"And even in our little enclave you get zapped for what you do, not for what you don't do. So we move unobtrusively and say nothing to nobody."

"That's our slogan."

• • •

Mid-morning I had a visitation from Phil Corliss of the Mexico City office. I'd last seen Fumblin' Phil in Norfolk and hoped never to see him again. He was an empty suit and a dangerous man on the street—not to dealers but to his partners, so naturally he'd been promoted into a cushy slot in Mexico City. Gray hair and coarse features with patches of busted capillaries. "*Mister* Novak," he greeted me before leaning on my desk. "You got a moment of your precious time for a listen?"

"Hey, Phil, all the time in the world. Following your example."

He flushed and flicked a thumb toward Manny. "This is private—unless you want the *cucaracha* to hear."

Stiffly I said, "Being as Mr. Montijo is my partner I'm glad to have him listen to whatever you have to say."

Corliss shrugged. "He co-author that fax with you?"

"My initiative, Phil. Mr. Montijo was elsewhere—on government business. What's yours?"

"That fax, calling our attention to Señor Aguilera. We know all about him, see, and he's a cooperative official. My boss don't want nothin' upsetting a productive relationship."

"And that's the message?"

"That's it. Whatever you mighta had in mind, forget it. We like Aguilera and he likes us."

Nodding, I scratched my chin. "Hear that, Manny? Phil's office gives Aguilera the strongest possible endorsement."

"I hear."

"Phil, what can I say? Far be it from me to upset a sweet symbiosis, and I'm deeply sorry. Also, ashamed of my suspicious nature."

His watery eyes regarded me uncertainly. "Then I can tell Pemberton you'll lay off?"

"Please do." I stood up, faced him and smelled the liquor on his breath. "Anything to reassure the Big Mexico City Chief, your boss, and by extension my superior. Guess you got enough grief with your do-nothing ambassador."

"What's that supposed to mean?"

"As I understand it the ambassador only does business with Mexican officials in social gatherings where drinks are served." I cleared my throat. "Not the venue I'd choose to twist Mexican arms."

He grunted. "Maybe that's why you're not an ambassador."

"Very likely, Phil. Message delivered, message received. That it?"

"Yeah, that's it. Still the Big Mouth, Novak. I shoulda known."

"Appreciate the compliment, Phil."

He sucked in a deep breath and looked around. "McManus in?"

"Check the back room—where *frijoles* are counted."

I watched him leave and eased down into my chair. Beside me Manny sighed. "Couldn't resist needling him."

"Hell, he asked for it. I almost recommended that joy house on the east side of town, that features young wetback *muchachas* he could work his way through—but prudence prevented me." I shook my head disgustedly. "So much for Mexico City."

The sterile phone rang, Manny answered in Spanish, listened, said, "Ten minutes, Frank," and replaced the receiver. "He's at the airport. I'll take him to the safe house to make arrangements with Paredes."

"If he cooperates and follows instructions you might lay a thousand on him for his trouble. But if he gets suspicious and balks, hold him until I get there."

"And then?"

"I've got some truth serum, non-prescription, to put him in the right frame of mind. Trust me. Oh, be sure to get the location of Paredes's *estancia* from him—so your pilot won't land you at the wrong spot. Ah—you have the buy money?"

"A hundred and forty thousand. I'll show him half as a convincer."

"Right—but don't turn your back on him—he killed Beverly for nothing."

"I know. Maybe things will go right and we won't have to hold him."

"Maybe."

Manny laid his DEA badge and true name ID on his desk, re-placed them with Pedro Vicente Mora documentation, patted his belt holster, and took off. Watching him leave, I breathed a silent prayer.

While waiting for word from Manny I pondered our next moves. Frank was to phone Paredes and tell him the buyer's plane would pick him up at his airstrip and bring him to Nogales for a sit-down with the buyer and a down payment of seventy thousand dollars. Our intention was not to fly Paredes back to his *estancia*, but to hold him in the safe house and obtain the identities of his South Ameri-can and Mexican suppliers. And, despite Phil Corliss's injunction, I had every intention of exploring his knowledge of *cuñado* Aguilera's drug connections.

On impulse I phoned the office of Assistant U.S. Attorney Fur-man Edison, and after a prolonged wait heard his voice on the line. "Mr. Novak?"

"Jack Novak here. Let me raise a hypothetical question: suppose my office were to produce substantial proof of involvement by a high Mexican official in protecting and facilitating narcotics shipments into the U.S. . . . what could be done with that evidence?"

"Well, if I were convinced the evidence was valid I could take it to the grand jury and ask for an indictment." He paused. "But I'm sure you're aware it would have no validity in Mexico."

"I am. Suppose the grand jury handed down a sealed indict-ment—and the target were found on U.S. territory?"

"He could be arrested, of course. Unless the Department of State objected."

"Then what?"

"State could ask Justice to dissolve the indictment. My superior, the U.S. Attorney for the southwest district, would order me to in-validate it."

"And the target walks."

"The target walks." He was silent for a few moments before asking. "You have a potential target in mind?"

"I'd rather not be specific at this juncture, just wanted to get a feel for the overall situation."

"Hope I've been helpful."

"You have, thank you." So it was about what I'd figured. We could almost depend on State to object to prosecuting Aguilera, especially if the ambassador's opinion were sought. So it would be non-productive to lure Aguilera to the U.S. as we intended to lure Paredes.

Reminding me that Manny and Frank Rodriguiz were at the safe house working out details.

I thought back to the death of Eddie Flanigan on Paredes's airstrip, a fate to be avoided. As I reconstructed the episode, Eddie and Rogelio Gonzaliz had flown there with buy money, the reception committee had gunned them and been gunned in turn. Poor old Isidro Moreno had taken the money from the death scene, but whether Paredes's gunmen had produced cocaine was known only to Paredes. Death ended that deal, warning me to be very, very careful when Manny and I flew in. I wanted plenty of firepower, and a .45 tommy gun wouldn't be amiss if things got ugly. Plus frag and stun grenades to maim and scatter a crowd. Manny was more reconciled to body armor than I was, probably because he had a family, but all circumstances considered I was going to take along a set.

At four o'clock Manny phoned to say negotiations had gone well and he'd brief me at the office.

"Frank?"

"Flying back to Phoenix. And you can cancel any plans for tomorrow, we're flying to Paredes."

Later in the office Manny said, "Frank was a little gentleman, took the thousand with gratitude, and phoned Paredes. Had to leave a message because Paredes was out riding around his *estancia* and didn't call back for two hours—that's what delayed me. Anyway, af-

ter some back and forth conversation to persuade Paredes a prof-
itable deal was his for the taking, Paredes agreed to come here tomorrow, collect half-payment and fly back with me to pick up the
keys." He grinned. "Felipe supplied direction and mileage that you
don't need, but he has no reason to think my pilot's been there before."

"What do we do about Frank?"

"Until we've finished with Paredes we keep Frank on hold. After that we tip the Vegas cops he's Beverly's probable killer. Any objection?"

"None. But we have to get down and dirty with Paredes, milk
him dry on tape before letting Edison have him."

"Agreed."

"What time is Paredes expecting us?"

"Between ten and eleven tomorrow. He wants to be back home
in time for dinner."

"We'll make sure that doesn't happen."

Just after dawn I took the Comanche on a test run to nine thousand
feet just under oxygen level, checked control responsiveness in
wingovers, loops, and power zooms. After landing I looked back at
my blue-and-white beauty and felt we'd been made for each other.
The mec added fuel and checked for oil leaks, wiped dust from nacelles and leading edges, and nodded admiringly. "Back today?" he
asked.

"Definitely."

"Just taxi in here and I'll check her over—and please don't get
her banged up—lotta fools in the skies these days."

"And on the ground."

After filing a flight plan to Hermosillo I got current winds and
weather to the south and decided to fly at four thousand. The vend-
ing machine dribbled a cup of last week's coffee that lasted until
Manny arrived with a picnic basket packed by Lucinda containing

chicken sandwiches, coffee, and soft drinks. Unseen, we transferred weapons and body armor from his car. Manny had his belt-holstered .38 Special loaded with armor-piercing Black Talon 124 grain ammo. My H&K .38 magazine held fifteen rounds of the same. "Take the passenger seat behind me," I told him, "M-14 on the aisle. The grenade box goes on the deck below the right-hand seat, lay my tommy gun on it."

"Jack, you're making me nervous. We want to bring Paredes back alive."

"More importantly, I want to bring *us* back alive. Our survival is a lot more important than that scumbag's." I looked at my wristwatch: 9:32. "Let's get moving."

Before closing the cabin door I said, "If Paredes gets sassy, lay your piece on his skull, will you? I don't like distractions when I'm flying."

CAVU—clear and visibility unlimited—and it really was. Once beyond smoky border factories the sky paled to an almost ethereal blue, and I took it as a good omen. I trimmed tabs, adjusted for drift, and flew south. Wearing a headset, Manny dozed behind me until I woke him for coffee. Far off and twenty thousand feet above me I saw a Boeing's contrails; otherwise, no neighbors in the sky.

Paredes's spread came into view slightly off the nose due to windage. The strip was easy to see, a narrow lane between rows of tall saguaros, and the junk pile had been cleared away. I pointed it out to Manny and said, "Time to load and lock." I charged the Thompson chamber—the fifty-round magazine carried soft-nosed bullets—and laid it carefully down. My H&K already had a chambered round, so I fitted on the black body-armor breastplate, while Manny did the same. Through the intercom he said, "Maybe this'll scare them."

"Maybe. At the same time demonstrating we're folks ready for a fight or a frolic. Now, after landing I'm going to turn around ready for takeoff and I won't cut the engines. If he wants to talk, tell him you'll talk on the plane, the deal's been made, nothing to discuss on the ground."

"I hear you."

"If any guns are pulled, I'm covering you, okay?"

"Okay."

Dropping down to a thousand feet I flew the length of the runway and over Paredes's hacienda and outbuildings, then did a wide, lazy one-eight-oh and lined up the strip.

From the hacienda a black limousine set out toward the airstrip, its wheels throwing up dust clouds as it sped along. I lowered flaps, pulled back the throttles and checked indicated airspeed: sixty-five knots. At fifty-five knots the plane lost lift and the wheels touched down. Throttling back, I braked a few times before reaching the end of the strip, and turned the plane toward the far end. Engines idling, I told Manny to get down and meet our target, so he was on the ground when the Mercedes pulled up alongside. A door opened and a *pistolero* got out, holding open the door for a short, rather stocky man wearing an ice-cream suit, white boots, a bolero tie, and an embroidered white sombrero. I couldn't see his entire face because of the brim shadow, but a black chin beard curved up into a broad Pancho Villa mustache. Behind him a second *pistolero* exited the sedan.

Manny walked toward the *charro* and they met halfway, shaking hands and giving each other *abrazos*. I set the Thompson across my lap and watched through the open door. The second *pistolero* handed Paredes a plastic bag, cut it slightly with his knife tip, and offered the powder to Manny. My partner took a pinch, tasted it, and nodded enthusiastically. Paredes snorted the remainder, and the *pistolero* returned the bag to the Mercedes. Manny pointed at the plane but Paredes didn't move. Instead, he had the other *pistolero* pat Manny down and remove his billfold. I assumed they were (a) looking for buy money, and (b) checking Manny's ID. Paredes inspected what was in the billfold, nodded, and returned it to Manny, who tucked it away.

So far so good.

Until the second *pistolero* moved behind Manny, pulled out Manny's holstered pistol, and pointed it at him.

Very un-good.

Paredes spoke to Manny, who turned toward me, cupped his hands, and called, "He wants you out of the plane."

"Get ready to duck," I shouted back, reached down for a stun grenade and pulled the pin. Lobbed it between the car and our three hosts and saw Manny drop. The three Mexicanos watched the grenade's trajectory, not moving until the blast staggered them. They were yowling and clutching their ears when I fired a six-round burst at the ground just ahead of them. Manny rolled over and picked up his dropped .38, jerked Paredes to his feet, and half-dragged him toward the plane. "Check him for iron," I called, and tossed down a pair of handcuffs, "then kick the scumbag aboard."

When Parcedes was strapped into the passenger seat next to Manny's I suggested relieving the bodyguards of their weapons. I fired another short burst at their feet and Manny told them to toss their guns toward the plane. Still grimacing in pain they arced big revolvers at us, and Paredes grunted. "You DEA?"

"Friends of the Morenos—Olivia and Isidro," I snapped, then sighted on the sedan's front tire and blew it, not wanting them to obstruct takeoff. "Everyone snug?" I asked, and Manny said, "Let's move."

With that I shoved the throttles ahead and the Comanche began jolting and accelerating down the strip. I'd just lifted off and the wheels were folding when a bullet zipped in under my left arm and hit the panel. I banked fast, looked back, and saw the *pistoleros* firing at us with assault rifles. Should have occurred to me they'd have weapons in the car. To Paredes I said, "Are they *loco* or just trying to kill you?"

"*Idiotas,*" he grated, and turned away.

Just then I saw oil pressure dropping in the right engine. Sure enough, black spray was coming over the wing, so I cut the engine and feathered the prop. Paredes said fearfully, "Are we going to crash?"

"If we do you can thank your *pistoleros*." I speeded up the port engine to maintain altitude and silently thanked the Lord I'd picked a twin-engine plane. Oil had stopped pumping out now, but no way to check how much damage the bullet had done. The mec would do that while cursing me for bringing back a shot-up plane.

Paredes was licking his lips. "Listen, we can make a deal."

"Too late," I said, "you queered it back there. The way you ripped off Rogelio Gonzalez and his pilot. You got no money then, you'll get none now. Frank Rodriguez tried, but all he did was kill a harmless dancer—for which he'll pay."

Manny said, "I think we're losing altitude."

"A little, but from here we could glide home. Trust me."

"Have to." He put his hand on Paredes's shoulder and said, "You're under arrest."

"For—for what?"

"Killing a U.S. citizen, Eddie Flanigan. That's a federal crime." He shrugged. "I didn't do it, wasn't there."

"You set him up, him and Rogelio," Manny said sternly, "and you had Isidro Moreno tortured and killed."

"He stole my money," Paredes said tonelessly.

"Dirty money from a thief. You'll pay for his murder, too."

"Not in Mexico, no capital punishment."

I smiled without mirth. "Another characteristic of a backward country. However, the U.S. is more advanced. Even get a choice: gas, chair, noose, injection, or firing squad. You'll get one of them, Felipe, count on it."

"And," said Manny, "after we're on the ground I suggest you behave yourself. No struggling, no yelling. Any of that shit and I gag you and break your arms. *Entendido?*"

Before crossing the border I called Nogales tower and asked for landing instructions. The controller gave me the north-south runway and a new heading. To Manny I said, "Blindfold him, *compadre,*" lowered flaps and nursed the throttle back. Tower control barked, "Your right prop's feathered. Need assistance?"

"Thanks, but we're doing fine. No cause for alarm." I trimmed the wings to add lift to the right side, and then the wheels touched down, and we were home. As I taxied toward the hangar I said, "Welcome to the USA, Felipe. You're one wetback who got here the easy way."

I taxied deep inside the hangar before cutting the engine. The mec came over, saw the oil-streaked nacelle and frowned. As I climbed down he said, "Any other damage?"

"There's a hole in the fuselage and a bullet in the panel."

"How soon you need it?"

"Sundown."

"Ummm. The engine could need to be changed."

"Sundown," I repeated, and handed him a hundred-dollar bill. Operational funds, confiscated from some dirty deal.

"You'll have it."

I helped Manny pull Paredes out of the plane and walk him to our van. Inside it, we cuffed him to a seat and let him sit down.

Manny went back to the plane and got out our weapons and the untouched picnic basket. We each had a cup of coffee, and then we got in the van and drove to the safe house.

In the bedroom we tied Paredes to a chair and cuffed his hands behind him, duct-taped his ankles together, and set a strip across his mouth. I got out my hypodermics and bleach, while Manny watched without emotion. Finally he said, "Your truth serum?"

"Right. He needs to be prepped for his confession."

"I understand—but why the rush repairs on the plane? I thought we finished flying for the day."

"You have."

He frowned. "Flying off to Cozumel and leaving me with this *mierda?*" He gestured at the bedroom.

"Far from it. We'll give Paredes a taste of what's to come, and let him think things over. What I do after that—don't ask, okay?"

We finished the coffee and ate our sandwiches before returning to the bedroom. I pulled off Paredes's blindfold and let him watch me load a hypodermic from a bottle of bleach. He squirmed in his chair and I could hear gurgling sounds in his throat. "So far," I said, "you haven't been booked, no one knows you're here. We have questions to be answered, there's work to be done." I pulled up his trouser leg and scratched the skin with my needle. He struggled and gurgled some more. Then I pinched a fold of flesh and eased the needle into it, injected a few drops of bleach. His face contorted and his body went rigid. The chair would have toppled had not Manny steadied it. Tears rolled down Paredes's cheeks. I pulled off the tape gag and said, "There's a half gallon of bleach and extra hypos if you break a needle."

"What do you want?" he sobbed.

"Information."

"Who—are you?"

"Law enforcement officers. We want your setup, Felipe: Frank's contacts in the U.S. and yours in South America. Who supplies your *cocaína*. How do they get it to you?" I paused. "And that's only a beginning."

"Let me go," he begged, "I'll give you a million dollars."

"No deal. But I'll give you your life—if you cooperate."

His features were working, lips trembling. "I want a lawyer," he croaked.

That made me laugh. "We're playing Mexican rules—no lawyer until you confess. Time to talk, Felipe." I jabbed the needle in a little deeper and fed a few more drops into his flesh. He howled again and Manny replaced the tape while Paredes struggled.

Gripping his hair, I jerked back his head. *"Cálmate,"* I advised. "If the needle enters a vein you're dead. Chlorine scorches the heart like a blowtorch." I let his head flop forward; his body sagged. I pulled off the tape with part of his mustache. He winced and whispered, "Luis Salazar."

"Who is—?"

"Banker for Frank Rodriguez."

"Where?"

"Arizona—Phoenix."

"All right. Now tell us where the cocaine comes from. Mexico?"

"No. Colombia, Venezuela."

"Names."

"Don't know names."

"I'll give you time to remember. And then you can tell us who you pay for protection."

"I don't pay."

"Why don't I believe you?" I pulled fresh tape from the roll and closed his mouth with it, replaced the blindfold. Manny and I left and shut the door. "He hasn't yet figured where his best interests lie," I observed, "but he will. Now, if you want to go home for a couple hours I'll stay here—you've got the night shift."

Manny nodded. "I'll shower and have *comida*. Bring you anything?"

"Double cheeseburger and coffee."

After he left, the place was silent except for occasional muffled sounds from Paredes. Off in the distance ranchero music was playing on some Tex-Mex station. Probably a broadcast from Heroica Nogales—Heroic Walnuts, I translated. What a name for a Mexican town, or a town anywhere. I was tired from stress and tension, my eyelids heavy. I closed them, crossed my arms on the table, and pillowed my head on them. The music faded and I slept.

When Manny returned with my bag dinner he said, "I think we ought to let him use the facilities, such as they are."

I finished my cheeseburger, washed it down with muddy coffee, and said, "Good idea—don't want him smelling up the place just yet."

So we freed his bonds and escorted him to the bathroom, stood just outside the open door while he answered Nature's calls. Then we tied him to the chair, cuffed his wrists behind his back, and taped his bare ankles. I held up his white, reptile-skin boots, and said,

"Maybe you'll get to wear these again—maybe not. Depends on you, Felipe. Been wanting a pair like this for some time. About five hundred *dólares,* I'd say."

"More," Manny remarked, "custom-made."

"From snakes on his own *estancia,* no doubt." I dropped the boots and looked at my wristwatch. By now my plane ought to be ready.

We gagged him again and blindfolded his eyes, left the room.

"Leaving now?" Manny asked. "When'll you be back?"

"Two, three hours, maybe more. Definitely by midnight. In any case I'll call you from the airport." I paused. "Strike that. I may call from anywhere."

"I'll be waiting."

When I reached the hangar the mec was applying a small fabric patch to the metal skin. "If you got time I'll paint it over."

"I've got the time if you've got the paint."

He produced a spray can and blended the patch with the white fuselage, capped it, and said, "I put in a replacement oil line and filled the reservoir—what happened was a bullet nick let your oil out. Coulda been worse."

"Plenty worse," I agreed. "Thanks again."

Together we wheeled the Comanche to the gas pump, added thirty gallons, and pushed the plane back into the hangar. He went back to his tool shack, and I drove the van alongside the Comanche.

From it I transferred grenades and tommy gun into the cabin, and taped four gasoline-filled bottles to four fragmentation grenades, figuring the gas would explode when the grenades did. I stowed them carefully below the co-pilot seat and started the engines.

Westward the sun was barely visible on the horizon. By the time I reached destination it would be gone.

Aloft, I set a now-familiar course to the south and thought about Molly in Cozumel. If all went as planned tonight I should be free to join her in a few more days, and I looked forward to our reunion.

She was pretty but not a world-class beauty. Her body was great but I'd possessed better. And her education left a lot to be desired.

Still, I mused, Molly had an innate honesty I'd encountered in no other woman of recent memory, and that quality made up for everything else. I knew she cared for me, partly out of gratitude I was sure, and I wondered how well she would wear spending a season with me in Cozumel—or longer. I was optimistic about it, though as far as her future was concerned it would only be marking time. Well, it was something to discuss after I got there.

Ahead below the flat terrain was losing its deep purple and giving way to shades of gray. I wanted more darkness before reaching the *estancia,* so I climbed to nine thousand feet and flew in an oval pattern until I thought the Comanche would be nearly invisible from the ground.

Then I throttled back and flew south of the *estancia,* losing altitude on the return leg until I could see the outbuildings coming into view. The altimeter showed seven hundred feet. I lost two hundred before starting my run, flaps down.

Very carefully I eased the pin from a grenade and tossed it with its gasoline bottle through the open window.

EIGHT

I tossed a second firebomb at the next building, and saw the first explode in a blast of flame. Before the next explosion I targeted two more wooden buildings, brought up the flaps, and gained speed and altitude away from Paredes's spread.

Looking back, I saw three outbuildings in flames—apparently one firebomb was a dud—and human figures silhouetted by the flames. I could see no effort being made to put out the fires; it would have been hopeless in any case. A huge explosion tore through one building, lifting the roof skyward and flattening walls to reveal a burning vehicle whose gas tank had detonated.

I hadn't targeted the main house because I didn't want to injure Paredes's family or servants. The bombing was intended to warn Felipe that worse things could happen if he stonewalled.

He would be made to understand that his family was hostage to his good behavior.

I taxied the Comanche into the dark hangar and left it, having been gone under two hours. Before returning to the safe house I stopped at the Embers for drinks and a thick strip steak with stuffed potatoes, hot rolls, and fresh asparagus. Along with coffee the waiter brought a double shot of Añejo, and when I felt replete and relaxed I phoned Manny at the safe house and reported I was back.

"Glad to hear it. Everything quiet here. You coming by?"

"Shortly."

Entering the safe house I told Manny we were going to let Paredes call home.

"Mind telling me why?"

"Doubtless they've worried about him. He can assure them he's safe and in good hands. And he thinks he's entitled to a call."

He looked perplexed. "That all?"

"That's half of it. Let's move him now."

We dragged his chair close to the phone so he could reach it, un-cuffed one hand, and removed his gag and blindfold. After blinking, he stared at us, then noticed the telephone.

"What's your home telephone number?" I asked.

Uncertainly he repeated the numbers and fell silent while Manny dialed. "Ask for your wife," he said, "tell her you're safe and well. Say anything more and it's the last call you'll ever make. *En-tiendes?*"

"Ya entiendo," he muttered, but his face was animated by the prospect of talking with someone other than his captors. At the other end someone answered the telephone, and Manny handed him the receiver, keeping it far enough away from his ear that we could hear what came through it. *"¿Quién es? ¿Quién llama?"* came a female voice.

"Felipe. Amalia. This is Felipe, your husband."

"O, *Dios,* where *are* you? Come home. The most terrible things are happening."

"Terrible—? What do you mean? Tell me, tell me quickly."

"Ah, Felipe, I can hardly believe it. But all our outbuildings are destroyed, horses and cattle running loose—" Sobbing came over the line. Paredes glared at us and snapped, "Control yourself, woman! *Tell me what happened!*"

More sniffling before she said, "An airplane flew over and dropped bombs. The fires are still burning. It's—it's *horrible.* Every-thing is destroyed."

"Everything? The house? You, the children? *You must tell me!*"

"The house—thanks be to a merciful Savior—was not touched, and no one was injured. I—I don't understand . . . where are you? When will you come?" Manny ended the call and took the receiver from Paredes's trembling hand. Fury on his face, Paredes spat, "You devils! You burn my home, injure my family . . ." Eyes darting from one of us to the other, he cried, "Criminals! Killers!"

"Your home wasn't harmed," I said mildly, "nor your family. They were spared, Felipe." I paused. "This time."

His face was anguished. Staring at me, he grated, "The airplane—you, *you* did it." Manny eyed me but I ignored him and said, "Who knows? You have enemies. You are a criminal and a killer. Did you expect no reprisals? Ever?"

He swallowed. "Our business is between men, leave women and children out of it."

"You're a romantic, Felipe. Was Olivia Moreno left 'out of it'? She's in a hospital, you put her there. And she's a widow—your doing. All you've lost so far are some buildings, no one was injured, be thankful."

Manny said, "Buildings can be rebuilt, but a human life . . . ? How precious is your family?"

His mouth was working. "I must save them. Whatever happens to me, I am a man of honor, a father, a Christian. I cannot let them be harmed."

"I respect that," I said, "and the way to keep them from harm is to answer all our questions. Now, tomorrow, and whenever more questions may be asked." I looked down at him. "You understand? Do you agree?"

After a long sigh he nodded. "I do—if you will swear not to harm them."

"Not as long as you cooperate fully." To Manny, I said, "Show time," and we moved him to the dinette table where the invisible camcorders could capture his confession. I freed his other hand and he began massaging his wrists. His ankles were still hobbled, but that wasn't going to be on film. From the table up he appeared free and unhampered.

"What will happen to me?" he asked in a subdued voice.

"That's not up to us," Manny answered. "Our superiors will decide the value of your cooperation."

His gaze traveled from Manny to me and back again. "Water," he said, "my throat is dry. If I am to talk I need a glass of water."

I brought him a cup of tap water, he drank it all, and then Manny read him the Miranda formula in Spanish and English. After that, Felipe gave his name and age, said he did not want a lawyer, and was willing to answer all questions without promise of preferential treatment.

He acknowledged that his *estancia* was used for transshipping narcotics into the U.S. from South America. His *estancia* was protected by elements of the Mexican army and federal police and he paid heavily for the franchise.

Coca leaf and paste came from central Bolivia and was flown from jungle airstrips to Colombia where it was converted into cocaine. Unsurprisingly, his Colombian contacts were in Medellín, and he was alerted to the arrival of an aircraft by telephone—message in open code.

"And you sold cocaine to Frank Rodriguez."

"From time to time."

Between us Manny and I explored his Colombian contacts; one name—Jesus Uribarri—was known to me as a second-level exporter.

Paredes asked for more water—he'd been talking for an hour—and Manny gave him a chicken sandwich. He seemed grateful for it, and asked, "Will I ever see my family again?"

"That depends on you," I told him, not wanting to mention the Federal Witness Protection Program while the cameras were recording. A defense sawyer might manipulate my words to his advantage, and I'd gone through too much risk and trouble bagging this murdering *pendejo* to have my own comments set him free.

I poured Añejo into a used coffee cup and gave it to him. Paredes swallowed in two gulps, wiped his mouth and mustache, and said, "Thank you."

"Ready to go back to work?"

"Yes. But please tell me I will see my family again."

I glanced at Manny who shrugged before saying, "They can come to your trial."

"Assuming there is a trial," I added, and Manny nodded agreement. So far we'd gotten fairly routine information from him, but not yet touched on the involvement of his brother-in-law. To me that was paramount because toppling Aguilera would deal a real blow to Mexican *traficantes* while improving the safety and status of DEA colleagues working in Mexico.

When we resumed interrogation Paredes gave us more names, including contacts in the Southwest states to whom he knew cocaine deliveries were made.

We listened without comment, and when he paused I drew Manny out of earshot and said, "He's just about barreled-out on this low-level stuff. I want to move on to Aguilera while he's still in a talking mood. If we break now and don't resume until tomorrow I'm concerned he'll stonewall."

Manny gave me a wry smile. "You could bomb his hacienda again."

"Who says I did? Speculate all you want, but I admit nothing."

"Okay, Jack, whatever you say." He paused. "We're probably as tired as he is, so we can't go on forever—but how's to start on Aguilera, get some admissions from Felipe, and build on that tomorrow?"

Stifling a yawn, I said, "Let's do it."

So when we went back to Paredes I said, "Your *cuñado* is Licenciado Pablo Antonio Aguilera—your sister's husband."

He nodded. "As is well known."

"What you don't know—and this information is very closely held—is that he's cooperating with the American Embassy in Mexico City."

He shrugged. "Liaison is his job for the Attorney General. Also well known." He glanced up. "What of it?"

I glanced at Manny and smiled. "Who do you think gave us your name, Felipe? Told us about your airstrip and the protection you pay for?"

Scornfully, he shook his head. "Not Pablo Antonio, never. He hates gringos."

"Oh? Then why does he go to all the embassy parties? Why are he and the ambassador such great friends? Think about it. Is that the way a true gringo-hater would behave?"

Paredes squinted at me. "My *cuñado* likes parties, likes being part of diplomatic society. That's no crime."

"Suppose I told you there was evidence against Pablo Antonio that could put him on trial in Mexico."

"What evidence?" he demanded.

"Bribe-taking, corruption, protecting *traficantes,* laundering money, making use of his office and influence to protect murderers."

Paredes licked his lips and looked down at the table top. Nothing there.

"But there's a possible problem with your *cuñado*. Some in the embassy feel he's holding back by identifying only his enemies, while protecting his government and party friends. Those who hold that view want to expose and crush him now; others say no, he's really co-operating."

"So—what is the problem?"

"Determining if he is being completely honest with the embassy."

Paredes frowned, ran one finger across his chin beard. Finally he said, "I don't know how that can be done."

"I can think of one way," I told him. "By comparing a list of the men he fingered with a list made up of those he *should* have named."

Paredes thought it over. "I see," he said after a pause, "but Pablo Antonio has many friends and associates, including the president of Mexico."

"Should the president be on those lists?"

"Oh, no," Paredes said quickly. "Pablo Antonio would have told me."

"Then," I said, "he told you other names."

His head jerked as he recognized the slip. "No."

"Why not? I think you know who he works with clandestinely, whom he protects, and the names of those he bribes."

"No, no, I know nothing," Paredes said, shaking his head for emphasis.

"But I believe you know a great deal. Now, if he named you, that's not a brotherly deed and you would have a right to reprisal. One the other hand, Pablo Antonio is a power in Mexican politics and could be of some service to you—but only so long as he retains his office."

Paredes listened impassively. Manny said, "So it's in your interest to help him with the embassy."

"I—I'm confused, I don't understand."

"Let me help," I said. "Your *cuñado* has given certain names to the embassy, names of figures he deals with in drug-related enterprises. The embassy is not sure Pablo Antonio has identified all his associates. A list of them made up by someone knowledgeable— you—would establish the extent of his cooperation. Whether comparison would benefit your *cuñado* remains to be determined. But your cooperation with us would definitely benefit you."

He swallowed. "I think I understand. Only—would Pablo Antonio have to know?"

I shook my head. "Absolutely not."

"And if I can't name his associates . . . ?"

"You can, and we know you can. But if you do not, the embassy will reveal evidence of his misdeeds to the president, and your sister—your whole family—will be disgraced."

"I—I'm tired, I must think."

"All right. You have the rest of the night, but in the morning we expect names." I gestured to Manny, and we moved Paredes back to the bedroom, let him lie on the mattress, and handcuffed one wrist to a water pipe. After gagging him we left the room and locked the door. Manny said, "So far so good."

"A giant step for mankind."

"How much do you think he knows?"

"Probably a good deal. Pablo Antonio could have boasted of the high-level figures he corrupted, and Paredes would remember."

"Speculation, Jack."

"Except that Paredes admitted knowledge of Aguilera's dealings. Okay, go home and I'll baby-sit our captive. In the morning bring two breakfasts and a monitor, and we'll resume."

He nodded. "When do you propose to bring in Furman Edison?"

"When we're satisfied Paredes has told us everything he knows."

"McManus?"

"He should watch the video tapes when Edison does."

"I mean, when do we tell him what we've got?'

"Maybe later tomorrow. He likes you, you do it."

"*Likes* me? He's on the *cucaracha* kick."

"Respects you, then."

Manny shrugged. "We'll see. *Buenas noches, compadre*."

"*Buenas noches* yourself."

After he left I made a pillow from my jacket and stretched out on the cleanest part of the floor. It was far from comfortable but fatigue overwhelmed me and I slept until Manny woke me in the morning.

We brought Paredes back to the dinette table for a Burger King breakfast, the scene duly recorded to eliminate complaints of bad treatment. Over coffee I said, "You're rested, Felipe. How many names do you recall?"

"Eight," he said sullenly. "How is telling you going to help me?'

"You might never see the inside of a cell. We could make that recommendation to the federal attorney."

He sipped coffee from a Styrofoam cup and pursed his lips. After a heavy sigh he said, "I told my sister not to marry Pablo Antonio, told her he would bring us trouble."

"You were right."

"So I have no alternative but to help myself." He looked up at us. "I have to trust you as honorable men."

"Yes," I said. "In helping yourself you help us, and in turn we will do what we can for you."

Another drawn-out sigh. "Very well, señores. My *cuñado* pays the chief of our customs service, General Ramón Vasquez; the head of immigration, Licenciado Juan Bermudez; the chief of air force operations, General Pedro Iglesias; the head of the army regiment in the state of Sonora, General Fidel Abreu; the director of all airport operations, Colonel Isaac Esposito; the chairman of the Foreign Relations Committee, Senator Angel Dominguez . . ." he paused to sip coffee before saying, "Licenciado Eduardo Rojas, the deputy foreign minister; Roberto Quiñones, director of consular affairs." He spread his hands. "Eight."

"There are more, Felipe. Who's Number Nine?"

He grimaced. "Very well, the assistant secretary of treasury, Israel Delgado. There, that is all. I know of no others. I swear it."

I looked at Manny. "Believe him?"

"For now."

We took him back to the bedroom, and while I stayed there Manny brought in the video monitor. He removed one cassette from the camcorder, rewound it, and slid it into the playback monitor.

Seated at the table, Paredes watched his confession unfold for a few minutes, then covered his face with his hands. "You didn't tell me you were taping me," he said brokenly.

"You didn't ask. But it's all there, Felipe, every admission, every name. Want to see more?"

"No. I feel sick."

Manny rewound the tape and turned off the monitor. He put the cassette in his pocket and said, "You did well, Felipe," and turned to me. "If I'm asked the status of the prisoner?'

"In protective custody. *Vaya con Dios*."

Forty minutes later Manny returned with McManus. By then I'd freed Paredes's ankles and returned his boots. Except for his cuffed wrists he looked like an average Mexican-American who needed a shave.

Glancing around, McManus growled, "Jesus, what a dump."

"Low-rent, Wally. You taking charge of the prisoner?"

"Damn right I am. I'm holding him at the office while Mr. Edison and I review the tape. If Edison says okay he'll take federal custody."

"Very quietly, I hope."

"Up to the U.S. Attorney how this creep is handled."

I smiled. "No congratulations on a job well done?"

"Maybe later, smartass."

"I won't hold my breath." After a yawn, I said, "I'm taking some time off, Wally, maybe more than a few days."

"Okay. I guess Manny here can fill in anything Edison needs to know?"

"Absolutely," I said, got Paredes to his feet, and watched Mc-Manus and my partner march him out to the office car.

After I heard them drive away I pulled over the telephone, called Cozumel, and heard Ramona answer. She recognized my voice and asked if I was coming.

"Maybe tonight, if not, tomorrow. Tell the señorita."

"Yes, she will be glad to know." Her voice lowered. "Very pretty and nice, señor, *muy mona*."

"Exactly. Plenty of food in the house?"

"Yes—she eats but little."

"Get some steaks and charcoal for the grill."

"I will. *Hasta luego*, señor."

"Luego," I responded and hung up.

I drove the van to my motel and parked it at the rear where it wouldn't be noticed. Then I got into bed and slept until noon.

Before showering I got on the phone with a travel agent and worked out a flight to Mexico City with a connecting flight to Cozumel. The first departure was at two-thirty, so I shaved, showered, and packed a suitcase for the trip.

A taxi took me to the Embers for grilled lamb chops with rissolé potatoes and artichokes, then on to the airport.

From the air it was easy to spot Mexico City because of the yellow-brown smog above it, making it appear that the entire city was under gas attack, not unlike Los Angeles in that era. Bus and automobile exhausts flooded streets with noxious fumes from the combustion of lousy government-produced fuel, so I avoided the city, stayed in the airport, and boarded a Mexicana DC-9 for Cozumel.

During the flight I reviewed accomplishments with Felipe Paredes, and thought that if his information were properly exploited, a couple of dozen agents would be occupied following up his leads.

But as to Pablo Antonio Aguilera I was not optimistic. Paredes's confession provided a framework for aggressive action, but whether the embassy would go along with defenestrating him was doubtful. And there were the probable objections from State.

Well, I'd done my work; it was up to others to follow through.

While sipping Veterano brandy I looked around at fellow passengers and saw the usual mix of young honeymoon couples; middle-aged businessmen and their much younger secretaries; grizzled sport fishermen; and scuba enthusiasts of both sexes. Cozumel offered something for everyone, and the offshore Palancar Reef was a worldwide draw for divers. Movie producers were increasingly lured to Cozumel because of its even climate, nearly cloudless weather, and tropical setting.

The combination brought anglers, too, and I'd invested DEA money in a charter fishing boat to establish cover for living in Cozumel. My partner, Carlos Paz, captained the *Corsair,* and was also one of Ramona's nephews. He chartered to anglers out for billfish, took salary and expenses from charter money, and settled monthly with me. Occasionally there was a profit, though hardly enough to live on.

My two-bedroom bungalow was about a mile outside the town of San Miguel, the only populated center on the island, and easy to reach from the airport. I'd chosen the location because of its isolation and the availability of the house when I needed it. Three sides were protected by a tall chain-link fence, and a long wooden pier stretched out from the water side. My old Fairchild Republic Seabee amphibian was snubbed to it. I'd replaced the original Franklin engine with a 260 horsepower Lycoming that could lift us off in thirteen seconds and climb to a thousand feet in sixty.

As the DC-9 turned and lost altitude on its approach leg I looked down and scanned my place, then we were on the ground and I got ready to exit the plane.

And elderly taxi took me to the front gate. I unlocked it and carried my bag to the front entrance. Molly had heard the taxi, and hurried out to greet me with a hug and a kiss. Behind her Ramona bowed in welcome, and insisted on taking my bag. Arms linked, Molly and I went inside, and she exclaimed, "Oh, Jack, I'm so glad you're here. Ramona's been wonderful to me, but without you I've been lonely. Now all that's changed."

"I've missed you, too. Have you been comfortable?"

"Who wouldn't be? Tiled floors, colorful serapes, and plumbing that works." She sighed. "I could probably be happy here forever."

We were moving toward my bedroom, the larger one, and I could see a nightgown folded on one pillow, makeup bottles and gadgets on the bathroom counter, and I recalled how Pam used to take over available space. "I'm hot and sweaty," I said, "and I need a shower."

"Then I'll make drinks. Are you hungry?"

"Not especially. Let's watch sunset from the patio and have something to eat later on."

She watched me undress, and while I was showering she brought a glass of iced Añejo which I drank appreciatively. Then I got into shorts, sandals, and a white guayabera, freshened our drinks, and walked out to a patio table. As Molly sat beside me she said, "Your plane—you'll really take me up?"

"Of course. If you like we'll fly over to Cancún tomorrow, check out the action there."

"I'd love it."

After a while, sun low on the horizon, she asked, "Did your business go . . . well?"

"So far. Manny and I bagged the owner of the airstrip where your brother was killed. We taped him confessing to a lot of things and turned him over to the Assistant U.S. Attorney for possible prosecution."

She frowned. "Possible? I thought—"

"Having Paredes in custody is only the beginning. The federal attorney has to like the evidence before he'll take it to a grand jury for an indictment. Defense lawyers are another problem and Paredes has plenty of money to hire good ones. They'll probably advise him to recant his confession, allege it was obtained under duress— that he was illegally brought to the States, and so on."

"Not encouraging." She sipped from her glass and sighed. "And Frank Rodriguez, the man you think killed Beverly?"

"The Vegas police can build a case. Manny is phoning them about Frank. He won't be long on the street."

"That's a relief—I've been worried about him stalking me, doing what he did to Beverly."

I finished my drink and asked, "Your money's safe?"

"I did what you suggested, put it in a safe-deposit box."

"Good. Don't lose the key."

After a while she asked why I'd come to Cozumel, and I said it was because DEA wanted someone to report on drug movements. "With the plane I can spot drug motherships coming up from Panama and Honduras."

"Is there a lot of that?"

"Any is too much, and yes, there's enough to keep the Coast Guard busy off the Keys. Cruise ships stop at Cozumel for a day or so, passengers come ashore, and some buy drugs to take back to the U.S., but the amounts are small and usually detected at Customs. If I hear of a major buy I report it to the Miami office."

"By telephone?"

"By radio." I gestured behind us. "In the house."

When my glass was empty I started the charcoal grill and pounded rock salt into our steaks. Before leaving, Ramona had filled a large bowl with fresh greens crisped in chlorinated water for safety's sake. And as Molly watched the beef grilling, she said, "I'm not used to having a man cook for me."

"If it bothers you, take over."

She waved a hand dismissively. "You know what you're doing and doing it very well. Ramona having set the table, I'll take care of our salads. I can bake a pretty good cake, though, and brownies. To-morrow?"

"Tomorrow will be fine."

We ate in a screened section of the patio to avoid mosquitos and nighttime bugs, and after a while Molly said, "When you said I should come here I had no idea how good it could get. You have everything here to make living enjoyable."

"No virtue in living like a peasant if you don't have to."

"No . . . no, there isn't. But you weren't ever poor, were you—I mean your family?"

"After Dad died, Mother worked in a department store. She earned barely enough to pay the rent and I worked as a bag boy, made deliveries and worked odd jobs." I shrugged. "Really poor? No, but we bought second-day bread and economized on other things." Light breeze blew across the charcoal, sparks whirled up-ward, and I glanced out over the dark Caribbean. "Why do you ask?"

"I—I guess I've never been really down-and-out poor, but once I thought I was. Eddie was sending me money from Vietnam, but I spent it on clothes, dance lessons, and rent. Paid for a modeling port-folio, too, but I only got a few jobs and they didn't pay much. I men-tioned it to a girl in my dance class and she said she could arrange modeling work for me if I didn't mind being photographed nude. Said the pay was five hundred for a few hours work, and I jumped at it." She laid aside her knife and fork and her expression was trou-bled. "Jack, I have—I'm afraid I have a confession to make. You'll probably be shocked, and if you want me to leave I will."

"Bad as that? Try shocking me."

"I wouldn't tell you, but I care for you so much that I want you to know the worst about me—I don't believe in false pretenses."

"Neither do I. Take your time—but, honestly, you don't have to tell me anything."

"I—I must, Jack."

I held her hand. "Let me guess. Your friend steered you to an escort service."

She shook her head. "No, wasn't that."

"You were lookout for a bank robbery."

"Jack!" She slapped my hand lightly. "Be serious."

"Okay, okay." I cleared my throat. "Adult movie."

Her face turned away. "Oh, Jack—I was so ashamed then, and I'm even more ashamed now."

"Was it . . . pretty raunchy?"

She breathed deeply. "In the man's hotel room . . . he had a camera set up—my friend was with me, I wouldn't go alone—and after I, uh, stripped, he handed me a can of shaving foam and—oh, this is so *hard* to talk about—"

"Go on."

Her eyes closed. "I had to—to shave myself. With a razor." She swallowed and her eyes opened.

"You mean—?"

She nodded. "Between my legs—you know where—while the man filmed it all."

"And that's all there was to it?"

"That was bad enough."

I shrugged. "You shaved your muff and went home with five hundred dollars. Only mildly kinky, Molly, and hardly a lifetime worry, so why tell me?"

"Because . . . I want everything honest and open between us . . . and because some day you might, just might, see it, and—"

"Forget it." I kissed her cheek. "Not a voyeur, okay?" I paused. "Weren't you pretty young at the time?"

"I—I was nineteen."

"Call it a youthful indiscretion. Ever do it again?"

"No, everything about it disgusted me. But the money helped me until I got a dancing job in a night club. But even if I'd needed the money I wouldn't repeat what I . . . did." She drew in a deep breath, and I said, "Because you were willing to confide in me I think even more of you than I did. So it's over, Molly, behind you, not to be resurrected."

"Then you don't—hold it against me?"

"Never," I said comfortingly, and kissed her lips. "Steak's getting cold, honey. We can swim off the pier or go to bed. What will it be?"

"What do *you* want?"

"I want to hold you in my arms, sleep with you, care for you."

She kissed the side of my face and whispered, "I want to sleep with you, be held and cared for. I'm crazy about you."

In the morning, after breakfast on the patio, we strolled down the pier and I pulled the Seabee alongside, opened the cabin door, and helped her in. She thought the plane was quaint and cute, descriptions I wouldn't normally have applied to my veteran aircraft, and when she was strapped into the right-hand seat I throttled forward and ruddered into the wind. Molly screamed at the sudden acceleration as I began our run into open water, gripped the seat and closed her eyes. Then we lifted off and flew smoothly upward. Cancún was only a few miles away, so I circled over Cozumel until reaching six thousand feet. She was looking down, absorbed in the view, when I tapped her arm. "Pants off."

"What?" she stared at me. "Did you say 'pants off'?"

"I did. Seatbelt off, pants off, and wriggle over here."

She began peeling off her pants. "Why?"

"Sit on my lap, eyes front."

"Oh." She smiled. "I get it. You want to make love."

"Don't you?"

"Actually, I do."

So, despite minor spatial difficulties we made love together, and as she wiggled back into her seat I pointed at the altimeter dial. "Six thousand feet."

She was pulling on her panties. "So?"

"So you're a member of the Mile High Club."

"Oh, Jack!" She blushed prettily. *"Really!"*

"A qualified member," I added.

"It was, well, an experience, I'll say that." She clicked on her seat belt. "How many have you qualified in this little plane?"

"Oh, fewer than a thousand." Before she could frown, I said, "Actually, honey, you're the first. I've been saving it for you."

"Liar. Oh, I don't mean a low-*down* liar, but how could you know you'd meet me?"

"I knew," I told her. "Believe me, I knew. It was in the stars."

Then it was time to lower flaps and spiral down toward a beach just west of the Hyatt. I landed into the wind, a few small waves bumped the fuselage, and then we were drifting toward a white boat buoy.

One of the lifeguards I knew from previous visits splashed out and snubbed the Seabee to the buoy, then carried Molly to the beach. He took me on his back to dry sand, I thanked him with a thousand pesos and asked him to shoo away *chamacos* who might try to board my plane. "*Sí, patró.* And with respect I must say the señorita *peliroja* is a formidable beauty."

"*De veras,* Marcelino, and not for you." I took Molly's hand and we walked away from the water to the hotel patio, where we had a light second breakfast of mixed fruits, *tostadas,* and strong coffee.

We toured Plaza Caracol shops for silver-and-turquoise trinkets, lizard-skin handbag, and leather sandals for Molly, an embroidered white-on-white guayabera for me; nothing acquired without congenial bargaining that Molly found entertaining.

After that we took a tourism van to Tulum where we strolled among Mayan ruins and speculated about the humans who had lived and sacrificed there. The driver/guide brought us bottles of cold Corona and we sipped them in the shade of a tall stele while waves crashed against the rocky shoreline below.

"The really famous ruins and pyramids are a hundred miles by jungle road from here—but we can fly over them and save ourselves a hot trip."

"Yes, I'd prefer that," she said, fanning her face. "This is all fantastic, but I'm perishing from heat."

So we returned to Cancún and had lunch in the hotel's air-conditioned restaurant. Marcelino ferried us out to the Seabee and we took off in a light breeze.

From there I flew west for twenty minutes and circled low and slow over the magnificent pyramids of Chichén Itzá until Molly had taken in everything. Then I reversed course, Molly dozing beside me, until Cozumel island was in view, and I set down the Seabee practically at my own back door. The landing jolt woke Molly and she snubbed the bow to the pier, then got out ahead of me. As we walked back to the house I said, "It's siesta time."

"It certainly is—but if we siesta together what will Ramona think?"

"Nothing at all."

"Meaning she's used to girls sleeping with you?"

"Didn't say that. You have to understand that Mexicans are generally relaxed, nonjudgmental people. And at her age Ramona is well aware of the way of a man with a maid—and vice versa. Okay?"

"Okay, I won't worry about it again."

As we entered the house I heard the radio buzzer sounding. To respond I had to open a false-front section of the bookcase and take out the handset. "Receiving," I said "what's the big emergency?"

From a thousand miles away Manny's voice came through loud and clear. "McManus wants you back right away."

"Whatever is is, can't you handle it?"

"Afraid not. This morning Paredes posted a quarter-million dollars bail and vanished."

"Predictable," I said bitterly. "I warned Edison to find a sensible judge. So, the bird's flown—what am I supposed to do? Close the cage door?"

"There's more. Our chief said Edison has problems with the confession, how it was obtained—alleged coercion, you know the defense formula."

"Only too well." I thought for a few moments. "Okay, the bail will be forfeited and Felipe becomes a fugitive—right?"

"That's how it goes."

"So tell Wally I'll be there tomorrow. Meanwhile, see if you can get a line on Paredes's whereabouts. I think it's safe to assume he returned to his hacienda but I'd like to make sure."

"Any—?" Manny began, but I cut off the question with, "Later. And since all that's wanted of me is a review of recent history I may not break my butt to get back. Besides," I continued, "plane seats are scarce between here and Mexico City—high season in the Caribbean, you know."

"I do, and you put the case so convincingly." He paused. "Your guest okay?"

"Better than okay," I told him. "See you fairly soon."

As I replaced radio handset and false panel I realized Molly had probably heard most of what I'd said. She looked up at me and asked, "You have to go?"

"Not immediately, so let's make the most of remaining time."

We made love in the half-dark bedroom and relaxation segued into sleep, the ceiling fans cooling our damp bodies while we slept.

By the time I woke, Molly had baked a layer cake and prepared salad greens. I marinated *róbalo* filets in lime juice before grilling them, and as I poured chilled Paternina white I thought of Felipe Paredes in his sanctuary and resolved to bring back the fugitive dead or alive.

NINE

Next morning we flew to Isla Mujeres, off the coast from Cancún, and spent most of the day at an isolated beach. We snorkeled for shells and ate a picnic lunch that included Molly's layer cake.

That part of the island was uninhabited, so we were able to enjoy sun, water, and each other in the buff, and when we left it was with a shared feeling of regret.

During dinner on the patio Molly grew pensive until she finally broke silence saying, "I wonder if I'll ever again know such a heavenly day?"

"Why not? We've plenty of time ahead of us, and I know other secluded spots you'll enjoy."

"But this was so perfect," she sighed. "Sort of once in a lifetime—for me."

"Think positively," I admonished. "Just let me know when you want to come back. Open invitation, just supply the dates."

"I will, Jack, don't think I won't." She stretched back and looked up at the sky's first evening stars. "And I'll never forget how wonderful you've been."

"You're pretty wonderful yourself."

"Thank you—we won't lose touch, will we?"

"No. Will you stay in Phoenix?"

"Probably. But first I need to close out the Vegas apartment and collect my things, then go to Phoenix and do a lot of thinking about what to do with my life."

I nodded approvingly before she asked, "Are you in a lot of trouble with your office?"

"Not a lot, and nothing I can't resolve pretty fast."

"You'll let me know?"

"I will," I promised, and our conversation turned to other things.

In the morning we taxied to the airport and boarded our flight to Mexico City. She was changing to a Las Vegas flight, and my flight to Nogales had a connection in Tucson. At her gate we kissed and parted reluctantly, with mutual vows to see each other soon, and then she was gone, walking quickly away without looking back.

Even as the Mexicana plane lifted above the city's yellow-brown smog I was still thinking of her, and wondering how long our relationship would survive. In her new life-to-be Molly could meet a more stable fellow than I and opt for a nine-to-five husband, something I could never be. Well, absence would be a test for us both.

I was in Nogales by noon, and after leaving my suitcase in the motel room I went to the office and noticed a lot of eyes taking note of my entrance. Manny signaled me and said, "Glad you're back, amigo. You're to see Wally without delay."

"Sorry I brought you grief."

He shrugged. "Part of the profession. But Wally tends to tread lightly around me—I'm a *cucaracha,* after all, and he wouldn't welcome a minority lawsuit. Guess he'll take it out on you."

I grunted. "My mistake was in not recognizing Wally as a clown. Next time I'll laugh at his jokes—if there is a next time."

"*Vaya con Dios.*"

McManus's door was partly open, so I went in and found him munching a fast-food sandwich with fries. He gazed at me, dislike in his expression, and said, "So you're back. I sort of hoped you'd defect—save us all a lot of trouble."

"Great greeting, Chief, been working on it?"

"Didn't have to—comes from the heart." He laid aside his sand-wich, drank noisily from a Sprite can, and said, "Furman Edison can't wait to see you, wants all three of us together."

"Fine with me. Unless there's a court reporter taking down what's said."

He squinted ate me. "So—what if there is?"

"Then I ought to have a lawyer present—to make sure all rights and proprieties are observed."

"You have a lawyer?"

"Sure, Emilio Fernandez—heard of him?"

"Not's I recall."

I smiled. My superior had just revealed his ignorance of Mexi-can culture, "El Indio" Fernandez being Mexico's best-known movie actor and director.

McManus finished his Sprite, tossed the can in a wastebasket, and said, "This ain't no Inquisition, Jack, just a get-together among professionals to discuss how evidence and confessions are obtained."

"Fine with me," I repeated, "since all I have to do is tell it like it is."

"Be sure you do, eh? Don't want to hear some cockamamie self-serving fantasy that Edison won't buy."

"Well, I'll have to make sure I relate a cockamamie, self-serving fantasy more to his taste. Like a campfire story."

His only reaction was to drag over the phone and call Edison's office. Hanging up, he said, "The AUSA will see us now. Ready?"

"Ready as I'll ever be. By the way, Paredes hasn't been men-tioned. Any idea where he fled?"

"South of the border, no doubt." He rose from his chair. "Cu-carachaland, where else?"

Assistant U.S. Attorney Furman Edison kept us waiting in his office anteroom for eighteen minutes before deigning to receive us.

He was the same sallow-faced, sharp-eyed functionary I'd met a few days ago but today his expression was aggressive. "Take a seat," he directed from across the conference table, and gazed at me with disapproval. "Afternoon, Mr. Edison," I responded. "You hauled me back from a deserved vacation so I hope you had ample reason."

"Not for you to question my motives," he bristled. "You're on the thin edge of sanctions, so behave accordingly."

I turned to McManus. "What kind of sanctions?"

"To be determined," he said uncomfortably. "Mr. Edison is in charge here. Listen up."

I smiled at them both. "I hadn't anticipated a who-pissed-on-whose-boots session, but since that seems to be developing I have to observe that Felipe Paredes is no longer in custody. Who let him go? Not me, I was a thousand miles away dreaming of merit awards and promotions for bringing him in and securing a confession."

Edison stoked his chin. "That's what everyone has a problem with—the manner of his arrival in U.S. territory, and the way his confession was extracted."

"You saw and heard him confess. I don't recall his registering complaints at the time."

"His attorney did that—based on what Paredes told him off camera."

"And you believed him?"

"More importantly, the judge did."

"If you'll recall, Mr. Edison, I suggested you select a hardass judge not likely to be swayed by the scumbag. Right, Wally?"

McManus shrugged, said nothing.

Edison cleared his throat. "Not a lot of choice around here. Judge-shopping is big-city stuff, down here it's the boonies. Anyway, your criticism of the bench is out of place. You're on the griddle, Novak, make no mistake about it."

"Sensed that," I responded, "seeing no coffee offered. So, what's the big deal?"

"The big deal—as you call it—is the likelihood you'll be charged with kidnapping a foreign national, flying him here, and coercing a confession that won't stand up in court."

"Well," I remarked, "the value of the confession is somewhat nugatory, wouldn't you say? I mean, the perp's gone so there's not going to be any trial. Right?"

"That doesn't mitigate your offenses, Novak," he said sharply. "Paredes might eventually be arrested on U.S. territory, in which case he could be brought to trial."

"Meanwhile," I observed, "our government has the usufruct of the quarter-million bond he left behind. Suppose I'd handed you the quarter-million dollars to use as your office saw fit—you'd be giving me wall plaques and damp kisses. Contrariwise, you seem to feel I should have trudged in here under a huge load of guilt. Well, think again. If I'm ever required to tell the tale—the full tale—to a properly constituted tribunal, I'll do so. While citing your halfhearted attitude as material to any misfeasances I may have inadvertently committed."

"Inadvertently!" Edison exploded. "You set out to kidnap Paredes, don't deny it."

I nodded thoughtfully. "Since we're reminiscing, let me remind you gentlemen that you both signed off on a project to bring Paredes to justice. He was brought to the bar of justice, but you couldn't handle him—that's the tale that *ought* to be told: how you let a major trafficker slip away."

Sullenly, McManus said, "You were supposed to lure him here."

"I lured his accomplice here. He persuaded Paredes to come here for a big buy. The scam would have worked but Paredes decided to stage a rip-off. I left and he left with me."

"Voluntarily?"

"His men were shooting at us. I got him out of the line of fire and saved his life."

Edison grunted. "And held him prisoner in a safe house."

McManus said, "What a safe house—a shithouse is more like it."

"I've never believed in coddling scumbags—but why are we all worried about ungentle treatment of a murdering bastard like him? You saw and heard his confession—it was clean, no flaws. What more do you expect?"

Edison considered before saying, "I expect a degree of professionalism you obviously don't possess, Novak."

I shrugged. "Blame it on insufficient training. I was taught to do a tough job and leave the niceties to Department of Justice lawyers."

He swallowed. "So you have no statement to make regarding the subject under discussion."

"Not at this time."

Edison eyed McManus. "I expect you to discipline your subordinate, Wally, make an example of him so others will refrain from similar misconduct."

McManus looked away, remained silent. I could have asked, *What misconduct?* but I was tired from the long flight and weary of Edison's white-collar bullshit, so I said only, "That all?"

"For now," Edison responded, opened a legal folder and began scanning the contents. To McManus I said, "Guess we're dismissed. We better hop it before gendarmes arrive."

Edison gave me a baleful glance as we rose, then looked down at his folder.

As we left the Federal building, McManus said, "I got to discipline you, Jack, you heard him."

"I heard him. Let the punishment fit the crime."

"Yeah, I believe in that. So how about copying the Bill of Rights in longhand? You can do it during your week's suspension from duty—with pay."

"I can handle that. No entry in my personnel file?"

"What could I say? It's a complicated situation, not all of which I understand."

"Me neither."

"Just stay out of the office, okay? Go back to Cozumel if you want."

"Nobody there," I told him, "but I'll make myself scarce."

He managed a rare smile. "You got a lot going for you: you're smart and resourceful and you got the balls of a rhinoceros. Just don't fuck up and ruin your career. Okay?"

·   ·   ·

We returned to the office, where I beckoned Manny to join me for a private chat. We held it over beer and tacos at Sol's Southern Deli, and after my summary Manny exclaimed, "*Carajo!* Until now I didn't think Wally was human. So, what are you going to do with your week's suspension?"

"Take it elsewhere. Ah—where's our van?"

"At the government hangar."

"Weapons?"

"Bagged and stowed in the plane's cargo—wait a minute, you going someplace?"

"Haven't thought it out yet. But you won't be involved."

"Suppose I want to be?"

I shook my head. "You're on duty, I'm not, forget it." I took a long pull of Corona and wiped foam from my lips.

Abruptly Manny said, "Bad news, Jack, I should have told you the Phoenix police haven't collared Frank Rodriguez; they think he's in Mexico."

"I hope so," I said, "because Molly's moving back to her Phoenix apartment and I don't want that killer anywhere near her."

"There's an outstanding warrant for his arrest. Vegas detectives found fingerprints on the door handle, and on the basin where he apparently washed blood from his hands. The warrant hasn't been made public, so Rodriguez may feel it's safe to move around."

"Yeah. Well, I'll have to call Molly, warn her." I paused. "Should have had her stay at Cozumel until Rodriguez was off the street."

"Good idea. Uh, did Furman Edison mention me?"

I shook my head. "It was a spirited colloquy but your name never came up." I smiled. "See, you bring me bad news, I bring you good."

"What do you make of Edison?"

"Your average, run-of-the-mill government geek prosecutor. The kind that won't docket a case for trial unless he or she is a thousand percent convinced of winning. Edison wanted to read me the rule book but I didn't let him get far." I grinned. "Doesn't like me, Manny, but few people do."

"Got that right, *hermano*."

"Okay, now tell me what if anything is being done about the nine knaves Paredes named."

"The ones he said his *cuñado* is paying off—yeah. Well, Mc-Manus sent the names to Washington and Mexico City—plus Aguilera's—but so far only silence."

I laughed mirthlessly. "They can't deal with it so they'll ignore it. Makes our work seem sort of useless."

"I try not to dwell on that. Anyway, I'm outa here and back to the office. See you . . . when?"

"Call you soon."

He left the deli and I paid the bill. From there I went to my motel room and called Molly's Las Vegas apartment. I let her phone ring a dozen times before hanging up. Thought I'd suggest she activate the answering machine on her Phoenix phone—then I could at least leave messages. I wanted to call her later in the day—after some business at the airport.

I drove an office car into the hangar where the mec was changing aileron cables on the hornet-infested Piper. I touched the horn to get his attention, and when he saw me get out he walked over. Today's uniform was fairly clean, and the top pocket had an embroidered name: Barney.

"Well," he said, "where you been? Flying today?"

"If there's nothing wrong with the Skyhawk I'll take it up for a spin." I looked around and spotted the Ford van parked between two abused-looking aircraft. "Follow me," I told him. When we reached the van I slid back the panel. "Need some interior alterations, Barney."

"Like what?"

"I was thinking of creating and camouflaging a hideaway space."

"How big?"

"Oh, a foot wide, four to six inches deep, and a yard long."

He pulled himself into the van and looked around, stamped on the metal floor, and said, "I can cut out a floor section next to the slide panel, hinge it inboard from underneath so's you can get to it when the panel's slid back. That do you?"

"It will."

"Needed when?"

"Tomorrow before noon?"

"You'll have it."

"Good, now let's get the Skyhawk outa here."

Together we rolled it out of the hangar, checked oil and fuel, and Barney ran up the manifold while I filed a flight plan to Hermosillo.

I took off on the east runway, favored by a ten-knot breeze, and climbed to five thousand feet before turning south. On course, I climbed toward nine thousand, reached altitude above Santa Victoria, and presently Felipe Paredes's *estancia* came into view.

The bombed buildings were still black carbonized ruins, nothing having been done to replace them. Horses and cattle were back in their corrals, and the big house looked lifeless and abandoned. That worried me, until I saw a pickup drive away from the far side of the house and take the dusty trail toward the airstrip where I'd met and snatched the owner only a week ago.

I maintained altitude, not wanting to alert anyone by dropping eyeball low, and continued flying south until the hacienda was almost lost from view. Then I noticed a twin-engine plane with wing tanks heading toward me on a reciprocal course. It was about two thousand feet above me when it started to descend. I lost a thousand feet for safety's sake, and the Cessna 402 passed over with plenty of space to spare. For a minute I continued on course, then made a wide bank to the west. Sure enough, the Cessna was approaching Paredes's airstrip, side-slipping to lose altitude until it lined up with the far end and touched down. The pickup headed toward it as the plane rolled the distance and turned around in a billow of tan dust.

I set my teeth and grimaced. Paredes was still in business, or his ranch hands were, because the Cessna's cabin door was open and bundles were being passed out and loaded on the pickup. No hay for starving cattle, the contents were a lot more costly and had come a long way. Like from Colombia, with refueling stops in Costa Rica and Honduras or Belize.

Paredes was like a snake that kept lashing and biting even when cut apart. And he was probably even more arrogant, having fooled the gringos and become convinced of his own invulnerability.

Well, I'd seen what I'd come to see—there was life and activity around the hacienda, and on the airstrip it was business as usual. Chances were pretty good that Felipe was overseeing the transaction and anticipated many more. No reason for him to abandon the hacienda—his family was there, and so was his business. I wondered what share of today's load Paredes would pass along to his brother-in-law. Twenty percent seemed a fair share for air force and army protection arranged by Pablo Antonio Aguilera.

Live in Mexico, I thought, where everything has its price and everything is negotiable.

Nearing Santa Victoria, I could make out the church tower from four thousand feet, and lost more altitude until Nogales airport was in sight and the controller told me which runway to use.

From the flight line I taxied as far as the hangar cut off the engine, and Barney helped me roll the Skyhawk the rest of the way. "See anything interesting?" he asked.

"Not much." But I went to the pay phone and called Manny to tell him what I'd seen. "If the Cessna was going to fly the load here it wouldn't have been unloaded, so it's probably going back south. I know one thing: Paredes isn't going to store the stuff forever."

"No. No money for him until the buyer pays for it. Uh—I want to report this, but I need a source."

"Say an informant of tested reliability phoned in the tip."

"Will do." He broke the connection and I went back to where Barney was wheeling welding tanks and torch to the van. He looked at his wristwatch and said, "I could have this ready by dark if you need it."

"Good idea."

From my room I phoned Molly again, and this time she answered. "Honey, I'm so glad you called. I was thinking of calling, but I thought you might think I was pursuing you."

"Not necessarily, but I like the idea of being pursued. You're doing everything just right. How about me?"

"No complaints at all. Except . . . I miss you badly."

"Mutual. Ah—I don't want to frighten you, but I just learned that Frank Rodriguez isn't in jail where I thought he'd be, because the Phoenix cops can't find him."

"Oh, God," she breathed, "now I *am* scared. Jack, what can I do?"

"Keep your door locked and don't open it to anyone you don't know. Don't go out after dark, shop were people are. Ah—got a gun?"

"No—I'm afraid of them."

"We'll remedy that. I was thinking of Cozumel. But I'd like you to take a handgun course and buy a three-eighty to keep in your handbag."

"What's a three-eighty?"

"A short thirty-eight caliber pistol. Yeah, do that. And for now I think you ought to stay clear of Phoenix. Have you got a girlfriend you could move in with? Temporarily?

"Maybe. I'll have to think about it."

"Or, you could go to Cozumel—you'll be safe there as long as you want to stay. If you decide to go, just go."

"But we won't be together," she objected.

"Honey, we're not together now." Though I wish we were, I thought.

"When could you come?"

"Weekends—maybe three-day weekends."

"All right, if that's a promise. I'll do everything you want me to. Oh, how long is a gun course?"

"Couple of hours. And you should fire off a few boxes of shells at the range to get confidence."

"I will, Jack. Now, are you in trouble at the office?"

"Hardly noticeable."

"I'm so relieved." She paused before saying in a low voice, "And when we're together you'll kiss me where it counts most?"

"And leaves a lasting impression. Depend on me."

"I do, oh, I do."

"I'll call when I can and hope to see you soon."

"I'm counting on it. 'Bye, love."

I hung up and visualized Barney in a shower of welding sparks. Good man. Reliable. Needed for what I had in mind.

So far everything was moving along on schedule. Tomorrow I had at least a four-hour drive ahead of me, but there was no hurry. I didn't plan to reach target destination until well after dark.

TEN

Having been banned from office premises, I had to assemble supplies and ordnance I could have requisitioned, had I not been out of favor.

At a gun shop where I was well and favorably known, I bought four boxes of .45 ACP ball ammo for the tommy gun and a box of Black Talon .38s for my H&K pistol. From a large selection of rifles I chose a .308 caliber FAL with flash suppressor and twenty-round magazine, and had it fitted with an 8-power Leupold scope while I waited. The clerk tossed in two boxes of metal jacket ammo and I paid with operational cash.

From there I drove to the barrio and bought two old blankets, a stained serape, a GI gasoline jerrican, and a fairly new looking Zenith TV. At a corner store I bought four gallon jugs of purified water, a loaf of sliced bread, a package of bologna, and two bags of ice. Ordnance was in the Comanche where Manny had stowed it.

By the time I returned to the hangar Barney the mec had left, but I was able to check out his work.

A small unobtrusive button opened the hinged lid he'd cut from the van's floor. I lined the cavity with a blanket and loaded it with the tommy gun and grenades, then the new FAL rifle and ammo boxes, and arranged everything snugly before covering the contents with the second blanket. I closed the lid and dirtied its perimeter, and covered the area with the shabby serape. On it I set the television cabinet and jerrican, and put water bottles, edibles, and ice on the floor beside the passenger seat.

I had everything I needed, why wait until tomorrow?

In my motel room I exchanged true name ID for the Matthew J. Barden phonies, got into old clothing, and drove back to the hangar. In the van I stopped at a filling station for a rim-mounted used spare, and stowed it in the back of the van. Then I drove to the border crossing point and was waved into the Republic of Mexico.

Heroica Nogales was no worse than the average Mexican border town. Smaller than Tijuana and Reynosa, it had the same narrow run-down streets bordered with shops selling everything from toy whistles to slaughtered hogs; barefoot, half-naked urchins smearing and wiping windshields in hopes of a few pesos; shabbily dressed whores aged nine to eighty; and everywhere the sight and stench of poverty. Always I felt compassion for the Mexican underclass but none for its corrupt governors who looted the country of its considerable wealth and enjoyed it in impunity.

Immigration and customs inspection took place ten miles into Sonora. At the checkpoint a uniformed inspector waved me over and had me slide back the van door. When he saw the TV set his eyes sparked. "Contraband, señor!"

"It's just an old TV I'm taking to a friend."

"Where?"

"Santa Victoria."

"Anything else to declare?"

"Nothing."

He frowned. "There is duty to be paid. One hundred dollars."

"I see. To the government."

"Yes. To the government."

"Hmmm. The set isn't worth a hundred. I can take it back to Nogales or give you twenty for your trouble."

"Thirty."

I handed him three tens and said, *"Buen provecho."*

"Gracias, señor. Have a good day." He thumbed me through and turned his attention to an incoming passenger car. The TV and the

prospect of a *mordida* had focused the inspector's attention as I thought it would, and my weapons were safely in Mexico.

As the sun lowered, the sky took on purplish hues. I drove the potholed, badly surfaced road whose shoulders were littered with peculiarly Mexican waste: disposable diapers and plastic shopping bags that fluttered in the evening breeze. Imperishable, they would endure through the next century.

Soon I was driving through a cactus forest whose tall saguaros stood out like gibbets against the darkening sky, and I thought of Eddie Flanigan, Molly's brother, killed in a drug rip-off and cremated in a pyre that had been his plane. His death attributable to Felipe Paredes, as was the murder of Beverly Dawn through the agency of Frank Rodriguez, now missing from his usual haunts.

Felipe Paredes was one bad *hombre,* no doubt about it. I'd bombed and burned some of his replaceable buildings and thrown a brief scare into his wife, but more had to be done. More did not include returning Paredes to U.S. jurisdiction; that had been tried, but his wealth and shysters had set him free, a formula that could be repeated endlessly.

I thought of Frank Rodriguez and prayed the Phoenix cops would collar him before he harmed Molly. And there was Licenciado Pablo Antonio Aguilera at the top of the corrupt pyramid, an embassy favorite, and a provider of protection for the traffickers who used Mexico as a base for operations into the United States.

Mexico was never going to prosecute him, and he was too big a fish for the U.S. to net. Why—the ambassador would protest—aspersions on Aguilera could destabilize the entire range of our cherished, carefully nurtured relations with Mexico: diplomatic, cultural, and commercial. Whatever his alleged crimes Aguilera was too important to offend.

We had Paredes's videotaped confession implicating Aguilera and his high-level accomplices but it was never going to be used against Paredes. The judge had set it aside without considering its merits, but the tape might be a useful tool against Aguilera. Eventually.

I pulled into Santa Victoria after nightfall, parked around the side of the church, and knocked on Father Gardenia's door. He opened it, gave me an *abrazo,* and invited me in. After pouring wine, he asked, "So, what are you doing here so late in the day, my friend? Can I be of service to you?"

"Mainly," I said, after sipping his wine, "I wanted to stretch my legs, rest a bit, and inquire after your health."

"Excellent," he said, and told me that Señora Moreno had relocated with relatives in the interior.

"Any more unwelcome visitations?"

"None, thanks be to God." He paused. "There was a rumor that Paredes was jailed in Nogales, but that must have been false, because I saw him only yesterday."

"Yes, he was briefly in jail, but forfeited bond and left."

"I see. While he was away from the *estancia* some of his buildings were firebombed. I heard he was in town to arrange for building materials."

"Logical," I said, and asked if he could use a televisions set.

"I could indeed. I have not had one for nearly a year."

So I brought in the Zenith and set it on a corner table. The priest clasped his hands and smiled. "Thank you, thank you. I believe it will be a good companion."

I realized then that it would be uncharacteristic of him to spend money Isidor Moreno had left on his personal needs or comfort. Unlike the Customs inspector, Father Gardenia understood what was right and what was wrong. We sipped wine silently until my host said, "Surely you did not drive all this way just to bring me the television."

I smiled. "True, Padre. I have ulterior motives, but they had best be left unexplored."

"Then I can only bless your journey and wish you well."

"Thank you. Now, if I can impose on you I'll make some food for myself and eat before I move on."

"No imposition at all."

So I made bologna sandwiches for us, and we finished them

with more wine. The protein pickup energized me, and as I bagged the remaining food the priest said, "If on your return you desire a place to rest, this house is at your disposal. You are always welcome here, señor. The door is never locked."

"I'll remember, Padre, and thanks."

From his doorway he watched me drive off, and then I was passing the village airfield and the last of the streetlights, with the dark, uncertain road ahead.

After six miles the road gave out and I slowly followed the bank of a small stream that I knew from overhead observation ran through Paredes's *estancia*. After a while I reached wire fencing and paralleled it until I could see in the distance faint lights that marked the hacienda.

In the night's silence, the old van's engine sounded as loud as a locomotive, but I recognized the amplification as due to the impact of adrenalin on my senses. I braked, turned off lights and engine, and opened the arms cache. From it I took my .38 pistol and the FAL rifle. Night air was cool and refreshing as I focused the eight-power scope on the distant lights. The sky was clear, stars brilliant; above the horizon a thin crescent moon. I had plenty of time.

After loading the rifle, I cut fence wire to let the van through and emptied the jerrican into the van's gas tank. Then I got behind the wheel and scoped the house from time to time as I waited.

From high above came the whisper of a jet aircraft, and as I watched its blinking lights I was reminded of the Cessna I'd seen landing at Paredes's airstrip. Was it still there? I wondered, and decided to have a look. With dimmed headlights I drove slowly through the fence opening, steering carefully around cactus stands and desert shrubs until I could see the airstrip. Starlight outlined the dark plane, glinted from its propellor tips, and I realized I had come across a target of opportunity.

More than that. Its destruction would draw men from the house into the open, while women stayed behind away from danger. An unanticipated plus.

Scope calibrations ranged the Cessna at two hundred and twenty yards. I scanned around the plane looking for watchmen, saw nothing, decided to drive closer without headlights.

Night vision had kicked in and I was able to make out a cactus stand about eighty yards from the airstrip. For concealment I parked the van beside it, and opened the weapons cache again. Bullets could hole the plane's gas tanks but might not ignite them, so I opted for a fragmentation grenade and set a thirty-second fuse delay. Then I walked slowly, quietly and carefully to the edge of the clearing, knelt beside a thick saguaro, and listened. Pounding in my eardrums echoed the accelerated beating of my heart and I breathed deeply to calm down.

The hoot of a cactus owl broke the silence, then there was rustling on the ground ten or fifteen feet away—probably a snake or kangaroo mouse. I shined my flashlight toward the sound and saw a big-eared hare standing erect, frozen by the light. I snapped it off quickly and heard the hare bound away. If he was lucky, I thought, he could forage through the night without falling prey to a diamondback.

Concentrating again on the next few minutes, I figured it would take at least four minutes for the pickup to arrive following the explosion, probably longer in the dark. Say five, maximum elapsed time.

Was my van too close to the scene? Conflagration would light the area, so I ought to move it farther back. Prone on the floor of the van, I could shoot through the door space; bullet trajectory at a hundred yards was close to impact point at eighty. Then, after downing my target, I had to cripple the vehicle to avoid hot pursuit, and if any stout-hearted men came plunging through the cactus I could spray them with the Thompson. Okay. I made my way back to the van.

Thirstily, I drank from a water jug and capped it before backing the van from the airstrip, positioned it broadside to the plane, and scoped the scene again before walking to the Cessna, grenade in hand.

I could tape the grenade to the near wing tank but I hadn't brought tape, and I didn't want it rolling off slanted surfaces and exploding on the ground. So I moved to the near engine and pried open the inspection port. There was enough ambient light that I could see the fuel line to the carburetor and its brass flange. I unscrewed the flange and fuel poured out, flooding the nacelle. I coughed from the fumes, held my breath, and was just putting the grenade through the port when the cabin door slammed open and a man called, *"Oye, ¿qué pasa?"*

I couldn't see his face, but I could see a gun in his hand.

ELEVEN

Checking the engine," I told him. "There's a gas leak, come see."

He was a middle-aged *peón,* unshaven, scraggly straw sombrero, baggy pants, stained pullover shirt bunched by a cord around his waist. He couldn't see the pistol in my belt, so he lowered his revolver, got down from the plane, and came around the wingtip. I withdrew my hand from the open port, still clenching the grenade, and gestured at the engine nacelle. "Smell," I said, and pointed. He stuffed the revolver inside the belt cord and shuffled forward, sandals scraping the pebbled surface. I stepped aside, and when he was peering into the nacelle I gave his neck a hard chop and he dropped without a sound.

The watchman was just a poor farmhand, not a *narcotraficante* like his employer, so I got both hands under his shoulders and dragged him off the airstrip and far enough into the cacti that he wouldn't be harmed by the coming explosion. But it would rouse him, and if I knew the inbred reaction of *peones* he wouldn't wait for Paredes's arrival, but would flee far into the night.

Leaving him out of harm's way, I went back to the Cessna and continued what I'd begun before being interrupted.

I drew out the grenade's safety pin and set the grenade inside the port, then closed it and jogged back toward my van. Before I reached it the grenade went off, instantly igniting and detonating fuel tanks. The shock wave whooshed past me, flames shot upward and lighted the area around me. Another tank let go and I heard pieces of aircraft hurtling out and beyond me.

From the van I looked back and saw a flaming, crumpled ruin that barely resembled a plane, and I thought how much it looked like the flaming finale of the plane Eddie Flanigan had landed and which had become his pyre.

Before I lay on the van flooring I emptied the weapons cache and set the tommy gun, grenades, and ammo within easy reach. I rolled the serape into a thick bundle and laid the rifle barrel on it. Then I assumed prone firing position and watched the burning aircraft through the scope.

About now, I thought, the investigating party should be setting off from the hacienda, and checked my watch. Four to five minutes travel time, I'd estimated—and they'd have no night directional problem, the flames were a beacon.

Paredes would have no reason to suspect sabotage from the ground; more likely he would assume a plane had flown over and dropped a bomb on the visiting Cessna.

The roar and crackling of the conflagration had died down, and presently I heard the racing engine of a fast-moving vehicle. At three minutes, forty seconds a big, high-axle pickup emerged halfway down the strip and slowed as it neared the burning plane.

The pickup stopped twenty yards from the fire and three men got out. Two had submachine guns slung from their shoulders, and the third was Paredes wearing black pants and his trademark white reptile boots. He walked toward the fire, then backed off from the heat and stood watching, bodyguards on either side. I had his torso in the crosshairs, not trying for a head shot with an untried weapon. Why wait? Fingertip on the trigger, I pulled smoothly, felt the stock buck into my shoulder, and saw Paredes stagger and drop.

His bodyguards stared at his body, and before they could unsling their weapons I drilled them both. One rolled and kicked, then his back arched and he died. The other was dead before he fell.

Next, the pickup. I couldn't see if a driver was behind the wheel, so I shot out a front tire, then a rear, and when no driver emerged, I exchanged the rifle for my tommy gun, grabbed a grenade, and jogged to the pickup.

The big fuel tank was set below and alongside the cab. I un-screwed the cap, armed the grenade, and dropped it down the fuel pipe. Then I walked back to my van.

The detonation slammed my back, and chunks of the pickup whistled through the air, one piece topping a nearby saguaro.

I didn't look back. No point in hanging around to see if rein-forcements arrived. I'd done what I'd come to do, and it was time to go. Felipe Paredes would make no more slimy deals, kill no more in-nocents. He was finished, along with two of his villains, and I had no regrets whatever. Eye for an eye.

I started the engine, and with headlights on, drove across the dead *hacendado*'s land, steered through the cut fence, and followed the stream until the cactus forest thinned and I found the way back to Santa Victoria.

At two-ten I drove around behind the church, parked and locked the van, and knocked on Father Gardenia's door. After a while he opened it, blinked at me, and said, "Come in." He was wearing a nightshirt and no slippers. I said, "I'd like to rest a while, Padre."

"*Estás en tu casa,*" he replied. "Are you thirsty? Something to drink?"

"A little wine would go well, Padre, help me sleep."

He poured us each a glass and we touched rims before drinking.

"Take my bed," he said, "I will sleep on the couch there."

I shook my head. "The couch is fine. I'm tired enough to sleep on the floor." And that was the truth. The adrenalin surge was gone, leaving me bone tired from the stress of everything I'd done. Señora Paredes was a widow now, but so was Olivia Moreno, who in time would learn that she had nothing further to fear from Don Felipe.

"So be it," my host said, "but . . . is there anything you wish to confess?"

"Nothing, Padre. I have no guilt this night."

"Then rest safely in the arms of our Savior," he intoned, crossed himself, and went back to his bedroom.

I made myself reasonably comfortable on the lumpy old sofa, and slept until I heard Father Gardenia making breakfast. Outside it was still dark. I washed up and shared his breakfast of boiled eggs, spicy *chorizo,* hard *bolillos,* and thick coffee. He turned on the television set, and while we ate we watched a children's cartoon program in Spanish. I thanked the priest for his incurious hospitality, we wished each other well, and just after dawn I took the road north to Heróica Nogales.

On the Mexican side there was no vehicle inspection, but at U.S. Customs I showed my false ID while a mirror was wheeled under the van and the underside checked for wetbacks. "No liquor to declare?" the inspector asked. I said, "Nothing," and he waved me on.

At the hangar I left the van near the Comanche and got into my office car. Barney the mec waved at me and went back to work.

When I got to the motel there was a message to call Manny, and when I heard him on the line he said, "You okay?"

"Sure, why not?"

"You were away last night."

"Was I? Who says so?"

"Never mind. Lunch?"

"See you at the Embers. Wait a minute—Frank Rodriguez still on the loose?"

"Afraid so, haven't heard to the contrary."

"Phoenix cops must be looking in the wrong places. Any ideas?"

"Maybe we can come up with something. Ah—his pal has been identified as Patrick Meehan, small-scale mugger, burglar, and crack peddler. Hasn't been charged with anything—lately."

"Let's think about him," I said, and hung up. Before turning in I showered, shaved, and bagged dirty clothes for the cleaner. Then I slept until nearly noon, and drove across town to meet my partner.

• • •

After the waiter had taken our orders he brought two bottles of Tecate and a pair of chilled glasses. I drank from mine and Manny said, "You don't listen to border radio, do you?"

"Not if I can avoid it."

"Then you wouldn't know about a small war on Paredes's airstrip last night."

"On it, or for it?"

He looked away. "A plane was burned. Paredes and some men were found dead nearby."

"Plane crashed?"

He shrugged. "What I heard was fragmentary. Apparently people at the hacienda phoned police after the bodies were found."

I smiled. "Welcome news, Manny. Shows you how ill-advised Paredes was to skip bond and run home. If he'd stayed in jail he'd still be alive, right?"

"Right. And while we're on the subject, I beat on your room door at zero-seven-thirty this morning—no response."

"So?"

"I figured you hadn't been there all night."

"Reasonable conclusion, but did you consider I might have gone out for early breakfast?"

"Actually, I didn't give it a lot of thought—until I heard the radio news."

"I don't see there's much to think about, *compadre*. Narcotics is a competitive business and *traficantes* have enemies. Seemingly, one caught up with Paredes and put him out of business. That's good for America and the DEA."

He nodded agreement, hot rolls arrived followed by salads and marinated fajitas. As I began cutting the tender beef I said, "Also, Furman Edison's office gained clear title to that quarter-million bond. He should be happy as a *chamaco* with a found copy of *Playboy*."

"Could be. I can have the Phoenix cops pick up Pat Meehan and squeeze him—if you think it's a good idea."

"More like a last resort. At this point Frank Rodriguez doesn't know he's wanted by the cops. If Meehan's bagged, he will." I chewed a mouthful of endive and avocado. "While you were scamming Frank you had his contact number."

"Been disconnected. His apartment was surveilled for a while but he never showed up. Probably went to Mexico."

"In his place I would." We ate without conversation until Manny asked, "Molly okay?"

"Hope so. I suggested she go back to Cozumel until Frank's behind bars."

Manny smiled. "You care for her, don't you?"

"And I'm concerned for her safety, so I suggested she learn to shoot a three-eighty and keep it in her purse. Just in case."

"Yeah. And I've been thinking how this whole Paredes thing developed because she came around asking about her brother. He died on Paredes's airstrip and so did Paredes—like they say, what goes around comes around."

"That's what they say."

After lunch I drove back to the hangar and cleaned the weapons I'd fired, and stowed them in the Comanche's baggage compartment—except for the scoped FAL rifle. I took it to the gun shop and told the clerk to put it back on the rack and give me its used value. He looked it over for scratch marks, found none, and squinted through the barrel. "Looks good to me, is there a problem?"

"None. It's a great piece. I decided I need it less than the cash, okay?"

"Suppose I knock off a hundred."

"That's fair."

He opened the cash register and handed me the bills. As I left he was polishing the rifle stock.

From my room I phoned Molly's Vegas apartment and after six rings left my name and number on her answering machine. Same with her Phoenix phone, so I began wondering if she was in Cozumel.

I called the house but Ramona didn't answer, nor Molly, but that proved nothing. Ramona worked part time, and if Molly were there she could be sunning on the pier.

Phone in hand, I considered what to do next. I had the best part of a week's suspension to do with as I chose, and if I hadn't earned time off before, last night's solo operation entitled me to some indulgence. Destroying Paredes should be worth a couple of in-house medals if I could talk about what I'd done. Hadn't lied to Manny, just evaded his queries.

If I left now for Mexico City I'd have to overnight there and take the morning flight to Cozumel.

That meant calling Molly's numbers again and leaving word that I'd be in Cozumel next afternoon, with an invitation to join me there.

Manny met me for an after-work drink and I told him my immediate plans. He said, "Sounds good. When you coming back?"

"Next Monday. And if you hear anything about Rodriguez, let me know."

"Of course. Regards to Molly."

The Mexico City-Cozumel flight was late leaving, so I didn't land until late afternoon. From the San Miguel airport I phoned my house expecting someone to answer—Molly or Ramona—but gave up after a dozen rings. I called the *Corsair* for Carlos Paz and a deckhand told me my boat was at the marina and Carlos had gone home. That seemed an example worth following, so I taxied to my place and entered a silent house.

After unlocking patio doors I went down the dock to check on my Seabee. It wasn't listing from leakage, and otherwise looked okay, so I went back into the house, unpacked, and changed into shorts and guayabera. I got ice from the fridge, filled a tumbler with Añejo, and sipped while I considered what next to do. I could go in to Morgan's for a thick steak or fly over to Cancún for a more elaborate meal, only I didn't want to leave the house and risk missing a call from Molly, or even her arrival. It seemed like forever since I'd seen her, and I missed her.

From the freezer I took a grouper fillet and had begun thawing it with lime juice when the telephone rang. I picked up the receiver and said, "Hello," expecting Molly to reply.

Instead, a male voice said in Spanish, "Listen carefully. Someone wants to speak with you."

I gripped the receiver. "I'm listening."

Then came Molly's tremulous voice. "Jack, oh, Jack, I'm so frightened."

"Don't be. Where are you?"

She didn't answer my question, but said, "I was kidnapped at the airport," and broke off to whimper before saying, "the men who took me say they'll kill me if you don't do what they want." By now my flesh was cold. I heard a brief scream as the phone was jerked from her hand. The voice said, "If she lives or dies is up to you."

"What do you want?"

"The tape of Felipe Paredes's confession."

The line went dead.

Book TWO

TWELVE

At Annapolis, Ben Somers and I were in the same Bancroft Batt. We played lacrosse together, Ben the star performer, me the average stickman, and were friends on and off the playing field. At graduation Ben chose a Marine Corps commission and went to Quantico, while I took flight training at Pensy. A few years later we came together in Saigon in an odd sort of way.

A Huey had ferried my squadron into the metropolis for a day's R&R, and I was walking along a back street looking for souvenirs to take back to Pam in New York. The shops and bars were shabby, and I'd been warned that it was a zone where you could get laid if you weren't careful. I was thinking about a sapphire ring or a filigree bracelet set with semiprecious stones, when a kid raced out of a doorway, almost colliding with me; I saw terror in her eyes just before the bomb blew out the front of the joy house. I dropped flat to avoid flying debris, and when I got up flames were flaring across the face of the three-story building. I was dusting off my pants when a fiery figure burst out of the flames and headed across my path. The back of his camo uniform was on fire, and so was his hair. He kept running until I tackled him, rolled him in the dust, and smothered the flames. The guy looked at me, burbled, "Thanks, that was close."

Ben Somers.

Through singed eyelashes he stared at me until a smile creased his smoke-darkened face. "Jack! Jesus man, am I ever grateful!" He got to his knees and began brushing away charred fabric. "How do I look?"

"Like a damn fool who used his cock for a compass."

"Oh, Christ, the old morality guy." He shook his head, patted burned hair from his forehead. "Let's have a drink."

Behind us roof timbers gave in, showering the street with cinders and sparks. An army ambulance roared past us. I gestured at it. Ben shook his head, "Some other time."

We had our drink—several of them—a block away from the fire, and parted.

So Ben Somers owed me, and not just for the restorative drinks.

From the Mexico City airport I phoned his embassy office and asked for Major Somers. The sergeant politely inquired my name, said "One moment, sir," and presently I heard Ben's gravelly voice. "Jack, a courier brought a package from you 'bout an hour ago. So I figured you'd show up sometime. You with, uh, DEA still?"

"Shhh—the wires have ears, big ones."

"We can talk here, the office is swept occasionally."

"Rather not. I'm in town, let's say unofficially."

"Got it. So, what's the drill?"

"Know that Hungarian bar on the Alameda?"

"Know it and love it. When?"

"Make it an hour."

"Roger—and the package?"

"Stick it in the vault for now. More later."

I got there first and took a corner table, ordered a Tecate, and looked around the goulash palace. It hadn't changed since my previous visit. Still the softly lit mittel-European decor featuring heavy red velvet drapes, red-and-black flocked walls, an ancient piano, and atop it a violin and bow waiting the attentions of the host.

Ben arrived in civvies, open collar and no tie, punched my arm playfully and sat down. The first thing he said was, "That bomb could have been a blessing, Jack. I hadn't even got my pants off when it blew. But half an hour later I could have dipped myself a spectacular case of Asiatic clap. The kind that jus' don' go away."

"So, count you blessings."

"I do. I was drunk to go in there—no excuses, I was in the boonies for four fuckin' months, but to sprint out flaming like a burning bonze until you knocked me down, old buddy." He ordered tequila from the hovering waiter and turned to me. "So, what're you up to, Jack?"

"Routine shit mostly," I told him. "Except that I'm here on personal business, and don't want the office or the embassy to know."

He nodded. "Woman?"

"Yeah, and that's all you need to know—for self-protection." I sipped my beer and waited while Ben kicked back a healthy slug of Cuervo. He shook himself, muttered, "First today, may it not be the last," and settled back in his chair. "So, what's with the package?"

"I'll ask you for it. Meanwhile, I need a printout on a fairly well known Mex—Licenciado Pablo Antonio Aguilera. Heard of him?"

"Hell, yes. Head of the anti-narcotics task force. Your office works with him."

"He's dirty," I said. "Very, very dirty, but no one in my circles wants to hear it. Nor in yours, I gather."

"Jesus, that's like saying the Pope has a wife, a mistress, and three kids." He stared at me. "Printout on Aguilera?"

"It's what I need."

He licked his lips, downed more tequila, and grimaced. "Won't be easy."

"Ben, in your moment of need I didn't hesitate," I reminded him.

"That's true, you didn't." He sighed. "Okay, buddy, I'll do it. Where'll you be?"

"Probably the Fenix. Wherever I settle I'll call you. And, Ben, I need fast action."

"No time for lunch?"

"Sorry, this is super-urgent."

He drained his glass, got up, and patted my arm. "Roger, Wilco, birdman," he said, and left the table. I finished my beer, paid the check, and walked out to the taxi stand.

The Fenix was on Calle Atenas not far from the embassy. It was an old hotel featuring breezeways, colorful tiles, and glazed Oaxaca urns. Maybe one-star, probably none; minimal amenities, but clean rooms and linen. I signed the register as Matthew J. Barden and paid cash for two nights. My third-floor room overlooked a tiled court-yard fringed with palms and potted plants. There were tables for open-air drinking and dining, and a wet bar at one side. I pulled off my jacket, money belt, and holstered H&K auto, stripped, and got under a lukewarm shower. After shaving I stretched out under the ceiling fan while I reviewed action ahead.

Manny had responded to my request by sending two copies of Paredes's confession tape c/o Ben Somers. Yesterday, a second phone call—same voice—had supplied a Mexico City number I was to call when I was in the city with the ransom tape. I wasn't ready to estab-lish contact with Molly's kidnappers, not wanting them to think I was frantically eager to make the exchange. Actually, I was, but I wanted to inflict pain and suffering on the *pendejos* responsible for hers. That was essential to the trade.

I was drowsy from travel and stress, so I phoned Ben, told him I was in room 303, and asked him to check the reverse phone book for the contact number I'd been given. He could send me the corre-sponding street address along with my package and the Aguilera bio printout. No problem, he said, so I pulled down the blinds and slept until wakened by a knock on the door.

At that point I wasn't expecting enemies to call so I opened the door and saw a burrhead in civvies who handed me a large envelope and said, "From the Major."

"Thank you, and thanks to the Major."

He executed a smart about-face, and I closed the door as his heels clicked down the hall tiles.

So, here it was, the whole enchilada: tapes, printout, and a hand-printed address: a house on Sierra de Guadarrama in the residential Lomas. No subscriber name—the TelMex system didn't work that way; phones were bought and assigned to houses or apartments whose occupants could be transient—but I now had the location of the contact number I was supposed to call. Was that where Molly was being kept? I figured chances were one in three. Was she still alive? Once they had the Paredes tape, would she be freed? Would they let her live? I was worried about her and disgusted with myself for underestimating Aguilera's capacity for reprisal. Clever wasn't the word for him; he had to be a super-coyote to have gotten where he was and amassed all that wealth.

Of one thing I was sure: Aguilera wouldn't be at the house whose address I now had. He would have issued orders and thugs would carry them out. Frank Rodriguez among them?

I carried the printout to the writing table and opened it. Began to read.

Pablo Antonio Aguilera came from a family of wealthy landowners in Sonora. Mysteriously, his family's holdings had been exempted from the *ejidal* confiscations so fundamental to the Mexican Revolution, so the Aguilera family continued to be wealthy landowners, with scores of *peone*s working their land instead of neighboring *ejidos,* communal farms.

After the American School in Monterrey, Pablo Antonio attended Tulane in New Orleans, then law school at the University of Mexico. There he formed enduring friendships and working alliances with young PRI-istas as ambitious and upwardly mobile as himself.

In Monterrey he married Sara Beltrán y Montes, of a prominent industrial family, by whom he sired three children: Diego, a student in Barcelona; José at Texas A&M; and Susana María Aguilera y Beltrán, seventeen and a student at the English School of Mexico City. I noticed that Susana had left previous girls' schools in Lucerne and Buenos Aires owing to unacceptable deportment and curfew violations. Her passport photo, badly reproduced in black and white, showed a somewhat pudgy, almond-shaped face, with thick eyebrows and black hair drawn tightly back from her forehead. Once the baby fat left her features, Susana was going to be a classical Latin lovely.

Her brothers, I mused, were out of reach, but Susana was only a few miles away and potentially accessible. The thought sparked a plan to blindside Pablo Antonio and promote Molly's release.

Yellow pages gave me the address and telephone of the English School in suburban Coyoacán, and the name of a limousine rental agency: Domos Vehículos de Alta Calidad on Ávila Camacho. I noted both, and resumed scanning the printout. The rest of it summarized Pablo Antonio's rapid rise to prominence—political, social, and financial—with due mention of his contacts within the foreign diplomatic community.

Enough, I thought; I had what I needed to begin.

My belt buckle was of unusual design. The buckle itself formed the grip of a sharp, double-edged, three-inch dagger concealed inside the leather as a back-up weapon. I detached the dagger and slit the far edge of the bed mattress to conceal my holstered pistol and money belt, less three thousand dollars I folded into my trouser pocket. I slid one video cassette into the opening and wrapped the other in its package to take with me. Then I replaced the buckle-dagger and tightened my belt. Now I was ready to go.

A taxi took me to the Domos rental agency, where I asked about the availability of a stretch limousine. The proprietor led me into a covered parking area where workers were washing and polishing a long white Lincoln limo. I wanted a less conspicuous vehicle but examined it before asking about a nearby stretch Mercedes. "That is more expensive to hire," he told me. "Usually I rent it for weddings—newlyweds who want privacy." He winked lecherously, and opened one of the doors.

All windows were darkly tinted, as was the privacy panel separating driver from occupants. I nodded approvingly and asked, "Car telephone?"

"Of course." He pointed to its back seat recess, and opened a panel to reveal an assortment of liquor bottles and glasses. Two bottles of champagne stood in a separate compartment from which cold air flowed until he closed it.

"This will do nicely," I told him, "pending the selection of a driver. I want one neatly uniformed, shaved, and discreet." I added, "Meaning incurious. Do you have such an individual?"

"I do. Raúl Medina." We began walking back to the office. "How long will you require limousine and driver?"

"The rest of the day."

He went to the counter and scratched figures on a pad. "Pesos or dollars?"

"Dollars."

"Half a day will be six hundred dollars."

"Including driver?"

"Yes, but he would welcome a *propina* for satisfactory service."

"Bring him in."

Raúl Medina was of average height with the dark skin and aquiline nose of a pure-blooded Mexican Indian. His gray whipcord uniform was pressed, white shirt clean, and black tie neatly knotted. He stood at attention, cap in hand, while I looked him over before nodding approval. I gave my Barden ID to the owner with six hundred-dollar bills. While he was writing a receipt I handed another hundred to Raúl and said, "More, if you follow instructions."

"Depend on me, señor. You have only to make your wishes known."

As I regained my ID I said to the owner, "I expect to return by nightfall. If unexpectedly delayed I will, of course, pay for the extra time."

"Understood," he replied, and I followed Raúl toward the limo.

Before getting in I went to a wall phone and dialed the English School. To the lady who answered in Spanish, I said, "I am calling from the office of Licenciado Pablo Antonio Aguilera. He will be sending a car for his daughter, Susana María Aguilera, on a family matter. Please have her at the gate and ready to leave within forty-five minutes."

"Of course. With her books?"

"As usual. Thank you." I hung up hoping she would not call Aguilera's office to verify the request. If she did, it was likely that more than a schoolgirl would be waiting for me.

I went back to the limo, Raúl waiting beside the open door. "We are going to Coyoacán," I told him, "the English School," and gave him the address. "There a young lady will be waiting. As soon as she is in-side, lock the doors, pull away, and take the highway to Cuernavaca."

"I understand, señor."

"Keep your eyes on the road. Driving is your only concern."

"*Sí, señor.*"

"Your discretion will be rewarded." I got into the limo and was pleased to find the air-conditioning functioning properly.

As we drove out onto Ávila Camacho, I reflected that I was embarking on an uncertain and possibly dangerous mission: kidnapping the child of an enemy.

Light traffic on Avenida Universidad allowed us to reach the upscale residential colony of Coyoacán in thirty-eight minutes. And as we pulled into the school's facing street I saw a girl standing inside the high grilled gate near a security guard. She wore a school uniform comprising black blazer, black pleated skirt, black knee-length stockings, black thick-soled shoes, black glazed-straw bonnet, and black floppy tie under the Eton collar of her white blouse. Through the intercom I told Raúl to stop in front of the gate and open the rear door. When he did so, the girl crossed the sidewalk carrying her book bag and got in beside me. "I don't know you," she said. "You work for my father?"

"We have business dealings," I told her as the door locks clicked and the limo drew from the curb. "My name is Novak. You can call me Jack, Susana."

She turned to face me, and I realized how little the passport photo resembled her. Her black hair was cut quite short, her cheeks were dimpled, and her light ivory complexion was unblemished. Her face was beautiful.

"Miss Stoneleigh, she's the school clerk, said it was a family emergency. What kind of emergency?" She began pulling off her jacket.

"She misunderstood. A family *matter,* Susana. I told your father I had in mind a trip to Cuernavaca or Taxco, and he said you could show me around. Do you mind?"

She shook her head. "I love it—anything to be out of that hateful school." Jacket off, she undid the big floppy tie and opened the collar of her blouse. "You're American?"

"Yes."

"From where?"

"San Antonio."

"You like it there?" She pulled off her clodhoppers and smoothed the pleated skirt over her thighs.

"It's okay. I'm not there much, I travel a lot."

"That must be interesting." She breathed deeply and I saw the swell of mature breasts."

"At times."

"My brother is studying in Texas."

"José," I nodded. "Texas A&M. Diego's in Barcelona, your father told me."

"He told you a lot, so I guess you're okay." She drew the skirt above her knees. "Have you been to Graceland?"

"Not lately."

"I'd love to go there but so far Papá hasn't approved. I've been trying to arrange a class trip but the school—English, you know—doesn't have much feeling for Elvis."

"Keep trying and they're bound to give in."

She smiled, showing perfect white teeth—and those deep dimples.

Susana was not a tall girl, five-four or -five, I guessed, and the severe school uniform camouflaged what I guessed to be a rather zaftig figure. Her English was almost devoid of accent and she seemed bright and forthcoming. Apparently I'd passed inspection, so I asked, "Shall I tell the driver Cuernavaca or Taxco?"

"Oh, Taxco, if you don't mind. I love shopping there." She paused and I saw a slight frown. "I don't have any money, Jack, do you?"

"Enough for both of us." I picked up the intercom phone and told Raúl to bypass Cuernavaca and head for Taxco. Through the smoked-glass privacy panel I could barely make out the back of his head as he nodded.

"Oh, this is going to be fun!" she said happily, stretching back her arms in a movement that, whether she did it consciously or not, lifted her breasts provocatively. "Jack, I'm thirsty, is there *anything* to drink?"

"Should be." A button opened the liquor panel and she leaned over to study the bottles. I said, "I'm afraid there's no Coke, but we can stop for whatever you like."

"That's all right. At home I drink wine and champagne."

I opened the champagne compartment and she clapped her hands. "I *love* champagne!"

She held two tulip glasses while I popped the cork and poured fizzy champagne into both. Things were moving rapidly, and in a totally unexpected direction. "Cheers," she said, and touched my glass with hers. After we sipped I said, "Since we're going to be out of telephone range fairly soon, why don't you call your father and confirm you're with me?"

"Must I?"

"I'd feel better if you did. Then we can, ah, do whatever we want without any concerns."

"If you insist," she sighed, and reached for the mobile phone. I noted the numbers she punched as she shifted to Spanish and asked for her father. To me she said, "This is his private office number, Jack, but I guess you know."

"It's how we do business." Through the receiver I heard a male voice. "Susana?"

"Yes, Papá. I'm with Jack Novak and I'm glad to be away from school. Thank you."

Before Pablo Antonio could yell I took the phone from her hand and said, "Licenciado, your daughter is thoroughly charming, and I don't want you to be the least concerned about her. We're enjoying the afternoon together and she's under my protection. *Adiós.*" I broke the connection and returned the phone as Susana gave me a somewhat uncertain look. I sipped champagne, she followed suit and said, "Are you *sure* this was Papá's idea?"

I shrugged. "I didn't say we were going out of the city, but it seemed like a good idea and you agreed."

She shook her head. "Some of the things Papá does are very difficult to understand."

"Parents can be baffling."

She held out her glass for a refill and fanned flushed cheeks with the other hand. "I'm hot," she complained. "Is that air conditioner working?"

"Well, it's German," I replied, "and not to be compared with American units."

"I s'pose. Anyway, do you mind if I get more comfortable?"

"Get as comfortable as you want," I offered, and saw her fingers begin unbuttoning her starched blouse, presently revealing a white lace bra that was taut under heavy burdens. Next, she unbuttoned her waistband and wriggled out of the skirt. What remained was a black lace trifle, too small to cover her luxuriant bush. Gesturing at the driver she asked, "He can't see, can he?"

"No way."

She drank more champagne and stretched back, catlike. After exhaling a deep breath she said, "This is much better, Jack. Yes, I feel so *much* better. I absolutely despise that school uniform—and the school doesn't have air-conditioning, so I'm miserable most of the time." I sipped from my glass and appraised her figure, now almost fully revealed. Below the narrow waist her tapered thighs were plump and appealing. Regular breathing lifted breasts that seemed to be battling their restraints, her naturally full lips were sultry, and the overall picture was of a desirably voluptuous young female. Swallowing, I licked dry lips and downed more champagne. One bottle was almost gone.

She watched me drain my glass, her dark brown eyes gazing directly into mine. The veil of innocence was gone, replaced by more than a suggestion of worldliness, and I wondered how many of her father's friends had taken advantage of her—as the euphemism goes. Her parents, I mused, as upper-class Mexicans, would never permit peer dating, and would look on her cloistered schools as fortresses against anything unseemly. And I felt I understood why Susana had been booted from previous schools. That wouldn't happen at the English School because of her father's power, wealth, and prestige. In Mexico foreign schools were dependent on government tolerance, an accommodation Aguilera could easily revoke.

So, here was this gorgeous, nearly naked teenager sitting beside me, sipping champagne and displaying her beautifully developed body so provocatively that I could only interpret it as a deliberate act of seduction.

I inverted the empty Moët bottle and uncorked its twin. Susan giggled and held out her glass. "How'd you guess?"

"You looked ready." I filled her glass.

Her smile deepened the dimples. "And I am." Her tongue

stabbed into the golden effervescence, tasting before she drank. "Do you really want to go all the way to Taxco, Jack?"

"Not if you don't. Why?"

She shrugged. "On Calle Sexto in Cuernavaca there's a lovely little inn with good food and cool rooms. We could have a bit to eat and relax upstairs for a while."

I cleared my throat. "Wouldn't that be . . . indiscreet?"

"Shouldn't be. Some of my girlfriends say their fathers take their girlfriends there—there's never been any scandal."

"None you've heard of. Look, Susana, I feel an obligation to your father, so—"

"Oh, who wants to trudge around dusty Taxco when we're so near a place I've always wanted to see? Of course—if you don't like the idea . . ." One hand reached around and unhooked the lacy bra. It dropped and freed two perfectly formed breasts the size and shape of young mangoes. "Well," I said, "since you insist," leaned over and took the nearest small nipple between my lips. Her back arched, she moaned and pressed my face deeper into her cushioning flesh. What ecstasy!

After saluting the twin, I reached for the intercom phone and told Raúl we'd turn off to Cuernavaca and stop on Calle Sexto—

"Posada del Viajero," Susana supplied.

I repeated the inn's name for Raúl while she shed the black bikini, then unzipped my fly. The invitation was hers and I took advantage of it as she positioned her thighs across mine, found what she sought, and nibbled the tip of my tongue.

It had been years since I'd made love in a moving vehicle, but everything came back to me as we surged rhythmically together. There was nothing strange or new except that my partner was very young, very eager, and far from virginal. She climaxed first, crushing my face into her moist breasts, and then it was my turn, and I spent with pent-up enthusiasm.

In the afterglow we held each other tightly, Susana murmuring and licking my face and lips as the limo rumbled over cobbles in the old part of Cuernavaca.

Gradually she detached herself, wiped her forehead, and said, "What a great ride! I loved it."

"Me, too." The limo turned up a small incline and stopped. Looking out, I saw a tall, wide wooden gate set between high stone posterns. To the driver I said, "Raúl, ring that bell and when the gate opens, drive in. If there's a back entrance, stop there. I'll tell you what to do."

"*Sí, señor.*" He pulled the clapper of an old, verdigrised ship's bell, and presently the gate opened wide enough for entrance. To Susana I said, "Better put on blouse and skirt, and—oh, yes—shoes."

Leaving bra and bikini on the seat, she made herself passably decent as the limo turned into a large, flowered, tree-bordered courtyard with a tiled fountain surmounted by a life-size bronze of Venus. Small jets of water arced from the lady's breasts, and I thought: this is the place. This is definitely the place.

Raúl steered around the side of a two-story building covered with vines, and braked at the rear. I told him to come around to my window, and gave him two hundred-dollar bills. "Get me a room," I instructed, "the best in the house, and tell them I'll want room service."

"*Entiendo.*" He took the money and walked back toward the main entrance. Susana looked around and said, "Jack, this is just marvelous. It's everything my friends said it was. Do you like it?"

"I like everything you do, *querida*. This place has *ambiente*."

After Raúl handed me a heavy room key I told him he was free for an hour. He thanked me and walked back toward the street. Susana and I got out and climbed a wooden staircase, heavily flanked by Bougainvillea, to the second floor. Ours was a corner room overlooking the courtyard on one side. Through thick branches I could barely make out Venus on her watery pedestal. I closed the blinds and looked around. The furniture was heavy rustic-style stained wood that matched the exposed rafters above. There were decorative tiles inset in the white plaster wall, and serapes were strewn across the tiled floor. On the tables stood an assortment of unfired clay pitchers, cups, and ashtrays, more decorative than useful. The large bed was covered with a tassled Indian serape, but the mattress appeared suspiciously thin—probably filled with feathers that long ago had lost their resilience. Well, we'd make do with what the house supplied.

Hearing a knock at the door, I called, *"Momento,"* and asked my guest what she wanted to order. "Oh, some sandwiches, white wine—anything, really."

As I went to open the door she disappeared into the bathroom and I heard running water. I gave her order to a nicely dressed señorita, and asked for a steak sandwich with *papas fritas* and a chilled bottle of white wine. "Undurraga, if you have it." I liked Chilean Riesling.

"As you wish, señor."

I closed the door, locked it, and heard the shower running. Susana was behind a translucent shower curtain, actively soaping her body, and I noticed a nearby bidet. The posada was a well-equipped casa de rendezvous, and I could understand why her classmates' fathers might choose it for an idle hour or two with their amigas of the moment.

I stripped, and when Susana emerged dripping from the shower I offered a large fluffy towel. At her request I dried her back, paying special attention to her glistening, pear-shaped buns whose taut solidity demonstrated how wrong I'd been to anticipate baby fat. She toweled her short hair and fluffed it with her fingers, then dried the rest of her body. I stepped into the shower and saw Susana gazing at my body. She said. "You have scars, Jack. Quite a lot of them."

"Vietnam," I said, and turned on the spray.

When I returned to the bedroom she was lying on the coverlet in a careless Modigliani pose, ceiling fan stirring her hair. "When's lunch coming?" she asked.

"Any minute. Hungry?"

"Suddenly I'm famished."

"Okay, when the waiter knocks, disappear." I had a towel

wrapped around my hips for appearance's sake, and from the bed-side leaned over to kiss her full lips. She responded voraciously until a door knock interrupted things.

With Susana in the bathroom, I opened the door and let the waitress set the table with our order. She uncorked the wine and re-turned it to an ice bucket, handed me a bill, and I paid her, adding an appreciative tip for prompt service. Then I locked the door and called Susana to come join me.

She began devouring a sandwich while I poured our wine, and then I drew up a chair and joined her. My steak was stringy but fla-vorful, the fries not McDonald's quality but I wasn't particularly hungry. I watched her enjoyment of the mini-*comida,* and refilled our glasses until the bottle was empty.

After finishing, she sprawled back on the bed and beckoned me to join her. As I lay down beside her, bodies touching, she said, "I really shouldn't ask, but are you married? Makes no difference, really, but I'd sort of like to know."

"The answer is no."

"Strange—because you're a wonderful lover any woman would be lucky to have."

"Compliment appreciated. Have I told you you're absolutely gorgeous, with a body that drives me out of my mind?"

"You haven't—until now." She regarded me affectionately. "Can we do this again?"

"Unfortunately, I'm leaving Mexico tomorrow."

"Oh? That saddens me. Where are you going?"

"Los Angeles," I lied. "Business involving your father and me."

"I hope you make a lot of money from it."

"So do I."

Reaching down, she fondled me and eased a breast toward my mouth. Before responding, I said, "What about pregnancy, *querida?*"

"I've got a 'fram, don't worry."

"Bet your mother doesn't know."

"She'd kill me—only my doctor knows." Her giggle told me the wine was hitting her. And when she rolled atop me we began the age-old game of ten toes up, ten toes down. and even the creaking bed didn't bother us.

It was almost dusk when we drove out of the posada courtyard, and I found myself wondering how often she'd been here with older men. No business of mine, really. I hadn't set out to seduce her, or even thought about it. The passport photo had been a downer and I hadn't really looked at her until she began stripping in the car. But once I had . . .

Mentally, I'd separated this precocious child from her evil father and so I felt no special satisfaction in having cuckolded him. If her mother would kill her for having a diaphragm, her father would kill me for having bedded his bodacious daughter. She was dangerous pussy, and though she didn't know it I intended never to see her again, despite the powerful attraction between us. I thought I'd covered my trail sufficiently to keep Papá from finding me before I was ready to be found, and neither Susana nor the Domos agency knew where I was hanging out.

But what an afternoon. I'd remember it the rest of my life.

So would Susana, I thought, and lie to protect us both.

She was yawning when we hit the expressway back to Mexico City, and in a little while her head rested on my shoulder, eyes closed. Just as well—wasn't much left to talk about. Besides, I had Molly on my mind, and the riskiest part of my plan yet to execute.

Before leaving the posada I'd told Raúl to drop me at the Hotel Reforma, then take the señorita home. Pablo Antonio would be glad to see her, then question her closely about her afternoon with the nefarious Novak. He would understand that having kidnapped her, I could have held her hostage, or worse—the point I wanted to make. I sought deterrence, elimination of any impulse for reprisal.

Beside me, Señorita Susana María Aguilera y Beltrán slept soundly, the unwitting instrument of my operation to free Molly. I kissed her forehead and she stirred, then relaxed again.

When she married or matured—not necessarily contemporaneous events—Susana was never going to be a traditionally docile upper-class Mexican wife or *ama de casa*. Already she had seen too much of the world and was well aware of the basic relationship between male and female—from her own experience—to accept anything less than equality. Demonstrably, she had a mind of her own with an independent view of life and the real world, remarkable in one of her tender years.

As I appraised her unusual qualities I realized that we were in metropolitan traffic, lights along the Paseo de la Reforma just winking on. A few more blocks and Raúl turned in at the hotel entrance, braked with engine running. I woke Susana then, and handed her the wrapped videotape. "These have been wonderful hours with you, and I wish you every happiness in the world. Now, one final favor. When you reach home, give this to your father. Can I count on you?"

"Yes," she murmured, and kissed me deeply.

"Promise?"

"I will," she said a bit crossly, "and I keep my promises." She sighed, "Jack, I'm probably in love with you—at least a little bit, do you mind?"

"I'm honored—and grateful for everything." I opened the door and got out. At the posada I'd given Raúl an extra hundred for his discretion, and now I waved him goodbye. Him and the young lovely I'd never see again.

From there I entered the hotel lobby, walked past the bar and out of the side doorway. By then the limo had gone and the tape of Paredes's confession was on its way to the corrupt official it implicated. Susana's father.

Well, there was more to be done, and the evening was young.

I taxied back to the Fenix, had coffee sent to my room, and considered the next sequence of events.

• • •

Around nine, and after a nap to let the champagne and wine metabolize, I walked to the María Isabela Hotel and called Susana's home number from a lobby phone. She didn't answer, a male voice did.

"*¿Quién habla?*"

"Aguilera?"

"*Sí, sí,*" the voice said impatiently. "Pablo Antonio Aguilera."

"Good," I said, "Novak calling to verify you have your tape."

"Yes, I have it, you *hijo de la Gran Puta,* and—"

"Spare the maledictions, Licenciado, and cut to business. You have the tape—enjoy it—and you have my friend Molly. Tell your thugs to drive her to the airport and put her on the next flight to Phoenix. Just do it, no argument. Because if you don't, and you harm her, I'll snatch Susana again, or your wife Sara, and I promise you the treatment won't be gentle." I paused. "Aguilera?"

I heard a heavy sigh before he spoke. "It will be done."

"I'll be watching," I told him, "and to keep you honest, the original tape is in a secure place. If you come after me, or bother Molly again, copies of that tape will be sent to your newspapers and TV stations. Understand?"

"*Sí, pendeljo,*" he said nastily, "I understand."

"And, please—my warm regards to Susana. She's a delightful young lady and we took an immediate liking to one another. So good of you to lend her to me for the afternoon."

He began yelling, but I replaced the receiver and walked away. So far, so good.

Back in my room I telephoned the embassy and asked the Marine night duty guard to have Major Somers call me. I gave him my name and room number and, while waiting, opened the mattress and removed pistol, money belt, videotape, and printout. I strapped on the money belt and put the other items in my carry-on bag, along with shaving articles. A few minutes later the phone rang and Ben Somers said, "Jack, what's up? You okay?"

"I'm fine, and my business here is concluded—but I have another favor to ask. I have a small bag I don't want examined by Mex airport security. Would you have Gunny pick it up at the desk tomorrow, and send it back to my Nogales office—pouch or courier?"

"Sure, why not? But—your bag would be safer if you bring it to the embassy tonight and leave it with the guard. I'll get it in the morning and have it on its way."

"Even better. Thanks, Ben."

He chuckled. "Are we square?"

"We're square."

Carrying the bag, I left the hotel and taxied to the embassy.

While the taxi waited, I told the night guard the bag was for Major Somers who would collect it in the morning. He took it from me and relocked the door. Then the taxi took me to the airport.

The next flight to Phoenix left in forty-five minutes. The next flight to Cozumel departed in an hour and fifteen. I bought a Cozumel ticket and positioned myself in the waiting room where I could watch Phoenix-bound passengers without being obviously close. Aguilera might have photos of me to circulate among his thugs but I didn't think so. He wasn't a detail man, and there wasn't enough time for him to issue orders and get results.

While eyeing the passengers I kept a copy of *El Universal* in front of my face, not wanting Molly to spot me when she arrived. *If* she arrived. Thirty minutes to go and no Molly. I began wondering if she was alive, or whether Aguilera had more dirty tricks in store. Had I been foolish to give him the tape without Molly? I hadn't been able to devise an alternate stratagem that would have secured her without risking my own capture—or death.

I was worried.

The announcement board showed the Phoenix flight was boarding.

Shit! Where was she?

Then at nine minutes before departure I saw two burly men elbowing their way among passengers, a woman between them. Yes, Molly.

Thank God.

Her escorts pounded the ticket desk until the clerk paid attention, and I saw one of them shove a credential in the clerk's face. That got fast service, and the clerk soon handed Molly her ticket. The thugs followed her to the boarding gate, and as she entered it, Molly turned and glanced around. Her face was pale, her features strained, and I silently cursed Aguilera. Like Susana, Molly was an innocent player in all this invisible action, and I was pretty sure she'd had enough of me and the troubles that accompanied me. Hell, I was sick of them myself.

I watched until she vanished in the boarding tunnel, and continued reading my paper. The two thugs scanned the waiting room, then walked toward the pay phones. One made a call—to Aguilera, I assumed—then both left the terminal. I stayed where I was until five minutes before departure, strolled to the gate, went through airport security unchallenged, and found my seat on the DC-9.

There was the customary Mexicana delay, during which I drank two iced Añejos and looked forward to a good night's sleep in my own bed. Eventually the plane took off, and I looked down at the lights of Mexico City blinking weakly through the perpetual smog; then we were beyond the valley and turning eastward toward Cozumel.

As I dozed, my mind began reprising the day's events: the startling, sweet encounter with Susana; forcing Aguilera to do my will; and finally seeing Molly free and homeward bound. I felt satisfaction over a job well done; mission accomplished without violence or bloodshed. And I thought wistfully that I would never forget how Susana looked as she came out of the shower, wet, glistening, and lovely as Venus emerging from the sea. I was wise enough to know that it was over, we'd had our moment together and there could be no sequel.

Still, every part of me wanted to be with her again, and I found myself wondering whether I was wise enough to stay away. Then my mind blanked out and I slept until the landing bump woke me.

As I left the cabin door and stepped out onto the dark tarmac, warm, humid, tropic-scented air enveloped me, and I knew I was home again.

THIRTEEN

For my first two days back I worked with Carlos Paz, Ramona's nephew, on the *Corsair*. He'd had it hauled up on the ways for bottom scraping and a coat of anti-fouling compound. While that was being done, boatyard mecs tuned the engines and blew out the fuel lines, Pemex gasoline being what it is. Blades on one of the propellers was nicked, so I had the edges brazed and buffed before replacing it on its shaft.

Carlos busied himself cleaning brightwork and spot painting topside, while I cleaned and lubricated the heavy VomHofe reels and replaced worn line with new. Nothing made a sport fisherman madder than seeing a line break and his trophy get away. Such losses were bad for business.

Keeping occupied diverted my mind from Susana, though from time to time I wondered why Molly didn't call to let me know she was okay. And though she hadn't seen me confirming her departure I felt she could have surmised that I was responsible for her freedom. The offset was her knowing that she had been snatched because of me, so I couldn't fault her apparent lack of gratitude. And I suspected it was over between us.

Anyway, I consoled myself, there was never going to be a long-term relationship. There was a social and educational imbalance that couldn't be easily overcome, and I sensed Molly was aware of it. The problem hadn't surfaced because we'd been emotionally charged by danger and the thrills of great sex—but danger was over, at least for her, and geography eliminated the rest.

And there was Susana: too young by far for a lasting relationship, her father aside, and I wondered what curse afflicting me placed females I cared for beyond reach. Maybe I'd find out sometime.

On the third day we returned *Corsair* to the water and ran it around to the charter fishing docks where customers were waiting. Carlos took aboard four sports from Oak Park, Illinois, and I took their charter money and tackle deposit before heading home.

Ramona had lunch waiting for me: grilled minute steak, sliced tomato salad with greens, and a glass of Beaujolais. She brought slices of hot, fresh-baked bread with a pot of butter, and said that, if I hadn't noticed, the radio light was on. I said thanks, I hadn't noticed and I'd take care of it after lunch. I added that Carlos was out on a charter in case his wife called.

It was siesta time, but I thought I'd better find out what the office wanted before stretching out for an hour or two. I didn't like radio calls because they usually meant a summons back to the office, or some moron checking on weather and girl-watching in Cozumel.

Grumpily I activated the transmitter, and presently heard McManus's voice hail me. "Hey, playboy, how ya doin'?"

"Chief, I was doin' fine—until now."

"Well, vacation's over. Consider this an urgent recall."

"Oh? My suspension hasn't run, Chief. See you Monday."

"Suspension? Forget that. Need you here ASAP tomorrow. I'm serious, Jack. Kiss the girls goodbye and get your ass on a plane."

I considered a provocative reply, settled for, "Mind telling me the nature of this emergency?"

"You'll get it all tomorrow. Don't ask the reason why, just get ready to do or die." His chortle told me he'd been drinking his lunch—if the false joviality hadn't told me.

"Roger, Chief," I said ill-humoredly, "and Wilco."

Replacing the radio in its cache, I looked around and decided the place was lonely without Molly, and I might as well be practicing my so-called profession as a law enforcement agent. The alternative was moping around and maybe getting more involved in charter fishing than I cared to. Besides, I'd subconsciously begun fantasizing how smoothly the hedonistic, nubile young Susana María Aguilera y Beltrán would fit into this tropical setting. Was it only a few days ago we'd been disporting ourselves at the Posada del Viajero? Seemed more like a month despite the clarity of memories. Just banish the thought, Novak, she'd been a gift from the gods, a one-time *don,* no sequel.

Her chronological age didn't bother me. In Mexican cities the age of consent was flexibly calculated at fourteen; in the countryside, considerably less, though I'd never heard of an instance of alleged child abuse. It wasn't a cultural factor the UN wanted to deal with.

But despite my irritation with McManus's call, and nostalgia over Susana, I managed to honor siesta, and got up for a refreshing shower and an iced beaker of Añejo that encouraged me to call for flight reservations and greet Carlos and his aficionados when they pulled in at the docks.

My billfish policy was tag and release, though I allowed every charter to keep one for dockside photos and wall mounting. (In Mexico, as everywhere, one hand scratches the other, and I got a cut from every taxidermy referral.)

Today's party had hooked and released two blue marlin and kept an eighty-pound sail. Hoisted for display, it looked sad, sail wilted along its spine, the shimmering mix of blue and white fading as the minutes passed. The Oak Parkers also racked six fine golden dolphin, two wahoos, a saw-toothed cubera snapper, and a small barracuda. Average catch for an afternoon in Cozumel's teeming waters, and the customers were well pleased.

After they departed, a dockside specialist autopsied the sail, saving bill, head, and sail for the taxidermist, and slicing the flesh into saleable steaks. Then he cleaned and filleted the dolphin, and reserved a pair of large fillets for my freezer. Carlos would take some home and sell the rest; already buyers from hotels and restaurants were crowding around. The poor of the town would get the rest of the catch, and be happy to have it.

I caught an evening flight to Mexico City, with a two-hour layover during which I bought two jugs of Añejo and had my suit pressed and shoes shined without leaving the airport. I left by the same departure gate as Molly used four nights ago, and wondered if I'd ever see her again.

En route Tucson I was offered a chicken leg with wild rice—both items cold—a hard roll and something resembling cherry custard. In lieu of the cold plate I drank iced Añejo and felt I'd made a prudent choice.

At Tucson airport I rented a two-door Ford, and drove the rest of the way to Nogales, arriving at my motel just before dawn. Leaving a call for eight, I turned in and slept dreamlessly until the clerk woke me.

After strong coffee and a good breakfast of eggs, bacon, sausage, and flapjacks at the deli, I went to the office and checked in with Manny. "Your package is in your desk drawer," he told me. "How'd things work out?"

"I persuaded Licenciado Aguilera to put Molly on a Phoenix flight, scoring one for the good guys." No point in mentioning Susana or her unwitting role—Manny wouldn't understand, much less approve, our brief encounter.

"Wally's waiting," he said, "with a couple of guys in his office who look like cartel killers."

"I'll let you know," I replied, and entered McManus's office without knocking.

As usual he was behind his desk, coffee cup in hand. He looked up and said to the visitors, "This is Jack Novak. Not what I'd call a smooth operator but now and then he gets things done. Jack, this here's Mose Gitman, and Vince Burgess. They're, ah, independent contractors." He paused. "You're replacing their partner who got himself a busted appendix in Tucson."

"Replacement for what, Wally?"

Gitman was short, dark, and built like a gorilla. Burgess was nearer my height, with prematurely gray hair, a caved-in cheekbone, and the upper body of a weight lifter. They looked ready for fight or frolic. I found a chair and asked, "Specifically, what's the deal?"

"Extraction op," Burgess said, "Agent Francisco 'Paco' Pazos got himself caught snoopin' around one o' them big Mary Juana plantations in Sonora three weeks ago. The state judicial police have had him, probably under interrogation and torture, and Headquarters wants Paco back. Alive."

"So," said McManus with a nasty grin, "in the absence of an agent who better represents DEA's ideals and operational methods I volunteered you."

I looked at the two heavies. "When do we go?"

Gitman stood up, brushed aside wrist hair so he could see his watch, and said, "If you made your will, Jack, let's go."

That briefing explains why we were driving at eighty miles an hour south from Nogales, where we'd crossed the border, toward Hermosillo a hundred and seventy miles away. Our target was the town of Mazatán's lockup—if he was still alive.

To sketch the geography, Hermosillo and Guaymas are in a line due south of Nogales, with Mazatán east, as I said, of Hermosillo. For lack of better cover, we were sport fishermen heading for Guaymas, poles, rods, tackle, and sleeping bags on the bed of our Charger pickup; fishing licenses bought just this side of the border.

My new partners—I was beginning to think of them as Batman and Spiderman—were ex–Special Forces sergeants from 'Nam, who'd spent time with the Contras in Central America, so their Spanish was fluent. Our Charger was a big 4WD rig with oversized tires, customized in San Antone for this kind of op.

The front fender wells sealed our ordnance: four Browning 9mm Hi-Power pistols with silencers and 16-round magazines; three AR-15 assault rifles; smoke, gas, concussion, and frag grenades; four bars of C-4 plastique, explosive detonators wrapped separately;

and two Uzi submachine guns. Plastic moneybelts wrapped around our middles—a source of hot, sticky annoyance—held sixty thousand dollars. DEA thought we might be able to bribe Pazos free, but DEA was the only party that thought so. While we were bargaining, the cops could be finishing off Pazos, the three of us agreed.

A big forty-gallon cooler held ice, beer, liquor, water, and sandwiches. Burgess had packed a first-aid box with bandages, antibiotics, morphine syrettes, and surgical tools—he'd been a platoon aid man and knew what might be needed.

Our road, Route 15, was ridged and pitted, but the rig's heavy hydraulic shocks absorbed a lot of the punishment. I sipped water from my canteen and munched a chocolate bar, thankful the cab's air-conditioning was working. Outside, it was around 115 Fahrenheit, and dust devils formed along the road, now and then spattering dirt and pebbles across the windshield. Gitman swore and wiped sweat from his face. Burgess nudged me and winked. "Hey, Mose, take it easy. Get uptight now, how'll you handle it in the jailhouse?"

"I'll handle it," Gitman growled, "don't worry about me, Vince."

I got out the Pemex road map and studied it. "If we're road-checked before we reach Mazatán, we say we're going fishing at the Novillo dam."

"Tell 'em nothin'," Gitman rasped. "Fuck them toy soldiers."

Burgess nudged me again. "Orders are to waste as few Meskins as possible—while carryin' out the mission."

"Yeah," Gitman said sourly, "that's what HQ always says. They want a neat, clean result, don't want to hear about blood and guts along the way. Those guys also believe in whorehouse virgins."

True, I thought, as I swallowed the last of the chocolate, leaned back, and closed my eyes.

In Hermosillo we were to eat and gas up, and check the Charger's fluid levels because we couldn't chance breakdown after leaving Mazatán.

Gitman said, "I hope the guy's still alive, Jack."

"The info was supposed to be current as of yesterday."

"What's the source?"

"Some little army poop, peed-off at his lieutenant for not passing along his share of the protection money. Anyway, that's what DEA says."

He grunted. "They been wrong before."

"Often." I shook out a Players and lighted it. "Anyone mind?"

"Your lungs," Gitman snapped. "Go ahead, die young."

I inhaled deeply and looked around. On either side of the road flat, arid desert, surface broken by patches of maguey and stands of saguaro cactus. Every mile or so there'd be a scattering of vultures from a bloated carcass off the shoulder; dead horse, cow, burro, or dog. Now and then an Indian trudging along, wearing sombrero or head-cloth and horizontal-striped skirt. Less often, a clump of campesinos huddled together waiting for a bus. There was a lot of waiting in Mexico.

This part of northern Sonora was desolate country and much of the rest of Mexico was the same. Between mountains and desert not enough tillable land to support an exploding population. Not enough jobs, water, irrigation, electricity or phone lines. But Mexicans were optimistic, I remembered a president saying. Why not? I thought; costs no more.

Burgess said, "If I was Meskin I think I'd shoot myself."

"Hell, you wouldn't have to," Gitman responded. "You'd die of thirst or starvation in this kind of country. How the hell do people live here?"

"Not many do," I remarked. "Most of them took off for El Norte when they were young enough to travel. What's left is old folks and Indians."

"Deal drugs or die," Gitman said bitterly. "Zero option."

"So we've got DEA agents in Mexico straitjacketed by State. Can't carry sidearms, make arrests, or do much but liase with corrupt cops. A guy like Pazos sticks his neck out and gets grabbed." I dropped cigarette ash on the floorboard. "DEA wasn't designed to be a covert agency, so they do things in a half-assed way."

Burgess grinned. "What we're doing isn't exactly covert."

"Not covert, deniable. "We're patriotic, public-spirited citizens trying to square a raw deal." I smiled and licked dry lips. "Strictly unofficial."

Gitman slowed to twenty-five miles an hour as we bumped and ground through a village with the odd name of Benjamin Hill. Both sides of the cobblestone street were lined with carts selling stewed tripe, hot *chicharrón,* fruit drinks, and boiled *nopal* leaves. Business looked good.

Outside village limits, Gitman floored the accelerator until we reached speed again. Burgess said, "What's the damn hurry, Mose? We got nothin' to do until nightfall."

"Hate to waste time on a lousy Mexican road," Gitman said grimly. "Anyway, we got to hole up and ready the weapons, right Jack?"

"Right." I thought of our Brownings' tungsten steel Teflon-coated bullets that could pierce metal and flak jackets. Manufactured by the KTW company, the cartridges were legally available only to law enforcement agencies. Somehow, *narcotraficantes* managed to have them, too.

Far to the east and low on the skyline spread an uneven ridge that marked the rise of the western Sierra Madre. The sun was now almost directly overhead, and the mountains undulated beyond the rising heat.

Hearing our approach, a dozen buzzards lifted awkwardly off the carcass of a Brahma bull. They'd been working inside the stripped rib cage, tearing out entrails. Its legs and hooves splayed stiffly outward. A beef that size, I thought, could keep a village in meat for a week; instead the Brahma was nourishing the buzzard population. I looked back and saw the buzzards settling down to resume their grisly feast.

Hot wind blasted dust across the road, making it briefly invisible. When we could see ahead there was a military roadblock. Slowing, Gitman muttered, "Tight assholes, men," and undid the hilt strap around his sheath knife. Burgess and I did the same. We pulled to a stop and an officer sauntered over with the arrogance common to petty officialdom. His uniform was olive camo, same as the four-by-four personnel carrier. He wore a billed camo cap and had an AR-15 slung from one shoulder. So did his five-man squad. In Spanish the officer said, "Where are you coming from?"

"Nogales," Gitman said politely.

"Where are you going?"

"Guaymas."

His dark eyes regarded us speculatively. Finally he said, "Everybody out."

Gitman left the engine on, and we got down into furnace-hot air. The officer pulled down the tailgate and began rummaging through our fishing gear. He opened the cooler and pulled out a can of Pabst. Opening it, he said, "Mind?" and began drinking.

"Help yourself, officer," Gitman said equably.

After a prolonged belch the officer asked, "You got fishing permits?"

"Sure." We produced them but the officer barely glanced at them. He was looking for something to fault us with but hadn't found it. "Officer," Gitman said, "we're in a hurry to reach Guaymas before the cooler ice melts." He handed the officer a folded ten-dollar bill. The officer took it and shrugged. "That's for me, what about my men?"

Gitman looked beyond him at the unkempt country boys in shabby uniforms. "Five each?"

The officer nodded. Gitman passed him a twenty and a five.

"Muchas gracias, caballeros," the officer said with an oily smile. "Have a good trip. Catch many marlin."

"We'll try," Gitman said, and we got back into the cab. A wave of the officer's hand parted the barriers and we drove slowly through. "Oh, that bastard!" Gitman grated. "That motherless *chingado!* When he ordered us out I figured he was set to slaughter us for the pickup."

"You played it cool," Burgess said approvingly, and began to laugh.

"What's funny?" I asked.

"That officer-prick'll never know how close he came to death," Burgess choked.

I smiled, too. "You know what the travel guides say—never drive in Mexico after dark. To which they should add: and infrequently by day."

We pulled into Hermosillo before things closed down for the two-to-four *comida-siesta* break, parked the pickup across the street from a restaurant with outside tables, and chose one in the shade. From there we could watch the pickup, an essential precaution.

The waiter said it would be a while before the kitchen could produce anything, so we ordered six bottles of Corona and quaffed them, along with peanuts and chips. The waiter left a stained menu on the table and wandered away. Beyond the pickup there were jacaranda trees in bloom, a lush scatter of yellow primavera petals, and big red bursts of bougainvillea. Hot breeze stirred around us, but the heat was dry, absorbing perspiration from my face and arms, and the cold beer was restorative. A flavored-ice vendor pushed his wheeled cooler toward us and offered us *Paletas* that we declined. "Who needs diarrhea?" Burgess asked rhetorically, smacked his lips, and drained a second bottle. "Damn, that's good beer!"

Gitman said, "Drink only beer south of the Rio Grande and you'll never get Montezuma's Revenge."

I got a cigarette going and eased elbows onto the table. "When we get to Mazatán we'll make a slow pass by the lockup, take a head count of visible cops, and drive out of town."

"Returning when?" Gitman asked.

"Gets dark around seven. I'd opt for midnight action, but every hour counts. Any objection to eight?"

Gitman shrugged. "We're gonna do it, let's do it. Vince?"

Burgess nodded. "Sooner the better."

A ragged shoeshine boy carrying a scarred workbox offered his services. He shined our boots and I noticed that he was barefoot so we tipped him lavishly. He didn't thank us, but nodded stolidly and trudged away. Burgess said, "I like a kid who works for his enchiladas 'stead of begging. Maybe he'll make something of himself."

"If he lives," Gitman remarked. "See those ulcerated legs? The kid's got yaws. Probably hookworm and TB." He shook his head. "Not much of a chance to see twenty."

The waiter returned to say we could order, and we asked for beefsteak with refried beans—no salad, thanks—and another round of Corona.

After lunch we found a *gasolinera* at the crossroads where the unnumbered road to Mazatán began, filled the tank with Extra, and added a quart of oil and a pint of water to the radiator. Tire pressure was okay. I bought twenty pounds of ice and was transferring it into the cooler when a police VW Beetle drove up behind us. Burgess groaned, "Not again!" as two blue-uniformed cops got out and came toward us, nickle-plated automatics slapping their thighs. One asked Gitman for car papers, and while he was scanning them his partner pawed through our exposed gear. "Any weapons?" he asked.

"Just fish knives." Gitman touched his.

"No shark rifles, shotguns?"

"No sir."

"Where are you going to fish?"

"We'll try El Novillo dam today, Guaymas tomorrow. Is there a hotel or motel near the dam?"

"There's a posada in Mazatán, but when you go through better make a reservation for the night." He stood facing Gitman, slapping the folded car papers against his open palm. "I appreciate the advice," Gitman said, "could save us time and trouble." He palmed twenty dollars to the cop and was handed the car papers. "How's the road?"

The cop eyed the pickup. "Four-wheel drive? You'll make it." He whistled at his partner who was picking through Burgess's first-aid kit. Holding up a pack of morphine syrettes, he said, "What's this for?"

"Gitman gestured at me. "He's a bleeder, that's coagulant."

"*Vamos,*" the first cop said, then to Gitman, "*Andale, pues.*"
Reluctantly, the other cop dropped the pack into the kit and closed
the lid. They got into their blue-and-white Beetle and backed away.
"Assholes," Gitman muttered. "Fuckin' extortionists."

Burgess got behind the wheel and started the engine. I bought a
six-pack of Tecate, paid for gas and oil, and joined my partners in
the cab.

Mazatán was old adobe walls and red-tile roofs. Shops were closed.
The little town lay naked under the broiling sun as we drove down
narrow, cobbled streets. Cur dogs twitched in the shade. A few na-
tives chomped *menudo* and *salsa verde* at sidewalk stands in the only
demonstration of energy I could see. Otherwise, a general air of lassitude permeated the town that seemed untouched by progress or
ambition.

"Not much of a place," Burgess remarked. "Reminds me of
Honduras."

"Yeah," Gitman said. "Tela. A place I never want to see again."

We were passing the sun-baked *zócalo,* the town square. At the
far side I noticed two police cars in front of a one-story building.
Over the entrance hung a frayed Mexican flag. Burgess drove slowly
around the square, and as we neared the building we could see its
barred windows. On one side of the doorway a chipped, weathered
sign read *Policía.*

"Ground zero," I said. "Pull over by the cantina and we'll see
who comes and goes."

We drank beer at a sidewalk table and watched the station. Gitman stretched and said, "I finally figured out what I wanna do most
in the world."

"Take a cruise around the world?" Burgess asked.

"That's number two—maybe. Number one is fuck Winona
Ryder."

"Uh-uh, she's married, has kids, too."

"Shit! She's so cute'n cuddly. Okay, Barbra Streisand, she gets me for free."

Burgess grinned. "Probably married, too."

"In Hollywood, who cares? Anyway, I'm not lookin' for virgins. Experience makes a man feel wanted, comfortable, y'know? Eliminates that love-me-forever bullshit."

Burgess said, "By the time you make it with Streisand I'll be president of the USA."

"Deal," Gitman said as two cops strolled out of the station. They stretched in the sunlight and drove away. While we watched, a barefoot boy in tattered trousers delivered a tray of food to the station, came out, and jogged around the corner. Another VW pulled up and three cops entered the station. Gitman said, "Jack, I think I'll go in and ask directions to the dam. We need an idea of the interior layout."

"Good idea," I said. "If you're more than ten minutes we'll come after you."

"Hey, I can talk my way out of anything." He drained his glass and crossed the *zócalo,* disappeared inside the station.

Burgess sighed. "Mose worries me, takes too many chances."

"He's right, though; we need to know numbers, where the cells are."

Burgess grunted. "And if Mose don't come out, whatta we use to get him?"

"That's a good question," I said, "so let's hope he comes." I glanced at my watch. Time was passing slowly. There was hardly any sound in the sweltering air. Across in the *zócalo* an Indian woman was drowsing under the shade of a flowering galeana tree, her suckling baby wrapped close to her breast in a dark shawl. I heard the eggbeater noise of a VW engine and saw a police car curbing at the station house. Two cops got out, and Burgess said, "Same two that braced us back there."

"Nine minutes," I said. "Maybe reconnaissance wasn't such a good idea."

"Sounded good at the time. Well, whatta we do?"

"Give him another couple minutes." I was stalling because there was no way we could get to our weapons from where they were sealed.

Burgess finished his beer and stood up. "Let's give Mose some company."

I laid pesos on the table and got up. We crossed the street and were entering the *zócalo* when Gitman came out of the police station. He saw us, motioned at the pickup and strolled toward it. We joined him there and Burgess snapped, "What in hell took so damn long, buddy?"

"Worried about ol' Mose? Hell, we were swappin' fishin' yarns, a couple of aficionados and me." He swung into the cab. "Couldn't just scamper away."

I got in beside him and closed the door. Burgess started the engine and hot air blasted from the air conditioner. Gitman grinned. "We're fishermen, right? Let's go fishin'."

Eight miles along the unimproved road toward the dam we came to an open field with a big shade tree. Its top was flat and spread out like an African thorn, giving shade for the pickup. With tire irons we pried back the metal covers that had been soldered in place to conceal our weapons, got them out, and checked each piece before loading it. We had shoulder-strapped weapons belts to hold magazines, grenades and explosives; while we were getting everything organized, Gitman described the station layout.

"From the street you enter a big room. On the left there's a table where the sergeant sits and takes phone calls. There's benches along the right hand wall where the cops snooze, and at the far end, a cabinet holds shotguns and rifles.

"While I was there a cop opened a metal-faced door in the center of the far wall, and that's the cell block. From what I could glimpse, there's three barred cells on each side. While the door was open I heard someone throwing up—probably a drunk—and then the door closed. It's locked with a key. The key and cell-door keys hang on a nail by the metal door. In all, there were six cops."

"Including the two who braced us?"

"They dropped by to bullshit with the locals, said they had to get back to Hermosillo, so I figure we'll face about four when we go in." He slapped a double magazine into the AR-15 and slanted the assault rifle against the car. "To grab anything heavier than their holstered .45s, they'll have to go for the gun cabinet, so that's a no-no for them. Vince, you got the Uzi silencers?" Burgess handed them over and Gitman screwed them into the muzzles of both pieces.

"What about radios?" I asked.

"There's a dusty transceiver on the floor with a lot of beer bottles on it. Probably hasn't been used in a couple of years. It's not even connected to a power source."

"So there's just the desk telephone."

"That's it."

"Flak jackets?"

"Too hot to wear, and I didn't see any hanging up."

I was screwing silencers into the Browning muzzles and wondering if there would be a firefight. After taking four cops by surprise and freeing Pazos—assuming he was there—we'd cut the phone line and lock the cops in separate cells, sabotage their cars, and take off.

With luck—a lot of it—we'd be in Guaymas by midnight.

After weapons check, we stretched out in the shade and snoozed through the hot afternoon. No human intruded or even appeared. I saw a stray burro in the distance chewing cactus buds, and there were echelons of buzzards riding the updrafts far above.

Half asleep, I found myself thinking of Molly Flanigan and Susana Aguilera, and wondering if I'd ever see either again. Both had entered my life through happenstance, yet were invisibly connected to each other through the dark figure of Pablo Antonio Aguilera, Susana's father and Molly's persecutor. As I reviewed the way things had been left in Mexico City, I doubted that Aguilera and I were finished with each other. Alive, Aguilera was a permanent menace to my life, as I was to his career. One of us had to go down.

McManus had volunteered me to go with these contract heavies for two reasons: he appreciated my willingness to get down and dirty with weapons, and he didn't care if I survived the mission. Well, I cared, and I was going to see to survival consistent with carrying out the job. Seeing the displeased expression on his face would be a psychic bonus for me.

Holding that thought, I drifted off to sleep, waking when breeze stirred the tree branches. The sun was setting and as upper air cooled, ground heat rose, creating a pleasant draft around us. I woke the others, we drank water, ate sandwiches, and in darkness started back to town.

FOURTEEN

urgess was saying, "Mose, you ever been in a small-town jail?"

"What's it to you?"

"Answer the question, willya? I got a feelin' about this place we're headed. So, tell me."

"Sure. I been in lockups, drunk tanks—longest two days. Why?"

"When the screws are off duty and there's maybe an empty cell I seen 'em bunk down between shifts."

"Me, too. So?"

"Well, this Mazatán lockup—they got an important prisoner there. I can't see just four cops guarding him—and the store."

I said, "Good point, Vince, and I'll bet Pazos is the only prisoner there. They wouldn't want drunks and bicycle thieves getting out and talking about the gringo prisoner—how he screamed when they tortured him." Fog drifted across the road, or was it smoke from some cooking fire? "We better figure on more cops back in those cells. Four in front, maybe another four in the cell block. Watching Pazos between naps."

Gitman said, "You're a good man, Vince, I don't give a damn what others say." They grinned at each other in the cab's near darkness. They'd worked together before, but with me it was first time out.

Now I had to rethink the plan to include more cops than we'd estimated. Stun grenades to neutralize the cell-block contingent before they could kill Pazos. Their chiefs wouldn't want Pazos telling his story over TV, so kill orders were logical. Concussion would affect Pazos, too, and I hoped he wasn't too frail to withstand it.

The dash clock showed ten before eight.

By now, I mused, after three weeks of torture-interrogation, Pazos would have spilled all he knew about DEA informants, and plane and satellite reconnaissance of marijuana plantations; names of DEA officers in Mexico; which Mex officials the DEA office had spotted as corrupt. Hell, I told myself, his captors would kill him anyway now that they'd squeezed out his total knowledge. That made me feel slightly better about risking Pazos's life in the breakout.

I saw the first faint streetlights ahead and steered down a narrow street with open sewers on both sides. I drove slowly, with dim headlights, avoiding the open *zócalo,* so that we pulled up behind the police station, out of sight.

I turned off the engine. "We'll take the front four silently, open the cell-block door and roll two grenades between the cells. Mose, you bring out Pazos while I cover the cops. Vince, you cover us while we withdraw. Shoot out the tires of any car you see, get in the flatbed with Pazos and shoot any following vehicle. Once those stunners detonate, the whole town will be awake."

"And scared," Gitman remarked. "Okay, let's do it. Semper Fi."

We trailed down the side street. Reached the intersection and scanned up and down, waiting until a kid on a bicycle pedaled off before we turned the corner. Two police VWs were parked in front of the station entrance. We went in shoulder-to-shoulder, rifles and Uzi leveled, covering four cops who were sitting down playing cards.

As they saw us, Gitman put a finger to his lips and hissed, *"Silencio, muchachos!"* None of them moved. I jerked out their holstered .45s and Burgess herded them against the wall, far from the weapons rack. Three of the cops were kids in their early twenties; the fourth, probably their *comandante,* was a balding older man with a broad Zapata mustache. Gitman took down the key ring and opened the metal-shod cell-block door. I activated two stun grenades and rolled them down the dimly lit floor. We both stood aside and covered our ears while the grenades went off. Their explosions shook the building and I was half deafened. All but one cell door was open, and four uniformed figures were writhing on the floor in agony. I collected their sidearms as Gitman opened the locked cell and went in. I was tossing .45s out the window when Gitman appeared with a half-naked man, their arms over each other's shoulders.

Dried blood patched his face and chest, his lacerated feet were swollen twice normal size. I locked the stunned cops in cells and helped Gitman with his burden. "Pazos?" I shot. "Yes." he managed, and began to sob. His cheeks were sunken from starvation. His eyes were wild, lips purple and swollen. Teeth missing.

We hauled him into the main room and paused while I broke open the gun cabinet and tossed weapons through the barred window. Burgess went to the entrance door and froze. "Company," he snapped and I moved quickly beside him.

A long, black Lincoln sedan had pulled up behind the two VWs, and three men were getting out. One wore civilian clothing, one was in army uniform—gold braid on the visor of his hat—and the third wore a blue Customs uniform, silver leaves on the bill of his blue cap. Their car had been too far away to hear the grenades go off so they were unsuspecting.

Until one of the front four—the *comandante*—shouted a warning. I whirled and cut him down with the silenced Uzi, but those three breathy pops startled the arrivals. As they halted, their driver got out and ran toward us, waving a pistol. He caught sight of us just inside the doorway and began running back to the car. Before he could reach it Burgess dropped him with a single round. He died yelling, but he died.

"Vince," I snapped, "get them into the cell block, the three slobs with them."

Burgess barked a stream of rapid Spanish and the three officials came toward us. I relieved one officer of his sidearm, but the army guy whipped out his glinting .45 and fired at me. His shot passed between my legs, but my shots hit him in the belly and chest and he toppled forward as I wrenched the Colt from his hand. It was silver plated, so I stuck it in my belt while Vince prodded his companion back into the cell block. Gitman ordered the three remaining cops to join them, and when they were all inside I locked the metal door and pocketed the key ring. Then I helped Gitman carry Pazos outside.

Burgess ran ahead of us but I shouted and doubled back to shoot out the tires of the three parked cars. Then he disappeared around the corner.

Pazos's battered face had a deathly pallor and his eyes were closed. Stay alive, buddy, I prayed as we dragged him along, suddenly noticing that the town had come alive. People lined up on the far side were watching us but not attempting to interfere. I lofted two smoke grenades into the *zócalo* and smoke spread rapidly, screening us from view.

Then we were at the pickup. Burgess had the tailgate down, two sleeping bags unrolled as a mattress for Pazos. We hauled him onto them, raised the tailgate, and I got into the cab beside Gitman.

"One detail," he rasped, and sighted his AR-15 on a pole transformer. A long burst and the transformer exploded. Every visible light went out. Except for our headlights the town was dark.

The pickup laid rubber accelerating down the pitted street, Gitman swearing at the potholes, while I looked back through the cab window for pursuers.

At the edge of town a few lights showed, but they came from gas lanterns. Earlier we'd spotted the TelMex central so Gitman braked near it long enough for me to shoot out the main phone junction box. Mazatán was now isolated from the rest of Mexico.

Gitman found the road to Hermosillo and accelerated to seventy muttering, "God help any critter in my way."

I looked down into the flatbed where Burgess had lifted Pazos's head and was helping him drink water. Because of the constant bumping a lot of it spilled, pooling on the skinny chest. Burgess got out a morphine syrette and sank the needle in Pazos's thigh. The

DEA agent winced, and I took that as a hopeful sign he wasn't in shock as I'd feared.

Five miles down the road Gitman pulled onto a narrow shoulder and turned off the headlights, leaving the engine running. We got out of the cab, urinated, and watched Burgess treating Pazos's feet and legs. "He's half dead," Burgess grated. "Wish we'd killed more of the bastards."

"Yeah," Gitman drawled. "Especially those fancy shits. I figure they were the real bad guys, the bosses."

"Probably came for a final questioning," I said, "before seeing Pazos killed." I got out a cigarette and my hand was trembling.

The air was cool, no visible clouds. Stars were diamond points in an indigo sky, the moon a silver crescent traveling the night.

I fumbled in the cooler for beer and a bottle of medicinal scotch. I uncorked it for Burgess who drank first, then dribbled a few swallows down Pazos's throat. Gitman and I flipped open Tecates and drank deeply. Overhead I saw the blinking lights of a far distant aircraft.

We waited a few minutes more while Burgess finished initial bandaging, then bundled his patient into a sleeping bag to keep him warm. Our wheels spattered shoulder gravel as we lurched onto the dark road, and we were on our way. So far unchallenged.

We were still a few miles from Hermosillo when we saw a military roadblock like the one we'd been stopped at that afternoon. Kerosene flares lighted the striped crossbars, and there was a cooking fire off the road, where soldiers were eating.

Gitman grunted and turned off the headlights. "How do you want to play it, Jack?"

"If it's the same squad they'll find it funny we didn't reach Guaymas. And we've got an extra man." I thought it over. "Maybe the best tactic is disarming them, disabling their PC and radios."

"Yeah, but maybe they've been warned by radio."

"Possible," I agreed, and rapped on the window. When I had Burgess's attention I called, "Trouble ahead. Don't shoot unless I do. Cover Pazos's face."

Gradually the pickup slowed. Gitman flicked on the high beams to blind the officer at the barricade, the same one who'd helped himself to our beer. He strode toward us with the same casual arrogance he'd displayed before, rounded the barricade, and stopped at Gitman's open window. "So," he said, "we meet again. No fish at Guaymas?"

"We got what we came for." Gitman shoved his Browning into the officer's startled face. "Now," Gitman rasped, "we took shit from you today, but that's finished. Line your men up in front of the headlights. They'll lay down their weapons, and you'll hand me yours."

The macho mustache quivered; light spots showed on the officer's cheeks. Surlily he handed Gitman his .45. "Tell them," Gitman said, jamming his piece against the officer's throat.

"Who . . . who are you?" the officer burbled.

"Bank robbers. But we're not splitting with you. Don't stall, niño, do what I say."

In a rough, uneven voice the officer barked out Gitman's orders. Wearing surprised expressions, his men trooped over in front of the pickup and slowly laid down their weapons. I got out of the cab and went over to the personnel carrier. Two soldiers were sleeping in it, so I disarmed them and prodded them over with the others. Then I laid frag grenades under the front and rear axles on the side away from the squad, and pulled the pins. The ten-second delay gave me time to get back into the cab before the grenades exploded. The off side of the PC lifted in loud blasts of flame, settled down askew minus two wheels. The officer watched in horror. Gitman said, "Don't forget radios," so I got out again and checked each man for a W/T, then searched the smouldering PC. Shrapnel had pierced the mobile radio, but I ripped out its wiring and shot up the transmitter for good measure.

Gitman poked the officer and snapped, "Get that fuckin' barricade off the road, General," and with the help of his men the officer did as told. Before I got back into the cab I looked into the flatbed and asked, "How's he doing?"

"Well as could be expected, I guess."

"Figure max three hours to Guaymas. Will he last?"

"I'm doing all I can. The liquor helps."

"Feed him more."

Burgess was raising Pazos's head as I got back into the cab. The officer and his squad stared into the headlights with stunned, incredulous expressions. This was as close as they'd ever been to war and it wasn't like what they'd been told.

To Gitman, I said, "Anything else, Massa?"

"Nada," he said and floored the accelerator. When I looked back I could see the kerosene flares, the cooking fire, and little flames spurting out of the ruined vehicle.

There was no way to bypass the road around Hermosillo, so we took it slowly, honoring stop signs and speed indicators until we found Route 15 south, which proved to be a hard-surface divided highway.

As we left the lights of Hermosillo I checked the dash clock: 9:45. The unexpected arrival of the three officials, our pit stop, and the army barricade had slowed us, but I wasn't worried. Not unless we had another roadblock to fight through.

The speed limit was fifty miles an hour, and we were making seventy-five, so I wasn't surprised when I saw a light bar flashing in the darkness behind us, twin headlights below. "Cops again," I told Gitman, who grunted. "I see 'em, and they've got a radio."

"We better parley. Pull over."

Parked off the road, we waited while two traffic cops got out of their VW and came toward us, one on each side of the pickup. They glanced into the flatbed and kept coming. Our windows were down, so when the cops were alongside, I covered my cop with the Browning, and Gitman did the same with his. Getting out, I tossed the cop's .45 into the dark shrubbery, came around, and repeated with the other's. While they were standing there I opened the VW and ripped wiring from the radio, shot out the tires, and smashed their flasher.

Not a word had been spoken. I asked Burgess how the patient was doing and he said he was concerned about dropping blood pressure. "What he needs is a transfusion—whole blood or saline with electrolytes. If you can give me a couple of minutes I'll get saline started."

"Do it."

Even with a flashlight it was hard to find an arm vein that wasn't close to collapse, but Burgess was competent and soon he had fluid flowing into Pazos's wasted body. Vince held up the plastic bag for gravity feed, nodded okay, and we took the road again, leaving the traffic cops with their ailing car.

Presently the highway worsened, deteriorating into two-lane blacktop that badly needed repairs. Twenty miles of it before the highway widened into four lanes, and arrow signs showed that Guaymas was only a few miles ahead.

After consulting the Pemex map, I said, "We have to go into town to get to the airport east of it. Airport signs should help."

"What if we're stopped before we get there?"

I looked at him. "Do I have to tell you?"

He sighed. "Guess not. You're a good leader, Jack; I'll work with you any time."

"Same goes for you, Mose. Let's pray word hasn't reached Guaymas."

At the outskirts of town we slowed to just under the limit and found an airport direction indicator. Now, so close to our goal, we were edgy, looking for anything that suggested ambush, but Guaymas went to bed early. Fishermen, foreign and local, rose before dawn to get out to the fishing waters; planes and vehicles from the U.S. were commonplace.

From outside the security fence the airport looked deserted. No night traffic, probably, but the sleepy guard let us drive onto the tarmac without questions. Our headlights picked out an AirEvac Gulfstream whose cabin and cockpit lights were on.

Gitman pulled up beside the fuselage that bore a large green cross, and shut off the engine. "Delivery made," he said. "Dead or alive."

We got down and dropped the tailgate as two white-uniformed

medics came out of the plane. "Still alive," Burgess told us, and eyed the medics. "Get a stretcher."

The pilot, co-pilot, and a government doctor left the plane to watch the transfer. A car drove up and a man in a blue guayabera hurried over to us. "Marston, DEA," he said, flashing a credential. "Any trouble?"

"Not so you'd notice it," Gitman replied, and winked at me. "But I wouldn't tarry here. Tell you what, Marston, you get our weapons into that plane and do what you want with the pickup. I'd suggest burning it, minus the plates. We left some pissed-off people behind."

So, while Pazos was eased onto a built-in cabin stretcher, Marston passed in our weapons. "I want to thank you men for all you did. Paco's a friend of mine and we'd just about given up on him." His face looked drawn, his eyes red. I said, "We left a few reminders behind. Maybe they'll go easier on their next prisoner—knowing we can reach out again."

"This is a shit job," Marston said with deep feeling. "No protection. But maybe this sort of makes up for Camarena."

"Know what you mean," Gitman said. We shook hands all around and got into the plane, finding seating space on built-in stretchers. The clam-shell door lifted and sealed the cabin as the twin jets whined.

"Dammit," Burgess snapped, "I forgot the scotch."

"But I didn't." With a grin, Gitman produced the bottle and we passed it around as the Gulfstream made its run down the unlighted strip.

After a while the co-pilot came back and said, "You ought to know that we left without clearance. An order came in to the tower saying we were to be held—especially you pickup riders."

I asked, "Where are we landing?"

"Tucson International. Ambulance waiting." He looked over at Pazos, whose eyes were closed; he seemed to be sleeping. A bag of serum was dripping into his vein as the doctor monitored his pressure.

Gitman leaned toward me. "How much reverb you figure?"

"From the Mexicans? If they're smart—always unpredictable—they'll squelch it or play it very low key. If they publicize the break-out someone's bound to ask who the prisoner was. And because the government never admitted holding Pazos—much less torturing him—they can't name him now." I lighted a cigarette, blew smoke at an exhaust vent. "I can see those late arrivals getting the townsfolk into the *zócalo* and telling them to forget what happened. They can control a small town like that."

He nodded thoughtfully. "One way or another."

I smoked for a while before I said, "When you report in, tell Mc-Manus I'm taking a few days of R & R."

"Sure. Where you going?"

"A small town in Mexico."

He drew on the scotch bottle and gave it to me. "After tonight I've had enough small towns in Mexico. You oughta, too, so I'd say there's a lady involved."

I let scotch trickle down my gullet before saying, "Probably."

I got out the silver-plated army Colt .45 and examined its flowery, over-decorative engraving. Under the light I read an inscription engraved along the breech: General de División Fidel Abreu, Ejército Mexicano, and smiled. Imprudently he'd tried to kill me and died in the attempt. I was glad he'd given me cause to shoot him, because Paredes's confession had named Abreu as one of Aguilera's principal paid protectors. And a key man in Sonora. All around, a good night's work.

I extracted the magazine and thumbed out the remaining rounds before taking the pistol back to Pazos's stretcher. To the doc and Burgess I said, "A souvenir for the patient, make sure he gets to keep it, okay?"

Both nodded.

"The former owner wore a general's uniform, but he was actually a rotten piece of shit."

Burgess said, "You knew him?"

"By name and reputation, Vince. Big-time *traficante*. Big loss to them, big plus for us."

•   •   •

At Tucson airport, after Pazos and the medical team were on an ambulance for the hospital, I asked the pilot if he could get into Nogales airport, which had only rudimentary facilities.

"Hell, I can try. Know anything about it?"

I gave him elevation, runway length and direction, and suggested he call tower frequency in case a controller was on duty.

Gitman and Burgess said they'd break off in Tucson; Marston was going to billet them and offer hospitality. So we shook hands, they left in Marston's car, and I got into the plane.

The pilot was ex-Air Force, so he knew something about getting a jet in and out of short, unlighted strips. An hour later we were on the ground. I got off fast, and the jet turned and took off while I entered Nogales terminal.

A security guard sauntered over and asked who-all came off the hospital plane. "Just me," I told him, "why?"

"Emergency landing like that—where's the stretcher?"

"Walking wounded," I explained, and kept moving.

Outside, a sleepy cab driver took me to the motel. I trudged up to my door and dropped across the bed. Slept without dreaming for ten hours—until Manny Montijo came in and shook me awake.

FIFTEEN

It wasn't a pleasant homecoming.

McManus had me standing in front of his desk (though he allowed Manny the convenience of a chair), and said, "Novak, your partner's here because I want he should know that, goddamit, Novak, you done it *again!*"

"Done what, Chief?" I asked, honestly perplexed.

"You and them out-of-towners—the gorilla and his pard—you shot up the police station, killed a bunch of cops, shot General Abreu who heads the Mex army in Sonora—or did—and threatened his two companions."

"True."

"Know who they are?"

I shook my head. "Brief encounter, no ID exchanged. So, tell me."

From under beetle brows he glared at me. "According to Mex TV one was General Ramón Vasquez, head of Customs, and the civilian was Eduardo Rojas, deputy foreign minister. Whadda ya thinka that?"

"I think they had no business being there. Abreu probably brought them along to enjoy the spectacle of a gringo being tortured and killed." I paused. "What's their excuse?"

He grunted. "They don't have to make any, being who they are."

I grunted back. "Fuck 'em, they're lucky to be alive."

"I'll grant you that."

"Chief, the point of the mission was to bring back Paco Pazos and we did. Last seen, he was alive and under intensive care."

"Yeah," McManus said grudgingly, "and apparently you three had to shoot up an entire town to do it."

I shrugged. "We did what was necessary. How are the Mexicans playing it?"

He frowned. "Officially, a gang of guerrillas attacked the Mazatán police outpost to free one of their buddies. By chance, General Abreu, Rojas, and General Vasquez arrived to inspect the station and got involved in the firefight that killed Abreu."

"About how I figured they'd play it. No mention of gringo killers?"

He shook his head. "Which don't mean the survivors don't know."

"So what? All they have to fear is Pazos getting on TV and telling his tale."

"Which'll never happen. DEA has been told to keep his mouth shut—in the interest of Mex-U.S. relations."

"Predictable. Anything else, Chief? Any little pebble left unturned?"

He sighed, "I hate this, Novak, but the Tucson office faxed a commendation for you, and so did Washington HQ, so you're outa this one by the skin of your teeth." He shoved two sheets of paper across his desk. Ignoring them, I asked, "And Gitman and Burgess?"

"They're contract, got no use for commendations. What they get is nice cash bonuses."

"Gee," I exclaimed, "maybe I should go contract and cash in heavy, not that the guys don't deserve it because they do. And the suit who selected them and got the op together deserves applause, too. Has he got a name?"

"Not's I know of." He sighed heavily. "Meanwhile, the Mex press and TV are going crazy over the Mazatán assault."

"Yeah," Manny said, speaking for the first time. "Army HQ

vows to track down Abreu's killers wherever they are. That worry you, Jack?"

"Terrified." I gazed at McManus. "I gather those three names don't resonate with you, Wally."

"Why should they?"

"Because if you'd paid attention to Paredes's confession you'd have heard them denounced as paid protectors of Pablo Antonio Aguilera. So they weren't just innocent drop-ins. That clarify anything?"

He looked uncomfortable. "I heard the tape, dammit, but you know my Spanish ain't that great."

In truth, it was practically nonexistent, but I'd made my point. "So," I said, "if there's nothing of equal gravity to detain me I'd like to get to my desk and check my mail. Maybe I've won the Digest Sweepstakes."

"Do so," McManus said reluctantly, "and I'll chat with HQ Personnel about your next assignment. You're due for a change, Novak, and not having you around will be a big relief to me."

"Your endorsement is always welcome, Wally. I've grown under your guidance. And, by the way, having been summarily dragged back from Cozumel I'll be returning there in a day or so."

"Keep Mr. Montijo informed."

I left the office then, Manny joined me, and we went to our desks. I got out my carry-on bag and extracted my holstered auto. After strapping it on I showed Manny the Aguilera printout and said, "The malefactor is definitely big-time but he's vulnerable where family is concerned."

"You found that out?"

"In the process of freeing Molly I had telephone contact with him. He's not a hard guy who clawed and shot his way to the top, more of a delicate businessman who pays others for dirty work."

"You figure on nailing him?"

"Right now we have a sort of cease-fire I wouldn't call a truce. But if anything happens to me, get copies of Paredes's confession to the media here and in Mexico, okay?"

"Sure, Jack, but I hope I won't have to." He paused. "I'd like to hear about Mazatán."

"No time like the present, no opportunity better than lunch."

So we chowed down at the Embers while I related all that had happened since he summoned me back from Cozumel. Manny listened, nodding approvingly from time to time, and when a newsboy passed our table Manny bought a paper. Sho 'nuf, there on the front page were photos of Abreu, Rojas, and Vasquez above a story on Abreu's shooting and his companions' brush with death. All at the hands of well-armed, anonymous guerrillas. I said, "There's a lesson here for readers: Mexico is a dangerous place even for high officials traveling on lawful occasions; imagine the risk to tourists and innocent travelers." I smiled and returned the paper to Manny. "This is one to file and forget, *compadre*. It's over. Pazos is safe and will probably recover. Too bad he can't tell his story to human rights groups that claim everything evil happens north of the border."

"Yeah, too bad."

I stayed around the office for two days trying to interest myself in low-level distribution cases, and when McManus hadn't announced an assignment change I figured I might as well wait out the paperwork where I was comfortable—Cozumel.

Of course, Aguilera knew where I lived and could dispatch villains to do me in. But I refused to be driven out of my home, no refuge being beyond his reach if he chose to assassinate me.

Through descriptions of their assailants, Vasquez and Rojas could identify me to Aguilera and confirm that I had taken down General Abreu. That would give Pablo Antonio something to think about. He might not seek revenge for Abreu's death, it having occurred in the heat of battle, but he could be convinced that I was more dangerous than seen and reported by daughter Susana, and the next move would be up to him.

His was a difficult character to judge. I had no psychological profile with which to predict his actions, but I sensed that as a lawyer and builder of a subterranean empire, Aguilera was probably not a man who moved precipitately. His forte was evaluating situations and deciding where his best interests lay; only then would he act.

Unless provoked intolerably.

That margin was one I had to calculate, and I believed that seeing Susana would be as risky as eating fugu, the lethally poisonous Japanese fish delicacy. Nevertheless, thousands of Japanese titillated their appetites with fugu morsels and lived to old age. It was said to be all in meticulous preparation; a false stroke of the knife and agonizing death ensued.

Anyway, I'd ruled out a reprise with Susana because, risk aside, the road led nowhere—so logic told me. But on an emotional level, I missed the sweet little sinner. Wanted to stroke, kiss and caress her voluptuous bod, feel the warmth and strength of her embrace. Undeniably, I was infatuated with Aguilera's daughter.

A psychologist, I mused, might suggest that after the violence and death at Mazatán I was subconsciously seeking an affirmation of life. But whatever the rationale, I knew it was pointless to keep thinking of Susana when I ought to get on with my life.

So I flew back to Cozumel, opened up the house again, and laid in stores for an extended stay. I flew the Seabee to Mérida for routine maintenance, flew back the next day. Carlos had been putting in long hours on *Corsair,* taking sport fishermen to the billfish grounds from dawn to almost dusk. The money was good, and charter captains believed in getting it while you could, but Carlos seldom got to see his wife and child by daylight. So I gave him a few days off and did the guiding myself with a dockside *chamaco* to cut bait and rig lines. The work was an antidote to my obsession, and sometimes as much as half a day would pass without Susana coming to mind and blotting out other thoughts.

I allowed parties to bring beer and soda aboard, but drew the line at hard liquor. I thought I'd made that clear to two St. Louis couples, but when they arrived dockside I noted three large jugs of Seagrams and told them they could board without liquor or stay ashore with it. The men shouted at me while their women simpered and snickered, but in the end they stayed on the dock and I took out a party from Dallas more interested in fishing than drinking. That season there were more customers than charter boats, so I didn't have to put up with unsolicited crap. From other operators I'd heard chilling tales of riotous, drunken fishermen at sea, and wanted none of it aboard *Corsair*.

One evening Carlos came to dockside, thanked me for his time off, and said he was ready to take over again. I gave him his share of what I'd taken in while he was tending family fires, and said I'd be home if needed.

That night I resumed thinking about Susana, and wondering why I hadn't heard from McManus about my next assignment. Neither subject elevated my morale, so I turned in early, thinking I'd call Manny next day for an update. I was both bored and lonely, and wanted to be doing something useful, even in Sioux City if it came to that.

I fell asleep weighing the pros and cons of acquiring another boat, and because I'm a light sleeper I woke to the tinkle of breaking glass.

The sound froze me for a moment before I reached under the bed and grabbed my 12-gauge auto shotgun loaded with alternate birdshot and buckshot shells. Belly down, I crawled through darkness toward the seaside doors and saw a man coming in. He was silhouetted against the lighter skyline, and as I sighted above him I saw a second man following. I fired a warning shot that took out most of the upper door glass. The intruders stopped and lifted their arms. I got up and told them to lie down. My heart was pounding, I was flushed with rage, which was why a third man came up behind me unheard.

Expertly, he laid a gun barrel across the back of my skull and I fell in a blaze of colors that faded into black.

Sixteen

Trough the blackness I was aware of motion, bumping, being carried and moved. I drifted off into unconsciousness again, coming to at the roaring of jet afterburners. I was tied in a seat, and my head was so painful I decided they'd cracked my skull. Couldn't help groaning, but I kept my eyes shut as the plane gained altitude. Nothing I could do strapped in an aircraft cabin, any attempt to escape would have to wait until we landed. Air currents lifted and dropped the plane and I nearly threw up, but I managed to hold down dinner not knowing when or if I'd get another meal.

There were cords around my chest and shoulders, my wrists were tied together, and so were my ankles. Where they thought I'd go—except by parachute—I couldn't guess. But they were thorough, these captors, and evidently resolved to deliver me safe if not entirely sound.

The plane lifted, and a spate of turbulence pushed me back and forth against my cords. I estimated we'd been airborne at least an hour, maybe two, ample time to reach the Mexican heartland, if that was where we were headed. Mexico City was a thousand-plus miles from Cozumel, so if the jet was making an average 600 miles an hour, two hours flight time should do it. Of course, we didn't have to be heading for the capital. Monterrey was a possibility, as was Acapulco, but there was no point speculating—I'd know our destination soon enough.

Turbulence ended as the plane reached calmer air and leveled off. Barely opening my eyes, I scanned what I could see of the cabin. There were only a few interior lights but I could make out luxurious, customized appointments: overstuffed seats, dining table, an L-shaped lounge, a dark galley, and a bar. Not a military aircraft, as I'd first surmised, but a private jet configured to the owner's taste. In Mexico there were a lot of wealthy people who owned their own jets, but I could think of only one who had motive for capturing me: Pablo Antonio Aguilera.

The forward door opened briefly and a man came toward me. He had a stocky build, and as he neared he pulled a pistol from his belt. He braced himself with one hand on my chair arm, and stuck the barrel under my chin, lifting my head, "C'mon, Novak, you're awake—I didn't hit you that hard."

"Hard enough," I grated and opened my eyes.

Same slicked-back hair, same pencil mustache. Frank Rodriguez.

"Water," I croaked. "I need water."

He shrugged, put away his pistol, and stepped back. "I was for killing you back there, but I had my orders."

I licked dry lips. "Nobody got killed."

"Maybe that was your mistake."

I swallowed. "Yeah. How about water?"

"Don't you recognize me?"

"No—should I?"

"We met once in a Phoenix apartment."

"Don't remember—Jesus, my head's killing me." I squinted at him. "Who are you?"

"Rodriguez. Frank Rodriguez. That tell you?"

"*Nada.*" I let my head slump, chin on chest. "Please, Frank," I mumbled, "get me some water."

With a grunt he turned away, went to the bar, and drew water in a paper cup. I tilted back my head so he could hold the cup to my lips, swallowed and coughed, drank more. "Thanks," I managed. "Why am I here?"

"Why?" He laughed mirthlessly. "Because you got crossways with the wrong man. To him you're dirt, Novak. He'll squash you like a bug."

"Who would that be?"

"Figure it out," he snapped, and went back where he came from.

Time passed. Frank hadn't challenged my apparent loss of memory, so continuing to play dumb could be useful. Oddly, the water somewhat eased my skull pain, allowing me to think ahead. Frank confirmed my theory that Aguilera was having me brought to him, wherever he was, for a face-to-face showdown. I hoped he didn't know I'd bedded his luscious daughter, so what he had against me was the confession tape and the death of his protector, General Abreu. In Aguilera's circles that was more than enough for a contract on my life. Threatening him hadn't gained me the immunity I'd hoped for, and my only remaining card was a copy of the confession tape that could ruin him and all his cohorts. The questions was how to play it.

I shrank into the seatback to ease the tension of my bonds, but gained only a few millimeters of play. No escape there. Next, I began twisting and turning my wrists until my right-hand fingers touched a knot, and began picking at it. In a few minutes I gained enough slack to start working my left hand on the opposing knot. Five minutes more and the knots were loose enough that I knew I could free one hand at a time, and that gave me hope. But until opportunity came I might as well relax.

Frank Rodriguez came back again, stood a few feet away, staring at me silently, an expression of hatred on his face. He moved closer, leaned forward to eyeball my bonds, grunted, and went back to the forward cabin.

A few minutes later the engine sound changed and I felt the plane losing altitude. Flaps opened, then the landing gear locked down. The plane banked left, straightened, and began landing approach. Still dark outside, but moments later ground glow told me we were heading for a big city. Updrafts rocked the plane as it closed with the ground, then the wheels touched and the jets reversed to slow and brake the forward motion.

As the plane turned around I realized we were in a far corner of a major airport, probably Mexico City, but I kept my head down until after the plane stopped and the engines died. Rodriguez came back with two men who untied my chest cords and jerked me from the seat, shoving me roughly toward the open door. They steadied me down the steps to the tarmac and pushed me into the back seat of a limousine. One thug on each side of me, Rodriguez facing on the jump seat. The limo backed and turned around, following the perimeter fence to a gate guarded by a uniformed soldier or policeman. He opened it quickly, stood at attention, and saluted as we passed through. Rodriguez chuckled. "Nobody stops this car, nobody."

"First class, eh?"

"All the way, Novak. You been on the wrong side."

"You may be right."

I recognized the *periférico* that girdled the city, and soon we were climbing the *paseo* that led up into the Lomas de Chapultepec. When the limo turned I glimpsed a street sign, Sierra de Guadarrama, confirming my hunch that my destination was the house whose phone number I'd been given. The limo pulled up in front of a grill gate, the driver honked, and presently the gate began moving aside. A cobbled drive led past the side of the house and the limo braked in front of the garage.

"Out," Rodriguez ordered. The door opened, and the two heavies hustled me into a side entrance. Down a passageway to a bedroom. "On the bed," Rodriguez snapped, and when I was prone his men bound me across the chest. They left the room, Rodriguez stared down at me with an expression of satisfaction and said, "Say your prayers."

The light went out, the door closed, and I was alone.

My wristwatch showed three-thirteen. A few more hours until dawn. From elsewhere in the house came the sound of mariachi music, men laughing, the clink of bottles and glasses. They were enjoying their mission's success, but I knew it wouldn't be completed until Número Uno gave final orders.

Normally he wouldn't leave bed until at least nine, but this was no ordinary occasion, and if he wanted me terminated it was best done by dark. Still, I had one very slim advantage: I knew where I was, and they didn't know I knew. That knowledge might gain me nothing, but it improved my morale.

I stretched, flexed muscles, and worked on my wrist cords again. If I'd had my belt I would have had the buckle-dagger, but when the assault came I was in shorts and while I was unconscious they'd pulled on a pair of chino trousers, a shirt, and Top-Siders, no socks. More important, no belt.

Well, useless to speculate on what might have been. No one would notice I was missing until Ramona came at noon. Carlos had no reason to come around, and he'd be at sea with a fishing party in any case. Even when my absence was noted along with the smashed doors, what could be done? Who would suspect I'd been taken on a plane? Theirs was a foolproof plan and I could hardly have staged it more efficiently. Though if I'd wanted the target dead I wouldn't have gone to all that trouble. One shot in the brain, drop the body overboard ten miles out.

I felt played out from the tensions of pain, fear, and apprehension. My mind slowed, seemed to stop functioning, and I dozed until the room light went on and Rodriguez slapped my face.

Reflexively, I tried to snap upright but the restraints held me down. Rodriguez leered at me, and I saw that he'd downed his share of tequila. Standing unsteadily, he pulled out his pistol and pointed it at me. With the other hand he clumsily untied my chest ropes and stepped back. "Sit up. Try anything funny and I'll shoot," he slurred.

Slowly I sat up. "Dime store Jimmy Cagney. The lines don't change, only the scumbag talkers."

He tried to slash my face with the barrel, but he was slow as I ducked and the barrel whistled past. Off balance, he seemed startled, stepped back and snarled, "I oughta kill you, Novak."

"You won't—because your *jefe* is a businessman and we could do business together. A corrupt DEA agent is better than a dead one, so slack off, Frank. Besides, you might end up working for me. Like the idea?"

His face was working, a finger wiped sweat from his pimp mustache. Finally, he blurted, "Won't happen."

"You don't know that, but it's something to think about. You and I will drive out to an isolated place, no guns or knives, and face off. Without them you're no match for me. You're soft, Frank, beer belly, flabby muscles, no steel in your bones. I'll kick the shit out of you and snap your neck like a toothpick. We'll go out together but only one comes back." I grinned at him and saw fear tighten his features.

With two hands I could have taken him, but what then? His companions had stopped roistering but they were still in the house. No, better wait. Besides, I had overwhelming curiosity about Aguilera, wanted to see him in action, take his measure even if it was my final scene.

Frank's hands chambered a cartridge and the *snick, snick* seemed loud as breaking glass in the quiet house. He pointed the pistol at me, had trouble keeping it steady, and then I saw a figure in the doorway behind him. "Put it away, Frank," the man snapped, "and get out."

Rodriguez spun around, jammed the pistol in his belt, and lurched through the doorway. Taking no notice of him, the man came into the light.

"Good morning, Mr. Novak," he said, "we're both up earlier than usual but that's as much my fault as yours."

He was about my height, slim build, trimmed chin beard, blue Nike jacket over a white turtleneck, and delicate hands. Polished nails reflected the lighting as they moved. He took a chair, sat, and regarded me. "No response?"

"What do you want me to say?"

That brought a slight smile, not a nice smile but one resembling a viper's before it fangs an easy prey. "You know who I am?"

I shook my head. "Tell me and dispel the mystery."

"I think you're being evasive, Mr. Novak, but you have a talent for deception. My own daughter was charmed by you. She said you were probably the nicest man she ever met. What do you think of that?"

"I'd say she was right—if the only men she knows are your associates. Not much charm there."

"And you deceived her so cleverly that Susana never realized she was being kidnapped—how did you manage that?"

"Wasn't easy."

"But why did you do it?"

I sucked in a deep breath. "To impress you, Licenciado Aguilera, and I did. You let my friend go and you got Felipe's confession in return. I hoped that would end it, but I was too optimistic." I raised my bound hands. "What happened to our cease-fire?"

He shrugged. "You violated it."

"How?"

"Shot Fidel Abreu, killed him."

I looked away. "I could deny it, demand proof, but it's true—I shot the general—after he shot at me."

"That so? His companions say the shooting was unprovoked."

"What do you expect them to say?" I looked back at him, saw traces of Susana in his features. "You and I know why Abreu, Rojas, and Vasquez were at the Mazátan jail—to finish questioning Pazos under torture, and kill him."

He grimaced. "They say otherwise."

"They arrived unannounced in the middle of an op to recover Pazos. None of that would have happened, Licenciado, if your people hadn't snatched Pazos, sequestered him, and denied knowledge of his whereabouts."

"Pazos was snooping where he shouldn't have been."

"So, expel him across the border, don't make snooping a capital offense."

Aguilera spread his hands. "I wasn't told of his capture until your embassy asked about him, and I made my own inquiries."

"You didn't order his release."

"By then the matter was too involved."

"Better to kill him than let him go," I said thinly.

"At that point, yes." He shook his head. "You're no amateur, Novak, you know the stakes in large-scale narcotics. Leaks have to be sealed, informants neutralized, credibility maintained. An example was being made of your man Pazos."

"So I gathered. In real terms what information could he have brought to us that we didn't already know? Marijuana plantations? Our satellites have them spotted—you know that, because the embassy shares satintel with your office. They'd have told you about the Mazatán raid, but they weren't informed."

He sighed. "I wondered about that. Well, that's history. And Pazos is recovering."

"So they say. Let's get to the point—did you have me brought here so you could apologize for Pazos—or to look me over before having me killed?"

His fingers stroked the point of his beard. He got up, closed the door, and returned to his chair. "I'm a businessman, and my money allows me to entertain political ambitions. Two years from now the president's term in office ends. Under our system he nominates his successor and I plan to be that candidate. The only obstacle to my goal is you, Novak, because of what you hold over me: Paredes's confession. Made public, it would ruin me."

"And your friends."

"So, you leave me a difficult choice. I would prefer an arrangement under which I pay for your silence—or refuse, and be killed."

I stared at him. "How much is my silence worth?"

"Half a million dollars paid anywhere in the world—and your freedom."

"How about a million?"

He nodded. "I won't haggle with you. If you agree then you must give me all the copies of the tape."

I shifted on the bed and looked around the bare walls; no comfort there. "The reserve tape is all that's kept me alive, Licenciado. Simple prudence tells me to hang on to it."

He looked down at the floor, considering. "If you gave your word not to use the confession against me I would accept it."

My expression must have shown my surprise. "Only that? Only my word?"

"From a man like you—yes. Despite my faults I can appraise character. Of course, should it develop that I misjudge you, reprisal would be quick and deadly."

I took a deep breath. "It's a big decision. I need time to consider."

He nodded. "I understand—the idea goes against your grain. But if you decide not to cooperate I must tell you frankly that you will not leave here alive. The choice is yours."

"When we talked before I told you that if anything happened to me the tape would be released to the media here and the U.S. Doesn't that concern you?"

He got up from the chair. "I have influence in both countries. If I have to exert it, then I will have to take my chances, won't I?"

In Mexico, I knew, he could censor and suppress anything. And the embassy could help him avoid exposure in the U.S. That he had so much power was a chilling thought. As Rodriguez said, I was a mere bug Aguilera could squash.

"I get your point. How much time do I have?"

He looked at his watch. "Twelve hours. I'll be away from the city. I'll call for your reply."

"Tell your men I need water. They're treating me as if I was a corpse."

"I'll do so. Think everything through, Mr. Novak. Your life in return for silence, or . . . death." He left the room then, and in a little while Frank Rodriguez came in with a cup of water. "The boss wants you treated good." He helped me drain the cup. After licking my lips I said, "A deal is in the making, Frank, so treat me with respect."

"*Cabrón,*" he yelled, "*puto gringo!*" Then he switched off the light and slammed the door shut. I sat in darkness, reviewing all that had transpired, and decided that, yes, Aguilera preferred doing business with me, against the deadly alternative. I had twelve hours, and the time was now four-twenty.

Rodriguez hadn't retied me to the bed, nor checked my wrists, so I picked at the knots until I could free my hands, and began working on my ankle bonds. I hadn't got far when I heard a scratching sound at the window. The sound ended, then resumed.

On heels and toes I made my way to the window, looked down through open louvers and saw . . . the face of Susana Aguilera.

SEVENTEEN

Hardly believing my eyes, I stared at her until she gestured me to raise the window. When it was open a few inches she passed me a small automatic. "What—what are you doing here?" I blurted.

"*Shhhh!* Get out of there, I've got a car. Don't waste time."

"Got to untie my feet." Sitting, I laid down the pistol and untied the knots. "Coming out," I said and, pistol in hand, got one leg over the windowsill.

"Hurry!"

I boosted the window upward, it creaked and groaned, and the door slammed open. In the light I saw Rodriguez, gun in hand, look first at the bed, then at me—partway out of the window. "Stop!" he yelled, and leveled his pistol at me, so I shot him. Two small slugs caught his upper chest and he dropped forward, pistol skidding toward me. I picked it up. Susana shrieked and I motioned her away as I climbed back into the room. Rodriguez was coughing and spitting blood as I stepped over his body to turn off the ceiling light. I closed the door behind me and started down the dark corridor, a pistol in each hand.

From the front room two men came bolting toward me. One had his pistol out, the other was fumbling at his shoulder holster. Dropping prone, I shot them with Frank's 9-millimeter Beretta and they collapsed in the awkward postures of sudden death. I waited a few seconds before walking between them to the living room. No one else at the table. Scattered cards, glasses, and tequila bottles were all that remained of earlier revelry.

Not knowing if there was external surveillance, I decided against leaving by the front door and backtracked to the room window. Outside, Susana was sitting down, weeping. I dropped beside her and said, "It's okay, honey, everything's okay now. Where's the car?"

She got up then, pressed her tear-wet face to mine, and I felt her body shiver. "Oh, Jack," she breathed, "I was sure they'd killed you. Thank God you're safe!"

"Thanks to you, *mi amor.*" I took her arm and she led me down the back yard, through a fence gate, and onto the next street. She began walking faster as we neared a sleek, low-slung red Ferrari parked in shadows at the curb. Susana got behind the wheel, I sat beside her, and she started the engine. It had a burbling, muffled roar, and in the stillness of late night the engine sounded like a freight train.

As she steered down the incline toward the city, she said, "Where shall we go?"

"I don't know, any ideas?"

"No time to think." She drove skillfully with the smooth motions of a driver integrated to the car.

"What were you doing at the house?" I glanced around—no cars following.

"I was half-asleep at home when my father's phone rang. He answered in a low voice and I heard him start getting dressed. Jack, I thought he was going to visit a mistress and I wanted to find out who she was so I could tell Mamí tomorrow—he's been very hard on Mamí, broken her heart with his mistresses—so if I could get proof that would help her."

I smiled. Tension was wearing off and I kissed the side of her head. "A regular Nancy Drew," I remarked.

"Drew? Who's she?"

"Girl detective," I replied. "So, what then?"

"Well, I followed him out here to the Lomas, saw him leave his car and go into that house. I parked around the block and came back."

"With the pistol. To shoot Papá?"

"No, no, of course not." She gave me an irritable glance. "In case a watchdog attacked me. In the Lomas nearly every house has a watchdog, a big one."

"Okay."

"I keep the pistol in the glove compartment."

"Good precaution, *querida*. Go on."

"I went to the lighted window, heard my father's voice, and managed to look in." Her features tightened. "Saw you tied up, heard what he was saying."

"All of it?"

She shrugged. "He offered you a bribe to do something dishonest, against your character. Then he threatened to kill you if you didn't cooperate." She faced me briefly, tears in her eyes. Her lips trembled as she said, "At first I thought he might have found out about our afternoon at the posada, or maybe forced you to tell him, then I realized it had nothing to do with me and everything to do with money and his ambitions."

"I see." I hated to tell her what her father's business really was, wanted to postpone it as long as I could. My God, this sweet little treasure had saved my life, taken a stand against her father to rescue me. How could I bring her unhappiness? Changing the subject, I said, "His men kidnapped me from Cozumel, flew me here, and stuck me in that house. They called him to say I was here, and that's the call you heard."

"Cozumel? What were you doing in Cozumel?"

"I live there—really, Susana. Ah—the initials DEA mean anything to you?"

"It's something against drugs, isn't it?"

"It is, and I work for DEA."

"Oh, then my father shouldn't be against you, he's head of the national antinarcotics force. You should be working together."

"In the best of worlds, yes, but I'll explain everything when we have more time. Right now, we need to figure out where to go."

"I can't go home, Jack. Papá will see my car isn't there, I'm missing, and he'll realize I had something to do with your escape. I can't think of a lie to convince him."

"Complicated," I agreed, "so what do we do now?"

"Wherever you go, I go with you."

"I haven't any money, *mi amor,* no ID, nothing. How far can we go?"

"I have cash," she told me, "and credit cards. Where do you want to go?"

I grunted. "I know where I'd *like* to go—the posada—but this car is too conspicuous. We'd be picked up by noon tomorrow."

She rubbed against me. "I'd love the posada, again, but you're right—not tonight."

"We ought to get as far from Mexico City as we can." Something clicked in my memory, and I said, "You know how to get to Toluca?"

"Of course, easy. But, what's there?"

"A small airfield."

"You mean, hire a pilot to fly us?"

"Uh-uh, I mean steal a plane—I can fly, I used to be a navy pilot. In fact, I have a plane in Cozumel."

She beamed at me. "Jack, is there anything you *can't* do?"

"There is. I haven't been able to get you out of my mind, *querida.* You've haunted me day and night ever since we said goodbye at the Reforma."

Her head moved incredulously. "Oh, Jack, you don't know how that makes me feel. I've been sick with love for you all this time—and I just knew I'd never see you again." She began to cry. I kissed her cheek and nose. She dabbed at her eyes and pulled over to the roadside. I kissed her lips, her tongue parted mine, and her full breasts pressed against me. "*Jesus,* I want you, Jack," she whispered.

"And I want you, honey—but let's get to the airfield, okay?"

"Okay," she said reluctantly, and pulled out onto the road. "From there where can we go?"

"A light plane with full tanks could probably make Guadalajara. Or Manzanillo. From either place we could fly commercially to the States."

"The States?"

"For protection," I explained. "Where your father can't find us. If we stay in Mexico we're easy targets."

"I thought you'd want us together in Cozumel," she pouted. "I've been thinking of you carrying me into your house—so thrilling."

"In time," I promised, "but they snatched me from there, so that's the first place they'd look for me. Ah, are we heading for Toluca?"

"We are," she said firmly. She stepped on the accelerator and we sped through the night like a missile.

We reached the airfield just before dawn. The hangars were shut, and maybe two dozen private aircraft were lined up along the tarmac. I said, "One of those is going to have keys in its lock, and if the tanks are topped that's the plane we'll take."

"And my car?"

I peered through gray mist, spotted a clump of trees away from the perimeter fence. "Put it there," I told her, "while I go hunting."

I used her keys to open the trunk, then the gas tank. There was a small built-in toolbox and a bundle of polishing rags. I selected wrenches and pliers, and made a yard-long strip from the rags. I stuck one end in the gas tank opening while she watched, frowning. "Jack, what are you going to *do*?"

"Burn this beauty," I said, "and, yes, it has to be done. No place to hide it, so it has to be destroyed." I tore off the license plate and threw it into the woods. "Get out anything you want to take with us, and say goodbye to your car."

Dutifully, she opened the glove compartment, got out cosmetics, cigarettes, sun glasses and other things. I thought I glimpsed a pack of condoms and thought, naughty Susana, but said, "Here's how it's going to be. I'm going to take a plane and taxi over here. When I stop, light the rag, get over the fence and into the plane, okay?"

"Okay." She looked despairingly at her Ferrari. "If I leave it, it will be taken away, so either way I'll never see it again."

"Good thinking." I opened the hood, unscrewed a coupling from the gas line, and said, "Stay out of sight." Then I climbed over the fence and began jogging toward the line of planes.

The first four were locked and secured. Plane five was a Comanche with full tanks and a key in the ignition lock. There was also a map rack and a list of airport call frequencies. I undid the tie-downs, kicked away wheel chocks, and got into the cabin. Before turning the ignition key I heard a car engine behind me, looked back, and saw a pickup heading for the flight line. Two men were in the cab, the back was piled with bags of what looked like grain. They drove along the flight line and stopped at the far end where a twin-engine Beech was positioned. They hadn't noticed me, so I started the engine and pulled out of line, heading for the side of the field where Susana was to be waiting. Because of low visibility I got within a hundred yards before I saw her waving beside the fence. I throttled ahead and reached the rendezvous point while she disappeared among the trees. I braked and opened the cabin door as she came running toward me. Her dress caught on the top wire, she tore it loose, and dropped on my side. I reached across the seat and took her hand to pull her in. She turned to me, face white with fear, and fumbled with her seat belt. "Take it easy," I said, "the hardest part is over," shoved the throttle ahead and gained speed as I headed for the end of the strip. By the time we reached it the controls were light in my hands; another eighty yards and we were airborne.

Susana was looking down, and when the explosion came it bronzed the side of her face. I didn't circle over the burning car, but gained altitude, anxious to be away from Toluca and Mexico City air control. For a few minutes I flew south, then changed course and settled on a direct heading for Guadalajara. At nine thousand feet I trimmed for level flight, kicked in the autopilot, and turned to my passenger. "You're wonderful," I said. "Anyone tell you that?"

"You. And you're wonderful, too."

"But look at all you've done: tailed your father, rescued me, taken me to the airfield, and sacrificed your Ferrari. All that for a man you hardly know. That's more than wonderful, honey, that's miraculous."

Her dimples deepened as she smiled, and I saw her blush. "Jack," she said quietly, "from the first moment we met you've made me feel more alive than any time in my life. You had to kill that man—those men—I know, and when I thought you'd been killed I felt my life had ended. But you came back, you've taken a plane, and now we're going—I don't care *where,* so long as we're together."

"I should have added you've broken with your family, at least with your father, and things can never be the same between you."

"I don't want them to be the same, ever. All he gave me was money. My mother, even my brothers, gave me more affection than he ever did." She breathed deeply, and those provocative breasts lifted and fell. The dress's dark material was flimsy and translucent, revealing the outline of her bra. No stockings, just *alpargatas* on her feet, for she had dressed hastily to follow Dad.

As the sun rose behind us I could view the ridged Sierras ahead, and got out the flight chart to check safe crossing altitude. Upper winds had drifted us off course, so I got back on the correct heading, and decided to fly hands-on the rest of the way. Susana opened the console compartment and brought out a pint of Jack Daniel's. Unscrewing the top, she offered it to me. After kicking back a healthy slug, I shook myself and said, "It's not champagne, but it'll do."

She drank from the bottle, coughed, shivered, and drank again. By the time the bottle was half gone, we were in a mellow mood; my skull pain had diminished, and Susana was pawing at my crotch. She opened the zipper, groped and fondled me, kissed me full on the lips, and bent over my lap. It wasn't the Fourth of July or even Cinco de Mayo, but fireworks exploded in my head as she had her will of me. In the aftermath I felt limp as a wet rag but managed to say, "Sweetheart, that was wonderful. You really know how to treat a man."

"Not *a* man," she corrected, "*my* man. Big difference." She curled up beside me until I saw the smoky pall hovering above Guadalajara. I called GDL tower then and was told to approach from the south, head wind twelve knots. So I made the prescribed approach pattern and touched down at the far end of a runway reserved for civil aircraft.

Briefly, I'd thought of running the Comanche to the side of the strip and walking in, but it was daylight now, and after we were seen questions would be asked. So I taxied to the area of private aircraft, found a vacant slot, and killed the engine. A gas truck approached but I waved it off and we got out and walked a little lightheartedly into the weather room, continued through it, and exited by a taxi stand. As I remembered it, there was a pretty good motel a couple of miles toward the city. When I told the driver where I wanted to go, he said, "Las Gaviotas. Baggage?"

I shook my head. "Let's go. *Andale.*"

After leaving the airport Susana opened her purse and gave me a thick roll. "How much is there?" I asked.

She shrugged. "Thousands and thousands of pesos. Enough to live on for a while."

Rifling through the bills, I said, "About six thousand dollars. Taxi fare, and then some." I grinned, and kissed her cheek.

She smiled at that and squeezed my arm. I leaned forward and told the driver to stop wherever liquor was sold. Another quarter mile and I was in a sleepy shop with dusty bottles on the shelves. I paid for two bottles of German champagne, one of scotch, and a dark Añejo. Getting back into the taxi, I heard the driver say, "Cheaper than in the airport."

"Besides, the airport shop isn't open."

Las Gaviotas was a two-story L-shaped building with a sparkling pool inside. I paid the clerk for two nights, a *chamaco* carried a bag of ice to our poolside room, and by the time I'd set the champagne in ice Susana had shed her clothes and was nibbling my neck. "Slow down," I said. "I'm filthy and sweaty, but a five-minute shower will change that."

"We've showered before—remember?"

"I remember everything at the posada. We'll call this Posada Number Two."

She helped me out of my clothes, turned on the shower, and beckoned me in. We soaped each other's bodies, rinsed, and began to embrace.

Then all the longing I'd felt for her surged through my blood. Her love, youth, and sweetness flooded my brain, and when she closed her thighs around my hips to bond us I felt that with her I could find all I'd ever desired in life. In that place, in that moment there were only the two of us and I would forever cherish and protect her against all the evils of the world.

EIGHTEEN

We stayed in the motel room until eleven, making love, relaxing, and making sketchy plans for the immediate future. At noon a taxi took us in to Guadalajara's Hyatt Regency.

In the arcade we bought fresh clothing and a blond wig for Susana, stopped at the travel agency for tickets on a flight to Miami, and had an excellent lunch in the Hyatt grill. Then, from a hotel phone I called Manny Montijo in Nogales and told him I'd been forcibly taken from Cozumel and flown to Mexico City for an unpleasant session with Aguilera. "I'll give you details later, *compadre,* but right now I'm in a fugitive mode and I need your help to get us the hell out of Mexico."

"Us? Who's with you?"

"The big man's daughter. But for her I wouldn't have gotten away from his killers—including Frank Rodriguez, who is no longer of this world—and I need temporary travel docs that will get us to Miami tonight."

I heard a protracted sigh before Manny said, "What should I do?"

"Telex our office here and ask them to have the Consulate issue two travel IDs, one for me as Matthew Barden, the other for—let's see—Frances Donovan, age seventeen."

"Seventeen? Jack, you outa your mind?"

"Manny, just do it. I'll pick up the docs at our Consulate office. Okay?"

"Yeah, but, Jesus, no one even knows you're missing from Cozumel."

"I know it and you know it, so does Aguilera. That's enough." I paused. "This is fallout from Mazatán—Aguilera took Abreu's death personally and had me brought in for judgment. Once he realizes his daughter helped me escape he'll probably put her on the hit list, too, so I have to protect her. In the States we have a chance but not in Mexico."

"Won't argue the point."

"Good. I'll be needing my personal ID, pistol, and moneybelt from my desk drawer. So I'll contact you later and tell you where to send them, okay?"

"Okay, Jack, but I have to say this whole situation sounds crazy."

"I agree. Just start the Consulate moving. We'll talk tomorrow."

I paid for the call, took Susana's arm, and led her outside. We crossed the broad street to a shopping plaza and took seats at an outdoor table. I ordered Tecate, Susana a Tequila Sunrise, and when the waiter left I said, "*Querida,* I hate to be the bearer of bad news, but it involves your father, and you have a right to know how I became involved with him."

She looked away, then back at me. "For years I've heard rumors about my father, the kind of rumors the press doesn't dare print. Now I have a feeling you're going to tell me the rumors are true."

"Hear me out, then make up your mind." I took her hand and told her how the crashed plane on Paredes's *estancia* had started it all; Molly Flanigan's search for her pilot brother; Frank Rodriguez murdering Molly's roommate; Paredes's taped confession that involved Aguilera and his corrupt associates; Molly's kidnapping by Aguilera's thugs that led to my ostensible abduction of his daughter, and Molly's release . . .

She listened silently, though her features tightened from time to time, expressing her inner suffering. I described the Mazatán mission to free DEA agent Pazos, and the unexpected arrival of three of her father's key associates. The firefight in which I'd shot General Abreu, provoking her father's reprisal from which she'd rescued me. "Your father revealed his ambition to be president of Mexico and said Paredes's confession was the only obstacle in his path. He offered me a million dollars for my silence and gave me twelve hours to reply—the alternative being death."

By then tears were streaming down her cheeks. Chokingly, she said, "It's—it's so hard to believe—but it's true, isn't it?"

I nodded. "All of it, *mi amor,* and I wish it weren't. But somehow out of all the death and deception we found each other, and that's what we have to cling to."

"Yes," she said quietly, "I know, I know. Oh, Jack, it all seems so impossible—but here I am, and here you are, and that's reality and nothing else matters." I kissed her cheek and she dried her eyes. "What are we going to do?"

The waiter brought our drinks and I turned to Susana. "First, we find refuge, then live a day at a time while we make plans."

She drank and nodded thoughtfully. "But we'll be together?"

"We will."

"And—what about my father?"

"He's evil."

Her eyes closed, then opened. "Will you try to kill him?"

"Only if he harms us. Mexico has always had corrupt presidents, one more won't destroy the country. Besides, in practical terms he's untouchable—and I don't think I could kill the father of the girl I love."

"I'm glad you said that, though if you'd killed him at that house I couldn't blame you." Her lips set. "My mother would welcome his death."

"Will she help you? Can she be trusted?"

"I think so."

"But you're not sure."

She shook her head.

I sucked in a deep breath. "We have your money, and I'll have more in a few days but it won't last forever."

"I have my bank card. I can go to a branch here and empty the account."

I thought it over. "Your father will find out but by then we won't be in Guadalajara, so I think it's safe to do."

"There's a branch in the hotel arcade. I'll go there while you're at the consulate."

I left the taxi at the main entrance of the Consulate General and walked up the steps. Inside, a Marine guard directed me to an anteroom where I filled out a slip of paper requesting an interview with Art Stimson, signing as Matthew Barden. A disinterested Mexican clerk took the request slip and told me to wait. As I cooled my heels I looked outside and reflected that Kiki Camarena had gone down those steps expecting to lunch at home with his family. Instead, he'd been forced into a police vehicle and had never been seen alive again, except by his captors, torturers and murderers. I wondered to what extent Licenciado Aguilera had been involved in that foul deed, and decided that if not at the beginning, he was a major player in the cover-up. The blood of Kiki Camarena stained the hands of Susana's father, and the blood of others as well. And still the perpetrators had never been brought to anything resembling justice, although their names were an open secret in Mexico and within DEA.

A door opened, Art Stimson peered out, caught sight of me and blinked. Then he beckoned me into a small interview room and closed the door. "Jesus, Jack, you're Barden?"

"For the time being." We shook hands and he handed me two yellow consular cards. "These'll get you into the States if that's all you want."

I read the typed names—Barden and Donahue—and pocketed both cards. "Without involving you beyond need-to-know," I said, "I'm escorting a narco witness who's been guaranteed entry into the Witness Protection Program. We've been on the run for two days and only got here this morning."

"No wonder I hadn't heard about it."

"Very tightly held," I said. "because high levels of the Mex government are involved."

"The witness—this Frances Donahue—is a Mex national?"

I nodded. "But will pass as a gringa." I looked around the bare room. "You like duty here?"

"*Más o menos.* The cops tail us, tap our phones, intimidate our wives and kids, but the perks are good." He shrugged. "The Mexicans hate us, and I guess you know they passed a law against our carrying weapons."

"Which you naturally observe."

"Oh, yeah," he sneered and tapped a holster under his jacket. "Anyone asks for this, I'll give it to him—bullet first."

"Good thinking," I said and stood up. "If something happens to me and my witness I recommend you say nothing about these ID cards. If there's an internal investigation, you got a request from a domestic officer—whose name you don't remember—and accommodated him."

He grimaced. "This op is official?"

"Has to be deniable, Art, so play it that way."

"Will do. Take care of yourself, Jack—and your witness."

I walked away from the consulate, hailed a passing cab rather than take one from the rank of waiting taxis, and rode back to the Hyatt.

In her blond wig Susana was easy to spot in the section where tea and pastries were served. She seemed totally at ease, leafing through a fashion magazine, and sipping tea with the aplomb of British royalty. This was one cool kid and I admired her boundlessly.

I sat across from her, she smiled and said in a low voice, "I was beginning to get worried." Pressed my hand.

"You don't look it. Okay, I've got our cards. How did things go at the bank?"

"No problem. But I've never carried so much cash before—should I have changed the pesos for dollars? I've got about sixteen thousand dollars' worth."

"No, would draw attention. We'll do it in Miami." A waiter approached, I ordered Añejo over ice, but Susana said she was enjoying her tea. "Besides, we can drink all we want on the plane."

I looked at her wristwatch. "Reminding me our flight leaves in five hours. Now, even in the wig you look noticeably spectacular so I think for security—and other—reasons we'll keep you out of sight for a few hours."

"How?"

"This is a hotel. It has rooms to rent. I'll get one."

In the cool, dark room we enjoyed a bottle of chilled Moët, made love, and overcame the stress and tensions of the day. Her finger trailed across my chest and she murmured, "Were you remembering the posada?"

"I was."

"And I've been trying not to think of all you told me—about Papá."

"Thinking about it won't change anything."

"I know. But I can't help wondering how it all will end."

"I think of that, too, but for now all we can do is care for ourselves."

"Yes. I'm happy with you. So happy. I was never really in love before."

"I'm happy with you, *querida*. Nothing else matters."

"Nothing."

A night flight seems endlessly long. We shared a split of champagne before Susana put her head on my shoulder and fell asleep.

I dozed, too, waking her when the plane came in over the coastline to show her the glittering skyline of Miami. "It's so beautiful!" she exclaimed. "I've never seen anything like it."

"But when you visited Disney World—?"

"Papá's plane flew directly to Orlando, so I never got to see Miami even from the air." Probably the same plane, I mused, that flew me out of Cozumel. "It can be a great city," I remarked, "even though drug money is everywhere. *Narcotraficantes* own the best restaurants and condos, some of the better hotels. They have jets and racing boats, anything pricey they're there."

"Papá doesn't come here."

"Doesn't have to, has his own empire." I took her hand. "I think you'll like where we're going."

"I always have, *querido*." Her brow wrinkled. "You mean Miami?"

"You'll see."

Getting through customs was no problem since we had no baggage. Her pesos were divided between us, concealed under our clothing and not declared. The INS inspector frowned at our consular laiser-passer cards, inquired about our citizenship—we both said American—and reluctantly let us through. So far, so good.

A foreign exchange bank converted a wad of pesos into three thousand dollars, and with them we taxied to the airport Ramada Inn where we took a suite and fell asleep moments after going to bed.

In mid-morning we had a room service breakfast and inquired about transportation to the Keys. A limousine called at the hotel at noon and we rode in comfort to Cheeca Lodge on Islamorada. After checking in we bought beach clothing and swimsuits at the boutique, and I phoned Manny to give him my address for Federal Express overnight delivery. "I'll get it off right away," he said. "So, the consulate came through."

"Thanks to you."

"How long will you, ah, be there?"

"Until I find a cottage where we can play house. Any word on my disappearance?"

"Nothing."

"I won't be returning until I think it's safe. Right now I imagine the Cozumel house is being watched, phone tapped."

"How's your, ah, companion behaving?"

"Magnificently. Couldn't ask for better. Anyway, we're safe for now and I've stopped looking over my shoulder."

"Oh, almost forgot—a short news item said a Ferrari registered to Licenciado Aguilera was found burned beside the Toluca airfield. Susana's car?"

"Right. I also borrowed a plane to get us to Guadalajara. Anything else in the item?"

"Said Aguilera was away from his office and couldn't be reached for comment. Nothing about his missing daughter."

"Good. The missing plane will be reported and Aguilera will make the connection—only he won't know where we went."

After a pause Manny said, "I worry about you. You take big chances."

"Have to," I said, and replaced the receiver.

To Susana, who had been listening interestedly, I repeated what Manny said. She asked, "Anything about dead men in that house?"

I shook my head. "There won't be. Papá will have it cleaned up, corpses disposed of. The house probably can't be traced to him, but it might—if the cops were interested. But, no bodies, no interest." I kissed her forehead. "You don't realize how powerful your father is. There's literally nothing he can't do and get away with—including murder. But because I'm loose he has to be plenty worried about Paredes's confession surfacing." Gently, I stroked her hair. "We can't let ourselves worry over what might happen, honey. Let's enjoy being safe together."

"Yes, I want that."

"And tomorrow we'll find a place where we can stay as long as we want."

"Really?" She smiled expectantly. "Can I help choose it?"

"Of course. I don't want to be where you're not happy."

In the morning I hopped a bus for the ten-mile ride back to Key Largo, where I'd noticed a used car lot the day before. But four or five miles along, I spotted a weathered Toyota parked in front of a run-down cottage. 4 Sale, was printed in white letters across the windshield. Below it: Cheep. So I got off the bus and walked back to the car. I walked around it, looked at the tires, and peered inside. While I was inspecting the car a man came out of the cottage and walked toward me. He was an elderly black man with white whiskers and curly white hair. "'Mornin', mon," he hailed me. "That's a good car."

"Has to be," I replied. "Got close to two hundred thousand miles on it."

"Sure ain't new," he said pleasantly, "but it'll get you aroun' where you want to go. I'm goin' back to Abaco, so make me an offer."

"Fire it up," I told him. He got in and started the engine. I got in beside him. "Let's drive a ways so I can hear the engine."

We drove half a mile south, then back. The engine didn't purr like a kitten or growl like a bobcat, but gears shifted without groaning, and when we were back in his yard I said, "Okay. Four hundred. Cash. Dollars."

He smiled. "Mon, you take advantage of my age and need. Four fifty."

"Got the title?"

He fished it from the glove compartment and showed me. Abraham Watling was the typed name. "Insurance card?"

That, too, came out of the glove compartment, and I saw that the car was covered, no-fault, for another three months. I handed him green bills, had him sign his name as the conveyor, and printed Matthew J. Barden as purchaser. We shook hands, he wished me luck, and I drove back to Cheeca Lodge, parking where it wouldn't attract attention. Let the upscale clientele think it belonged to a servant.

In our room I found Susana still sleeping, so I shaved and got in beside her. I moved against her cool body, but there was no reaction. I fell asleep, and slept until I heard Susana in the shower. She came out toweling her hair, and said, "I had the strangest dream—that you'd gone and left me."

"I did." And told her what I'd been doing. "It's far from the kind of car you're used to, but it'll do for our needs."

"House hunting, right?" She leaned over the bed and kissed me warmly.

"Right. Lots to do today, so let's have breakfast and get moving."

I watched her get into panties, bra, a white linen shirt and faded denims that fitted her like paint. Seeing her dress and undress was something I looked forward to every day and night the rest of my life.

At the buffet we helped ourselves to sliced mangos, omelets, sliced ham, and biscuits with honey. After two cups of coffee we went back to the room in time to receive a Federal Express delivery.

From it I extracted my holstered pistol, the moneybelt with nearly thirty thousand in operational funds—written off by DEA but critically needed now—and my billfold with Barden ID and pocket litter in the same alias. "Now," I said, "we can do business."

She giggled at the dusty car but got in beside me, and said, "This is such an adventure for me, Jack. My first real lover is going to find my first real house." She bit my ear lobe, and said, "I'm so happy. My life before you seems like a distant dream."

Driving off US 1, I took the parallel road on the Gulf side, looking for rental signs. I wanted a place isolated from possibly nosy neighbors who might disapprove of a girl living with a male twice her age and call in the authorities. I'd seen her driving license and knew she'd be eighteen in two months, when cohabitation would be legal. Until then we needed to lie low.

The Gulf side offered nothing, so I crossed US 1 and headed back along the parallel road that bordered a thick wall of mangroves and casuarina trees. Half a mile and I saw a sign with an arrow that pointed toward a crushed coral lane. For Rent, the sign said, so I turned in. Less than a hundred yards along, the access lane gave out on a clearing beyond which I could glimpse ocean and a stretch of beach. At the far end of the clearing stood a two-story house of weathered cypress, outside stairs leading up to the second story.

"Shall we check it out?" I asked.

"Please. It looks wonderful."

So we got out and began walking toward the front door, when it opened and a white-haired lady in flowered housecoat came out and said, "Good morning."

"Morning, ma'am," I said. "Is your place still for rent?"

"It is. How long would you need it?"

"We'll talk after we've seen inside."

"Then come in."

As we entered I thought she eyed Susana suspiciously, but business is business, especially in the Keys, and she said nothing.

The first floor had a large living room strewn with Navajo rugs, Indian relics on the walls, television set, and a working fireplace. The dining room adjoined. There was a kitchen with gas stove, refrigerator-freezer, and cypress cabinets for dishes, utensils, cutlery, and pots and pans. From there we were shown a small office lined with bookshelves. The desk had a telephone, an electric typewriter, radio, and a smaller TV set. The owner said, "I just put the sign out yesterday, and you're the first caller. My sister died in Minneapolis and I need to go there tomorrow."

"I'm sorry about your loss," Susana said politely, and the owner nodded appreciatively. "Thank you. Shall we go upstairs?"

Two large bedrooms joined by a large bathroom. The windows had Bahama shutters letting in ocean breeze. She pointed at overhead fans and said, "I seldom need them, the breeze is so steady. No air-conditioning, of course, and no mosquitoes so close to the ocean."

We looked down from the balcony and saw a sandy path leading through sawgrass and seagrape to a divide in sand dunes. Beyond the dunes, slanting beach and a line of white foam. I asked, "How long do you want to rent?"

"At least two months—I need to take charge of funeral arrangements and do something about Maude's estate. Will you want the house longer?"

"Perhaps," I replied, "if the price is right."

"Furnished as it is I'm asking eighteen hundred a month. If you'll take it for three months and pay in advance you can have it for forty-five hundred." She paused. "Plus a deposit of two thousand against breakage."

Susana asked, "Linens?"

The lady pointed to drawers and cupboards, opened them, and said, "Washer and dryer are just below the balcony."

"I'm interested," I said, "but I'm not sure we should lay out so much cash."

"Then talk it over, I'll be downstairs."

After she left Susana said, "I'd be happy here, Jack. Will you?"

"I think we could look longer and be less satisfied." I opened my shirt and took off my moneybelt, counted out sixty-five hundred-dollar bills. After replacing belt and shirt I kissed Susana and said, "Home at last."

Susana went out to wait in the car while I concluded business with Mrs. Jessie Evans. As she filled out a stock rental form I said, "We're the Bardens. Matthew and Frances." I showed her my Texas driving license, and counted out the rent money. Mrs. Evans re-counted it, noted the amounts on the lease, and wrote her Minneapolis address and phone number on a pad. "You're planning to move in tomorrow, Mr. Barden?"

"I'd like to."

"Say, after one o'clock." She handed me keys, and said, "I hope you'll enjoy my house. I have—and so did my late husband. If you have any problems don't hesitate to telephone me."

"Thank you."

We walked to the doorway and shook hands. She looked at Susana in the car, and said, "Married long?"

"Not long." With that I went to the car and we drove out to the highway. Susana rubbed against me and said, "It's perfect, isn't it, the house, the view . . ."

"And the isolation. By the way, can you cook?"

She laughed. "I don't know. I never tried. Can you?"

"You be the judge."

Back at the lodge we got into swimsuits and lounged beside the pool. Susana's bikini top barely held her breasts, and the thong bottom was almost invisible. I noticed admiring glances from men, envious stares from poolside women. Well, I thought, youth comes only once, so take advantage of it. All the way.

At the far end of the pool a scuba class was forming and Susana said she'd like to learn the sport so she could dive with me. The instructor checked her swimming ability—she knifed through the water as smoothly as a porpoise—and enrolled her. The short course was two hours, lunch break, and two final hours before qualifying dives. Auditing the course, I was satisfied Susana could handle scuba equipment and emergency breathing. I could show her finer points when we began open water diving.

The qualification certificate showed her name as Frances Barden. She waved it delightedly saying, "I always wanted to do scuba but Papá wouldn't allow me. Even though our Acapulco place has all kinds of equipment for him and his guests. My brothers dive, of course, but not their little sister."

"Until now."

"Jack, every day I learn things from you that make my life fuller than I thought it could be. Don't ever stop teaching me, showing me everything you like."

"No way."

From the lodge we drove a mile to the Green Turtle for dinner: conch fritters, a bottle of Chardonnay, Florida lobsters, and shrimp salads. She liked the informal atmosphere and I told her it was one of many similar eating places along the Keys. "After we settle in at our house we'll visit Key West, maybe fly over to Fort Jefferson for a day in the sun."

"Anything you want, dear." She kissed me lightly. "Our house—I love the sound of that—and this new life you're showing me. Until a few days ago I had no idea the Keys even existed—it's all so, so un-Mexican."

I smiled. "Between here and Key West you'll see a dozen Mexican-style eateries with dishes as good or better than anything in Mexico, so the influence is here—in case you get homesick."

"So long as we're together I never will."

We ended dinner with Key lime pie and Cuban coffee, turned in at the lodge, and in the morning had another ample breakfast before checking out.

Our first stop was the Publix supermarket where we bought prime meats, green vegetables, coffee and tea to stock our larder. Next stop was a sportsmen's store, where I looked over a rack of shotguns and chose a 12-gauge Winchester semi-auto for home defense. To it I added two boxes of high-base birdshot and two of buckshot, then checked the action of a used Colt .380 from the display cabinet. "I'll take it," I told the salesman, "with two boxes of soft points and a nylon holster."

"Cleaning rods, oil and patches?"

"Absolutely." I counted our currency while he got everything together, and as he rang up my purchases he said, "Heading for Key West?"

"Uh, uh. Miami—where men of good will should be armed."

"How right you are. Have a good day."

After visiting a liquor store for champagne, rum, and cognac we drove toward our home-to-be until Susana pointed at the Fish House restaurant and said, "Mrs. Evans may not have left, so let's have conch fritters and cool drinks until it's time."

I parked by the door where I could watch the car, and we feasted and drank until after one o'clock. Back in the Toyota I said, "The pistol is replacement for your twenty-five. It's a heavier caliber that'll stop any intruder, and we'll keep the shotgun by our bed."

She gazed at me. "Expecting trouble?"

"Not from your father, but there's a lot of burglary and house-breaking along the Keys, and we don't want to be victims."

I flashed back to the night I was snatched from my house. My

shotgun hadn't helped me then, but my attackers hadn't been burglars.

Presently I turned off the highway onto the parallel road and
steered along the crushed coral drive until the house came into view.
The front door stood open. Above it hung a sign that read: Welcome. Hope you'll be happy here.

"What a nice lady," Susana remarked as we walked toward the
house. On the porch she turned and waited. It took me a moment
before I caught on, then I lifted and carried her into the house. She
clung to me, murmuring, "I love you, Jack. Don't ever leave me."

"Never."

We spent an hour putting away provisions and changing bed linens.
Then we stripped to bare essentials and strolled down to the beach.
Along the coastline in either direction there were no visible humans,
only a few fishing boats far offshore and on the skyline a lone
freighter. So at water's edge we dropped what we were wearing and
entered the ocean hand in hand.

The day was idyllic. Hot sun, almost cloudless sky, and low
waves. For a while we swam together, then went back on the beach
to dry in the sun. "Next time," I said, "we'll bring beach towels and
sun oil."

Her fingers moved slowly along my spine. "I love this way of
life, so carefree, so relaxed. Just thinking of the English School
makes me shudder—I could never go back to it."

"You won't have to," I said, and kissed her lips.

At sunset I fired up the charcoal grill outside the kitchen door and
put on teriyaki-marinated fajitas. Susana made salad, and we dined
at a small table near the grill. Gradually, silently, the sky turned
from purple to indigo, and when the stars came out we went upstairs
and watched the phosphorescent sea from our balcony.

Early to bed then; love-making began with kisses and warm

embraces and soon became urgent and ultimately satisfying. We fell asleep in each other's arms, hearing the soft rhythm of breaking waves, the lonesome hoot of an owl in the casuarina pines, and the far-off sound of a dog baying at the new moon.

So ended our first day in our first home.

NINETEEN

For a week we swam and fished, snorkled, made love, saw the dolphin show, made breakfast at home, lunched at roadside restaurants, and cooked late dinner, usually on the charcoal grill.

We devoted a day to visiting Key West, took the tour through Old Town, the Audubon House, and Hemingway's storied shrine. After the turtle kraals we inspected Mel Fisher's Spanish treasure display, and then I walked Susana to the old naval base crowded with small boats and fragile makeshift rafts that had left Cuba with desperate refugees, not all of whom arrived alive. Finger to chin, Susana said, "Jack, I really don't understand why those people risked their lives to leave Cuba."

"To escape the miserable lives Castro condemns them to."

She looked puzzled. "But Mexico and Cuba are friends and—"

"So they are. Mexico is Socialist and Cuba is Communist, two branches of the same poisonous tree. But in Mexico you don't hear the evil truth about Castro; the government is traditionally anti-American so Cuba is praised, its crimes ignored. Mexican funds help Castro stay in power, so does the oil Mexico sends Cuba at cut-rate prices."

She nodded thoughtfully. "I heard Papá discussing oil shipments to Cuba on tankers he has an interest in. Actually, I was introduced to President Castro by Papá at a government reception."

"What did you think of him?"

She giggled. "I wanted to pull his beard, see if it was real."

I laughed at that. "Political reeducation is in order—when we have time. And you should know that Cuba is a convenient stop for narcotics en route the U.S."

"If it's as bad as all that, why doesn't America do something about it?"

"Because Cuba is a protectorate of the Soviet Union, and ever since the Bay of Pigs the U.S. has been too frightened to make a move."

She looked at me. "Bay of Pigs?"

"Happened before you were born."

Definite generational gap that needed filling.

In and out of bed we told each other of our earlier lives, and while Susana had much less to relate than I, it was interesting to hear her describe the growing up of a pampered only daughter in a very wealthy family.

Without preoccupations or obligations, except to each other, we slipped into an easy, seductive way of living, congenial to us both and especially to Susana, deeply tanned and beautiful, effortlessly exuding an aura of radiant sexuality.

But despite our enjoyments and diversions I began to feel uneasy, dissatisfied, unfocused. Goals and objectives seemed to have melted away, and I was unable to project our future. Her father would pursue us relentlessly—to regain his daughter and exact vengeance on me. Maybe not next month or the next after, but I feared eventually Susana or I would make a mistake that would bring Aguilera to our door. And I lived with that fear.

Finally I wrote Manny giving him our location and phone number, said we were well and enjoying life together, and asked that he take charge of Susana's welfare, should something happen to me.

I wasn't sure the Toyota would make it all the way to Miami, but we started out and drove to Bal Harbour without the old car overheating or breaking down. Susana shopped for clothing and accessories in boutiques, and while she was trying on dresses in a shop I went to a jewelry shop next door and bought a simple gold band for her ring finger.

During lunch I took her hand and slipped the ring on her finger. She stared at it unbelievingly, and her eyes welled with tears. "Oh, Jack, I love you so much—you couldn't have made me happier." She dried her eyes with a napkin. "You can't imagine how much this means to me," she said huskily. "I'll love you forever."

I hadn't sealed my letter to Manny, so I told her he was my partner and closest friend, and had her read what I'd written. She handed back the letter and said, "I understand, though I pray we'll always be together."

"He's a good man, honey, the best there is." I licked the envelope flap and sealed the letter. "Thought it safer not to mail this from the Keys." I picked up her shopping bags. "Shall we go?"

On the way to our car I dropped the letter in a mailbox, and then we started back to the Keys.

At a gas stop I bought a copy of *El Nuevo Herald* for Susana to read while I drove. A few minutes later she exclaimed, "Jack—listen to this: 'Licenciado Pablo Antonio Aguilera, head of Mexico's anti-narcotics task force resigned yesterday. The President of the Republic congratulated him on a successful tenure, and American Embassy sources expressed regret over the loss of a close and effective collaborator in the drug wars.'" She glanced at me. "It goes on to say, 'Political observers suggest the timing of Aguilera's resignation frees him to advance his presidential ambitions over the next two years.'" She laid aside the paper and sighed.

I said, "Well, he's a man of his word."

"Jack, do you think he'll actually become president of Mexico?"

"Why not? He has influence, and enough money to bribe the president to nominate him." I shrugged. "That's tantamount to election."

"And what happens to Mexico?"

"It becomes open country for drug trafficking. One enormous landing field, a million times larger than your uncle Felipe's hacienda in Sonora."

"You've seen it?"

"Flown over it."

There was a pause before she asked, "Do you know how he died?"

"I read he was caught in crossfire between drug runners."

She nodded. "That's what I heard, too. Papá seemed very upset."

"Of course. His brother-in-law was a productive accomplice."

Susana looked away. "What a family," she said bitterly, "and what a hypocrite my father is."

"Well," I remarked, "he doesn't seem concerned over the possibility of Felipe's confession surfacing. Otherwise, he wouldn't have resigned his position so soon."

"Or," she suggested, "he's afraid it will become public and force him from his job."

"Just as possible," I acknowledged, "but either way he's not going to stop looking for us."

"No. I'm afraid he won't." She paused. "I wonder what Mamí thinks of it all."

"She's probably too accustomed to his political maneuverings to give it much thought—unless she knows the dirty side of his life."

"Oh, I'm sure she doesn't," she said quickly. "Her family is honorable, respected. If she knew the truth I'm sure she wouldn't have stayed with my father."

There was no point in prolonging speculation so I said nothing until, on Key Largo, I pulled in by the Holiday Inn and suggested we come back for the moonlight dinner cruise on the showboat at the pier.

"I'd love it, Jack. Once at Acapulco I went on a dinner cruise with my family, but I was too young to be allowed champagne. This will be much different—because I'll be with you."

So I bought tickets for the cruise leaving at eight and returning after midnight. Then we drove back to our house.

After a brief swim in the ocean we climbed the outside stairs and made love in the bedroom. Susana delighted in sharing some of the less acrobatic erotic positions, and I found that she liked having her bottom spanked until the cheeks were red, provoking a randy reaction.

The moonlight cruise took us through Florida Bay, close to mangrove islands populated with white egrets and herons. Tarpon fishermen in skiffs waved at us, and we watched a large Silver King tail-walking and churning up spray as it tried to throw the hook.

The seafood dinner wasn't bad; properly chilled champagne compensated for the average cuisine. Most of the couples were young, some obvious honeymooners, but there were a few seniors as well, and I felt that nostalgia had drawn them to the peaceful starlit cruise on a cut-rate Love Boat. Watching them, I wondered if Susana and I would grow old together. That entailed a formalized relationship—marriage, a house, children and their schooling, a job that could support it all, and further education for Susana. None of it possible while we were fugitives; a death threat hanging over me.

I noticed Susana occasionally turn the new ring on her finger and realized that subconsciously she was becoming accustomed to it. The symbolism was unspoken, but we honored its deep meaning.

I refilled our glasses with the last of the champagne, and said, "Tomorrow we might take an airboat trip through the Everglades, see raccoons and deer, huge gray herons, manatees and such like. I haven't done it since I was stationed at Boca Chica, and I think you'll enjoy it."

"Then we'll go."

But when we got back to the house Susana found a note she'd written to remind her that novice cooking classes were starting the next day. A southern lady was holding them in her house on Plantation Key. "Starting with boiling water," Susana laughed, "so I can do my share."

"Well, you wash dishes, make the bed, sweep the floor, and do laundry. Me, I grill stuff and put gas in the car—you do way more than your share. But I think you'll enjoy the classes."

"It's ten to two every day for two weeks—we eat lunch there—then another week if you want me to learn baking."

"Uh-uh, not now."

So the next day I drove Susana to an old frame house with peeling paint, set back from the road in a grove of old oak trees dripping with Spanish moss. A couple of old cars were rusting to one side of the house; there was a pen for chickens, and a hound dog lazing in the shadows.

I saw Mrs. Jefferson greet Susana and show her inside, then other students were arriving, so I went back to our own house.

That night I phoned Manny at his home and told him I'd sent a letter with contact information, and asked how things were going at the office.

"Good. So far, Wally hasn't asked about you, but if he does what should I tell him?"

"Say I've taken my plane to Mérida for engine overhaul and you don't know when I'll get back to Cozumel."

"Okay, that'll hold him for a while. Ah, glad you called because the Mexico City office finally got energized enough to put loose surveillance on Aguilera. Then, couple of days ago he showed up at the embassy and got a diplomatic visa for travel in the States."

"Any idea where he was going?"

"No destination given, he wasn't asked and didn't say. But it's likely he's drumming up electoral support in San Diego and Los Angeles and other large Mexican colonies along the border."

"Or establishing drug contacts to replace Paredes."

"That's possible, too." He paused. "Everything going okay with—well, you know what I mean?"

"First rate. I think this is going to turn into a longtime thing."

"So long as you're happy, Jack. You can be a mean bastard when you're not."

As I hung up, the thought of Aguilera in the U.S. chilled me. He was a focused, purposeful, and hugely successful criminal. As president of Mexico he would be perfectly positioned to do incalculable damage to the U.S. while making himself a megabillionaire like some of his predecessors at Los Pinos. If I could see that why couldn't our embassy? And do something about it?

In her first week of cooking classes Susana learned to boil and scramble eggs, make an omelet, fry bacon, grill steaks and fish, and sauté shrimp and mushrooms. Potatoes and vegetables were for the second week.

On Saturday we took the postponed airboat trip through the fringes of the Everglades, seeing lots of crocs, snakes and birds, a few manatees, but no panthers or deer. Back at the airboat shack we dined on sautéed frogs' legs, fries, and greens, washed down with cold beer.

Sunday we drove the short distance to Grassy Key, north of the Marathon airport, and flew in a pontoon Piper to Fort Jefferson down in the Dry Tortugas. It was a barren, isolated island, no water or tourist facilities, and the caretaker couple kept to themselves. But we'd brought along water jugs, snorkeling gear, and sunblock lotion and chose one of the narrow beaches that bordered three sides of the old red brick fort that was now a national monument. We enjoyed ourselves snorkeling in the shallows, bringing up colorful shells to take home, and drying our bodies under the hot sun.

Before the plane returned we went in again, saw a flurry of bait fish just offshore, and spotted a yard-long barracuda chasing slow learners. Susana shrieked, I grabbed her and snapped, "Get your hand out of the water. If he sees the ring he'll strike."

She shivered in my arms, gasping until the 'cuda whipped around and headed out to sea. Releasing Susana, I said, "They're meaner than sharks and mentally unstable, hit anything that shines or moves. And there's a deadly disease in their flesh—ciguatera—incurable, so don't eat barracuda." I paused. "When we're diving we'll see them occasionally. Never interfere with their feeding, or attract attention." I grunted. "One time a 'cuda attacked my dive knife—

the blade was bright stainless steel I'd neglected to paint black." I lifted my leg and pointed to faint dimple scars in the calf. "Never made that mistake again."

She sighed and moved aside. "Let's go on back and get dry, Jack, I've had enough excitement for one day."

Tired from our day of sun and swimming, we went to bed earlier than usual. The night air was warm and humid, no ocean breeze, only the ceiling fans cooled our bodies. Around midnight I half-woke to the burbling exhaust of a power boat offshore. But the sound of a passing racer wasn't unusual, so I lapsed into sleep as the sound diminished.

What woke me next was a harsh voice barking, "Don't move, Novak, you're covered." A powerful light blinded my eyes.

TWENTY

Beside me, Susana screamed and clung to my arm as the light struck her eyes. Dimly I made out three figures standing beside the bed. Armed.

"Susana," the same voice ordered, "get up and get dressed."

"No!" Shivering, she held me more tightly. "I won't."

"You will. If you don't I'll kill him now."

Slowly she sat up, covering her body with the sheet, and now I recognized the voice as her father's. Sobbing, she left the bed and began pulling on clothing. One man picked up my useless shotgun and began shucking shells from it. The other began binding my ankles with duct tape. He turned me over and taped my wrists behind me. Then pulled me on my back.

"Novak," said Licenciado Pablo Antonio Aguilera, "the situation is this. You abducted my daughter and seduced her. For that alone I should kill you. And you've been conspiring to destroy me—another reason to kill you."

Standing erect, boldly facing her father, Susana cried, "Don't, Papá, I'll never forgive you."

"Forgive?" he snorted. "You should beg *my* forgiveness. For betraying me. For being a little slut. You may have planned to spend the rest of your life with this gringo but I would never permit it." Bending over, he stuck the pistol muzzle under my chin. "A nobody. You betrayed me, humiliated me for a nobody—after all I've done for you." The pistol withdrew, and Aguilera shook his head. "Unbelievable ingratitude."

Susana sneered, "For ignoring me? For giving all your affection to your sons?"

"*Silencio!*" he roared. "You never lacked anything. You had the finest schools, unlimited money, everything a girl could want. And you run off with this . . . this . . . *pedazo de mierda.*" The words seemed to choke him. "This is the end of all that, no more humiliation. You're coming home with me and I'll make you into the kind of daughter you should have been."

"The daughter of a drug dealer," she said scornfully.

"Rumors. Unproven rumors."

She shrugged, gathered her purse from the bureau. "I'll go with you because you force me to. But if you harm Jack I'll vanish, you'll never see me again."

Aguilera said, "He lives for now—but if you try to see him I'll have him killed. I have better plans for you, *mi hija.*"

"I can imagine," she said hotly, and Aguilera turned to me. "Interfere and I'll kill you both. Understand?"

I nodded. "One question—how did you find us?"

He gestured at Susana. "She called Mamí. I traced the number."

To Susana I said, "You did that?"

She began to sob. "Jack, I'm so sorry—I shouldn't have, but I didn't want Mamí to worry." She turned away. "I ruined everything."

Aguilera took her arm, pulled her toward the doorway. Susana looked back at me and said, "I love you, Jack, I always will."

"I love you," I echoed, and watched them leave, heard their footsteps descend the outside stairs. The end of the affair, I thought, sat up and began pulling at the ankle tapes with my fingers. Aguilera had boxed me in, stripped away my options. Things were to go his way, or else . . .

Presently I heard the cough of an engine starting, then the engine's full-throated roar as the boat backed from the beach. Cleverly, they'd come by sea—where would they go now? His jet was probably standing by. A few hours and he'd have Susana home—a prisoner.

I pulled and plucked at the ankle tape as the speedboat gained speed and roared away. No slack in the tape, pulling it only tightened it. I needed a knife, had to get down to the kitchen . . .

Steps on the outside stairs, heavy steps coming up. Fast. Through the door came three masked men. Aguilera's staybehind clean-up crew. To murder me out of Susana's sight so she'd never know.

All three stood at bedside. One produced a knife, sawed through my ankle tape. "You're a sorry sonofabitch, Novak," a rough voice observed, "but you're alive."

I held out my wrists, he sliced the tape, freeing my hands, and I stood up. Gitman. "Christ," I said, "where were you when I needed you?" I lowered my legs over the bed edge and sat there naked, dazed. Too much was happening.

They pulled off their hood-masks and I saw Burgess and— Manny Montijo. "Where were we? Outside, Jack, keeping out of sight."

"Why, for God's sake? They could have killed me."

"But they didn't," Burgess observed. "Any gunshots an' we'da been here in a flash."

"A too-late flash," I said sourly, and stood up. "They took Susana."

"As her father had every right to do," Manny replied.

"Kidnapped her."

"Get real, Jack, you're the kidnapper if it came to that."

I pried myself off the bed and got the Añejo bottle from the bureau. After a long pull I shook myself, swallowed again before putting the bottle down. "How about some explanations? You guys are turned out like a fucking SWAT team but you did nothing to stop a crime in progress," I said disgustedly.

"What crime?" Manny asked. "Nothing stolen, no one harmed.

As far as the U.S. is concerned, Aguilera is a diplomat—we couldn't arrest him even if we wanted to."

"Even if he'd killed me?" I growled.

"Right. Even if he'd killed you. But we'd have done the others."

"And given the Licenciado a one-way ride in his pretty boat," Gitman added. "Make you feel better?"

"Okay," I said, "so much for what you might have done. What brought you here?"

"Jack," Manny said, "I told you Mexico City was surveilling Aguilera. On a phone tape they heard your girlfriend call her mama. She didn't realize Dad had caller ID recording it. His office traced your phone number, and when I learned he had it I realized something had to be done."

"Why not just warn me? Or was that too easy?"

"That would have told Aguilera his phone is tapped. Anyway, McManus okayed us coming here to keep you alive—if we could."

"You guys were a big help, can't thank you enough," I sneered.

"Jack, you got into this on your own—absconding with Aguilera's minor daughter wasn't the smartest move you could have made."

"She came voluntarily—after getting me out of that death house her Dad had me stashed in. She insisted. How could I say no?"

"Chivalrous to a fault," Manny remarked.

"Aguilera's making her a prisoner."

"He's her father. Lawfully, he can discipline her."

"Don't quote me the law, *compadre*," I snapped. "Her father's an outlaw and we all know it."

Manny shrugged. I said, "Aguilera's threatened to kill me if I try to contact Susana."

Burgess grunted. "Then, *viejo,* I guess you better not try."

Gitman nodded agreement. "Especially since Manny says he's likely to be the next Mex president. He can throw all kinds of shit at you, have you offed without trace."

"I know that," I said irritably, "but it gravels me to think of her locked up in a tower like Rapunzel."

"Me, too," Manny said, "but not every problem can be resolved. You had a good run with her, Jack, but it's over. Be reasonable. Mourn her, yes, but get on with your life."

"Thanks for all the advice and comfort, guys. You've been as helpful as a team of UN observers. So, what's next for you?"

"Nogales for me," Manny replied. "Houston for our friends. And you've been reassigned to San Antone."

"Starting when?"

"Wally says take your time getting there. Yesterday I talked to Carlos, your boat captain, told him you'd be getting back soon. He was relieved, having heard about the broken door from your house-keeper."

"Yeah, I better tidy up things there—before San Antone. Stay here tonight if you like."

Gitman said, "Our plane's at Marathon, parked near Aguilera's jet. We knew he was flying here, didn't know about the speedboat until we heard it come in. You're alive, we'll leave."

I shook hands with them, gave Manny an *abrazo,* and followed them down the stairs. As they walked down the access path darkness swallowed them. Presently I heard a car engine start, pull away. My rescuers were gone, leaving me resentful they hadn't intervened before Aguilera's party took off. As I went into the house I reflected that they had their reasons for inaction, though I took a different view.

Without Susana the house was more than empty, it was dead, along with our plans for a happy future. Susana's fault for calling Mamí, but she was young, hadn't been out in the world before, and in some ways was still a child. I couldn't criticize her too harshly but the sense of abandonment was strong, permeating my thoughts, par-alyzing them.

I poured a glass of milk and carried it up to the bedroom, added Añejo, and drank in the darkness. Alone.

After a while I gathered up the scattered shotgun shells and re-loaded the Winchester. Big help the shotgun, big fathead me. I hadn't rigged any warning system because I didn't believe Aguilera could ever find us.

And he wouldn't have but for Susana's naïveté.

Her father's threat would keep her from contacting me, but I was a poor loser and yearned for one more try at the Licenciado.

Even if it killed me.

I drank enough Añejo to make sleep possible, and in the morning woke with a pounding headache. In the kitchen I applied ice to head and neck and began listing Things To Do. Several sips of iced Añejo helped organize my thoughts, which I tried to divert from Susana.

The idea of cooked breakfast food was revolting, so I ate a mango and drank a glass of orange juice. Not soul food, but it was what I needed, and carried me into the office, where I typed a letter to Mrs. Evans, my landlady. I explained that a family crisis required us to vacate her house, and that I was not requesting a rent refund. I enclosed a front door key in the envelope and found stamps in her desk drawer. That much accomplished, I went upstairs and packed my clothing in one suitcase, Susana's in the other. After all, I mused, it was possible she'd come to Cozumel one day and find everything ready for her.

Next, I unloaded the shotgun and broke it for packing in my suitcase. Knowing Cozumel Customs of old, I was pretty sure I could get it through.

For a last time I looked around the bedroom where we'd spent so many happy hours—and where defeat had come unexpectedly last night. Then I carried the bags downstairs, locked the front door, and put the bags in the Toyota.

From the house I drove to Abraham Watling's cottage and honked the horn. Abraham didn't appear, and the place looked deserted and even more neglected than before, so I continued up US 1 to the used car lot on Key Largo.

From the office shack came a short, well-fed man with mustache and slicked-back hair. "Good morning, sir," he said, "also *buenos días*." Stepping back, he surveyed the Toyota before saying, "In the market for something newer?"

"Not exactly," I replied. "Actually, I'm receptive to an offer."

"Wanna sell, eh?"

"You got it?"

"Figure in mind?"

"You tell me."

He fingered his mustache, kicked the tires, and came back to me. "I know this car. Sold it to Abe Watling."

"So you know it's a good car."

"Not so fast, sir. It *was* a good car." He winked and gave me an oily smile. "Two hundred, sir. It's a trash car now."

"But a good trash car. "Two fifty."

"Two twenty-five. Cash."

"And a ride to the bus stop."

"Done."

I followed him into the office shack, signed transfer papers, and received green bills in exchange. He drove me to the bus stop, I unloaded the suitcases and waited twenty minutes for the next northbound bus. Needless to say, the a/c wasn't working so I sweated all the way to Bayside Park where I caught a taxi to Miami International Airport.

As usual, the airport was crowded with travelers, Europeans with rucksacks and schlepsacks, Americans with suitcases and backpacks. Nobody looked particularly happy, or eager to board their flights. At the Mexicana counter I got in line behind ten members of a scuba club from Oshkosh, paid for my ticket, and posted my letter to Mrs. Evans; the airport postmark would lend credence to my tale.

Two and a half hours to takeoff, so I went up to the hotel restaurant and lunched on lamb chops and asparagus with a split of Beaujolais. Inevitably I visualized Susana across from me and that depressed my mood. After Cuban coffee I went down to the departure gate and found myself wondering where she was. Her father wouldn't be sending her to a Spanish convent, or back to the English School; he'd want her under his eye and thumb until satisfied her spirit was broken. Susana was smart enough to simulate submission and eventually regain her freedom. Doubtless Aguilera would have her rabbit-tested to make damn sure his daughter wasn't pregnant by the hated gringo. If she were (and I was certain she wasn't) he'd simply have the baby aborted. Focused as Aguilera was, it would still take him a while to organize the situation to his satisfaction, and that interval gave me time to ponder and consider his vulnerabilities.

If any.

During the flight, the scuba club got pretty rowdy on free drinks. The cabin attendants didn't seem to care, but I thought the club members would be prudent not to dive until that night when metabolism and blood alcohol levels were normal. Every month or so some imprudent diver had to be pulled out of the strong Palancar current exhausted or dead, having dived too deep and stayed too long.

During a boring stopover at Mérida, most passengers got off and bought liquor, Cuban cigars, and comical straw hats. I stayed in my seat drowsing until the plane took off on the short hop to San Miguel airport.

From there I phoned *Corsair* and raised Carlos, who said he was glad I was back, not dead as he'd earlier feared. I asked him to come to my house later, and took a taxi home.

Everything was tidy; broken doorglass replaced, buckshot pits in the wall painted over invisibly. Freezer still stocked with meat and fish, and ample Añejo to take me through the rest of the month.

In late afternoon Ramona arrived, alerted to my return by Carlos. Rather than have her ask directly, I gave her a sanitized version of my unexplained departure that seemed to satisfy whatever curiosity she had. In the bedroom she unpacked my suitcase, hung up clothing, and took laundry off to the washer. When she opened Susana's suitcase she asked what to do with the señorita's clothing. I wanted it available but I also wanted it out of sight to avoid constant reminders.

For dinner Ramona sautéed a dolphin fillet and served it with salad on the patio. From there I could see my Seabee turning with the tide, and reflected that I hadn't flown it since qualifying Molly for the Mile High Club. I loved my little plane and felt happiest when I was at the controls.

Carlos arrived after dinner, we exchanged *abrazos* and had brandy together while we talked. Business was excellent, he said, and pulled out a large wad of pesos—my share. I told him I'd been thinking of buying another sport fishing boat, and asked if he knew any for sale. He wasn't aware of any, he said, but would look and ask around. "Same size," I told him, "or possibly a bit smaller for parties of four." Sensing his concern that I might want to invest his equity in a new boat, I said, "I can make a down payment, and look to the bank for the rest."

That cheered him, and after finishing his drink he got up, saying he had an early party booked and wanted to get to bed. Briefly I considered going out with him to divert my mind, then decided I ought to check out the Seabee before doing anything else.

So he went off, Ramona left a little later, and I was alone in my vulnerable home.

Again, I drank a lot of Añejo to ease me into sleep, suffered a morning hangover that subsided after I swam a dozen lengths alongside pier and plane. After a mainly-fruit breakfast I got out my moneybelt and counted remaining cash. Between Susana's contribution and my op funds there were more than forty thousand dollars. Enough for a healthy down payment on a second boat.

Later I was hosing down the Seabee, rinsing off crusted salt spray from control surfaces, windshield, and propellor, when I noticed a man standing at the end of the pier.

He wore a straw hat, shirt, tie, and two-piece suit. Not customary attire on Cozumel, so I cut off the hose and walked toward him. One hand slid inside his jacket and I felt a prickle of fear. One of Aguilera's thugs? "What do you want?" I called, and saw him bring out a credential with a gold-blue shield. "I want to talk with you, Novak. Things need to be said."

He tilted back his hat brim and I saw the unsmiling face of a man who had once been my supervisor.

"Hello, Fred," I said, "let's go inside."

TWENTY–ONE

In the living room Fred Dorschner took off hat and jacket and loosened his tie. A tall, thin-faced man with hair that had grayed since I'd last seen him. After looking around, he said, "Nice place."

"Comfortable, but as I found out, vulnerable. Drink?"

"Why not?"

In the kitchen I got a bowl of ice, grapefruit juice, Stoli vodka and Añejo, and brought them to the coffee table. "No bourbon," I said, "sorry."

"Who could turn down cold vodka in the heat of the day?"

We made drinks, sipped, and looked at each other. "So," I said, "what brings you to this off-the-track Caribbean colony?"

"You, Jack. And your recent capers." He paused. "Since we worked in San Diego I've become regional supervisor out of Houston. First, I want to thank you for your part in rescuing Paco Pazos—he's doing well, by the way. Out of hospital, and recovering at home. But we won't be sending him to Mexico again."

I drank Añejo and said, "Good decision."

"I think so. He's being allowed to choose duty in the States or South America. You've been assigned to San Antonio, but that could change."

"In what way?" I was feeling my way carefully with Fred. I hadn't know him well before, and now he held a position of considerable power. The regional supervisor could fire me, give me a dead-end assignment, or impose restrictions on what I could do. At that point I wasn't ready to accept any such career changes.

"Well, Jack, to say the truth you've become something of a hot potato. I'm not one to cavil at unorthodox methods—as long as they're successful. But when the heat gets intolerably hot in Washington, part of my job description says I should look into the cause."

"And right now you're looking at me. Tell me more, Fred."

"More involves some sort of vendetta you have with an important Mexican politician—to wit, Pablo Antonio Aguilera, who until recently headed our sister—or brother—antinarcotics task force in Mexico. You're aware of all that, of course."

"His late brother-in-law put Aguilera in our sights."

"Paredes's confession." He took a long pull from his glass and said, "Really appreciate your hospitality, Jack. We should have socialized more in Dago but I was—let's say, caught up in some difficult situations." He shrugged. "Neither here or there. To get down to basics, Aguilera has told the Ambassador—and of course our Mexico City office—that working in Mexico could be dangerous to your health."

I grunted. "He told me so himself—and more."

"After you ran off with his daughter."

"He said that?"

Dorschner shook his head. "For sociopolitical reasons he could never admit such a stain on his family honor."

"He makes delicate self-serving distinctions. It's okay to orchestrate massive drug running and corrupt the upper levels of his government—but intolerable to acknowledge the actions of an independent-minded daughter."

"Yeah." He spilled more vodka into his glass. "The code of Mafia chieftains."

I sipped more Añejo. "How'd you hear about Susana?"

"Grapevine."

"He broke into my house the other night, held a gun on me

while his thugs tied me up. Made nasty threats before taking Susana away. Plays the outraged parent but I wasn't convinced."

"You tell him that?"

I shook my head. "I was concerned for Susana's safety."

"Then Manuel Montijo and your two friends arrived."

"Too late to do any good. But you know that."

"I know it because I authorized them to go, and take charge if necessary." He looked around the room. "Now you're recovering from battle fatigue. How's it going, Jack?"

"Slowly." I added ice to my glass.

"Washington says you're to stay away from Aguilera, forget he exists. His future is a matter for the highest levels of government."

"His government?"

"Ours."

"Knowing what you do about Aguilera, you go along with that?"

"I go along with lots of things I'm not comfortable with—that's on the ticket we signed."

Dorschner had aged since I'd last seen him in San Diego. There were bags under his eyes, and the whites showed spidery veins. He wasn't known as a booze fighter, but in DEA anything was possible. I said, "Did this grapevine also tell you Aguilera had me kidnapped and flown to a drug house in Mexico City?"

"No comment."

"He made me an offer I couldn't refuse—but Susana arranged my escape. That's why we went to ground, Fred, to stay alive."

After a while he said, "I can understand that. You owed her."

"Still do."

"Payment may be uncollectable." He finished his drink, built another. "Any salt?"

I brought a shaker and watched him put the finishing touches on a Salty Dog. He drank with the concentration of a thirsty man. Then he said musingly, "You remember San Diego?"

"No good memories."

"Me either."

I waited a while before saying, "One memory stays in mind— I don't talk about it but it's there." Dorschner was studying the surface of his drink; he seemed not to have heard me, so I went on. "There was this doctor, a pediatrician, who hooked a young girl patient on Percodans, and debauched her. She was only, oh, maybe thirteen, and too frightened to tell her parents." I paused. "Until she was pregnant. Well, the law being what it is her parents knew the doctor couldn't be convicted of statutory rape on her word alone. And because of her father's position they didn't want the embarrassment of a trial. Remember any of that, Fred?"

"What's the rest of the story?"

"The doctor kept a boat down on the marina, often stayed on it overnight. So, one Monday morning he showed up dead, neatly shot in the center of his forehead."

"Guess I read about it."

"No suspects, no trial, no conviction, and the doc had no known enemies—except the anonymous parents of girls he'd se- duced and abused. And they weren't telling about their personal tragedies."

He licked his lips, "You said something about her father's posi- tion."

"I heard he worked for the government in some capacity, state or federal, but he was never publicly named, so that was probably rumor, too." I finished my drink and set aside the glass. "Whoever shot the doc paid off a debt of honor." I watched his taut features. "Wouldn't you say?"

He drew in a deep breath, expelled it. "If that was the situation I'd say the doc had it coming, the killer did right."

"That's what I'd say, Fred. I knew a couple of SD cops on the case. Drinking buddies. Heard the tale in smoky bars and diners. They weren't looking too hard for the guy who drilled the doc be- cause—see, they'd talked to the doc's nurses and office help, learned

SONORA

enough about the doc's predilections to persuade them his death was a rare instance of justified reprisal. Eventually the cops filed the case away—no leads, nothing." I swallowed. "You had a young daughter in those days, didn't you?"

His hands had knotted until the veins stood out. "Still do. Jennie's in college now. Sophomore at Rice."

"Glad to hear it. If I marry again I'd like children."

"They make a difference," he said tightly. "You'll see."

For a while we drank in silence. Then I said, "If you have no further warnings for me, how about staying overnight—at least for dinner? I'll throw a pair of thick primes on the grill while we watch the sun go down."

"Like to, but I'm due back in Houston tonight. My family expects me."

I added ice to my empty glass, splashed Añejo over the cubes, and lifted it. "Have a good flight."

"I'll drink to that." He did and we did. Then I said, "To make sure I got the instructions right—nothing was said about Susana?"

He shook his head. "Nothing. But here's a curious thing, Jack. After all the trouble Aguilera went to tracking you down, taking her back to Mexico, you'd think he'd have her in garret in the family home."

"That's what I'd think."

"Instead, he took her to his Acapulco manse—like rewarding her with a fun vacation." He drank from his glass, very little left. "Ever see Aguilera's Acapulco showplace?"

"No."

"Built on a cliff overhanging the ocean. Lower rooms carved out of solid rock, steps leading down the cliff face to the water. He keeps three or four speedboats there. Takes out movie stars, singers, diplomats, politicians. Big party guy. Entertains all the time. I hear his daughter is a real beauty; maybe he wants to show her off to his guests."

"Maybe." My hands tightened.

"Any way I look at him, Aguilera is very bad news. I'd like to send Gitman and Burgess after him, but that's not allowable."

"Too bad," I remarked. "Guy leads a charmed life."

"Maybe some competitor will put him down. A Cali baron, or a rival politico who wants the presidency enough to assassinate him."

"He's bound to have enemies."

"Which is why he keeps good security around the Acapulco place—electronic surveillance, guards . . ." He looked at his watch. "Good talking with you, Jack. Glad we're not back in San Diego." He got up, and I walked beside him to his waiting car. Before getting in he said, "Incidentally, the pediatrician practiced in La Jolla—the girl's family was in San Diego."

"I'll remember."

"You've got some good years ahead of you, Jack, so don't fuck up now. And, watch your ass." He waved as the car pulled away.

Walking back to the house, I pondered the strange visitation. Fred had done as ordered—warned me away from Aguilera, while describing his Acapulco setup in detail, and indirectly letting me know where Susana was. I'd brought up the doc's unsolved murder to check Fred's reaction, but he'd given nothing away—unless you count body language. And body language doesn't convict. He'd left a lot of rage and sorrow behind him in San Diego, and I was glad his daughter was doing well. God knows how much deep therapy she'd had to undergo—but young minds heal faster than old, so it was Fred who carried unclosed wounds. And the girl's mother, his wife.

On the surface, the perverse pediatrician, and Licenciado Aguilera, seemed to have nothing in common. Until you considered that for their crimes both men deserved to die.

After a while I wandered along the pier and watched the Seabee bobbing in a gentle breeze. Direct flight to Acapulco over the

Tehuantepec jungles was a thousand miles, twice the plane's fuel range. If I flew there I'd have to land at Oaxaca to refuel, stop there again on the return leg. Each way I'd be airborne five hours, barring headwinds, and no emergency landing sites in the jungle. In 'Nam I'd had more than enough jungle, so the prospect was unappealing. Besides, I had only a sketchy idea where Aguilera's lofty palace was located. On a cliff, Dorschner said. Well, there were plenty of cliffs to choose from, many topped with luxurious homes facing the sea.

Realizing that on-the-ground reconnaissance was essential, I reserved a seat on the morning flight to Acapulco, and spent the rest of the day at the docks and boatyard, checking the availability of a second boat. The only one for sale was on the ways, and the hull showed considerable toredo worm damage. Not for me. Well, maybe Carlos would locate one through other boat captains.

Before noon I hired a tourism driver to take me along the waterfront and point out homes of the rich and famous. He gave me a map of the area, and as we went along named homes of Pedro Armendariz, Ingrid Bergman, John Wayne, María Felix, Tyrone Power, "El Indio" Fernandez, Lucho Gatica, and Dolores del Río. After his recital, I said, "Some of those folks are dead."

"Dead?" He shrugged. "Who knows? Maybe just hiding."

It was a good Mexican answer but I hadn't gotten what I came for. After a while, the driver turned up a road that paralleled the ocean and pointed out retreats of prominent Mexicans who were not professional entertainers. Here, the home of the Pemex union chief, there the head of Mexicana, beside it the Minister of Finance, and finally a long stuccoed wall topped with broken glass and barbed wire that, he said, protected the mansion of Licenciado Aguilera, head of the government's antinarcotics enforcement program. Dividing the wall was a wide grilled gate through which I could glimpse a roving guard, and beyond him a large two-story manse topped by a seaside campanile and a satellite dish. Several homes had screened jai alai courts, and Aguilera's was one of them. Turning the car around, the driver said, "Many people believe the Licenciado will be the next president of the republic."

"Is that good?"

He shook his head. "They're all *bandidos,*" he declared. "Maybe Aguilera won't steal as much as the others, he's already a wealthy man."

Wealth seldom stifled greed, I reflected, but said nothing as we descended the road.

"Anything else you like to see, señor?"

"I've seen enough, thanks," and marked Aguilera's pleasure dome on the map. "Take me to the beach."

"No girls? I can take you where girls will give you a good time."

"Too old, too tired," I told him. "Just the beach."

As we neared sea level I wondered if Susana was behind the peach-colored wall, locked up inside the peach-colored house. Only one way out, by water—like Alcatraz. Susana's father had her where he wanted her.

On the beach I rented a clothing locker and stripped down to the swimming briefs I'd worn under my pants. The parasail concession was located near the water, where thrill-seekers donned parachute harnesses and were towed aloft by the power boat idling offshore. My turn came half an hour later, and as I strapped on the harness I told the operator where I wanted to go. "To impress a lady friend," I explained. He gave me a thumbs-up, the rope tightened, and I followed it into the water, the multicolored chute billowing out behind for a smooth liftoff.

As the towboat accelerated the chute rose, and presently I was moving along a couple of hundred feet above the ocean, exhilarated by the rushing wind. Two minutes later I spotted Aguilera's peach-colored palace, his jai alai fronton, tennis court, garage, guest house—or guard barracks—and the mansion itself with a flat area for sun lounges. A guard with binoculars studied the surroundings from his campanile post, another guard sat halfway down the stairway carved from the cliff face. At the bottom of the stairs a landing stage separated three speedboats. No one in the boats or on the stage.

As my towboat turned back I saw that the upper stairs ended at a grilled gate set into the rock, sealing off a passage behind it. To reach the mansion's upper regions from the ocean you had to climb the stairs and pass through the security gate. By land and sea Aguilera's retreat was immune to unwelcome arrivals. In a word, impregnable.

Nearing the beach, the towboat slowed, and my chute and I lost altitude. Presently, the pilot maneuvered the boat so that I came down on warm sand, and heard applause from onlookers. After unhitching the chute harness, I paid the beach boy and tipped the boat pilot for following instructions. Then I retrieved clothing from the locker, and caught a taxi to the airport.

By nightfall I was home.

After dinner I worked at the dining room table sketching the layout of Aguilera's *palazzo* as seen from above, then a slant view of the cliff face with its stairs, guard, and floating boat stage.

I'd seen one roving guard from the road, two from the air, so I estimated four guards working around the clock. Four on duty, four sleeping in the guest house/barracks. Eight minimum.

I scanned the map provided by my driver for landmarks visible after dark and recalled a tall microwave relay tower north of Aguilera's manse. I marked it on the map, figuring if I could spot its blinking lights through the darkness, a reciprocal bearing would intersect Aguilera's place. Okay, Novak, you can locate it by night—what do you do then?

Why, very simple. Set down the Seabee near the landing stage and scale the steps, neutralize the guard, and force your way through the grill. Inside, go room to room until you find Susana, take her down the stairs to the Seabee, and fly away. A fantasy scenario, Novak, dream on.

I was yawning. No more Añejo tonight. I was tired from compressed travel, the adrenalin rush of parasailing, the blaze of the Acapulco sun. Time to rack down for the night and postpone serious consideration to *mañana*. But not before charging my shotguns and laying them on the bed, where Susana ought to be.

After breakfast on the patio I went down the pier and peered through the planking at small fish nibbling barnacles on the pilings. The Seabee bumped the pier, and I gazed at it, wondering if the little plane could haul me all the way to Acapulco—and back. I'd never flown it that far before, and four five-hundred mile legs were a real challenge to plane and pilot. Was the whole idea insane? Was I so infatuated that I'd lost all sense of proportion? Though isolated, Susana was safe from harm, and logic told me that my chances of leaving Acapulco alone and alive were as slim as winning the national lottery. Leaving with Susana reduced those chances even more.

As I sat on the edge of the pier I told myself that going for her through armed guards was close to suicidal. Surely there was another approach drifting somewhere in my mind just out of reach.

Trying to phone her or reach her with a letter was futile. Her phone—if she had access to one—would be monitored, mail intercepted. Forget it. Bribe a servant to carry a message? Equally dubious. Aguilera's servants would be well paid; they'd take the bribe and report it to their master. The Licenciado would laugh himself sick—before having me wasted.

As the Seabee turned I noticed something I hadn't seen when I hosed it down two days ago—a slight oil smudge on the engine nacelle. I hadn't put it there because I hadn't opened the inspection port in the last month. But if someone had opened and closed it in the dark he wouldn't have noticed the oil trace.

Now I felt neck hairs prickling.

Slowly I pulled the Seabee to the pier and stared at the smudge until convinced a finger had left it. Mouth dry, I hesitated, then opened the hinged port and looked inside.

Bright sunlight illuminated the interior, showed fuel lines, distributor cap—and two sticks of dynamite wired to the magneto.

TWENTY-TWO

As bombs went it wasn't a complicated rig. Two wires from the magneto led to detonators inside the two red sticks. Turning on the ignition would send current into the detonators, exploding the dynamite and demolishing the plane and anyone inside; in this case, me.

Rage flooded my mind. My reflex impulse was to rip out the deadly device and fling it far into the ocean. Then reason prevailed. Treating the bomb roughly might detonate it, so I stepped back and thought things through. Hands unsteady, I got wire clippers from the plane's tool kit, looked and peered around and under the bomb until satisfied it was as uncomplicated as it appeared. With a pocket knife I cut through the adhesive tape binding the dynamite to the magneto until it was in my left hand. Just then a gust of wind bumped the plane's nose against the pier, almost overbalancing me. But I managed to hold on, and when the plane stopped swinging I focused on the two electrical wires. Sweat dripped down my face, stinging my eyes; my palms were damp with their own perspiration. I wiped my right hand on my trousers and gripped the wire clippers.

After studying the wiring again, I sucked in a deep breath and snipped the nearest wire. No explosion, so I cut the second, freeing the bomb with my left hand. Exhaling, I stepped back on the pier and lowered the bomb to the planking.

As I gazed at it I reflected that it could be a decoy bomb, one of several undiscovered. Meaning I had to check the plane thoroughly before flying again—and in that moment I had no desire to fly.

To fully inspect the Lycoming engine I had to remove the nacelle and examine the interior with a flashlight. That took an hour of hot, sweaty work, accomplished slowly and carefully. Next I checked the control cables, and drew the radio from its housing. Then rudder pedals and yoke. Looked under the seats and their cushions, wound the wheels partway down to expose their wells, and in the end found nothing.

Stripped, I went into the water to cool down, swam around the plane, and submerged to look under it in case an explosive limpet was stuck to the hull. Finally I decided I'd found the only bomb, got out of the water, and dried off in the sun.

As I looked at the dynamite bomb I realized it had been placed the night before I went to Acapulco, or while I was away. Aguilera hadn't actually put the bomb in my engine; he'd ordered it done. Had to be the Licenciado—nobody else bore me such virulent hatred.

What to do about him? What could I do? He'd kidnapped me and issued a death threat, tracked me down to Islamorada and rendered me helpless, again threatened my life, and taken Susana. I wanted to kill him outright—destroying his reputation with Paredes's confession tape was no longer enough. But I had to consider Susana. Because of her, Aguilera enjoyed a high degree of immunity. No matter how much Susana might despise her father, my killing him would cause a barrier between us, and that was no way to begin a life together. Nor could I live comfortably and securely as long as Aguilera lived. So I was faced with a dilemma that had to be resolved.

Hot and sweaty from the sun, I cooled off in the water and went inside to dry off and dress, having left the inert bomb on the patio.

As I was putting on sandals, Ramona knocked on my door and said I had a visitor. Not expecting any, I said, "Come in," and when she entered I asked, "What visitor?"

"I don't know, señor, but she asked for you."

"She?"

"*Sí—una dama, señor.* Very well dressed and—how shall I say it?—aristocratic looking."

Not knowing anyone on Cozumel answering to Ramona's description, I was curious about the unexpected visitor. "Show her into the living room, and I'll be there shortly."

Shoes on, I combed my hair and went to the living room, where a lady was seated on the sofa. Her black hair was pulled back from her forehead, Spanish-style, her face was oval with prominent black eyebrows, accenting an ivory complexion. She wore a coarse linen blouse colorfully embroidered with Aztec glyphs, and as she rose I saw that she was in long, flowing, pleated linen slacks, cork-soled high-heeled shoes on her feet. Around her neck, a long strand of coral beads, and diamond rings on her fingers. "I'm Jack Novak, Señora."

Extending her hand, she said in English, "And I am Sara Beltrán de Aguilera—Susana's mother." She smiled. "Her *Mamí.*"

I swallowed. "Señora, I hardly know what to say. I'm delighted to meet you, having heard a great deal about you from your daughter. Please be seated."

"Thank you." She crossed her legs and looked at me. "To say I've been curious about you is putting it mildly. Susana told me so much about you that I decided it was past time to meet you and form my own opinion." She paused. "My husband's departure for New Orleans this morning gave me opportunity to come here without his knowledge."

"I see. Ah—may I offer you something cool after your journey?"

"Oh, iced tea, lemonade, anything if it's not too much trouble."

Ramona, who had been eavesdropping, nodded at me and left for the kitchen. I said, "As you probably know, your husband and I are not exactly friends."

"As my daughter gave me to understand. She also told me

things about Pablo's life that I had never known, and said you were the source of her information."

"I thought she ought to know why the Licenciado is determined to silence me."

She sighed. "Susana mentioned a videotape of Felipe Paredes confessing to a life of crime, naming my husband and a number of his associates as drug traffickers and worse. Is—is there such a tape, Mr. Novak?"

"There is—Susana took a copy to your husband."

She eyed me. "Wasn't that rather bold of you? I mean, to stir up trouble for yourself."

"I regarded it as an effort to prolong my life."

Ramona came in with lemonade glasses on a tray, set the tray on the coffee table, and withdrew. "Such a good idea, Mr. Novak," she said, and drank deeply.

"Call me Jack, won't you?"

"With pleasure—if you'll call me Sara."

To avoid rudeness I hadn't been staring at her, but as I drank, I saw how much her features resembled Susana's. Her sons were of college age, and Susana was seventeen, so I estimated Sara's age at forty-four or -five, though she looked younger. Her face turned toward a window and she said, "I can believe anything bad about Felipe Paredes, but I'm not yet used to seeing Pablo Antonio as a *narcotraficante,* and I suppose it will take a while." She sipped lengthily. "I've watched my husband's political rise, known of his aspirations to the presidency, neither of which I can condemn him for. But I have little in common with most of his associates—army people, politicians, merchants, promoters . . . and their wives."

She turned back to me. "Pablo Antonio has not been what I would call an ideal husband. I knew of his infidelities and attributed them to his Hispanic machismo. I resented that side of him less than his treatment of our sons and daughters. Our sons—*gracias a Dios*—are being educated away from his influence, but Susana—he's always regarded her as a material possession, obligated to do his bidding. In return he showered her with what he thought were compensations—foreign schools, jewelry, the Ferrari, and as much money as she could possibly spend." She paused. "So I can't criticize her for the things she's done to show independence. We've always been close—which is why she telephoned to assuage my fears and unwittingly gave my husband the clue he needed to find the two of you. I'm very sorry about that, Jack, and I imagine you're much sorrier."

I nodded. "Because I lost her."

"You care for her, don't you?"

"Deeply."

"And she swears she loves you—do you believe that?"

"I do."

She breathed deeply. "Supposing Susana were to marry you—what sort of future do you see for the two of you?"

"It's something we were discussing when the Licenciado took her away. Since then I haven't wanted to focus on something so problematical . . . virtually hopeless."

Her head tilted as she said, "You don't seem to be a man who gives up easily. Are you?"

"Never thought so."

"And my daughter describes you as very determined—commendable if not carried to extremes."

"My life has known extreme situations, dangerous moves, but so far I'm alive. I try not to act impulsively but sometimes I do."

"So do we all. Susana's going off with you was an impulsive act. At first I was heartsick, then hearing Pablo Antonio raging against the two of you I realized she feared her father's anger. So—" her hands spread "—I couldn't criticize her."

"She saved my life that night."

She nodded. "And now that I've seen you I know how right she was. All right—" she sat forward "—now that I see how *simpático* you are I understand her plunging into a love affair with you. I don't want to interfere, Jack, by no means. But as a mother my interest is in her happiness, solely that. I also understand the compulsions of a deep physical attraction between you. But five years from now, ten years—will each of you still love and honor the other?"

"I can't predict the future, nor can you. The life I live, the only one I know, is how I earn my living. I'll always be able to support Susana, though not in the luxury she's always known. She would be an American wife, not a Mexican one, with freedom but lesser expectations. If that's not enough for her then we ought to leave things as they are: me at loose ends, she a prisoner in her father's castle."

Her right hand was worrying the coral beads. She looked down at them before saying, "Is that satisfactory to you?"

"Of course not," I said angrily, "and let me ask this—is it satisfactory to you that your daughter is a prisoner?"

She looked away. "A fair question—and the answer is, of course no."

"So—what's to be done about it?"

She held up her empty glass. "May I have a little wine? White and very cold?"

"I'll have some, too." In the kitchen I took a bottle of Murrieta from the fridge, opened it, and carried it on a tray with two glasses. My visitor was standing at a window looking out at the sea. I hadn't seen her profile before, but now I saw that she was narrow waisted and generously endowed above. I guessed that her unclothed figure could be described as voluptuous, probably more so than Susana's which was not yet fully mature. Taking her glass, she said, "A lovely view, Jack—and the tranquility so relaxing."

After our glasses touched I said, "Before you arrived there wasn't much tranquility."

"No?"

I drew her to the side of the window for a broader view of the patio. "See those two red sticks taped together?"

"Yes."

"Dynamite."

"*Dynamite?* What—?"

"Recovered from the engine of my plane. Wired to explode when I turned the ignition key."

"Oh, Jack!" she exclaimed with a horrified expression. "Who could have put it there?"

"Who hates me enough to want me dead?"

Her eyes closed. "You—you mean my husband."

"He could easily order it done. No Novak, no *problema*."

She found a chair and sat down. "I don't want to believe that, but I must believe you," she said tremulously, "after everything you and Susana have told me." She reached for my hand and squeezed it. "I'm so very glad you weren't killed."

For a while we drank in silence. Then she set aside her glass. "We were discussing Susana's situation. I sense that her father intends to keep her a house prisoner for weeks, perhaps months."

"How's she taking it?"

"Pretends submissiveness, but she resists and is bitterly resentful—and she longs for you."

"Can't you get her out of there?"

"If I could I would—but though I'm free to come and go, the guards would never let Susana leave." She leaned forward and her gaze searched my face. "Is there nothing you can do?"

"I've thought about it, believe me. And I've studied the mansion from ground and air. It's well fortified and well policed. So far I haven't conceived a plan that would let us escape together, alive."

"But you're willing to try."

"More than willing."

She rose, and holding her glass walked slowly back and forth. "Perhaps I can help. Next week Susana will be eighteen. Her father is planning a big fiesta to celebrate it—we've invited more than a hundred guests." Halting in front of me she looked down. "Why don't you come, too?"

"Me?" I stared at her.

"There's no one Susana would rather see at her party, Jack, and it can be done."

"Tell me how."

She smiled and took a seat beside me. "An invitation would get you into the house, and you'll see me and Susana in the receiving line."

"Beside her father, Sara—be sensible. After Pablo Antonio sees me I'm finished."

"Jack—didn't I say it's a costume party? Everyone wearing masks until midnight."

"That's better," I said, relieved. "Okay, I'm inside, unrecognized. What then?"

"When the fireworks begin I'll leave the line with Susana and take her to a private room. You meet us there, and I'll take you to a passageway that opens through the side wall. I thought it strange when my husband had the tunnel made, but now I suppose he expected the police to come one day, and wanted a way to escape."

I nodded. "Seems likely. All right, we're outside the wall. What then?"

"You'll have a car, won't you? Drive to the airport and take the first flight from Acapulco. Or take the highway to Mexico City and fly from there."

"Fine, but where do we fly to?"

She grimaced. "Oh, Jack, do I have to do it all for you? My husband won't suspect you were even at the party. You could come here."

I thought it over. "Not a bad idea." I was beginning to like it.

Opening her purse, she took out an invitation engraved on cream-colored stock and gave it to me. I said, "You came prepared."

"I did. And while you fill my glass, I'll sketch where the meeting room is."

I refilled our glasses and noticed Ramona in the hallway. When I went to her she asked, "Will the señora be having lunch here?"

"I don't think so, and you can go now."

"Is there nothing else, señor?"

"Nothing, and thank you." I returned to Sara, who explained the diagram she'd drawn. After that I said, "Susana shouldn't travel in her costume."

"Of course not. She'll change in the private room and be ready to leave with you."

"I'll wear a tux to get in. Outside it will be less noticeable than a costume until I can change into street clothes."

"And mask," she smiled, and looked at her platinum wrist-watch. "My flight to Acapulco leaves just after six. May I just stay here and relax until then?"

"Wouldn't have it otherwise."

"You have no appointments, commitments?"

"None, Sara."

She drained her glass and stood up. "I'd love to see your plane, Jack."

So we went down the pier, and as she gazed at the Seabee she said, "I've never seen a plane like it."

"Not many still flying. For maintenance I take it to Mérida. I don't think there are more bombs in it, but I'm not ready to take it up."

She removed her shoes, pulled up her slacks, and dangled her feet in the water. "Feels wonderful. Mind if I swim for a while?"

"Not at all."

"If I'd embarrass you, say so."

"Takes a lot to embarrass me."

Smiling, she removed her watch and the strand of coral beads, and pulled off her embroidered shirt. Then she wriggled out of her slacks and dropped into the water. Like her daughter she wore a black lace bra and matching panties. Her figure, though more mature than Susana's, was equally well formed. I gathered up her clothing and jewelry and took it into the guest bedroom, bringing back towels, a terrycloth robe, and an iced glass of Añejo.

Watching her swim around the plane I reflected that my future mother-in-law and I were getting on surprisingly well. Apparently I measured up to her standard, and she more than exceeded mine. She glided to the pier, held to it, and asked, "What are you drinking?"

"Añejo." I held out the glass, and she sipped. "Ummm, I'd like some."

So I left and brought back a filled glass with the bottle, and extra ice. She came out of the water and sat beside me as we drank together. After a while she said, "I suppose you know my family is in Monterrey."

"Susana mentioned it."

"I went to the American School there, then Briarcliff Manor on the Hudson."

"That explains your perfect English."

"Thank you." Her glass clinked against mine, sun glinting on the floating ice. "I want Susana to have more education than she has."

"So do I."

"Good. Mexican men usually prefer uneducated mates they can dominate. Americans are very different." She paused. "Susana showed me the ring you gave her, so I suppose you plan on marrying."

I nodded.

"I'll be very happy to have you as my son-in-law."

"And your husband?"

She shrugged. "The less he knows, the better for us all."

My shirt was soaked with perspiration. I pulled it off and stretched it on the planking to dry in the sun. Sara said, "You should cool off in the water. I feel terrific."

So I shed my slacks and slipped into the water, wearing my jockey shorts. The current brushed us together but Sara made no effort to move away. We sipped our drinks and looked at the light blue, nearly cloudless sky. After a while she said, "You know, Jack, we could be on some deserted Caribbean isle, anywhere. The quiet, isolated setting appeals to me. So unlike Acapulco. You're happy here, aren't you?"

"Usually—but it gets lonely at times."

She took a long swallow of Añejo. The current seemed to press her more closely against me.

"So, you're always welcome," I said.

"Thanks, Jack, I appreciate that, and you're very hospitable." She drained her drink and set the glass on the pier. "I don't believe in miracles, but you and Susana meeting and falling in love—that's a modern-day miracle."

"I've thought of it that way." I added ice and Añejo to our glasses. The heat was metabolizing blood alcohol, but not so rapidly that I couldn't enjoy its glow and the sense of well-being. After a sip Sara said, "Susana said you were in the Navy before DEA. That you joined it because of your wife's addiction and death. So your life has had tragic moments."

"I guess we all do."

"And happiness is the only compensation."

"Certainly helps."

She sighed. "I've long thought of my husband as a soulless animal—and now I learn that he's a criminal as well."

"Bigtime," I added.

"Not easy to live with that knowledge. Our estrangement can only deepen. Meanwhile, I must do all I can to secure Susana's happiness."

"I'm sure you will." It was getting increasingly hard not to be aware of her cleavage between splendid matronly breasts. The Licenciado was a fool not to treasure what he had.

Suddenly she squealed and lifted her leg, grasped me for balance. "Something's biting me!"

I peered into the water and smiled. "Little fish, Sara, just nuzzling your leg, haven't any teeth."

"You're sure?"

"I'm sure."

Tentatively she lowered her foot and when she was standing firmly again she said, "I'm sorry I was so foolish—but for a moment I was frightened." She kissed my cheek. "Thanks for being here."

"My pleasure. Incidentally, if you're hungry I can fix something for us."

"I don't want to cause you any trouble."

"No trouble at all. Just say when."

"I may—but I'm not at all hungry." She lifted her glass and

turned it. "Actually, I'm enjoying midday cocktails with a charming young man, and feeling totally relaxed."

I was feeling pretty loose myself and enjoying her company. I said so, and Sara smiled. "I hoped we'd be compatible, Jack, and so we are."

"I can't thank you enough for coming. Oh, I should have mentioned I brought Susana's suitcase from Islamorada—in case she ever showed up here. But you might look over her things and take back anything you think she'd like to have in Acapulco."

"Yes, I'd like to see them even though she'll be here very soon."

"When we go in I'll dry what you have on now, and if we take to the water again, wear Susana's bikini."

"I'd like to finish my drink first."

After a while I got out of the water and handed her a large fluffy towel. She dried her body carefully, and though her thighs were well rounded my gaze detected no cellulite. Doubtless she enjoyed the services of a good masseuse.

I held out the bathrobe for her, and then we walked back on the pier and into the house. I led her into the guest bedroom where I'd put her travel clothes, and indicated the closet with Susana's things.

"While I'm showering," she said, "perhaps you'd fortify my drink. That Añejo is delicious."

"Gladly." I turned to leave as unconcernedly she undid her bra and peeled down her panties, displaying full-frontal nudity. Unlike Susana's luxurious delta, hers was neatly trimmed. And unlike Susana's small pink nipples, the mother's were the size and shade of ox-blood cherries. She handed me her wet underthings and walked toward the bathroom, unbraiding her hair as she went. I left then, dropped her things and my shorts in the dryer and turned it on. I wrapped a towel around my hips, made fresh drinks, and carried them back to the guest bedroom, wondering how the hell this progressively strange afternoon was going to wind up. Susana's mother was certainly uninhibited, to say the least.

She was in the shower, steam rising above the translucent panels through which I could make out a distorted image of her moving body. I knocked on the sliding door, and when she opened it I handed her a glass of iced Añejo. She drank deeply, and said, "Jack, would you mind soaping my back? Susana often does."

"Glad to," I said, and stepped into the stall behind her. With soap and washcloth I covered her back until it was foamy from neck to furrow, rinsing with the shower nozzle. Her black hair fell below her shoulders in a dark fan that seemed almost Oriental. Sodden with water, my towel dropped from my hips, leaving me as naked as Sara. She moved back against me, and her hands came around to press me closer. Turning off the shower, she murmured, "I've been so lonely, Jack, so long . . . I—I can't help myself. Do—you understand?"

Throat dry, I managed to blurt, "I do." Then, almost as though my hands were not my own, but those of a guided robot, I found her breasts and cupped them. Throatily, Sara said, "I'm being bold, but I need affection, Jack, dear—human warmth and understanding. I didn't expect to find it here but I can't think it's wrong."

"Hardly," I managed, and nibbled the back of her neck. She swayed against me, her buttocks moving excitingly until she spoke in a dreamy, detached voice. "You killed Felipe, didn't you? Felipe Paredes."

The question startled me but I said, "Yes, I killed him."

"I'm glad you did." She pressed against me. "Years ago when I first married he almost raped me—I've hated him ever since. And you gave me what I couldn't do by myself." Her head turned and she licked the side of my face. "It thrills me to be with his killer."

The lady was full of surprises. Turning, she moved into me, breasts spreading against my chest, and whispered, "Whatever happens here has nothing to do with my daughter—this is for me, Jack, you and me, and I swear Susana will never know."

Taking my hand, she drew me out of the shower, gulped down her drink, and began toweling my body. Then she dried off and together we went to the bed. Lying back, she welcomed me with open arms and thighs, and when I entered her, she locked her legs around my hips and climaxed almost at once.

As I made love to her I saw tears welling in her eyes. "I'm so— so grateful, dear," she whispered, "please don't stop—I'm in heaven."

So we visited heaven several more times during the long afternoon, and each time she became increasingly aroused, pounding my back with her fists, biting my neck and lips as ecstasy overwhelmed us. Then, on her knees, she bucked and twisted like a wild pony, guttural cries coming from her throat.

During calmer entr'actes she seemed almost apologetic, saying, "We're not depriving Susana, dear, it's not as though she were here." And, "I didn't want Susana marrying a man who wasn't a great lover—and I've found that you are. Perhaps being ignored makes a woman realize how important the physical side of love is. And I've never taken lovers, Jack, believe me. In my position it was too risky, and I was too proud." She nestled her head in my armpit. "After I leave, Jack, don't feel guilty—you didn't seduce me, I seduced *you*."

With all of which I allowed myself to agree.

Sara had me lie face down, got skin oil from the bathroom, and scrunched her crotch on my buns. Slowly, expertly, her hands probed and massaged my back from neck to thighs. As she rocked back and forth her crotch ground into my *derrière,* and I could tell from her sudden gasps and shivers that she was exciting herself— and me.

A little later, *en bouleversé,* Sara cradled my head and, crooning "Love Mamí," fed a sweet, swollen nipple into my mouth.

So I reflected that, attractive and exciting as this woman was, an added aphrodisiac was knowing she was the mother of Susana, and my future mother-in-law. But my mind was going to have to partition off this episode and not revisit it. Or repeat it another time. Our secret—guilty or not—was ours, ours alone. We were bonded. I hadn't invited her here or made erotic advances. But Sara had come unbidden, and aroused me beyond the point of no return.

Not unlike Susana's disrobing in the limo that memorable afternoon.

Her mother was half asleep beside me, damp hair on my arm. Her flight was leaving at six so she should leave for the airport no later than five twenty. I kissed her full lips and she moved closer. My God, how much she resembled Susana! Was it like this in upperclass Mexican families—mother-in-law-to-be exercises the *droit de seigneur* before her daughter's marriage? Did Mexican fathers bed their sons' fiancées to taste first fruits and ensure continuance of the family line? No, just fantasy, but as I gazed at Sara's spectacular body I had to wonder.

And I mused that I had now made love with Aguilera's wife as well as his daughter. Humiliations for him, were he to know. And Sara—she'd praised me for avenging her with Paredes, but unspoken was her revenge on her husband, a far more powerful factor in our love-making. While making the beast with two backs we'd made him a *cornudo*—and every time she saw him she'd have the inner satisfaction of remembering how she'd set horns on his head.

Ah, Woman, how devious thou art.

Presently we made love again, and while she was relaxing I brought her scanties from the dryer and placed them on the bed. She sat up, kissed me lengthily, and said, "I'll miss you more than you can possibly imagine." Then she got up and looked through her daughter's clothing in the closet, said, "We'll leave it for Susana," and slowly dressed.

I called for a taxi, and while we waited at the door she hugged me and murmured, "I admire you, Jack, for all you've done and are. To be truthful, I envy Susana." Her loins pressed into mine, and she reached down to stroke my groin. The taxi honked, Sara said, "See you in Acapulco," blew me a kiss, and went outside.

I watched her enter the taxi, saw it drive off, and closed the door.

Again I was alone when I didn't want to be. But as I poured a shot of Añejo I told myself that it wouldn't be for long. Thanks to Sara, regaining her daughter was no longer a remote possibility. I picked up the engraved party invitation and studied it. Sara's scenario sounded simple enough to execute, but while hoping for the best, I thought it only prudent to prepare for the worst.

Because if Pablo Antonio found me in his home he would shoot me on sight.

And get away with it.

Twenty – Three

Acapulco! ACA to jet setters, but a hot, glitzy, overpopulated seaside town to me. Only midmorning when I drove my rental Buick from the airport, but already the streets were sun-baked, the air still heavy with humidity, and the discomfort level at an all-time seasonal high.

I was heading for the Hotel Neptuno, where I'd stayed a couple of years back while interviewing an informant from Guadalajara. The hostel wasn't big and showy—no nightclub acts or rave cuisine—but the rooms were clean and the air-conditioning was usually working, a large plus in Mexico. Its hundred and twenty rooms drew mostly commercial travelers and families who couldn't afford lodging in a seafront palace. Enough people came and went through the lobby that my comings and goings were unlikely to be noticed. And for the next fourteen hours I wanted anonymity.

Tonight was Susana's birthday party, her eighteenth, and, I hoped, the occasion for her—and my—escape.

In the days following her mother's departure from Cozumel I'd memorized the internal map she'd drawn showing the meeting room and the secret exit tunnel. I'd bought a lightweight dark gray tux, patent leather shoes, black bow tie, ruffled shirt, and a full-face mask. It would be hotter to wear than one covering only eyes and nose, but I couldn't chance Aguilera recognizing my lower features.

My travel bag held a change of street clothing and two .38 pistols: one to wear, the other reserve. And a box of soft-point ammo.

I steered the Buick under the hotel cupola, got out, and opened the trunk. A uniformed *chamaco* hurried down the steps and got out my bags while I gave my keys to the parking valet. He gave me a ticket stub and took off for the hotel parking lot with a sickening scream of rubber.

The lobby doors were open in case a stray breeze should waft in from the water, but the beach was three blocks away, and a lot of high-rises in between. I hoped my room would be cooler than the lobby—a lot cooler.

I registered at the desk using Matthew Barden ID, and paid cash for two nights. The clerk gave my room key to the waiting *chamaco* and we set off for the elevator. Three-twelve was the number of my corner room, and when we went in the boy immediately turned on the a/c. Then he showed me the bathroom, whose counter featured four bottles of Pellegrino water, and assured me that hotel ice was purified. I gave him ten dollars and asked him to bring me a load of cubes *muy pronto*. Then I pulled off my jacket and shirt, and wiped perspiration from face and throat. The air conditioner thunked noisily and gave off a moderate breeze. I hoped it wouldn't expire while I was using the room.

I set my bag on a collapsible rack and opened it, taking out a liter of Añejo, a beverage that tasted good, metabolized well in tropic heat, and produced only minor hangovers. My drink of choice. I recalled how Sara Beltrán de Aguilera had favored its flavor and relaxing qualities. After ice arrived I built myself the day's first drink and lay on the bed while the a/c rumbled away. So far, room temperature had dropped perhaps half a degree. Ominous sign.

I'd been up since dawn, packing and reviewing every aspect of tonight's enterprise. I went over each step backward and forward trying to find vulnerabilities, but finally satisfied myself that if Sara did her promised part two lovers would be safely reunited.

It was unreasonable to expect the Licenciado to accept defeat gracefully, but this time there would be no giveaway calls to Mamí or other careless clues to our whereabouts. Rather than go to Cozumel as Sara suggested, I'd decided on a night flight to Miami where we'd be unnoticed among the hordes of Hispanics and multicultural tourists.

The air was cooling somewhat and my iced drink helped lower body temperature; I wasn't perspiring so freely.

Last night I'd phoned Manny at home and outlined what I planned to do. "You're *serious?*" was his first response. "Bro', you're really asking for trouble."

"Hell, it's a short life, might as well be a merry one," was all I could think of. "And if I can pull this off, with Susana, my risk-taking days are over."

"Well, that's a real plus," he remarked. "I was there for you in Islamorada—"

"Much good it did me."

"—but this time you're flying solo."

"You're a master of the obvious, Manny, a real cliché expert."

"*Coño, chico,* take care of yourself, okay?"

"Okay."

"And—best of luck, *hermano.*"

There hadn't been much point to the conversation; mainly I wanted someone I trusted to know what I was up to. In case I needed help along the way. Or to pen my short obituary.

I got up to refill my glass and glanced at the small bag I'd packed with selected items for Susana: jeans, slippers, bra, panties, a Busch Gardens T-shirt, and the few cosmetics she'd acquired on our travels. Minimal baggage to resume what I considered an interrupted honeymoon, but she was an uncomplicated and undemanding young woman despite her regal upbringing.

I wondered if her mother had told her the plan or decided to withhold it lest Susana's demeanor make her father suspicious. Nothing to be gained from prior knowledge; Sara could brief her as they went to the private rendezvous room.

I recalled Susana saying her mother would be horrified if she knew her daughter had a diaphragm, and smiled as I thought of Sara's active sexuality. A smidgin of hypocrisy there? No one would ever know of our Cozumel afternoon, so even mothers and daughters kept some things to themselves. Sara seemed fully reconciled to our relationship though she'd asked my intentions and future plans. I felt her relaxed attitude boded well for our future relations.

I hung up my tuxedo and evening shirt, got out my shiny new shoes and wondered if I'd ever wear them again. Who cares? I asked myself; they were fully expendable items.

In the inside pocket of my evening jacket were two first-class tickets to Miami. The flight left at 0115, allowing us plenty of time to shake off any pursuers. I didn't expect any because our leaving the mansion was to be clandestine and unobserved. If all went as planned.

These and other thoughts revolved in my mind as I lay on the bed and heard the a/c thumping rhythmically away. Something had given it new life, for the flow of cold air was noticeable and improved my disposition.

I wasn't hungry but I thought I ought to get something in my stomach, so I had the valet bring my car, got directions to Sanborns, and drove there. In addition to providing quality American-style food, the establishment offered a wide variety of Mexican silver, turquoise, and jadeite. I ate a grilled cheese sandwich with a malted milk shake and looked over the display cabinets. After a while I bought a silver brooch fashioned to resemble a sailfish, nicely set with turquoise. Gift-wrapped, the package was small enough to fit easily in my tux pocket, though it would go unnoticed on a table piled high with birthday gifts for the señorita.

From Sanborns I took the cliff road to the mansion and drove slowly past, observing large trucks coming and going through the entrance gate. Several trucks carried tenting, tables, and chairs; others brought catering equipment and food for the affair. On the street two blue-uniformed policemen in white helmets and polished puttees directed traffic. A resentful public called them *mordelones* and *voladores* in recognition of their avaricious pursuit of bribes. Others, I assumed, would be working as the party got underway.

From the street I couldn't see strolling guards, who were probably snacking with catering help, so for the moment, at least, internal security seemed loose. Driving on, I checked for a parking spot conveniently close to the mansion, and made mental note of an area on the inland side of the road. To claim it I ought to get there before both sides of the road were occupied by party-goers. Upper-echelon guests would be chauffeur driven, but the younger element—Susana's peer group—would drive themselves. Especially the pampered *muchachos de bien* as they were contemptuously called: sons of the wealthy, immune to the constraints and limitations of ordinary folk. I didn't want a street argument with drunken, drugged-out rich kids, so I'd stake my claim before they arrived.

Well, I'd seen all I could from the road, knew where I was going to park; I turned around and drove back to the hotel.

My room had cooled down considerably. I took a shower and got into bed, slept for the next four hours.

After shaving, I got into party wear except for my jacket, charged the chamber of my .38, thumbed a replacement cartridge into the ten-shot magazine, and set the safety. My black nylon holster was a slim, quick-release model spring-clipped to my belt. I put it on, then my jacket, and checked by mirror to make sure there was no revealing bulge. The other .38 pistol I left in my bag on top of street clothing for easy access while driving. The black face mask I folded into a jacket pocket, and decided I was ready to go.

I scanned bathroom and bedroom, saw I'd forgotten nothing, and left the room carrying both travel bags. I tipped the valet, who loaded them on the rear seat, handed him my room key, and got into the Buick.

Fifteen minutes later I reached Aguilera's citadel and parked in the chosen spot. The time was only six-forty, but cars were arriving, directed by cops with flashlights. A catering van pulled up and servers began carrying pans of prepared food through the open gate, observed by an armed guard. Masked guests showed invitations to the guard and entered the premises wearing a variety of costumes. There were black-faced Moors with plumed turbans; women in glittering body stockings, whose masks simulated the colorful heads of tropical birds; hoop-skirted courtesans with feathered masks; a top-hatted ringmaster in scarlet cloak, carrying a coiled whip; a muscular, loin-clothed Tarzan leading a furry ape; a torero in glinting *traje de luces;* a caped Spanish grandee; a mustachioed seventeenth-century pirate with a brace of flintlocks in his scarlet sash; a nearly naked Aztec slave girl roped to a helmeted Conquistador; a red-suited, long-tailed Satan; and a scattering of men in tuxedos.

After putting on my mask, I crossed the road and joined the tuxedoed group. We produced invitations for guard inspection, and filed in. No metal detector, no patting down.

Already a mariachi band was playing in the distance. Guests buzzed excitedly as we walked to the broad, open entrance of the mansion, and when we were inside I saw a long table bearing presents already delivered. This party was a Mexican bat mitzvah. I left my small package and got back into line. Edging slowly forward, I was able to see the evening's hosts receiving us, the three of them costumed in a Goyaesque tableau: Queen Isabela—Sara; King Fernando—Aguilera; and the Infanta—Susana, who wore a plain black floor-length smock with white ruffled collar. Her parents, however, were royally costumed, even down to Ferdinand's jeweled, antique sword and dirk. Sara's queenly gown sparkled with jewels, and when I bowed to kiss her extended hand I murmured, *"Qué fiesta más imponente."*

"Gracias, señor," she replied, giving no indication that she recognized me. I bowed next to Aguilera, who said, *"Bienvenido, señor,"* and smiled. Then I was before Susana, and kissed her hand without meeting her eyes. She said, *"Gracias, señor, por haber venido."*

"Feliz cumpleaños," I replied, and moved on.

From there I followed guests through the house into the garden where mariachis were playing on a raised bandstand. A long refreshment bar drew the crowd like a magnet, and when there was space I asked for a glass of Pellegrino. Taking it, I moved toward buffet tables served by toqued chefs who carved large roasts and added delicacies to proffered plates. I nibbled a stalk of stuffed celery and found a seat at a small table that gave me a view of the reception line. One guest, presumably female, wore the feathered costume of a macaw; her escort was disguised as a turtle. There were going to be a lot of surprises when masks came off. Under mine, my face was beginning to perspire. I tilted the mask up from the chin and blotted without showing my face. A man in army uniform, head concealed by a Mayan ceremonial mask, sat down across from me and thumped his glass on the table. "What an extravagant affair, think of all the money it costs."

I shrugged. "Their daughter is eighteen only once—and her parents can afford the celebration."

He nodded, slurped his drink through the mask's mouth opening, and asked, "Friend of Aguilera's?"

"Of the family."

"Mexico City?"

"Saltillo."

"I'm Esposito, Isaac Esposito, chief of airport operations." He extended his hand. "Jorge Spelvin," I replied, recalling that Esposito was a close associate of Aguilera's.

"The mask annoys me. When can we take them off?"

"I was told midnight."

"Long wait," he grumbled, "and I need a drink." The general got up and walked away.

Mariachis had left the stage, replaced by a rock and roll band. Couples began dancing; both buffet tables were crowded. I saw Aguilera come into the garden with a tall, masked man wearing a white, silver-ornamented *charro* costume and a wide-brimmed, tassled sombrero. Some notable, I thought, and when the band began playing "The Star Spangled Banner" I realized that we were graced with the presence of the American ambassador.

As the music played, the *charro* bowed sweepingly to the crowd and received mild applause. At the end of the song, he turned to the band and called, "Thank you, thank you. *Gracias, gracias.*" Probably the only Spanish word he knew. Aguilera, aka King Ferdinand of Spain, led the ambassador back into the house, the crowd closing behind them as rock music resumed.

It was now eight-fifteen and I wondered when fireworks would begin: my signal to commence Phase Three of the night's operation. The sky wasn't yet fully dark and I supposed the pyro technicians would hold the display for better contrast. I went to the bar for another Pellegrino, and glass in hand approached the entrance and saw the royal family still receiving arrivals. Susana looked radiant as she acknowledged birthday wishes from each guest. This was her natural element by breeding, fortune, and sense of self worth. If we hadn't kept house at Islamorada I would have doubted her ability to become an American housewife, but she'd adapted without complaint, and willingly done her share of household chores. I was eager to have her out of the citadel, leaving with me for a new life, and as the first fiery rocket pierced the sky I tensed; the time had come.

Explosion followed explosion, the night sky erupting into a panoply of starbursts and golden drops. The crowd oohed and aahed, applauding as the display became more fantastic. I looked through the doorway and saw that Susana and her mother had left Aguilera alone to receive guests. I went inside, detouring well around him, and made my way to an arched doorway that opened into a dark hall. Fourth room on the left, Sara had told me; I counted carefully and stopped before it.

Looking around before pressing my ear to the door, I listened and heard low voices inside. I sucked in a deep breath, turned the door handle, and went in.

TWENTY-FOUR

Sara saw me first, snapped, "Close the door, and come here." Susana had dropped her costume and was pulling on jeans when her mother's voice made her turn. I pushed up my mask, she yelped with joy and threw her arms around me. "Oh, Jack, Jack, I didn't know you were coming until just now." She began to sob. Her mother said sharply, "Get dressed, Susana, no time to waste," and turned to me. "The car's ready?"

I nodded. "With a bag for Susana." I kissed Susana's cheek, she shivered and wiped tears from her face. "I can't believe I'm really going—with you. Mamí, I can't thank you enough, I'll always be grateful. So very grateful."

"I pray you will both be very happy. Don't tell me where you're going, and don't call me for a few months." She gathered her gown with one hand and went to an almost invisible flush door in the wall. She turned the lock with a key and pulled it open. "This is my birthday present to you, Susana—and you, Jack." reaching inside, she found a switch that illuminated a narrow tunnel. Jeans and sandals on, Susana pulled on a blouse as her mother said, "Hurry, hurry." Susana went to her and covered her face with kisses. "It's the greatest present I could ever want." She took my hand and we started for the tunnel entrance.

Just then the hall door opened and King Ferdinand burst in. He stopped, stared at us, and yelled, "So this is what you do when my back is turned. You betray me, all of you!" From a costume pocket he jerked out a pistol and pointed it. "Novak, you're the cause of all my trouble," he grated, as Susana screamed, "No, don't, don't, I beg you." She started for him but he shoved her roughly aside, and in that moment I flipped out my .38. Aguilera's finger pressed the trigger but I heard only the click of a misfire. I aimed for his right shoulder, but Aguilera half turned toward his wife and my bullet hit him in the chest. Impact made him stagger back, a disbelieving look on his face. As he dropped to the floor, muscle reflex pulled the trigger. Another misfire click. Both women shrieked as I knelt beside him. His carotid was still, his eyes held the blank stare of death. The women were crying in each other's arms. I took the pistol from his hand and ejected the magazine. Empty. How could he have made that fatal mistake? I holstered my pistol and got up. Sara left her daughter and locked the hall door. I said, "What do we do now?"

"Leave, both of you. Leave now!"

Susana gazed at her mother beseechingly. "But Papí . . . ?"

"I'll take care of everything. Just go." She picked up Aguilera's pistol and slid the magazine into place, dropped the gun beside him. "A burglar," she said in a hard voice, "and my husband knew so little about guns."

Whimpering, Susana seemed frozen in place. Her mother said, "Listen to me. He was your father and my husband but he was an evil man and I don't intend to mourn him. I suggest you do not, either."

"But—" Susana protested, until I grabbed her arm. Tugging it, I said, "If you're coming, we have to go. Now. Now, Susana."

Choking back sobs, she went slowly into the tunnel. Sara closed the door behind us. I said, "I have confidence in your mother, she knows how to arrange things."

Susana said nothing as I half dragged her toward the door at the far end of the tunnel, but she seemed to be holding back. Shock and grief; combined, a big emotional component. She was dwelling on what had just occurred, not thinking ahead as I was—had to. Licenciado Pablo Antonio Aguilera was dead. *Requiescat in pace,* I thought, and take all your evil to the grave.

At the exit door we halted while I lifted from its guides the heavy bar that blocked the exit, shoved the door open, and looked out. "Let's get to the car," I said, but Susana was a yard behind me, immobile as before. Exasperated, I said, "Are you coming?"

She blinked and her gaze focused on me. "You killed my father," she said dully. "I can't go with you."

"You were there, you saw how it happened," I pleaded. "He fired at me and I shot to disable him, not kill him."

"But he didn't shoot you," she said stubbornly.

"He tried—but his gun misfired. Would you like it better if he'd killed me?"

She thought it over, shook her head. "Maybe I'll come later, Jack."

"Not good enough. Now or never, Susana."

Half turning from me, she looked at the far end of the tunnel. "Mamí needs me."

"Like hell she does. She's got it all figured out."

Her head lifted and she faced me. "But you killed him. How can I live with the man who shot my father?"

"Your decision," I told her as gently as I could. But her expression was vacant, nothing registered. Presently she began walking back toward the death room. "I love you," I called, "we can work it out," but she seemed not to have heard me. Finally I said, "Goodbye, Susana," went outside, and shut the door behind me.

For a while I leaned against the wall, aware of the night air's coolness, the cheerful strains of the mariachi band. The fireworks were ended and only music rose from the citadel. I walked beside the wall to the road, crossed, and got into my car.

I sat there, scenes kaleidoscoping in my mind. Nearby, traffic cops were smoking in the darkness; a cloud smeared the face of the moon. I felt utterly alone. A loser. I wondered how long before Sara broke the tragic news to her guests. Doubtless, she'd withhold it until they were gone, inform someone of influence who could allay suspicions, present the episode in a positive light. Of one thing I was certain: the widow of Pablo Antonio was not going to be stained by her husband's death.

A few guests emerged from the grounds. Limos picked them up and drove off into the night. I roused myself, started the engine, and steered toward the airport.

Partway there, I pulled off the road and changed into street clothes, putting evening garb in my bag. I threw both pistols into the bushes and drove on.

At the car rental office I turned in the Buick, and carried my bags into the airport. After checking them at the American counter I wandered into the café bar for a cold glass of Añejo and sat in a booth reflecting on the recent past.

I wasn't accustomed to the role of patsy, but Sara had chosen carefully and well, working out a quadrangle that involved her loathing for her husband, his hatred of me, my hatred of him, and my love for Susana, who she'd used to draw me into it. Her steely words after the shootout: *"I'll take care of everything . . ."* Then, *"A burglar . . . and my husband knew so little about guns."*

Oh? I couldn't imagine Aguilera knowing so little about guns that he wouldn't check his pistol's magazine. His expression when he pulled the trigger told me he *expected* it to fire. Was he forgetful enough to unload the magazine and carry an unloaded gun? Or had someone unloaded his piece, anticipating his trying to fire it? Sara had stage-managed everything else, why not neuter the gun as well?

Reluctantly, I found myself admiring her coolness and craftiness; her paranormal ability to fit everything into place. She'd established place and setting, anticipated her husband's reaction when he discovered us. The outcome hadn't surprised her, and once Pablo Antonio was dead she showed indifference to him . . . hadn't even denounced his unintentional killer—me. No, for by then her mind was rocketing ahead, framing the calculus of disposal and explanation.

For weeks I'd wrestled with the problem of living happily with Susana while her father was alive; aware that killing him would be unforgiveable, no matter how she despised him in life. Well, that paradox was resolved—by Sara. Aguilera was dead, and I'd lost the girl I loved. What a rotten solution.

I ordered a second Añejo, and after that a third. Adrenaline was leaving my bloodstream and I felt exhausted. Perhaps if I hadn't been so hot for Sara that Cozumel afternoon, I'd have taken warning from her bringing me the party invitation. Call it foresight, intuition—her guiding hand was everywhere, and I was the instrument chosen to rid her of a hated husband. Like the third act of a play, everything came together in that private room. Had she told Aguilera to join them there? Why else had he come?

In letting me escape Sara had rid herself of a possible witness who could never even prove he was there. Unnamed on the invitation list, unseen by anyone who could conceivably recognize me, I was the useful fool who blindly followed her script. And she would drill the cover story into Susana: the three of them had gone to the room for a brief interlude from guests, surprised a masked intruder who shot Aguilera and escaped in the confusion. The ladies hadn't seen his face, couldn't identify him—so sorry, wish we could be more help.

I grimaced at the melted ice in my drink, thought of ordering another, and decided against it. Couldn't look too drunk to board the plane.

At twelve forty-five boarding for Miami was announced. I got up heavily and trudged to the gate, showed one of my two tickets, and was shown to my first-class seat. The empty one beside me was a poignant reminder of the girl who hadn't come. I looked out of the window and tried not thinking of her. Then jets whined into life, the plane lifted over Acapulco Bay and headed for Miami.

Leaving part of me behind.

We landed in Miami before dawn. I was too tired and mentally disorganized for onward travel, so I slept a few hours in the airport hotel and took the next flight to Phoenix. The feeder flight to Nogales put me there in early afternoon.

My motel room was musty but undisturbed. I turned on the air-conditioning, got into the shower, and after drying off called Manny. He was surprised to hear from me so soon after my other call and said he'd come over after work, maybe we'd have dinner together.

"Tell Wally I'll report in tomorrow. Right now I can't handle it."

"Will do. He's been asking about you."

"He need ask no more."

So in a secluded booth at the Embers I told Manny most everything that happened beginning with Sara's unexpected visit, excluding our orgy. As he listened, he put aside knife and fork, and said, "I'd say you were set up, *compadre*."

"So was Aguilera. Any publicity yet?"

"None I know of." he paused and said thoughtfully. "At least Aguilera is finished. His organization will be in disarray for a while, but we know the remaining players."

"If anyone cares." I sipped from my glass and set it down. "I like it that the ambassador, Aguilera's big buddy, was on hand when he went down. Wonder what he'll report to State?"

"Probably nothing."

I reached over and claimed the dinner check as Manny asked, "Was it worth it, Jack? All of it?"

"I'm not sure," I told him. "There's enough angst to go around, but maybe time will tell."

EPILOGUE

The passage of time told me only that I was getting older and less alert, but not the least forgetful. I was a failure at suppressing memories of the Aguilera women, and while I was bitter at Sara for exploiting me, I felt only understanding and regret for Susana. I wanted to seal away the whole episode, bury it deep like nuclear waste, but I was still too close in time.

After the birthday party Mexican media portrayed Aguilera's death as probably the work of a hit man commissioned by a vengeful Cali Cartel. The president of the republic went on government-controlled television to denounce his friend's cold-blooded murder and vow his administration would not rest until the killer was identified and Aguilera's assassination avenged. Standard verbiage. I yawned, grateful I hadn't been named.

Aguilera was given a state funeral attended by the president and his political claque, the American ambassador, four Central American ambassadors, and diverse Mexican and regional dignitaries. Airborne TV coverage showed the cortege passing the monument to the national lottery, perhaps the one institution Aguilera had lacked time to corrupt. And of Pablo Antonio Aguilera I thought that nothing became his life so much as did the leaving of it.

At the cemetery TV cameras showed his two sons and black-veiled widow and daughter placing flowers on his mahogany coffin. As it was lowered into the grave an honor guard fired salutes and I

turned off the TV. To me the ceremonial atmosphere was redolent
of hypocrisy. Enough already.

I accepted the San Antonio assignment and rented an apartment
near the office on a month-to-month basis. My caseload was pretty
routine: I'd been given three informants who fingered dealers and
middlemen, whom I arrested and tried to flip à la Paredes. Some
took the offered deal, others stayed silent and took the rap, afraid to
identify wholesalers and distributors. Their reluctance was something I understood; they had enough street smarts to know they
didn't face much jail time, especially if they were Hispanics tried by
an Hispanic judge. I didn't let myself get emotionally involved in
outcomes.

A month after I reached San Antonio Fred Dorschner came
through on a final inspection tour. He was taking early retirement,
he told me, and planned to enter a substance abuse clinic before alcohol destroyed his Golden Years. DEA ruled his addiction job related and agreed to pay for treatment. We didn't discuss it, of course,
but we both knew his problem began back in San Diego with his
daughter's seduction and the killing of her debaucher.

I told Fred I felt he was doing the right thing, and wished him
and his family a happy future.

Too often at night, alone in my apartment, I'd think back and recall
how it had all started: with Eddie Flanigan's drug flight to Sonora;
Isidro Moreno's discovery of the drug cash and his murder; Padre
Gardenia; Frank Rodriguez and the killing of Beverly Dawn; Molly
with me in Cozumel; Felipe Paredes's confession and death; Licenciado Aguilera; Susana and Sara—so many players in a drama that
turned tragic; so many things I preferred not to remember . . . I did
my daily work without joy or satisfaction and eventually, because I
was a bachelor, was given roving assignments that took me to Los
Angeles, Chicago, Caracas, Ankara, and Cyprus. At times I thought

how cleverly Sara had manipulated me. With Susana as unwitting bait she'd drawn me into her net without resistance, made me her husband's killer, and gotten everything she wanted from her lethal design—including her daughter.

For a while I thought—and hoped—Susana might call saying she wanted to forget the past and rejoin our lives. But the call never came.

Eventually I gave away her clothing to the Salvation Army, and when I spent a weekend in Cozumel I had Ramona clear out the rest of the clothing from the closet and do with it as she chose.

Seven months later, while waiting in a Tex-Mex barber shop, I scanned a copy of *Excelsior* and saw a photograph that quickened my pulse: two people standing by the mainmast of a large yawl. The caption identified them as Signor Pietro Bonacelli and his bride Sara Beltrán y Montes, widow of assassinated Mexican presidential aspirant, Pablo Antonio Aguilera. The newlyweds were cruising the Aegean Sea aboard the Italian financier's yacht, and planned to spend part of each year between homes in Rome, Acapulco, and Mexico City.

The barber had to call me twice before I got out of my chair and into his. Sara hadn't waited long to resume life's pleasures, I reflected, less than the conventional year of mourning.

But why should she dissemble? Sara believed in the present, in sucking from each moment every dram of pleasure that came her way. *Carpe diem* should be engraved on her jewelry and escutcheon. A good Roman motto.

Months later it was Manny who sent me additional Aguilera-related news: a *Mirasol* photo layout showing the Madrid cathedral wedding of Susana María Aguilera Beltrán to Conde Alfonso Federico Gomez Peña of the Gomez international hotel chain. My lost love looked gorgeous in bridal lace and mantilla, and my heart seemed to choke in my throat. She was taking her proper station in life among the world's rich and famous, and we commoners could only stare through the bake shop window at unattainable delicacies beyond.

I poured a long drink, lighted a candle in her memory, and let the flame consume her photos—until only ash remained.

> *Ring the bell,*
> > *close the book,*
> > > *quench the candle*

Four long years passed before I met her equal. And through them all I never forgot Susana.